The Bloody Awakening of the Anaxagorum

The First Expedition of The Six Fingers.

***

By John Y. Graham

ISBN: 978-1-7379611-4-7

Acknowledgements

Five million thanks to my editorial staff: Patty Szelest, Linda Arnest, Karen George, Katie Hushbeck-Shneider, Ian Ruel, John Stevie, Robyn Storm, and the interdimensional Ryck Neube.

Cover art: The ever patient and brilliant Curt Tweddell

Map and concept art: David "Beam Me Up" Butterfield

FAELLAR
TULAS
ARQONIAS AND THE KNOWN WORLD

Part I

The Myth of Reason

To the Curious:

If curiosity has not led you to this volume, set it down, move along. I write for those chasing the truth, not for the indifferent or the coerced. Herein, I record the events leading to the rise of a new force in the world, one seemingly intent on taking from us our understanding of nature, logic, and reality.

Per the traditions of the Librasts of Northem, I avow here in writing that the following events happened as I witnessed them. Some will appear fabrications or embellishments, but they are not.

You came for the truth. Prepare yourself for it.

- Anonymous, for now

Lexica I

The sarcophagus entombing the blood book required a lengthy ritual involving solvents and great finesse to open its marble cover intact, so Ryckerd's men used pickaxes. The clang of iron against stone hammered the eardrums of the six in the undercroft. They hoped to hack a small hole in the slab quickly and pry it off, remove the forbidden tome and flee. Whoever had applied the seal three hundred years earlier knew their art well, for the lid refused to come loose. A full mark of the clock passed before it cracked open.

Ryckerd peered inside. The blood-red Anaxagorum, strewn with white fragments of marble, peered back. Five men-at-arms stayed a prudent six paces away.

The tome measured roughly the size of a small chest and appeared, in construction, a normal book: a spine, a front and back cover, and the ridges of pages between them, all seemingly drenched in blood. No human had touched the thing since its interment, so Ryckerd's hand, although sheathed in leather and iron, hesitated. Did blood actually swirl on the surface of its cover, or was light from the party's lanterns making it appear so?

A vigilante mob had beat them to the Imperial Library and set fire to three thousand years of manuscripts in the five upper floors of the tower. They hadn't bothered trying to destroy the Anaxagorum—if that were possible. Mayhap they assumed debris from the collapsing floors above would block intruders, for the nonce.

While rack after rack of scrolls, tomes, and tablets burned, the structure had yet to ignite. The undercroft maintained its dank closeness, but enough heavy smoke from burning velum above sank into the closed space to set eyelids fluttering and throats rasping.

Ryckerd, being massive of physique and broad of face, seemed an armored bear risen on two legs. Sweat streamed his cheeks and into his beard, even though he wore only a chainmail coif that left his face open to the air—his visored half-helm hung from his belt. Prescient hairs on his nape prickled. As all children of Northem, Ryckerd had been taught the nature of the book and, upon confronting it, could not discard the possibility that life quivered within its pages. The Anaxagorum might be living evil, but it held knowledge, and Northmen were sworn to protect all knowledge.

A young man-at-arms with the spindliest of mustaches availed himself of Ryckerd's hesitation to whisper, "Leave it!" He searched the other faces for support. "Nobody wants it. We can say the fire overtook the horrid thing."

"Quiet!" Ryckerd snapped. "Take your gally-wagging upstairs."

The young man retreated a pace toward the way up. His companions looked ready to follow him.

Ryckerd had been raised to be a scholar but grew more adept with the blade than the book. A hulking grump to strangers, he was fiercely loyal to his brother knights, his retinue of stray cats, "the noble rogues", and, with effort, his sister.

Lada, two years younger than Ryckerd but millennia beyond everyone in ambition, appeared with a chirping cough at the bottom of the stairs, a spectre in the noxious gloom. Her hooded cloak of twilight blue hid all but her sharp chin. The garment was a magnificent specimen of her own making, and like all of her work, left the seamstresses back home envious.

"Why do you tarry, Ryckerd?" Much shorter and leaner but possessed of a volcanic impatience, she shouldered her brother aside and gripped the side of the sarcophagus. "Time we do not have!"

The warrior bear growled. "Have you gone wobbly, Sister? Get to safety."

"I am saving this."

When he turned to share an exasperated sigh with his men, she tugged the heavy glove from her right hand and lay her palm upon the tome's cover. Warm, red liquid flowed over her fingers and up to her wrist before she jerked away with a gasp. The red flowed back to the book.

Ryckerd whirled. "You touched it bare-handed?"

She rubbed thumb and forefinger together. "Dry."

"Move, and I'll lift the thing."

"No!" She tugged the glove back on. With a breathy grunt, she lifted the volume from its marble bed, only to slide it onto the unbroken part of the lid to rest. "It must weigh an eight stack, at least."

The others gasped, expecting to see a wet, red streak where the book had touched.

Angry at himself for hesitating, Ryckerd laid an armored paw on the book. "You said the burning wouldn't begin for a week."

Lada pushed away his hand and tilted the monolithic tome, until it stood upright. Firelight swam in its covers, and although it seemed to have pages, the thing was more block than book. "I underestimated the strength of the usurper's supporters."

"I told you and Father the loyalists couldn't hold long against Draman's zealots."

"I thought having a plan before rushing into a hostile city was prudent."

"Speed wins battles."

"Haste loses them."

Smoke hissed from the central beams just an arm's-span above them. The young man-at-arms moaned. "Are you to let us roast?"

Ryckerd snapped, "Stopper yourself!" and then stooped to eye his sister. "You notice there is fire, yes?"

"A bit more firelight is welcome." The young woman examined the upright Anaxagorum. If she sweated, it was nowhere in evidence. The glistening crimson tome presented no symbol or rune on front, back, or spine. It had no clasps or bands to keep it closed, yet she could not pry it open.

Ryckerd motioned to the half-circle of men. "Bring the bag."

One shrunk closer to the steps up to the library vestibule on the ground floor. Three stood motionless, as firelight licked in and out of their eye sockets. A fifth handed the bag to Ryckerd. Twas a sheathing bag of woven vegetable fibers infused with elum sap, giving it a red-brown luster. Such bags were made to protect books from the elements, although the blueskins back home believed such efforts of nature couldn't harm the Anaxagorum. They said the ageless thing was an element of nature, itself.

As huge brother and petite sister wrestled the blood book into the sheathing bag, the young man near the steps bolted up to the ground floor, the slap of his boots on stone as crisp as a lash against flesh. The others looked to Lada. Obscured by her cloak and seemingly in no hurry to leave, she strapped the bag closed. "This structure was built to withstand fire. Have patience." One hand lost its grip, and the book thumped flat onto the lid.

Ryckerd asked, "So now we have time for patience? This is my responsibility. Yours is the Traillus upstairs."

Lada glanced from under her hood, face uncharacteristically vulnerable. "The Traillus is destroyed, Ryckerd, probably the first tome burned by the mob.

The Traillus had been written thirty-five hundred years ago, when humans first became enlightened. It praised, in epic poetry, the ideas, arts, and gracious comportment that had lifted them from a primitive society to a civil society. Fulfilling the potential of the human mind became as important as fulfilling the human appetite. The upright beasts on two legs could be beautiful. The Traillus would always remind them how.

"Destroyed?" exclaimed one of the soldiers at the base of the stairs. "Gela help us!"

Another asked in anger, "Why do we tarry, then?"

Ryckerd pressed his sister. "You are sure?"

"Its vault is open and filled with ash and blackened clasps." Lada placed both hands on the sheathed tome. "That is the reality of it."

The angry soldier regarded the bag as if it were an organ just ripped from its host. "We're risking our lives for...that bloody horror?"

Lada glared. "Tis your duty to preserve knowledge."

"Even when it's shite?"

Ryckerd thumped his fist onto the intact half of the marble lid. "Find your balls, man." Then he leaned in, broad head shadowing his sister's. "I say we leave the benighted thing to the inferno."

Lada's face, pale and hatchet-sharp, met Ryckerd's, making up in menace what it lacked in size. "Am I to tell Papa you failed to respect your little sister's authority?"

"You won't carry this thing ten paces."

Lada rose to full height—a half span shorter than her brother—fingers standing in ownership on the enshrouded tome. "I am the Librast In Situ, and I will carry the book! You are my protection, so protect."

Ryckerd gestured to his men. "Lead the way up."

Lada's reason said she shouldn't be able to carry the massive book far, but her intuition disagreed. Difficult enough to be the first woman to assume the post of Librast In Situ, she couldn't allow her brother to make it harder by questioning her in front of others. She pulled her leather-hemmed hood forward and, with both hands, slid the standing tome onto her hip where it would ride, she hoped, like a bundle of faggots. A groan rose as she rose. Her legs turned to boiled carrots.

Ryckerd waited at the top. The beams crackled above her, and she took the first step with a squeaking groan.

Ryckerd called down. "Shall I carry it?"

She nearly stumbled on the next step and had to consider relinquishing the tome. Suddenly she rose to her full height, face aglow with wondrous puzzlement. "It grows lighter, a bundle of feathers."

"Then hasten!"

Up she trotted to the smoky ground floor, Ryckerd a shadow in front of her.

He said, "You misled me as to its weight, then?"

"It misled me," she replied.

He ushered her to the main door. "Odd thing for a book to do."

She slipped past him. "Not so odd." Under her breath, she added, "It wants to be saved."

***

The moon remained hidden behind a gray fleece, so the night was black beyond the circle of firelight radiating from the towering library. The summer air felt as cool as autumn, and the emerging group stopped to bathe in it. Three more knights from Ryckerd's military order, and twelve soldiers of fortune hired in the north crouched outside the light. Lada's heart sank when she saw the near-empty bags in their hands.

"How many?"

One of the group rose from the flittering shadows. "We were only able to rescue thirteen manuscripts from the upper floors."

Lada regarded the long face of the Imperial Library. Once the pride of a golden age, with its flying buttresses and crown of golden spires, it now gazed down on her, cheeks dark, eyes burning, and hair billowing sooty-dark against the clouds. "There were fourteen thousand."

Although the moon cast no light, the flames did, and those who shouldn't have seen, saw. Five soldiers of the city watch, carrying long, axe-headed halberds, stepped into the light. "Who are you lot?"

Lada stiffened, the Anaxagorum on her shoulder. Ryckerd whisked his broadsword from its scabbard. Arrows jumped from the group of waiting Northmen and into the men of the patrol. One took an arrow in the eye and collapsed where he stood. The others had the good fortune of being protected by their armored hauberks, but the bad luck to be within swinging distance of Ryckerd. His long blade whipped red swaths through the air, and two men fell. The other knights rushed in to slay the others.

Lada detested violence but understood its necessity. She retained a hope—woe be unto any who called it naivety—that men and women could be raised from their ignorance into the light of reason and unity. But that would take more generations, so until then....

She gazed upon one of the dead soldiers. "You were on the wrong side of history, this night."

The desperate score-and-a-half of Northmen bundled through the dark alleys, like so many raccoons. This part of the Lower Town was stacked with tenements three-stories high, their occupants the poor of Tule: the imperial capital's hulking wharf-men and urine-soaked dyers, toothless seamstresses and untouchable gutter farmers. Most would be sleeping. The younger, more energetic ones would be in the Upper Town helping the patrols drag heretics from their homes to be burned or hanged. Their victims were guilty only of believing reason over faith, those who put more stock in their learning than in the tutelage of Askerat and the Ninety-Nine Ascended, those accused of bringing drought and plague to the land, because of angering the god. The Askerati believed this purge would set the world right. The poor would "see their progeny thrive and their larders overflow with loaves, meats and sweet gums." Draman, the new emperor promised it would be so.

The local watch, often drunk and always talking, was easy to avoid. Lada, veritably bounding along with the inexplicably lighter Anaxagorum, followed Ryckerd's vanguard through the streets to the wharfs lining the river, the odors of muddy water and rotting wood surrounding her. The raiders slowed when they entered the fog enshrouding the lakeshore. Soon, the pale, crushed stones of the jetty into Lake Rado loomed ahead. The armed gang guarding the point opened the way for them. Not all Tulians backed the emperor. These in particular risked their lives helping the Northmen rescue their now-outlawed texts. All were men, some with their sons, armed but ill-trained.

Their leader reported, "All quiet, lady, but you're a welcome sight nonetheless."

"Booker." Lada squinted into the murk, as her companions arrived behind her. "Not Lady Booker. Not Librasta. Just Booker."

"But the Traillus is explicit in how a gentleman should address a—"

Ryckerd's lantern-bearer doused his light, and the dark swallowed them. Slowly, eyes adjusted to the moonlight reflecting from the gravel. Every ear searched the fog for the tell-tale crunch of feet or rattle of armor other than theirs.

The jetty marked the terminus of the Tule River and the beginning of the great lake that separated the imperial south from the ancient north, not that one could see much of it. From the tip of the jetty, a barrier of thick cables woven through massive pilings blocked vessels from accidentally entering the estuary. Cold water from the Eridus Mountains flowed north into the warm equatorial waters of the lake, so fog was ever-present—at least, that's how scholars saw it. Many others believed the lake to be cursed and that it fumed in fury at the intrusion of the river.

The leader of the local Tulians, a dour man with a red, bulbous nose noted the bagged item on Lada's shoulder and brightened. "Is that it, the Traillus?"

"The Traillus was burned to ashes," Lada replied without thought of cushioning the blow. "Have you signaled our boat?"

The man darkened. "If the Traillus is lost, then are we all."

A long-bodied young man with big eyes and a small mouth, that reminded Lada of a praying mantis, stepped from the gang to within touching distance of the shrouded Anaxagorum. Even in this dark and desperate moment, he was dressed as finely as the hero in a child's story: high, turn-top boots, black leather jerkin chased with black-on-black needlepoint over its chest and shoulders, and red lace at his neck and cuffs. "Is this the other, then, the blood book?"

Lada addressed the leader but couldn't take her eyes off the man. "Tend to the signal."

The leader cuffed the young dandy. "Get to it. What's wrong with you?"

The young man leapt away. "Worry not." A glance at Lada. "Have you opened it?"

The leader raised his hand. The young man evaded and headed for the end of the jetty, all legs and toothy smile and glimmering buckles. "Worry not."

Lada's interest perked the day before when she learned a luminast had joined their party. "You are the luminast?"

"That I am." He paused and stooped to peek, unsuccessfully, under her hood. "And from what face issues that comely voice?"

"Lada of Northem and Librast In Situ for this expedition."

"A spiff like me, then?" He turned his foot to show off an ox-blood boot, nearly black in the low light but obviously of quality. "It's a genuine Ruprecht. He only cobbles twelve a year, you know."

"Light the signal, strange person." Lada could not decide if the leggy fellow were ugly or attractive. Cleverness shown in his eyes, and a strong jaw gave manly support to his crowded face. Almost forgetting the burden on her hip, she followed in his wake, the crunch of gravel beneath their boots unwelcome in the quiet.

She had never met a luminast, but his craft fascinated her. Those seeking the secrets of fire-play had to travel far to the southeast, beyond the five severed kingdoms of the old empire to the forests of Haramdum and their pale worshippers of the fire god Unathar.

He walked to the end of the jetty, where she could no longer see the stones for the fog. The gurgle of water running around pilings and the creak of the great hawsers forming the barrier told her ears what her eyes could not see: the river barrier was nearby. It had to be an impressive feat of engineering. Word was, one could only view it on rare days when a determined wind thinned the fog. Lada had only visited Tule twice and on calm days like this one, so she had yet to see it.

From his shoulder bag the luminast withdrew a crystalloid geode cut in twain, so it resembled the hollow pit of a halved cantaloupe. The man hid his exact machinations, but from her viewpoint, it seemed he produced a tongue of fire from his fingertips that ignited the geode's core. Light leapt forth and painted a wide circle on the fog.

Lada, her voice imperious, as from the moment she was born, asked, "Tell me how you do that without a fire box?"

The young man, narrow face barely containing its expansive smile, tried again for a glance at her face. "A kiss, ten seconds, at least. No pulling away."

Lada could not find words disdainful enough. "I…I would rather kiss the stinger-end of a gut fly."

"Nah, you wouldn't."

What cheek! A total stranger to a woman of merit?

She was too offended to consider whether his kiss might be pleasant. Her younger brother, Jonne, of all people, had recently become a serial kisser of young women, as if he had the right!

"I'm not sure you're pretty under that hood, so I'm the one taking the chance."

"I am pretty enough…but you…." To say more would only amplify her fluster. She waved him away. "Turn about and make your overtures to the fog."

The man only half-turned, raised the lamp-thing, and said, "I am called Pulumbonk." He grinned. "I've heard one or two things about you."

"Pulumbonk? An odd name for an odd fellow."

In better times, Tule's lighthouse beacon was lit monthly for the incoming ship from Northem, ancient riches in her hold and a knot of eager fortune hunters waiting on the pier to sail back with her. The pier and lighthouse were invisible somewhere to their right. Northern things were no longer welcome there.

Lada jumped at Ryckerd behind her. Even his whispers were large.

"I don't doubt the tome on your shoulder carries such dark knowledge, the conjuring of unnatural light and all."

"Papa would cuff you for being superstitious, Ryckerd. I wager the young man's trick and all the arcana in the Anaxagorum can be learned with study."

"So we've been taught, but…." Ryckerd set the point of his broadsword into the gravel and rested his hands on its crossguard. "As I see more of the world, I find it hard to believe reason is the only thread weaving reality."

"How are you my brother?"

Ryckerd snorted. "You'd rather I be pillowy and grim, like Jonne?"

Lada smirked. "If you spent more time with learned people instead of with your cats, you might not fall prey to piffle."

"How are we not arrogant thinking the human mind can comprehend all things?"

"This young man wants a kiss. Perhaps you can shut up and service him."

Ryckerd's eyes snapped to the back of the man with the light. "Did this man-shape force himself on you?"

The young man's head turned, face aghast. "No, oh no no no. I wouldn't disrespect a lady, by all!"

"Not lady. Just Booker."

Ryckerd glared at the young man a few seconds longer and then tip-toed crunchily back to the troops.

Lada regarded the luminast's circle of light and recalled a passage from Agular's Philosophies of a Wanting Man: "Where there is fog there can be illumination." Ryckerd had always been contrary, but this bothered her that he—

A man's face, scaly as a fish and with raptor wings spreading from it, jutted into view. She chided herself for being afraid, for it was but the prow of the boat sent for them. The figurehead was a traditional depiction of a mares (maw-rees), a water spirit, a holdover from primitive times.

The luminast darkened the geode and, placing one, pretty ox-blood boot gingerly into the water, guided the prow to nuzzle into the jetty. The way his long fingers cupped the mares' round face sent a shiver through her. Lada was not prone to girlish shivers.

Pulumbonk hopped clear of the water and bowed to Lada, sweeping his arm toward the boat. "I hope we meet again."

"That is in the hands of fortune."

When she stepped next to him and prepared to board, Pulumbonk raised a hand. "One quick moment, yea?" He lifted the hem of her cloak and wiped the lake water from his boot, as she looked on in disbelief. "The lake water not only kills men, it kills the shine on boots, as well."

Lada wanted to tug her cloak away, but one arm clutched the Anaxagorum, while the other was in the grasp of a helpful oarsman. She had no choice but to concentrate on climbing into the boat. The weight of the blocky tome reasserted itself, the boat yawed, and Lada crumpled, with the book, to the water-sloshed bottom between the boat's thwarts. The book approved of the spot. Lada sensed it was so yet stiffened as the water touching the book's sheath turned to a cloud of steam around her ankles.

Nine others of her party followed her aboard with the few rescued manuscripts. Three trips would be required to ferry all the Northmen from the jetty to the awaiting cog anchored in the lake beyond the mist. She feared for her brother, although none of her companions would see it on her face. If the emperor's men found his band on the narrow jetty, they might never see Northem again. The oarsmen hauled, and the boat slipped back into the fog, the stones of the jetty instantly invisible. They needed no exhortations to hurry them.

Ryckerd had rejoined his circle of kneeling men, when a horn, muted by fog and distance, bellowed from the direction of the city.

He glanced toward the now-departed boat. The ursine warrior held no delusions about how fast a man could row or how quickly an outnumbered party could be cut down. His hand rose. "Fortune be with you, Lada, and, I beg you, look after my rogues."

Chronicler's Illumination: Emperor Draman the First

As the chronicler of this history, I will, at times, find it expedient to step outside the tale to teach. In this instance, I speak of Draman, the man who would take the world for himself.

Draman had served the king of Tulas as chancellor for seventeen years. His position allowed him influence on trade, shares in lead and tin operations, and on a network of powerful people in every kingdom of Arqonias. He was known by all as a man enamored of himself and relentlessly ambitious, which makes one wonder why the world didn't see his grab for power coming.

Two months prior to the raid on the Imperial Library, after years of spending his wealth on the disenfranchised, Draman summoned an army of Askerati zealots from the backwaters of the continent to march on the royal palace at Tule. He imprisoned the king and crowned himself Draman the First, Emperor of Arqonias, Master of the Severed Kingdoms, Hand of Askerat. He claimed he would lead all who followed him out of despair and into a new age of enlightenment and prosperity.

I take exception to the emperor's definition of enlightenment. The people of Northem considered enlightenment to be the embracing of knowledge and reason. Draman condemned thousands of books and people to the flames for being "in conflict with the right-minded." Along with the followers of Askerat and the Ninety-Nine Ascended, his supporters included an expanding circle of nobles from leading families around the continent, men and women expecting to be amply rewarded.

Nobody, including Emperor Draman, could cross the steep and inhospitable mountain ranges to either side of Lake Rado. Should he ever find a way to cross the lake safely, the irreplaceable archives in Northem and the truly enlightened who protect them will be erased from history.

Lexica II

Ryckerd knew the horn call meant the enemy was near. He hated to think the men he had led thus far might meet their ends at the very moment of their escape. Such a tragedy would be a blight on the honor of the Order of Man.

He and the three knights accompanying the raiders were pledged to protect the archives of Northem as members of the Order, should a serious aggressor take arms against the scholars there. Its members were required to gain actual combat experience, something rarely available around Northem. Ryckerd earned his when fighting for Draman in the wars to unify the five severed kingdoms, while the future emperor still followed the King of Tule. By that night on the jetty, the ursine man had worn the Order's livery of an orange sunburst against a divided field of red and white only four years.

In the mist with the knights were trained men-at-arms from Northem, experienced soldiers of fortune from many lands, and the Tulian loyalists, only thirty-three men—thirty-three dead men, if the Sutthers caught scent of their presence.

"Sutthers" was a derogatory term used by many in the north when referring to those in the imperial south who had turned to Askerat for guidance instead of the reason nature gave them. Some in the south referred to Northmen as Bombees, after the cult of defiant heretics exterminated by the growing Askerati a century earlier.

Ryckerd deduced that whoever had blown that horn must have found the bodies of the guards outside the library, but would they think to search the waterfront? He thought it obvious. Any foe at the library must be after the books, and who would want them more than the custodians of the north, and how else could Northmen come to Tule other than by the lake?

Something back toward the wharfs caught his attention. A mote in his eye? A trick of the fog? The thing became a distant dandelion puff of the palest orange. Then three. Soon a line of six or more.

Torches!

He pointed silently. His brother knights nodded and began arranging the men.

One of the Tulians groaned, "We are discovered,"

"Not yet, we aren't," said a knight. "We're more invisible than they."

The twelve soldiers of fortune displayed a variety of armor types and weapons, but they all carried bows. They knelt, nocked arrows, waited. Ryckerd placed his men-at-arms and knights to block the land approach to the jetty. He kept the Tulians on their bellies behind the bowmen. Ryckerd took his place in the middle and watched the approaching puffs of light. He hoped nobody coughed.

The fog that sucked the warmth from his cheeks also absorbed details from the torches, but he guessed there were at least eight. The newcomers were disciplined, as they betrayed not a stifled sneeze or scuff of a boot.

Someone whispered. "How long till the boat returns?"

Ryckerd turned to see the young man with the spindly mustache who had fled the undercroft earlier, a normally steady lad, probably wishing to hear something affirming.

Ryckerd said, "Flee from us again, and I'll kill you."

"But?" The man's eyes bulged. "That...that bloody abomination? It will end us all and—"

Ryckerd slapped his hand over the man's mouth and pushed him onto his back. The point of the stubby knife from his boot dimpled the man's throat. The man stiffened, hyperventilated, calmed.

The torches grew close enough to become distinct. Eight torches could mean five times as many men following them. One halted, then another and another, until all eight were spaced several paces apart. The nearest was an easy arrow-shot away. A distant voice muttered, two others repeating the utterance up the line of torches. Each interval between the torches suddenly flared with smaller, diffused dots of orange.

"Fire arrows!" The knight whispered.

The men put as much space between themselves as the narrow jetty allowed. The Tulians watched in confusion. All heard the twang of the strangers' bowstrings and saw a flight of soft orange balls arcing up and then diving down. The first six went long and hissed into the lake. Three others fell short, also into the lake. Five, each a terrifying meteorite, stabbed among them into the gravel. One struck a Northman's shield. One caught the back of a Tulian's doublet and hung there. He screamed, and the enemy knew they had found their quarry.

The soldiers of fortune rose on a gesture from Ryckerd and fired back at the torch-bearers. Not a lobbing shot, theirs was a flat trajectory with the power to kill. A wet gurgle through the fog signaled a hit.

The next flight of enemy arrows came straight in with lethal intent, ripping through the fog but missing any mark.

Ryckerd ached to counterattack, but the fog-shrouded terrain would defeat them before they reached the enemy. He repositioned his men with shields in front of the soldiers of fortune to offer some protection as they fired. All ducked to offer only the glancing surface of their helmets and their shields to the missiles. The knights wore knee-length hauberks of high-quality chainmail with steel plates added to shoulders and elbows, a gambeson of sturdy fabric underneath. Still, every armor had weaknesses.

Behind Ryckerd came the crunch of iron arrowhead against iron chainmail. The wearer groaned, but the arrow shattered and fell away. To his side, the meaty thump of an arrowhead into leather followed by the crunch of another into bone. A Tulian who had defied the order to lie prone fell to his knees howling. Ryckerd hated archers.

He calculated the risks of charging the enemy or trying to slip north as far as the cliffs would allow, but when men couldn't see the ground before them, how could either succeed?

An arrow pierced the forehead of the soldier of fortune next to him. The man fell like a plank onto the gravel.

Ryckerd thought of his cats, his noble rogues, all twenty-three of them. They deserved to live, as cats were the only beings he trusted to be themselves. Dogs were useful, but they required too much attention. He felt the same about women.

Where was that damned boat?

The lightly armored among them were simply targets waiting to receive. If the enemy archers began lobbing their arrows, the wall of shields wouldn't help them. With luck, the enemy would run out of ammunition or patience soon.

More voices. More points of light joined the others. More shafts hissed, one so close, its blue feathers sung along the metal of Ryckerd's helmet.

Where was that boat?

The soldiers of fortune went prone, either out of missiles or out of the courage to die standing. He considered ordering the charge. One had no time to be afraid in a charge. Yet, to die saving that accursed book!

The dour-faced Tulian leader duck-walked to him. "If we are captured, our deaths will not be swift. We volunteered to help because of the Traillus, not for the one you saved."

"No one's been captured, have they?"

If the man requested, Ryckerd would kill him quickly. The followers of Askerat felt justified in prolonging pain for non-believers. The crunch of wood into gravel heralded the return of the boat.

To the Tulian, he said, "Choose your three youngest."

To the mercenary leader. "Pick three deserving."

To Brother Poonal, the next senior knight. "Take two. Leave me two."

Poonal shook his head, his voice reduced to a shred of sound by an old wound to his throat. "You too valuable. I stay with our men and the Sutthers."

"Tulians, Poonal. They're fighting for us." Ryckerd dismissed him with a wave.

Brother Poonal knew not to argue further. With the other nine lucky souls, he hustled up the jetty, the jingle of chainmail and harness surely audible to the enemy. Once aboard, the boat pulled away and received a parting gift of arrows thunking into its side, joining the half dozen already there.

Whatever was about to happen would be over before the boat could return. Poonal tipped his head in respect to those left behind and then turned toward the lake. After a dozen heartbeats, a gauzy dot of orange revealed the position of the waiting cog. A few more tugs on the oars brought them into fog thin enough for him to make out the ghost of a ship and two masts anchored a quarter-league away. The night grew cotton quiet, until a sailor from the deck called.

"Are you followed?"

"Not followed and not going back, neither," answered an oarsman. "They'll all be dead as Waning Day geese."

Brother Poonal cuffed the back of the man's head and croaked, "We go back and forthwith!"

Lada's voice carried over the dark waters. "By truth, you shall not leave anyone."

The small boat bumped against the hull of the ship where a ladder of netting hung, and men clambered upon it. Brother Poonal refused to leave and clutched the necks of two oarsmen. "Row."

The oarsmen protested with whimpers of dismay, and then back they slipped into the fog.

Lexica III

Lada had made her pronouncement of not leaving anyone behind knowing the chances of any of Ryckerd's group returning were infinitesimal. She had been taught that leaders said such inspiring things in dire times. Still, she hoped that, by some whim of fortune, Ryckerd would return safely. While she played at being indomitable, Ryckerd was indomitable.

Howls went up from the invisible shore. Ryckerd must have ordered his charge, something he would do only if no other options were available. Her brother was no romantic who dreamt of valiant last stands and heroic deaths.

Five marks passed before the small boat reappeared and bumped against the hull with no additional passengers, only a greater accumulation of arrows in its sides.

Lada helped steady heavily armored Brother Poonal, as he climbed aboard. "You could not have stayed in his stead?"

Poonal squeaked. "What you think?"

She raised her chin. "I think fighting is foolish."

"Foolish? Your brother was—"

She swiped her hand. "Tis all foolish. Why is it the benighted Askerati cannot see reason? Do they wish to plunge the world into devastation? What progress comes from that?"

"Your brother's a hero."

"He is just another corpse now."

Poonal's voice squeaked higher. "What's wrong with you? Ryckerd—"

She shut her eyes. "Please, Brother, no more." Memories came unbidden. Her big, bully of a brother, the same who had slapped her belly pink when she was a girl, the same who had carried her on his back for two months while the bones in her foot healed, the same who turned into the gentlest of bears when with his cats, he was out there somewhere facing death. Her eyes fixed on a random spot beyond the stern.

Ryckerd wouldn't ask for glory in his epitaph, only that he died doing his duty. Lada, as Librast In Situ, would be responsible for chronicling the raid and his last moments facing Draman's zealots.

Oh, how I hate the ignorance that makes religion possible!

She suddenly regretted taking the Anaxagorum from Ryckerd in the undercroft. Her intent had been to save him from the infamy of bringing it home to Northem. One couldn't allow the destruction of a book, no matter what its contents, but saving that one might be unforgivable. Chronicles needed heroes. She could bear the weight of "villain" far better than Ryckerd—not happily, but better.

The blood book lay two decks below her in the moist blackness of the bilge. She could sense it, even with the silty smell of the lake in her nose and the night breeze on her cheeks. Not a taste or odor, it was a presence that had seeped into her after she first touched the book bare-handed. It existed now as a slight tingling at the nape of her neck, noticeable only when dwelling on it.

She left the ship's stern to find comfort in the circle of light under the main mast lantern. Sailors had tacked the sail to catch the northwesterly breeze. The waters of the lake did not heave and drop as they had on the way south, and her stomach appreciated the change. The ship rolled easily, ropes and planks creaking in rhythm with the waves. She glanced at her feet, as if she could see through the decks to the book. The planks between the toes of her boots grinned: a semi-circular crack in the wood for a mouth, the ends of two fastening pins for eyes. She glanced about for a nearby soul, seeing only one of the crew heading toward the bow.

The blueskin Guides crewing the ship were indifferent to her, as they were to all whiteskins from the castle, but she trusted them. Generations of them had sailed that cursed lake, one or two taken by its toxic waters every few years. People said they got their knowledge from the Anaxagorum centuries ago, but, people also said dragons lived along the edges of the world.

Even the lowliest manure carter of Northem asked for proof, when told something fantastical. The librasts of the castle would accept the book with intellectual curiosity, others with trepidation, some with protest. Would any of them feel its presence, as she had?

A familiar voice jerked Lada from her rumination. "I've not seen hair so orange before, orange as the fruit."

Long-legged Pulumbonk, the luminast, stood a span away, one hand on a belaying pin for balance and the other holding a stylish leather cap at waist level. His hair looked black, except at the crown where the light picked up a strand of plum. His wide mouth, when not talking, made a warm smile.

"You again." She raised her hood and pulled it forward.

"I took off my cap, seeing how your hood was down, but I guess I can put it back on, now that you have." He snugged the cap onto his head and cocked it at an angle.

"Do as you will, but I would prefer you do it elsewhere."

He glanced about. "Not a lot of 'elsewhere' on a ship, but I'm sure I can find a deep shadow, if you wish."

"Why are you here? I hoped you were a Tulian and would stay behind."

"Me? A Tulian? I'm from Atmaa, or perhaps I should say, I escaped Atmaa."

Atmaa was one of the five severed kingdoms that had seceded from the empire forty years earlier. Draman, the new emperor had conquered and re-assimilated two of the kingdoms as a general for the ruler he had just deposed. Atmaa retained its independence, for the nonce.

"I thought luminasts were from Haramdum."

"Yea, I've been there, all right, twelve years as an apprentice. Barely made it to Tule in time to catch this ship. My eyes have been set on the north since I first heard of ancient ruins full of treasure. Wasn't gonna let a civil war stop me, by all."

"Half the adventurers who delve into those ruins die, you know."

He winked. "Half don't."

"Is wealth worth such a risk?"

"Even a slog like me can come back from there well-trimmed."

"Are you not already...'well-trimmed'?"

"A man of merit must always replenish his means to stay so."

"So, you are a lolly who does not care to get his hands dirty."

His smile faded. "Yea, I've done plenty of that. Watched my brother die a slave in the Krekk iron mine."

"I thought slavery had been outlawed through the empire."

"Who's gonna care what happens to an orphan, yea?"

"Oh, dear, so...you are an orphan?"

Pulumbonk's grin reappeared. "I'm a luminast."

Lada couldn't help smiling with him. When his gaze remained on her, she turned lest a blush betray her. "You have seen me without my hood. Am I pretty?"

"I have a short memory, Perhaps you can turn to me again. The way lantern light plays tricks, you could be hideous."

"Like you, then?"

"Ack! I wouldn't even kiss me."

"Well, do not expect me to." She wondered if he still smiled.

The double-masted cog carrying them and the other survivors of the raid was one of only two to ply the great lake. It was known as the Drowned Hag. The name was chosen for two reasons, or so the tale goes. A drowned thing could not be drowned again, and what would be a less desirable thing for slipperfish to drag into their aquatic homes than a toothless hag? An arbor of rope netting woven over her deck was proof against slipperfish, should they actually exist. No crewman or passenger could be readily drawn through its tight web.

The twin moons, Homm and his little sister Humu, peeked from behind the clouds through the netting to cast a cross-hatch shadow over Lada. She found it comforting and sinister.

Legend said slipperfish formed from the spray of a ship's wake and would curl as a wave over the gunwales to gulp sailors. Nobody on six generations of ships bearing the name and the netting had been lost. Why did that not calm Lada? Or was it fear for her brother that heightened her uneasiness? Or mayhap Pulumbonk's attention unbalanced her. And why let that bother her? Her romantic needs were taken care of well enough by Brillix, the Lance Captain of the Order. They had spoken of marriage after her tenure as Librast In Situ. A short tryst with another would not be frowned upon, but really? With a lolly from Atmaa?

The water in every direction lay dark. Landfall was at least two hours away. The rear of the cog had a captain's quarters and a cabin for special passengers, but Lada chose to stay on deck. Accepting privilege would appear weak.

Pulumbonk remarked from behind her, "Your brother seems a good man…bit of a terror boy, really, but good with that sword, yea?"

She turned, happy to talk about Ryckerd. "He is a good man…or should I say 'was' a good man." She mulled the grammar. "I believe I will stay with 'is.'"

"Does he ever smile?"

"Oh, yes!" She recalled her brother singing when around his cats. "A big bear like that should have stag hounds, would you not a agree?"

"I suppose."

"He has cats." She wanted the pleasant moment to linger. "I find one cat to be agreeable enough, but twenty-three. Thank Gela he has servants to clean up after them. You look qualified."

The Drowned Hag bumped to a halt. Lada lurched. Pulumbonk fell to his knees. The ship had struck something in the water. Firm but giving, like day-old porridge. Mud, mayhap? But the middle of the great lake had no shoals or reefs. The hide of a beast?

The waters around the ship shuddered. Lada forgot about Ryckerd, forgot about Pulumbonk, and gripped the netting beside her. The tingling at the nape of her neck grew ferocious.

The blood book was apparently unhappy with its accommodations.

Lexica IV

When the Drowned Hag listed to port, the deck fell aslant. A nearby crewman seized the netting to keep from crashing to his face. "Drok!"

The vessel lurched to a halt. The contents of Lada's stomach took flight, only to be lost in the incoming spray.

Pulumbonk fell into the port-side netting, now below Lada.

The rudder man, near where she clung to the netting, shouted. "The steer board's free! We've high-centered!"

Lada's feet slid free of the deck, so she was hanging, one elbow hooking the net, one hand grasping it. She had not known panic during the raid on the Imperial Library. Having her eyes and ears, hands and feet at her disposal gave her a sense of control. She felt now as if she were a leaf in the wind, a groat caught in the talons of a hawk, a babe being torn from its mother.

The possibility of death didn't present itself. The possibility of losing her position as Librast In Situ emptied her. She was the first woman to achieve the post, and mayhap the first to lose it after one time in the field.

The blood book was to blame!

She knew, by a sense beyond those nature gave her, the Anaxagorum was calling to eldritch things of the lake she had been taught were myth. Mayhap it wanted them to drag it and its liberators beneath the waves. But that made no sense, for it would be lost again after just gaining its freedom. Mayhap it did not wish to be lost but free of human hands, free to command the lesser things of the world.

I am to blame!

Lada knew the touch of her bare flesh had awakened the thing, and fate was punishing her.

"Stop!" She screamed not at the waters of the lake but at the superstition driving reason from her. Fate was not a force. Fate was merely a term describing a concatenation of events.

A wave crashed over the gunwale, through the netting, and onto her. Not water. Thicker. Like oil or syrup or mucus. The power of it pulled the ship's starboard side down, and violently, until the deck was nearly level again. The force slammed her legs to the planking and ripped her hand from the netting. Her right shoulder screamed. The liquid around her lower legs opened in a circle, like a mouth, curdled into opaque lips that gulped her to the armpits, and pulled. Her shoulder screamed from its socket, as her torso slid through the netting and hung over the roiling lake. She hooked the ropes with her legs, fearing the force would break them and mayhap tear her in half. The slipperfish, or whatever held her, tried with everything it had. The world became awash with pain.

A figure appeared above her at the ship's gunwale. She recognized the outline of the bobbed, silver-gray hair belonging to one of the females of the crew, a young woman named Remi. Lada has seen her dance many times in the grove of Gela during festivals. Time slowed as the young woman raised both arms and cried words Lada did not understand. "Ballus e horendun!" From the woman's hands hurtled a missile past Lada's face, a melon-sized carved effigy of a ship's hull etched with strange markings from stem to stern. She did not hear its splash. She did feel the watery lips release her and the wave of pain that swept from her knees into her brain, and the undertow of blackness that dragged her from consciousness.

***

The blue-skinned woman's cobalt blue eyes were encased by naturally black lids and lashes, and were the first things to greet Lada's return to the light. "Do you know me, Librast?"

Maybe. Somewhat. Are you, "The dancer?"

"I am also the warder on this voyage."

Warders were blueskins skilled in casting invisible wards to protect a companion or to knock a threat away. Lada and the others of Northem with untainted skin refused to call the ability "magic," although they had no explanation for how wards were summoned.

"You're sore hurt but you'll live."

The wrenching pain below Lada's thighs confirmed both the seriousness of the damage and that she was, indeed, vividly alive. She tried to hold the pain with clenched teeth, but no normal person could remain composed suffering so. A touch of her fingers and a peek revealed a left leg attached by naught but a tendon and a right calf twisted backwards. A scream rushed forth, until Lada's breath grew thin. Remi inserted a hank of coiled leather between her teeth. Moans continued, low and pitiful.

Two of the blueskin Guides crewing the Drowned Hag and Brother Poonal had disentangled Lada from the netting and laid her on the deck. Moving her farther would only have encouraged more bleeding.

Poonal stepped into view above her, his voice vaporous. "The wave carried away two men whole-husk."

Remi's voice sounded deep in comparison. "Yanked them right through the netting, like tomatoes through broad cloth."

Lada's stomach wobbled.

"Not you, though. A stronger kind of fruit you are, I'd say."

Her lids pressed back together. "Were they...slipperfish?"

Remi bent close, talismans of polished rock suspended by tiny leather strips dangled from the braided grass tiara holding her hair back, colored blurs inches from Lada's face. "I am not a skragging woman, but I can dull the pain, if you allow me to invoke."

Invocations suggested magic, so any other time Lada would've said no.

"Please."

Remi produced a star the size of a biscuit made from woven plant material, breathed heavily on it, and pressed it against Lada's forehead. "Ansa, Lada non."

Lada felt as if her brain had been kicked to the side of her body, which left her pain in the distance.

"Thank...." Lada said, unable to finish the "you."

Poonal squatted. "Castle herbalist will help you properly. No more blueskin tricks."

Remi rose, all olives and browns in her jerkin and trousers. "As I am not wanted here...." She glided out of sight.

Poonal's hoarse voice didn't offer comfort, just explanation. "Twas not a slipperfish. Just a wave."

"No, Brother Knight, twas something unnatural."

"Like her." He nodded toward the prow, and Lada felt a pillow of hands lift her head enough to see over her chest, past her mangled legs, down the deck, to where Remi stood watching the waters ahead. Her tiara held a fan of three red-and-white great ruyk feathers splaying over the back of her neck. The weak moonlight turned everyone's skin blue, so the woman's looked normal.

"Remi?"

"She, too, is unnatural, yes?"

"I do not understand her skills, but I do not find her unnatural."

Remi was one of many female children given to the Sisterhood of Gela, a sorority dedicated to the celebration of nature and the maintenance of Gela's Park, a pristine tract of trees and streams off limits to agriculture or logging. Unwanted male children usually went to work as hands on the farms and ranches, or as apprentices to tradesmen. There were no true orphans in Northem.

"Not curious? Her incantation saved you."

Lada did not have the energy to discuss. She knew there was a natural explanation why the slipperfish backed off. She might not know it. Humans might not learn the reason for generations, but the logic of it would come clear someday. There were even enlightened minds of Northem all too ready to ascribe the warders and skragging women healers to magic.

"I like her." Lada's face compressed, as the pain swelled...and then ebbed on a long sigh.

"Relief is nigh." The voice belonged to Pulumbonk.

Lada tilted her head back, so she could see the person pillowing her head. A familiar wide mouth and big eyes crowded a narrow face. He might have been smiling. She croaked, "Still want that kiss?"

The luminast said, "No, Booker. I never take advantage of the infirm...or the upside-down."

The comment was no doubt intended to charm, but it brought a burning to her eyes. Who would want to kiss such a twisted horror as she? Tears squeezed onto her cheeks. She hoped Pulumbonk and Brother Poonal did not notice. Best to keep her eyes and mouth shut, until they reached land, if they reached land.

Time needed to pass. She forced an image of Ryckerd to the fore of her brain...and there he was: broad, hairy, bear face with close-set brown eyes gentle and violent.

Do you feel I abandoned you? Did you hate me as you died? If you had carried the blood book, it would have been you on the boat first. You would have lived. But...really, you are Ryckerd, and Ryckerd does not leave first. And I am Lada, she who also puts duty before family. A pair destined to unhappy ends, it seems.

Her eyes popped open at the press of lips on her forehead.

Pulumbonk smiled down at her. "Your face looked like it needed that."

She gazed stupidly at him. The kiss had felt good, but that somehow made the pain more excruciating. Her back arched as she moaned and crushed tears from her eyes.

"Nah, nah, listen to me, not the pain."

Forget the pain? Was he joking?

The expression on his upside-down face wasn't easy to read, but his voice sounded genuinely curious. "Tell me, how did the early folk of Northem know to look for the Anaxagorum? I can't imagine it walked up and introduced itself, yea?"

"Of course not," she croaked and turned her face away.

Brother Poonal invited her to speak. "You tell the tale well."

Lada did not wish to speak, yet, as a booker and historian, it was expected. "It called to them."

"In a voice?"

When she didn't reply, Poonal croaked, "'Like the keening of a bereft mother."

"That is how the chronicler of the time described it." Lada sighed, relieved to feel the pain distance itself again. "It came from underground, up through the settlement wells as my ancestors slept."

Pulumbonk winced. "Rather unsettling."

"Whatever…whatever it was, guided them over the hills to a plain of towering spikes. Its cry rose from a deep slash in the soil, a pit…black and soundless." She half-chuckled and half-whimpered. "How curious they must have been, for they lowered themselves into the nothingness…three men…two torches and…and a lantern."

"Did they know what they were following?"

She shook her head. "Nobody knew of the blood book then."

"But they found it underground, yea?"

"In a vault beneath a buried city of great antiquity, part of the long dead empire of Faellar."

"I am here to see such a place."

Pain nudged at her, and she bit her lip.

"Nah, nah, look at me, lady. Talk to me."

"Stop calling me 'lady'."

Remi's strong voice came from the prow of the ship. "Land up!"

Lada opened her eyes to an intensely bright light from the shore that practically blinded her. Pulumbonk threw a hand over his eyes. Both asked, "What is that?"

Poonal squinted at the light. "The eye. The tower eye."

The luminast peered through his fingers, but the glare slapped his lids shut. "The great Faellic eye?" His mouth stretched wide. "Oh, I must see that as fast as my Ruprecht boots can take me there."

Lada laid her palm over her eyes, and released a long, braying moan. Was the reason the ancient eye had come to life only obvious to her?

Chronicler's Illumination - The Six Fingers.

The Six Fingers wasn't always a tavern. It began as a lighthouse. We know who built it but little about them. Thousands of years tend to bury details. The few letters of their alphabet our scholars have identified are yet to be understood as a language. Four of them appear together in several instances, usually etched into draysalt towers, and resemble, somewhat tenuously, our letters:

F A E L

We don't know what they called themselves, but to us, they are the Fael. The ruined cities hiding beneath millennia of rock and dust north of Lake Rado are all that is left of the Empire of Faellar.

Calling the coastal structure a lighthouse is deduction, not fact. But what else could it be, a single tower rising eight stories from a foundation of solid rock on the long unpopulated north shore of the toxic lake? The only marking on the tower is the image of a hand with six fingers, blood-red and stamped into the lintel over the open entrance. Did a door ever exist? Stairs wound up the interior walls to a dizzying view from a cupola at its apex. There rests a large crystalloid sphere of a thousand facets in an immovable cradle, a wide-open eye asleep for ages. How it projected enough light to warn incoming ships during its day we don't know. In the current time, the Society of Guides lights a brazier whose light is reflected toward the lake by the crystals of the eye, but it is a modest illumination.

Moonlight bouncing from that eye was enough to guide the first southerners to shore five centuries ago. Those new aboriginals were a polyglot of diseased and outlawed souls desperate enough to flee persecution across a lake that killed other travelers, but that is a tale for another time.

I have yet to tell you of Lada's return to Northem.

Lexica V

The sun had risen to mid-morn before the anxious throng waiting above the Northem pier parted and four litter bearers hustled through them to collect Lada. Only she, the captain, and the Anaxagorum remained aboard the Drowned Hag. The blood book would be removed to the castle vaults by a special retinue later.

All one hundred and fifty members of Northem's legislative and custodial Collegium, including three recently inducted females, had gathered. The sight lent Lada an instant of joy. She had been the first female inductee five years earlier, an achievement some say was only possible because her father was the Librast Superior, head of the Collegium and acting regent of the realm.

The litter bearers carried her down the gangplank, a sheet covering her lower half. She rode propped on an elbow and waved to show strength, although one shred of will away from squealing like a scalded pig. Remi's invocation had placed her pain in the distance, but with wounds so grievous, no distance was far enough. The herbalist and the relief her medicine would bring were no doubt held up by Papa, who thought nobody could do their jobs without him.

Mama and he were easily visible in the crowd, as they and the forty-seven knights from the Order of Man who had remained at home sat astride horses. The gonfalon bearing the flaming eye of Northem hung over them. Horses had been introduced from the south over a century ago, a gift from the King of Tulas in better times. Papa was portly, bald—save for a circlet of trimmed, gray hair—and only a thumb taller than the average twelve-year-old. He rode his black-and-brown-swirled gelding, Jules, whenever in public. The beast had no will of its own and dutifully served every whim of its master. Papa preferred people to be that way. Many of the bodyguards around him were in excess of three spans tall, armored and broad-shouldered, and each of them knew exactly who the biggest man on the scene was.

Papa had always regaled Lada with his own glories without encouraging her to achieve her own. The household ate what Papa ate, dressed as he dictated, and learned to listen to his monologues without yawning. Growing up had taken an effort for her not to feel small. That said, Papa had never been mindfully unkind to her, and when he saw her on the litter, he galloped to the pier, eyes as large as hard-boiled eggs. The Herbalist Superior, in her grass-green robe bearing the monogram G for Gela, followed.

"Lada, by all that is good, tell me you do not suffer much!"

Lada had gotten the word "I" out when Papa stabbed his stubby right hand at the surgeon who followed the litter. "Put more men on her litter. Four's not enough." He looked around to Mama who trailed the herbalist. "Why do I have to tell people this?"

The surgeon, having dealt with the Librast Superior for years, waved away Father's aides. "Tis a four-man litter and tis made for four men because more than four men twitch it all up."

Papa turned from the surgeon and his grievously injured daughter, when the captain of the Drowned Hag prepared to descend the gangplank.

"Hold there!"

The captain held forth a weary hand in protest. "Might I report later?"

Papa placed one fist on his hip and struck an imperial pose from his saddle. "I don't wish a report. I wish you to turn that ship around and go back to Tule. I've a son missing."

"It's been a whore of a night, celestial one, and my crew's already ashore."

"I'll have them brought back."

"And Remi, my warder, dances in the grove tomorrow."

"I'll find you another."

"And I'm exhausted."

"Put one foot on the shore, and I'll have you arrested."

The captain sucked down his anger, and let it sigh slowly out. "I'll be in my cabin."

"Find Ryckerd and any other survivors, and bring them back, fast as fire!"

The captain disappeared below decks before Papa finished. As though there had been no interruption, he pulled Jules alongside his daughter's litter. "Your Papa is here, sugar cake. I shall see nobody botches your care."

Lada looked past him to Mama. Once beautiful, she had withered to old fruit after three decades as wife to the tallest short man on the planet. She had patience and the strength of water, flowing around Papa without a burble but always a current that carried him unknowingly to a destination better than that of his choosing. Unlike devout women of the south, she wore her hair uncovered and festooned with shiny red beads and golden ribbons. She shared a defeated smile with her daughter. The woman surely ached to be at Lada's side, mayhap holding her hand, certainly wanting to ask about Ryckerd, but she had accepted second place to her husband years ago.

Lada stretched a hand toward her, crying openly and without shame. "Mama."

Papa and his horse remained between them. He swiveled to shout at the herbalist. "You cannot help my dear daughter back there. Dismount and stop making her wait!"

The herbalist, one shoulder raised and one eye squinted as if forever about to be struck, slid from her horse and hastened to Lada's side. She burrowed into her shoulder bag and did everything in her power to not disappoint the Librast Superior—a doomed chore, as she would never be fast enough or knowledgeable enough to please him. Who was?

Lada's father had overborne her since she slid from her mother into his world. "Papa, back off! Let the expert do her work."

"And let her work at a snail's pace? She has not even prepared her ingredients!"

The woman was a master of herbs and, even though liquid in the bowels most of her life because of the Librast Superior, she would not be hurried. Her compounds were best when mixed just before administering. She knelt, spread bowls and bags before her and began grinding saffron and fennel, mint and bloodberry, and purple Valens powder she tapped from a vial. Only select people among Papa's sphere received Valens powder, as lives had been lost more than once collecting the ingredients for it.

Papa watched from his saddle, his shadow darkening the woman's work space. "The mint is only for flavor and will slow you down, so—"

Lada snapped at the herbalist, "Keep the mint," and then at her father. "Stop! Stop being so...so much like you."

Papa turned to Lada's mother, someone he could boss without sass. "Back! Give the woman space to work." He waved back his bodyguard and retainers. "All of you, back!" They were already well back, but the man loved giving orders.

Lada watched the powders being mixed, aware of the pain all the more as she waited. She wiped away her tears and composed herself. "My pain will pass. You should be worrying about Ryckerd."

"Why?"

Lada grimaced. "Surely, you were told of our Ryckerd's predicament."

"Did you see him die?"

"No, but—"

"Then shush. Ryckerd's death is not a fact. What is a fact, you failed to retrieve the Traillus, and I am not happy about that."

"And I should care how happy you are?" She would've apologized for the remark, if the pain hadn't killed her ability to care. "Move and let Mama come to me."

Papa gestured to the castle rising on its hill, the massive central keep and its surrounding ramparts picketed with towers and rimmed with gold from the morning sun. "I shall send your brother to get your account of the expedition while the surgeon tends your wounds."

"Listen to me," Lada pressed.

Her father looked bemused. "Always."

"No, really listen. I cannot bear being with my light-sucking brother, right now. Send Mama."

The Herbalist Superior stooped over Lada's litter, hands trembling as she offered the bowl of green-gray paste. Lada tilted it to her mouth and sucked in as much as she could. It tasted gloriously of mint.

Papa pressed. "I will need your report. Did you see any ships being built? It will happen someday, a Guide will defect and Lake Rado will no longer protect us from Draman and his rats."

She slurred wetly. "I can barely focus."

"You are my daughter. You will focus as needed."

"You pain me nearly as much as—" A razor ran up her right leg to her brain.

Papa's mouth, perpetually in a pout, frowned epically. "I shall not let you stay in pain long. Only a worthy few—"

"Get Valens powder…I know." Lada grimaced when she swallowed, as the taste went from mint to mud.

"I will also send berries and cream with Jonne."

"No Jonne!"

Papa recoiled without comment. He had not seen his daughter weep in red-eyed rage since she was an infant.

Lada, head lolling dreamily, said, "A journeyman luminast named Pulumbonk made the crossing with us. You may send him and Mama only…and the berries and cream."

Papa re-inflated himself. "A common adventurer can stay at The Six Fingers, not in my castle."

Lada smiled tearfully, as Mama craned her head over her father. The woman's plump face seemed always pained, so to weep would be gratuitous. She did offer healing sympathy with her eyes that Lada drank as deeply of as the medicine. "We will send word to the young man, if that is what you wish."

Papa did not address his women, only the day at large. "We will NOT."

A man aboard the Drowned Hag called from the gangplank. "Your Glory, we are ready to bring the book ashore."

"Not before I inspect it." He dismounted and strode up the gangplank, a giant in miniature.

Mama slipped her mount into the spot he had vacated. She was not one to show overt tenderness, but her voice was soft. "What does the young man look like?"

With Papa descending on other, lesser beings, mother and daughter were free to reunite properly.

Chronicler's Illumination: The Man Behind the Pen.

This is where I enter the tale as a player in my own right. I am Jonne the Booker, Librast Custodian of Northem. I have been much more comfortable writing from anonymity, scribing the previous events from Lada's dictation with a shoom blanket over my legs, a cup of bloodberry tea, and an orange cake within easy reach.

Because of her accident, I fear the title of Librast In Situ shall devolve to me. I'm no adventurer. I fare poorly away from my own bed. I know the nooks of this castle, where the deepest shadows are and how to glide among them to avoid others. I'm happier that way. They're happier that way.

A Librast In Situ must stride into the world boldly with an unquenchable curiosity and a constitution suited for cold nights upon the ground and hot days in heavy armor, for remaining collected when terrors arise. I have only the curiosity, and I find it well sated by my life among the archives of the castle. The most terrifying things I might encounter there are girls. Without a substantial quantity of ale in me, I am butter before their fire, melting quickly to goo and running back to invisibility through the cracks in the cobbled floors.

Lada was born for the job. I know because she is my sister. Ryckerd my brother. Life was in balance with her as the seeker, he as the fighter, I as the forgettable.

Protest though I might, history calls.

Lexica VI

The Collegium called me to a special conclave a week after Lada and the raiders returned. They needed to interview candidates to replace Lada as Librast In Situ, and I was one of five bookers in contention. Each of us must have served as a librast custodian for a minimum of three years, be under twenty-five, and have been recommended by a senior librast who was satisfied with the candidate's dedication and proficiency. I am but twenty, the youngest of my siblings, the youngest of the candidates.

The one hundred and fifty members of the Collegium of Northem have one vote each. Father, the Librast Superior, who chroniclers call—at his insistence—Arno the Celestial, has no vote, except in case of a tie. He does have a driving desire to get what he wants, as I've shown. No doubt he was behind the scenes cajoling members into voting for his choice. While he can be a pestilential force, Father never sinks to bribery. Being a bringer of emotional misery usually works. My question is: who was his choice? He nearly lost a daughter to the job. Was he all that keen to push for his youngest son to be next?

Possibly.

Each of us five candidates was asked to present an impromptu argument as to why he or she should be selected. For my argument, I held forth about how a Librast In Situ must be physically fit and enthusiastically engaging with others, so he or she can get all sides of a story. I made a point to mumble often and rarely look at the person to whom I was speaking. Once finished with my presentation, I slunk back to my bench in the collegia and pretended to fall asleep. Several someones at the table of judges chuckled, which I took as a sure sign that they saw dumpy Jonne as beneath consideration.

As I have stated, I am not a forthcoming fellow. My left ear is to blame. It has been malformed from birth, resembling a tiny flesh flower with its three petals laid open and flat. Father refused to recognize it as a problem. Mother told me it made me special. Lada and Ryckerd, and half the people in the castle called me Blossom, not an empowering moniker for an impressionable lad. Girls never looked at me.

As my siblings matured, they began defending me, but the damage had been done. I lived inside books and shadows. I begged for years to be allowed to grow my hair longer, but blueskins often wore long hair and Father wouldn't have that.

I'll define Librast In Situ as a chronicler situated within a group embarking upon an expedition expected to be of historical significance. Lada joined the library raiders, and as Librast In Situ, was responsible for chronicling the expedition and accounting for saving the Traillus and the Anaxagorum. The holder of the title must possess a high calling to the preservation of knowledge, a mental catalog of extant volumes, great physical endurance, and the ability to use a weapon if things went bloody. Lada trained with the poniard and stun darts, I with throwing knives and the short sword. There have been many a fight in the darkened tunnels of Faellar that turned on the stroke of a librast's blade.

A majority of eighty-seven members voted for me, twenty-nine for the runner-up, and the drippings went to the rest. When my name was announced, I shrunk and accepted the astonished stares and jibes of my peers. Blossom wilted.

Everyone, including Lada, believed Father was behind the vote. Members of the Collegium refused to reveal their reasons to me. Father is not a habitual liar, and when he does get his way, he usually gloats. He has been atypically mum on the subject, only stopping by my chamber after the vote to say, "I expect you to embrace the post with diligence and honor."

A great deal of prestige goes with the title and puts the bearer in line to be Librast Superior, a position I desired only tepidly, and one Father could only wish me to occupy if out of his mind with fever. Anyone desiring to be a leader needed to be like Father, confirmed in the righteousness of their own opinion and impervious to their own toxicity.

On the bright side, the job of Librast In Situ will kick me from my happy routine into the presence of new people and places, whether I want them or not. As I have inadvertently repelled every eligible maiden in Northem, mayhap I can find one elsewhere in the world who can see past my ear to the mind behind it.

***

When the litter bearers set Lada next to me on the high porch of the great keep, she smiled dreamily at the blue sky. "A beautiful day. Thank fortune!"

Not a cloud sullied the canopy. Sunlight brightened the patchwork fields of green, yellow, and brown stretching in all directions from the castle. I spied gray gathering at the horizon. "I see rain clouds."

"Of course you do, oh jaundiced Jonne."

"Just pointing out a fact, La-la-lada."

Whatever concoction the nervous Herbalist Superior had been giving Lada, it was more potent than anything I'd received. My sister was almost enjoyable to be with, not the sharp, officious Lada I'd grown up knowing. She acted far too happy for someone whose legs had been removed a week ago.

I offered her a grape from the platter resting on my lap. "You're feeling no pain?"

"Oh, no, I am raging with pain." She accepted the grape, said, "I simply do not care," and popped it into her mouth.

"I'm glad. Well, not glad, but it's good you're not suffering as you should be." Too many grapes caused me to break out in bumps, so I finished the last sliver of roasted groat.

She abruptly declared, "I have decided to quit sewing."

"Nonsense. You're quite accomplished at it." I cocked my leg to see what little of my pants showed between tunic hem and boot top. The inseam stitching was strong and uniform.

"I do not fancy sewing stump covers. Full pants are complete and rewarding. No more sewing."

"What about sewing for me?"

"Ah, so this is about you. I will be happy to mend certain things for you."

I nodded. "My gratitude."

"Not your clothes, your speech, drip-spittle. Even in your writing I see: 'You're,' 'it's,' 'I'm.' You are the Librast In Situ now, not a blithering blueskin."

"Blueskins have other talents. They don't blither, in any case."

"I liked the alliteration: blue, blither, blue."

"People speak in contractions, and contractions are easier on the reader. We've discussed this."

"Our job is to lead the people in learning, not follow." She rolled her gaze back to the sky. "Oh, well...."

"I am to renew my combat training with Brillix this afternoon."

"Brillix?" Her mood dimmed. "He has proven himself a sorry paramour, as he has not visited me once, but then...." Her eyes fell on the vacant place under the sheet.

"I don't know why you ever entertained that preening ham as a possible lover."

"He is a man of ambition and value." She giggled. "I rather imagine he's bold between the sheets, and....matters not now."

"Is that the most attractive trait of a man, lust?"

"What goes on inside you, Jonne? I have pondered that much this last week, the things we think and feel, what we humans are about. Do you feel things about other people, as in things other than hunger or fear, things like…say, do you ever have good thoughts about me?"

A mace to the face wouldn't have stunned me as much. "I…I consider things, people. I try to be rational. I do have thoughts of you, but not a preponderance of them. I imagine, as I write about your exploits in Tule, I will think deeply on the person you are."

"What kind am I?"

"I haven't thought on it, yet."

"You have had a lifetime to think on it. What kind of person am I?"

This was a different Lada, for sure. We had been taught by kin and culture to be curious, to learn whenever possible, but to keep our thoughts to ourselves until we had something valuable to say. "I think you are a capable woman."

"Capable? Am I nothing more? How capable am I with no legs? Do you have an inkling what I am feeling?"

"You are in great pain, of course."

"In my head, in my heart, the pains are worse."

"I'm sure you feel a certain loss of independence. You can still write, however, and read, and—"

"Do you think I am pretty?"

"You're my sister."

"And if I were but another face among the women at a festival dance, would you give me a second glance?"

I was on thin ice. "Possibly."

"You have become quite the bold lover, or so I hear."

I was glad she didn't notice my blush. "Too much ale is the culprit."

"You kissed three girls in one night. Three!"

My whole body shrank. Three girls had kissed me at the Festival of the Twin Moons, not the other way around. I was wholly receptive, at the time, wholly embarrassed since. I was certain it was a cruel joke among the girls to hurt me. They'd surely prefer a man like Brillix.

"Kissing." Lada said flatly, growing despondent for a moment before the concoction lifted her back to her happy perch. "You know, Ryckerd would have volunteered to help carry this litter, were he here."

"Have I done something to upset you?"

"You knew, I believe, that for many years, I had a standing invitation from him to spend each Waning Day evening with sweet drinks and his cats. It was my favorite night of the week."

"Ryckerd never had any patience with you."

"Wrong, Jonne, wrong. He loved me, as do Papa and Mama. Who loves you?"

"If I had known you wanted to be moved here when you summoned me, I would've volunteered to carry you."

"Oh, pish you would. You never once invited me to an evening of anything."

Was that true? I couldn't tell her it wasn't. "If you wish to call me terrible, do so."

Lada's hand inched toward me only to halt at the litter's retaining rail. "You have moments that feel brotherly. You held my hand when I was in pain last...what was it, Skyday? Waterday? Days ago, in any case."

"Actually, you held my hand, but I didn't mind."

"So unlike me. Is our family broken, Jonne?"

I gazed beyond the low wall of the high porch to the lazy sails of a windmill in the mid-distance. The day was nice, no doubt a boon to the farmers.

"I don't know how you mean."

"Do you love me?"

I glanced to her then immediately back to the windmills. "I don't have to answer a question like that."

"You have a brilliant mind, Blossom, but a heart too small to hold anyone but you."

"I don't like that name."

Her smile seemed to belong on someone else's face. "I meant it in a sweet way."

"Are you saying I love only myself?"

"Perhaps a bit, but mostly you have little desire for others to love you. Sad."

"You don't know what I desire."

"You have many admirable qualities, but few friends. Blueskins, mostly."

"Why do you care about these things, of a sudden?"

She closed her eyes, her smile not joyous but happily complacent. "Perhaps this tincture is too strong or," she giggled, "I am simply out of my mind."

"That would explain it."

One eye opened, a tear trembling in its corner. "Do not wait until you are legless to crave the warmth of others."

The last time I saw Lada cry was when Father ordered her to marry a prince in the south for political reasons, and those were tears of fury. He was a toad of a man with a penchant for beating his servants. More distressing to her, marriage would've ended her dream of becoming Librast In Situ. I felt relief for my sister, when a runaway cart of melons ran over the fellow, leaving him as inarticulate as the fruit it carried. "Does crying make you feel better?"

"I am not crying."

"Yet, it seems you are."

"Would that be a weakness in your eyes?"

"To Father it would. To you, as well."

She wiped her eyes. "I am a broken thing, and what adventurer, what lover wants a broken thing?"

"I didn't think you cared for anything but being right."

She sank into her cushions. "Being Librast In Situ meant everything to me. Bring honor to it, Jonne, not bile. Revel in it. But do not let it be all that you are."

"I'd give your legs back to you along with the title, if I could."

"Out of another mouth, that might be sweet."

"Sweet or not, it's the truth. You'd be happier. I'd be happier. As it is…we both have unpleasant futures to face."

She remained silent, almost convincing me she had fallen out of consciousness. I was half standing when she spoke. "There is a man who travelled over the lake with us."

"A man?"

"He is called Pulumbonk, and he looks a bit like a praying mantis…a bit, big eyes, long parts. Anyway, he is a luminast come to seek adventure in the ruins. Mama has made arrangements for him to visit. Please tell him to desist."

"I can speak to him."

"Do not be too harsh, only tell him it is not in his interest to see me anymore."

I glanced at the sheet where it sloped from her knees to nothing. "Has he a fondness for you?"

"He is a pleasant young man but silly. I see no room in my life for that…silliness, you know…silliness…." She faded.

I sat by her litter, expecting her to awake again. If it might make her feel better, I would be there when she opened her eyes. The leftovers in my lap offered grape stems, a shred of spinach, and a bit of cheese. I modified the materials with my thumb nail and spelled LADA in the middle of the plate. I had no idea how to make a girl happy, but it gave me something to do.

Lada's handmaiden, a lovely young thing with strawberry hair and blushing-peach cheeks, rose from her place near the door leading to the hall circling the stairwell, and crossed the floor. Her name was Myrle, and she hated me. "Lada is sleeping now. You may leave."

She had kissed me full on the lips during the feast of the twin moons three weeks earlier. I thought I was appropriately appreciative to her, especially since I bowed drunkenly to her. Ironically, I was drinking more than usual to bolster my courage to kiss another girl at the festival. Myrle, I learned later, had witnessed my kissing that girl and another later in the night. I couldn't blame her for thinking me the scoundrel.

As I left Lada's chamber would've been the perfect time to explain myself to her, but words failed me. I set the newly monogrammed plate on Lada's litter. "It's for Lada. Don't disrupt it, please."

She held the door open for me.

When avoiding her glare, I noted a thick tome recently set on Lada's reading stand. "Did you bring this up from the vaults for her?"

"That's our business."

The cover of the book was thick, aged leather, its title spelled from grooved letters filled with gold filigree: Festur's Theories on the Anaxagorum. Festur had been Librast Superior after Arno the First three hundred years ago, just before the book was requisitioned by Julius the Wise in Tule. He spent his life, from the time he entered the Collegium, gathering clues from archeological relics and primary sources in Faellic literature—what little he could read—to surmise the content of the blood book. The Librast Historian of the time wrote that Festur was murdered by his successor, because he refused to let the Anaxagorum leave Northem. Evidently, the majority wished the book gone, because the murderer lived on for thirty-five years as Librast Superior Arno the Second. Reading between the lines of Festur's book, scholars of the Collegium believe the author learned how to open and read parts of the Anaxagorum. The first generation of blueskins happened to be children of Festur's hunting friends, which makes many wonder if he shared what he learned.

Why would Lada, a beacon of reason, wish to know more about a book that gets men killed and others turned blue? If we'd just left it in the Imperial Library, it would be the problem of the Askerati now.

***

Lance Brother Brillix was nearly a perfect physical specimen. He was also a perfect ass. When I wandered into the training yard that afternoon, he muttered "What...is...this?" He wore a gray gambeson of quilted heavy fabric and carried a lacquered wood baton capped at one end with a bronze orb etched with a human eye on each hemisphere. Every lance brother of the Order of Man carried one. His hair was cut in the style of the Tulian court, shaved at the temples, medium at the bangs, and short elsewhere. No facial hair interrupted the godly line of his jaw.

I wore a mustache and jawline beard to add gravity to the otherwise roundish features of my head. My hair was long enough to be clubbed in the back and free to hang over my ears, when Father was elsewhere.

"Greetings, Lance Brother," I said, dipping my head, as if politeness would persuade him to be merciful with his training.

His reply was to pace slowly around me, eyeing me from tip to toe. "This is the first time I've seen you in the training yard in many a month." He stopped in front of me. "How is the bakery, these days? I see a fair amount of its pride swelling over your belt."

"It is, I suppose, as all bakeries are."

"I could say, 'My how you have blossomed', Jonne."

"Very clever."

"But Blossom does not adequately capture your new rotundity, so I shall call you, 'Plumpkin.'"

"I'm not obese. I just—"

"If you last an hour, I won't mock you. Last two hours, and I'll be impressed. Last three, and I'll give you my sword."

I dropped wheezing before the sun's shadow passed the first half-hour on the dial. He tested my sparring form on the dummy we called a "ginny." I had little to display. He ordered me to raise a catapult stone to my chest ten times. I failed to make three. He assessed my throwing arm. My knives hit the bullseye four out of five times. Before I could feel any vindication, he ran me to ruin on the tower steps.

"I thought you custodians ran your scholar's manuscripts up from the underhalls all day."

I had no breath to reply.

"Did I say 'all day?' I meant once in the morning. You sit on your dumplings the rest of the day reading and eating."

"We...do more...than that."

"Custodians are encouraged to spend two hours every Skyday and Waterday practicing combat arms."

I had made myself indispensable to my scholar by helping him from his chair, steadying him up and down steps, rubbing his feet when they grew cold, and so on, so he had never reported my neglect of training.

"Do you plan to stop an enemy's weapon strike by quoting philosophy?" He mimicked an actor holding forth. "Doth the blade approaching my face exist outside my own perception? I shall closeth my eyes and find out."

I wheezed my defense. "To wage war without understanding its place…in the human experience…is to be no more than—"

"A brute?" He booted me in the bottom until I rose. "Learn to stay alive, then learn Orlon's Soliloquies or Ak-Franick's Treatises on Being."

Whenever I flagged, he indented a different area of my corpulence with his baton. On my right side: "Sweet gums here, mayhap?" On my left: "Sugar cakes?" Square in the belly: "An appetite for everything but hardening yourself."

I admit that writing, reading, cataloging, and a predilection for berry tarts and sugar cakes had plumped me up and slowed me down over the last two years. I should have hated myself, but it was easier to hate him. The man had oft declared his affections for Lada, and she encouraged them, which made me despise her a little and him a great deal.

I looked up from my wheezing stoop. "And yet you are no more man than I."

I don't know if his smile was evil or if I only chose to see it that way. A gentle push with the toe of his boot toppled me. "Tell me of this new kind of manliness you display."

"It is the manliness of character. You've not once visited my sister, since her return. Your overtures of affection run false."

His smile didn't falter. "At least they can run."

When he walked from me, I noticed something. He had a pronounced sway to his back. Nothing grotesque but he did walk with his chest out and his arms back, as if a wind were blowing into the small of his back. Was it petty of me to feel cheered by the imperfection?

***

By the time I arrived at The Six Fingers, I could barely lift my arms to pass the reins of my horse to the livery attendant. A light rain had begun, so I scraped my soles clean on the boot bar by the front step. I banged the heavy, coiled serpent door knocker, and the peekhole in the floor of the overhanging room above the porch clicked open. I looked up from under my dripping, floppy brimmed hat. "Jonne the Booker."

I could see no eye in the dark hole, but I heard the muffled clang of an iron bell. The front door, built to withstand a battering ram, swung inward, and the one twinkling eye of Merf greeted me. Merf was a bartender and one of the few people I connected with as a friend. My opposite, he seemed forever in a merry mood, big gray eye set in a soft-blue bubble of a face. His black, silk eyepatch detracted little. "No orange cake tonight, Jonne. Do you think you'll make it through the night alive?"

"Luftberry tarts?"

"By the loads."

I removed my hat and stepped inside. "I'm saved."

"For the nonce, mayhap. No sugar from the south for who knows how long. Trade won't begin again till after what's-his-name is deposed."

"Draman."

"Right, Draman. Maybe the south will continue to hate us even after he's gone."

What a depressing thought.

The mood of the alehouse and eatery was an effective antidote. Sometimes the noise from the revelers and joke tellers, singers and arguers blasted one at an unwelcoming volume. That late afternoon, the noise was moderate, which allowed the senses to savor the pleasures of the place.

Jutting from the buffer wall that concealed the interior from newcomers were two magnificently grotesque figureheads removed from past versions of the Drowned Hag and the Bloated Shrew. The ships had long since decayed, but the figureheads proclaimed their years of service with deep cracks and rot pits in their surfaces that made them almost venerable. The craftsmanship shown in the leering hag's face and the snarling shrew's muzzle made me proud to be of the same blood as their carvers, and thankful my blood didn't carry the tendency to blueness.

The fragrances of baked goods and ales, wood smoke and roasted meats inhabited the wooden walls, becoming intensely fresh as I rounded the buffer wall into the east circle hall. Ornate columns as thick as tree trunks spiked the space. Carvings of beasts of the forests and under-dwellers of Faellic ruins, assorted ships, boats and sailors, the poisonous fish of Lake Rado, mares and other mythological creatures, and ancient

Faellic letters yet to be understood swathed the columns from floor to ceiling.

The Six Fingers entertained commoners and foreign adventurers almost exclusively, but they suffered my frequent presence, as I lost myself among them. I knew almost all of the locals, so I was used to their smells. The fare was simple, filling, and pleasing to the palate. The bench seats were passably comfortable, the fires soothing, and the laughter plentiful. The castle teemed with pretension and expectations.

Mealtime was an hour off, so the hall was underpopulated. The eleven passengers who had crossed the lake with Lada sat bubbling with enthusiasm at one long table, separate from the nineteen battered treasure hunters in from the wilds with nothing to do but loiter at two other tables.

The fifteen at the nearest table sat slump-shouldered and blank-eyed, listening to one of their number saw a dreary tune on her violette. That was the usual state of new adventurers returned from Faellar. Most of them couldn't bear another trip into the undergrounds, and until the south grew friendly again, none would be going home. I had always wondered what drove people to leave what they knew and risk everything. Treasure seemed a paltry reason.

A knot of four recently returned adventurers sat laughing and joking at their own table. Three were veterans I knew, men who lived for the thrill and hardship of expeditions. Riches seemed of secondary importance. The fourth, a lean man so tight with muscles the air around him quivered, wore a coat of pelts stitched together into a crude garment that covered his boiled-leather cuirass. His hairless pate rippled with badly healed skin. A long nose flanked by bright, round eyes and long, orange side whiskers gave the look of a fox. He rose from his bench and adopted a wide stance and comically serious expression, which drew expectant grins from his companions.

One said, "He's gonna blow!"

The man thrust one hand in front of him and blew a crispy trumpet note from his rear-end. He locked the pose, punched his other fist out and trumpeted a squeaky coda. He held the pose, hands in the air like a conqueror, and his companions guffawed. The morose woman sawing the violette ceased playing.

The hawkish man grinned at her. "And ye thought ye were the only one makin' music today."

More laughter as the man took a bow and threw a glance at me before retaking his seat. I didn't know how someone could take pride in being so foul.

A lovely, young, blue serving maid with a shock of ebon hair barely contained by a head band swished gayly toward me. When I turned myself fully toward her, she halted, rolled her eyes, and stomped away. Her name was Eela, and like Myrle, she hated me. She had always been flirtatious with me as a serving girl, but I supposed she was that way with every man. Minutes after Myrle had kissed me that night at the festival, Eela had charged me a kiss as a tip for bringing me an ale. She inserted her tongue into my mouth, which I found simultaneously revolting and titillating. I jerked away and made an icky sound, not an advisable move when on the cusp of romance.

Pulumbonk proved easy to identify. He found me, signaling his discovery with a yelp, a leap to his feet, and the thrust of a long finger in my direction. He did remind me of a praying mantis, if such a thing can look debonair. "Lada's brother, true? Jonne the Booker, or is it Blossom, or librast, or…mayhap I should ask what moniker you fancy, before I make an enemy."

"Jonne is best. You are Pulumbonk?"

He approached with a gangly man's stride, noodley but fast without appearing hurried. The lumen light highlighted veins of plum in his hair, exotic for these parts. "Your sister told you of me?"

I held out a hand to slow his ardor. "Your excitement is misplaced. She wishes you to desist in your advances."

The man's smile was so wide and toothy it made the plunge to a frown all that more epic. "But…I feel sure she—"

"She has no legs. You understand that, yes?"

"But…she is still beautiful to me."

Not the way I'd describe my sister. "You'll be happier if you keep your mind on your treasure hunting."

"Treasure's not the main target for this next run."

What next run?

His voice dropped to an excited hush. "They say we're going to Dunkelgrau."

Dunkelgrau? Of all the ruins, why there?

The under-dwellers guarded their lairs especially fiercely in those lethal passages. It was where Arno the First discovered the Anaxagorum. "Would this be your first expedition to Faellar?"

He set his jaw. "And I stand ready, mind and body."

"I have my doubts."

"Lada said you were a dark cloud. Me, I have trained my whole life for this."

"Allow me to remind you, the Anaxagorum is back in the North. You should fear entering any ruin of Faellar, especially that one."

"They say it is medicines we seek, medicines available only in that place, medicines men will pay a fortune to possess."

Valens powder! The purple mold forming its base ingredient must be in Dunkelgrau. No wonder it cost so dearly. I had only to recall my sister's being pain-free to understand why adventurers would risk their lives getting it. I knew exactly who had ordered the expedition.

"Father." I didn't mean to say it aloud. If the supply of Valens powder were running low, Father would be at maximum toxicity until his daughter's well-being was ensured. "When is this expedition supposed to launch?"

"Are you frightened?"

"Do I seem so?" I felt so.

"I say freely, I'm scared to my pits. Prayers to Unathar give me strength."

"Unathar? And you evaded the Askerati inquisitors long enough to make it up here? They hate him more than any other rival god."

"They should fear him."

"Up here, talking of gods will get you ridiculed."

"I hear the people of Northem have no god. I'd feel mighty lonely with nobody to watch over me, by all."

"I have my wits and those of my allies to watch over me." I held up a finger in warning. "You should stay away from Lada."

"What about Gela? You worship her, yea?"

"Gela is not a goddess. Gela is the name we give nature. We sing and dance, and meditate in a grove set aside for such purposes."

"Are you not trying to win her favor with such goings-on?"

"That would be praying. We expect nothing from her she doesn't already offer. So when does the expedition leave?"

"A fortnight or less." He pointed.

I recognized the slick, tied-back hair of Merf behind the bar. Whereas my hair was clubbed into a short whisk, his fell like a horse tail to the top of his belt. Many blueskins wore their hair long, believing it to be respectful to nature. He chalked names onto the expedition register with pale blue fingers.

The bar deserves a brief description, as there is no other like it in the known world. Not carved like the columns, it was assembled from bones large and small, most of which I can't identify. Ribs and spines are obvious. The two tusked skulls capping the front corners are humanoid, but everyone around The Six Fingers has a different answer when asked what kind. Not human is the consensus. The lot of them are held together in a resin block, as if trapped in an amber glacier. The countertop is of stained and rutted blackwood, and has been replaced but once in the bar's three hundred and fifty years.

The only names I recognized on the list of sixteen members so far included in the expedition were those of Pulumbonk and the two just being added: L. B. Brillix and J. Booker.

My inner coward awakened as a pounding in my chest. I always expected to have Ryckerd at my side on my first adventure, should I ever take one.

"Merf, why am I on the list?'

"Brillix sent word. You're Librast In Situ now."

I forgot Pulumbonk and wandered to the bar, feeling the need for something to drown my sorrows. "I'll have that tart now."

I couldn't tell whether the look on his face was pity or amusement. "Apologies, Jonne. Runner just come from the castle, saying 'no sweets' for Jonne the Booker."

"Who this time?"

"Your friend Brillix, again."

"My friend?"

"You've never said a good thing about him, as long as I've known you, so...humor, my boy."

"Not the funny kind." I put my soggy-brimmed hat on and stepped outside.

The clouds I'd seen earlier had rendered but a trickle. The ones behind them had moved in, dark and fat and disgorging with a fury. I stepped under the livery portico to collect my horse, Thunderhoof. I named the horse four years ago when I was sixteen. It seemed dashing then.

At the rail where Thunderhoof should've been tied leaned a figure in muddy boots and a knee-length cloak emblazoned with the flaming eye of the Order of Man.

It had Brillix's voice. "Gloomy Jonne no more. You're walking up to the castle with me...in the rain...the way men of sturdy constitution do it...Plumpkin."

In a misguided way, I envied Lada.

Lexica VII

Thirty-six names ended up on the Dunkelgrau roster, ten more than a normal expedition, but not nearly enough, in my estimation. Most were mercenary adventurers from the south: rogues and warriors, and Pulumbonk the Luminast. Some were specialists from Northem: a smith; a cook; the Fletcherson triplets, Certe, Berte, and Aethelbert, blueskins with preternatural skills in hunting and scouting; a clinker who knew locks and traps; a field herbalist and her two apprentices; and to my chagrin, a comely warder who hated me. Atypically, ten lance brothers from the Order of Man, including Brillix, were going. I'd never known more than five to go on any expedition. Its members were entrusted with the defense of the castle, thus not expendable for just any mission.

The party presented an impressive array of fighters and survivors, and a less-than-impressive me who would probably get everyone killed. We left in twelve days.

***

The chest muscles I had trained to manliness during my teens had abandoned me for the fleshy delights downstairs at my belt line. Moonsie, the thick-armed, thin-nosed, annoyingly self-amused armorer, placed my tailored jerkin back on its stand.

"Sorry, Jonne, your gear was crafted for a thinner man. What happened to him?"

I wiped sweat from my eyes. "Re-fit me." The forge lay outside the storage room, but the heat of its continually stoked coals sucked rivers from me.

"Within a fortnight, you lolly?" A tattoo of a semi-clad woman on his upper arm transfixed me, as usual. Her buttocks swelled a bit each time his bicep flexed. "I could do the vest, but fashioning the bronze reinforcements will take weeks."

"I assume you don't intend sending me to Dunkelgrau naked."

"Well, I'm not sending you, am I?" He chuckled, as if something funny had been said, a quirk of his.

I scanned the walls of his armory. Helmets, gauntlets, greaves, along with various metal scales and splints, sheets of chain armor and leather strapping, all tinged orange from the lantern light, hung from pegs or peeked from bins.

“I look at all of this, and I wonder why we’re wasting our time. I’m a dead man.”

Moonsie motioned to a stool. “I have something for you. Sit and raise your arms.”

I sat but didn’t raise my arms. “What is it, a reject no worthy man will wear?”

“With your attitude, you probably will die, but this’ll give you a chance.” He chuckled again and lifted a long, chainmail coat from its T-stand. “I just finished this for a strapping fellow from a village south of Tule. Got skewered by a Raka spear in the pits of Stonebrook last week. Shame. This would’ve stopped a weapon like that. Raise your arms.”

The long coat of tiny iron rings looked, even in the low light, exquisite. Every ring was riveted, not every fourth. He lowered the jingling cascade over me, and I slumped under its weight.

“Stand.”

With a grunt, I did. The hem reached almost to my knees.

“A belt will help distribute the weight. Margie and her girls will sew you up a sturdy gambeson to wear under.”

The thought of walking even a quarter league in the thing exhausted me.

“Wear this all day, every day, and walk up and down in it, till your expedition departs. Get your body used to it. You will be mounted, yes?”

“Of course.”

“Then thank Gela for strong horses.” Moonsie punctuated the statement with a quirky chuckle, although the humor was lost on me.

***

Simply walking from the armory up the steps to the castle’s main courtyard in the chainmail hauberk set me thinking about finding someone to carry it for me, but I’d only be cheating myself. In twelve days I was bound for Dunkelgrau, and while the armor couldn’t protect me from every weapon and ripping claw, I would wear it. With luck, it would cripple me, and I could stay behind.

The early fall morning was dry but especially chill after the inferno of the forge. I caught my breath then headed out through the barbican and down the cobbles. Downhill was only a little better than up. Having an ox slung over my shoulders couldn’t have been much worse. The metal rings chinked with every step, an annoyance I’d get used to or go mad.

Down the hill. Toward the village. Plod, plod. Chink, chink. Ugh, ugh.

For the last two years since I reached my majority, I elected to take breakfast at The Six Fingers. Father and the near-pious formality of dining at the castle suffocated me. At The Six Fingers, I could keep to myself, eat, drink, write or sketch without molestation.

The village spread below me. Its thirteen hundred structures were mostly homes that doubled as shops for smithies, weavers, cobblers, leather workers, fletchers, and other trades. From my perspective, it was a chaotic sprawl of stone rectangles and circles roofed in burnt-orange tiles or blond thatch. Stone lay in abundance in large quarries beyond the farms and a lesser pit near the castle behind me. To the east of the village, separated by a robust creek that ran from the Erle River to the lake, squatted the urine-sloshed dyeing vats and drying stalls. Dyers, with arms stained up to the elbow in a muddy mix of reds, purples, blues, and greens, claimed they didn't notice the smell. Chandlers workshops were forced to set up there, as well, as making candles meant boiling animal fat from bones day in and day out, an also less-than-pleasant addition to the atmosphere. Smoke from all the chimneys rose a hundred spans, grew lackadaisical in the still air, and lay over the village in a flat cloud.

The road leveled where it bisected the market. The stalls on either side, once bright with merry reds and oranges, had weathered to mere suggestions of the colors. They were shuttered and silent. Their butchers, grocers, and dry goods sellers wouldn't open for business until noon. There were no beggars in Northem. Those unfortunate enough to suffer physical or mental disabilities and had no families to support them lived in a group home funded by the Acolytes of Gela. They worked by day in whatever capacity they could manage. Deformed or unhealthy newborns were given back to Gela right after birth.

I usually enjoyed the morning peace of the place. That morning I heard singing. Malefactors of a less serious nature were often placed in public view along the road here at the market. Dangerous offenders went to the quarries. Drunks and other nuisances spent a day in the market with their feet restrained in the stocks. Petty thieves, brawlers, and practitioners of superstitions stood for ten hours with their heads and arms restrained in pillories. Castle children who didn't attend their studies were locked in cages from mid-morn to mid-afternoon to contemplate their indolence.

I noticed only two "guests of the market:" Ottus, the habitual drunk who had the ability to sleep while sitting on the narrow rail of the stocks; and a woman in the pillories singing a haunting tune, low and slow, in a language I didn't recognize. Bobbed, silver-gray hair. Striated blue hands. Shapley form. Head down. I reckoned her to be one of the blueskin acolyte dancers at the grove of Gela, as they were often speaking of magic and defiant about it. As I chink-chinked past this one, she looked up.

My heart jumped sideways. She was Remi, a lovely surprise in the midst of so much ill fortune. Remi and I had shared clandestine glances at festivals throughout our adolescence. Neither of us could marry, she being dedicated to Gela and I to serving the library until thirty years of age, but we still had desires. I wasn't sure she actually felt the way I did about her, until she took the initiative at the Festival of the Twin Moons, the very same at which Myrle and Eela kissed me. I can't say I wasn't excited by the fact that two comely lasses found me kissable, but it wasn't until Remi led me by the hand into a storage shed that I knew bliss. When I saw her face, lit only by a sliver of light through a crack in the door, I forgot all about Myrle and Eela.

We didn't touch, just stood, she gazing upon me, I gazing at my feet.

"So, you've found yourself in a dark shed with a blueskin girl. What now?"

Twasn't courage but mayhap need that propelled me to take her gently by the shoulders, my fingers delighted to feel her warmth. She teased with a soft giggle then surrendered with closed eyes and parted lips. The spit of our mouths turned to honey. Until then, I had never expected to know such ecstasy.

And what lips! She had a slightly rodent-esque overbite I found adorable but Ryckerd would've found a deformity. He liked his women tall, full, and perfect, like his bride-to-be, Suellt of Kamsala, who he said was gorgeous and had a head of bouncy red curls. It seemed I'd never meet her and my brother would never enjoy her charms. I'd like to see bouncy curls on a woman some day, as we descendants of the Tulians sprout only straight hair. But why think of other women, when I had the wonder of Remi an arm's length away? Her kiss had been life-changing, so I felt it sad that what I remembered most was thinking, Why me?

I stopped dead at seeing her. "Remi…I—"

"Die, dog!" she hissed.

My eyebrows leapt. This from the winsome girl who'd twirled her finger in my hair while we kissed. When I had asked if I could see her again, she smiled up at me, eyes soft gray in the shadow. "I don't let anything stop me when I want something."

Now, her cobalt eyes seemed as sharp as icicles, a startling contrast with the naturally blue-black lids and lashes encasing them. "Did they send you to make my day worse?"

"No…I'm…." My wit failed me.

Her head couldn't rise very high, so her eyes strained from under her brow to reproach me. That eminently kissable mouth could, by the slightest change in curvature, turn cruel or delightful. I got cruel. "Don't gaze on me. I deny you the right."

I glanced away and then back. "But I thought we were—"

"Were what? We're nothing, that's what. You, though, are a rotten thing."

"Rotten?" Hurt turned to anger. "If so, I'd be pilloried with you."

"A milky skinned snittle from the castle? I'll never live long enough to see it."

"What have I done to so enflame you? I have displayed only warmth and tenderness to you."

"Drunk and handsy is more like, grabbing any village lass you like, cuz you know she can't stop you. I had to gargle piss to get your taste out of my mouth."

From the shed, she had led me to the dance floor. We had danced two rulays and a twinka, giddy the whole time and heedless of the disapproving eyes upon us. I had ached to see her again, but my inner coward didn't dare seek her out. Father would've had me impaled, should I so much as suggest a dalliance with a blueskin.

I stood heavily in my chainmail. "I don't think I was drunk."

"You were!" she sang.

"I…I wasn't. I think now you may have cast a spell on me." The words were out before I could stop them.

"A librast who believes in spells? Perhaps you will stand some time out here."

"I didn't mean that, didn't mean magical. I meant that glamour you and every comely female can cast by nature."

"All females can do that? Well, pibbly bibbly."

"Is that some form of eldritch curse?"

"What? Pibbly bibbly? That's what I think of your opinion."

That burned. "My opinion has value, and—"

"I should've clapped a ward on you."
"Can you?"
"Of course not. They pillory people who believe in wards."
"As it should be."
Yet the enlightened of Northem had no problem with wards when they were used for the protection of sailors and adventurers.
Her head shook. "Jonne, rotten Jonne. Rotten hypocrites the lot of you castlers."
I stopped myself before blurting, I'm not a hypocrite, and examined the possibility. My gaze shifted to the pearlescent black tower of The Six Fingers rising from the woodsmoke of the blueskin tavern and dwellings built around it. My body reoriented in a likewise direction, and I stepped off.
Chink, chink, chink.
She called almost merrily. "If you want to know how to treat a woman, ask Brillix."
I wish I could say I kept walking, but I turned, adopted an idiot's posture, and said, "Uh." That was it. "Uh."
During the rest of my walk to breakfast, I thought on a quantity of things I should've said. I should've defended myself better. I should've blamed her for false affection. I should've offered her a drink of water. Brillix would've done that. I hadn't even asked why she was pilloried. "Oh, darkest of Jonnes," Lada had said. Perhaps it should've been "densest."
Remi, I soon learned, was the warder on the Dunkelgrau roster.

***

My breakfast of eggs, seared groat, bread, and berries was delicious but served in a half-portion by order of Brillix. A double portion would not have filled the hollow in me, anyway. While I might not have been able to have Remi as a bride, I did want her to want me. Selfish, I suppose, but I realized I was angry at her for denying me the satisfaction. A blueskin and a warder, with a tongue less than eloquent in speech, could only be a trickster to avoid. Logic said she would, under no circumstance, be a good match. Damn my nature, as I still wanted to bed her. Lying with her afterward teased as a glorious fantasy.
I struggled to make myself loathe her all through breakfast but failed badly. She looked lovely even in the pillory, those eyes, those dangerously playful lips, that ornery silver-gray bob. How was it possible she had turned on me? In the dark of a Faellic tunnel, a blueskin woman with a grudge might be more to

fear than Raka. I had no sense at all for how to talk to a girl meaningfully. Remi said Brillix knew how, but I'd rather be eaten by corpse lice than ask him.

Lada though....

Rising from my bench in the chainmail after sitting for half an hour reminded me, brutally, of forgotten muscles. My back and shoulders, legs and buttocks mewled.

Merf's single eye regarded me as I hobbled for the exit. "That fine mail's wasted on you, Jonne. Give'er here, and you'll eat free for a year at the Fingers."

"If only I could."

"Ah, shush that twaddle. I don't want your armor, and I don't want any part of you on that mantle."

Crowding the mantle over the nearest fireplace and nailed to the bricks above it were memorabilia from those lost on quests into Faellar: a scrap of mail, a snapped clay pipe, a belt buckle, a single ankle boot, a Raka skull with the name ODO painted on its forehead, necklaces, knives, gauntlets, battered lanterns, and snuff boxes, a signet ring from the Order of Man, a note written in blood on velum reading LOVE J, a sword pommel, and some fabric items so old they'd become indistinct. All four grand fireplaces, each in a different section of The Six Fingers, were so garnished.

Merf escorted me to the door and laid a hand on my shoulder before I started up the road. "You've made me laugh more than most. You've made me think—and you know what an uncomfortable thing that is for me. I can't return the favor in kind, but I can say, listen to the veterans who lead you. Don't listen to the warty little shit inside you who says you can't do it. You can. You will. And you'll tell me about it when you're back."

"If there's never to be sugar again from the south, I'm not sure I want to come back."

His boot to my backside forced me to windmill forward to keep from falling.

"It's good armor, Jonne. You've twelve days to earn it."

***

The road up to the castle seemed longer than usual, the hill steeper. As I passed Remi, head down and no longer singing, I thought to ask, "Might I share water from my flagon?"

She glanced up and immediately back down. She spat into the dirt, the foamy white turning into a brown ball. "Ask me when I'm out of spit."

"I could talk to the Warden of the Collegium to have you released."

Her head rose, as did her smile, the cruel one. "I was caught dancing naked in Gela's Grove singing in the ancient tongue with my sisters. I was the one who didn't repent. I am the one who'll account for her actions."

I'd seen her dance many times but never totally naked. I trembled at the thought. "Why did you do it?"

"Why did you let me kiss you after you'd toured the lips of every other lass at the festival?"

"What? Well...because...I don't know."

She regarded me, spat, and dropped her head.

So, I'd been caught by her, too. Did girls talk to each other about the boys they'd kissed? Seemed a private affair to me.

Half of a tart I had begged Merf to give me rested in my purse wrapped in albon bladder. I had planned to enjoy it as a reward for surviving the day, as soon as I was out of my chainmail and comfortable in my chamber.

I asked, "Do you favor luftberry tarts?"

Her eyes rose warily. "Mayhap."

I unfolded the bladder to reveal the golden-brown cake and its crimson filling. "I brought this for you."

"Now why would an oxey poxy castler do that for a blasphemous blueskin?"

"Because, uh... you must be hungry."

Her eyes closed in reverie. "Enough to eat your shoe, were it offered." Then they opened with a grateful twinkle. "You'll, er...need to hold it for me."

I raised it to her in the bowl of my cupped hands.

She tried her best to get a nibble of it, but gave up. "Just shove a pinch in, if you would."

I did, and she chewed in ecstasy.

I knew I was ruining the moment as soon as I opened my mouth. "I don't believe 'blasphemous' is the word you wanted to use."

Her jaw continued to work the tart, but her eyes regarded me incredulously.

That was my chance to stopper my remarks, but, as I was man of words trapped in a nervous boy's body, I continued. "Blasphemy refers to one who disrespects another's religion. So, you're not so much a blasphemous blueskin as an incorrigible one."

She swallowed and then said, “You’re always better than us, aren’t you?”

“I didn’t mean it that way. I simply—”

“Feed me another bite, and try to think of something better to say while I eat it.”

I broke off another piece, and she sucked it from my fingers. How could someone so blitheringly impolite as I be expected to say something better? I hadn’t a clue. She took another bite and watched me, as if waiting for me to fail.

After I fed her the last of the tart, I said the one thing I couldn’t imagine her disliking. “I think you’re pretty.”

Her expression softened, and she stopped to chewing to smile.

***

If I didn’t die from the exertion of climbing back up the road to the castle, I’d fetch Lada to Ryckerd’s chamber. We could sit among the rogues and talk of female mystery and the perils of being Librast In Situ. For all my intellectual conceit, I doubted I’d understand the one and would probably underestimate the other. If that didn’t crush my spirit, I planned to go into the vaults and confront the blood book. Perhaps I’d gain courage from standing in its presence and coming away unscathed.

Nobody I knew had figured how to open the Anaxagorum. I might not be up to competence in swordplay, but I might be able to outsmart a book. Yet, who was I kidding? The thought of seeing what that book held horrified me.

I stopped five times to retrieve my wind, but I did make it to the castle and to Lada’s chamber, her empty chamber. Neither Mother nor other occupants of the great keep had seen her leave. Father was in bed with a headache, an event I never expected to witness. Being confined to bed reduced the number of minions he could order about.

I decided the Anaxagorum could wait for my visit and repaired to Ryckerd’s balcony. The view over the battlement took in multiple farms and the oak-lined lanes that boxed them into parcels, all free of the haze over the village. if I craned to the right, I could also see out to the edge of the distant lake where the tower of The Six Fingers dominated the landscape, dead black even under the noon sun. Big, orange Theodoric lowered to a hunker near my feet, viewing the same through a firing embrasure at floor level. The view must not have interested him for a leg shot up, and he licked its long fur vigorously. I wondered what the cat might think of me. They hold their opinions close.

I noted a tall figure in a stylish black jerkin trotting along the quarry road that ran around the base of Leper Hill, a good quarter-league below the castle. I knew from the easy lope it was Pulumbonk. The hat he wore was new, one of the kind they made in the village: wide brimmed and sporting a trio of crest feathers from the great ruyk, a giant flightless bird from the far north, a cousin to our domesticated groats. What would he want at the quarry? The only other destinations along that road were farms and, interestingly, the barred exit from the underhalls of the castle.

A suspicion arose, and I'd have to move fast to verify it. Removing the armor was a challenge for one man, but I managed, after much huffing and puffing.

I felt as light as a mouse, an achy one, as I hustled down the nearest of the two spiral staircases enclosed in square towers on either side of the great keep. The regular TOFF, TOFF, TOFF of leather soles on stone seemed loud in the enclosed space. The library vaults lay in the four underhalls below. An attacker would need to take the castle walls, the inner ward, and then the great keep to gain access. The single guard outside the double gate had his helmet off and his finger digging in his ear. He didn't say "halt." He didn't say "hello." Even two days ago, as a mere librast custodian, I would've been stopped, but as Librast In Situ, I was in the third rank of librasts now. I knew the guard. He knew me. We held no affection for one another.

The light feeling passed, so I plodded with numerous grunts down the wider, zig-zag stairway to the fourth underhall, where the recently reinforced sarcophagus for the Anaxagorum waited. It would not be sealed for another four days, so the librasts historian and academician (third rank, as I was) could study the physical attributes of the book and write a description for posterity. The moan of a female in anguish rushed up the steps and down my spine.

Lada?

I deemed it highly improbable that her litter could be carried down those stairs without endangering her.

My bravado to see the Anaxagorum evaporated, but my curiosity to see who else might be sniffing around it tugged me out of the stairwell and into the hall of arches, each arch leading to a different category of manuscripts. The first underhall contained maps and manuscripts in known languages from the last three thousand years. The second and third underhalls were dedicated to manuscripts found in Faellar. They held what we deduced to be histories, catalogs of items, ledgers of quantities, religious tracts, census information, political treatises, and others. Some were obvious. Some could only be categorized by educated guesses. The fourth and lowest underhall held the most brittle manuscripts, ones we knew the least about and, it seemed, my sister.

I had been told the Anaxagorum waited at the end of the hall inside the special manuscripts vault on a temporary viewing table. A cavity carved from the floor's bed rock waited for the marble sarcophagus that would encase the book. Diamond-shaped lumen fruit, set in sconces along the wall, held back the darkness with languidly pulsing orange light. Those in the south had to make do with lamps, rush lights, and candles for illumination.

A creaky voice I knew to be Lance Brother Poonal's ghosted into hearing range. "Why would they tell me? I am not a policy maker." The knight was tasked with guarding the Anaxagorum.

Lada's voice, without mistake: "It should be here. I need it to be here."

"Talk to your father, then. It has been taken at his orders."

Lada sounded near panic. "You know something. What is it? Where is it? It must be somewhere I can see it."

Brother Poonal, long-chinned and self-righteous, was losing patience, so they'd been talking a while. "If you were still Librast In Situ, I could tell you, but you are not."

Brillix's voice surprised me. "Would I have carried her down here, if we thought her father would allow her a viewing?"

"Why, Brillix? Why did you carry her down here, as in, why you?"

"I owed her a favor."

"Do me a favor and carry her back up and never, never let another commoner, or anyone else, in through the quarry exit."

That would be Pulumbonk.

"Else I'll be sure others hear of it."

Pulumbonk spoke excitedly. "Do you know if it's been opened, the blood book?"

"Silence, boy! Brillix, get them out of here."

Brillix said, "Pulumbonk, help her onto my back."

The thought of my sister's arms around that rectum of a man sickened me. As quietly as possible, I started up the stairs, feeling heavy again with new questions as well as sugar cakes of months past.

***

An hour passed, before I sent a paige with a request for an audience with Lada. He returned before the water clock above my fireplace had noticeably reduced its twelve-hour capacity. Request denied. I thanked the paige and walked the twenty paces around the stairway shaft to Lada's door directly across from mine. I rapped at her door with my new Librast In Situ's ebon baton, capped at either end with silver rondels so it resembled a scroll.

The face of her handmaiden, Myrle, appeared in the crack, her lips in a snarl and the peaches in her cheeks nowhere to be seen. Without a word, she pushed the door shut. As there were two other chambers on this level with occupants who might hear me, I slipped a prepared note under the door and rapped again. I hadn't waited long when the door reopened and Myrle, eyes trying their best to burn holes in me, allowed me in.

Lada sat lengthwise on the pillowy dove-gray couch Father had commissioned for her on her fourteenth birthday, a now-soiled sheet over the stumps of her legs. "You overheard us in the underhalls? How gentlemanly of you."

"I hadn't intended to eavesdrop."

"Are you here to blackmail me?"

"If necessary. I originally intended to ask you how females think and, secondarily, for insights into being Librast In Situ."

"Girl problems, brother?"

"I'm going mad wanting to be with one of you strange creatures, but I find you more inscrutable than the Anaxagorum."

"But now you are more interested in why I wish to penetrate the book."

"Neither you nor I know its true contents. I admit, I find the tome fascinating, but you, you're Lada."

She studied me intensely before speaking. "What if I could give you your old life back? No more combat training. No risking your tenders in Faellic ruins."

I had no answer.

"If you tell Papa what I am about to tell you, I will deny it with all the considerable charm I can exert upon him."

"No promises."

"Then I will tell him of the infatuation you have for a blueskin lass." My shock must've been easily decipherable, for her face lit. "Oh, my, you do have a wicked blue love! The warder or the serving maid? You kissed them both."

"Ah, and you're the one who told them. Myrle, too?"

"You needed to be taught a lesson. Three girls in one night is not how a librast of any rank comports himself."

"They kissed me."

"Inconsiderate oaf."

"So I am. Now, what is in the Anaxagorum you want?"

"My legs."

I knew instantly what she meant and felt stupid for not seeing it earlier. "By Gela, that is a dangerous pit to plumb!"

"Brillix discovered that your expedition will take the book back to Dunkelgrau. No fair, Jonne, no fair I cannot have a chance to recover what I was."

"You don't know how to read the thing or even know if it purports to reverse such a loss."

I'd seen the light in her eye, when she was a little girl and told me, as if it were destined, "I shall be Librast In Situ when I grow up." With the same surety, she proclaimed, "In Festur's book, he cites a scroll found in the ashen temple at Verdana." (Northem scholars name each Faellic ruin by its most memorable feature: Verdana for the lush vegetation obscuring its entrance.)

"What we believe is a temple."

"A line in it reads, 'Behold codex fifty-seven, in which the Master of the Infinite, at a word, might restore any creature of flesh to its natural whole.'"

I can't let shame stop me from admitting that Lada's offer enticed me. "What might I do, abscond with the blood book at night and rush it home to you?"

"You will need to watch for opportunities to take it, and you will not be alone. Others of your party are interested in its…remaining available."

I thought of the men in the vault with Lada. "Not Brillix!"

"No, no. He is done with me. He only carried me to the underhalls to atone for his ungentlemanly avoidance of me. His love is limited to women with more parts than I."

"Tell me you don't want to restore yourself for him!"

"Ridiculous! I want to be whole, so I can fulfill…why don't you lose your legs and tell me you would not do all in your power to have them back."

"Father will ostracize us both from Northem. Then what, go south and be burned or hanged by the Askerati? Go north and live in the wilds of Faellar with the Ruyks? Perhaps we can live with Pulumbonk in Atmaa. Have you thought this through?"

"Down to the paean I shall sing to Papa for overcoming his fear and accepting the knowledge of the Anaxagorum for the betterment of all. He shall be as pliable as horse hair after that."

"For all you know, you'll turn yourself into a headless dog that views the world through the hole under its tail."

"No cynicism from you. Will you or will you not help me?"

Brillix, the preening wart, would no doubt reject the proposition without a second thought and walk away with his honor. I, however, said, "I shall think on it."

Chronicler's Illumination: Gela and Askerat

Gela was the mother goddess of the Doranites in the south of Arqonias over three thousand years ago. Their empire enjoyed one century of stability and then three of strife that left them ready to collapse from the lightest blow. It came from the horse-riding Tulians from the large western island of Tulos. They swept away all opposition on the continent within thirty years, and made their capital in the grandest city of the north, now named Tule. Those who didn't bow to the horse warriors fled into the jungles of Kush to dwell among the headhunters who worshiped the blood god Ugra, an unsavory lot who reportedly drank the blood of their fourth-born child from the child's own skull. The victorious Tulians outlawed all other gods, but kept the nature goddess Gela to placate the hordes now under their rule.

Over the last five hundred years, the cult of Askerat and the Ninety-nine Ascended, which had thrived in the forests of Haramdum since prehistory, began capturing the imagination of common folk. It promised equality in the afterlife and the death of all oppressors, if they crushed rival gods and accepted their personal insignificance in this life. Askerat is depicted as a vaporous entity who covers the world with his clouds. The Ninety-nine Ascended were the souls of his family whom he murdered and absorbed into himself. The kingdoms of the south outlawed the growing religion, but it lived on in the shadows. From those shadows fled a handful of Gela worshippers and two-score lepers who braved Lake Rado to found a religion-free north in the abandoned lands of the Fael. They named their settlement Leper Hill, but it's known today as Northem.

The grove of Gela in Northem was set aside to venerate nature, but were an Askerati to witness the nude dancing and mass meditations in the grove each month, they would see little difference from their own rites. Askeratis offered themselves naked and en masse to their god. Gelans thanked nature for its bounty and, unlike the Askeratis, held that the thinking human was the highest of all nature's creations.

As taught, I'm a staunch believer in reason above religion, but when beasts kill a family of eight or the best among us are stricken while the wicked thrive, or one is alone under a lightning-lit night sky, it's hard not to believe a superior force is at work. Mayhap it speaks through the Anaxagorum.

Lexica VIII

"Tough luck about Lada," said Merf, his left eyebrow humping vigorously to scoot his eyepatch back into position.

I hurried him to the end of the amber bar of bones where we could talk in private. "You're just now mentioning it?"

He wiped his hands on his greasy red and black kilt. "It's only polite to wait a piece before discussing grim news about family."

"I've always encouraged you to speak your mind around me, but yes, a great shame about Lada. She deserves to be Librast In Situ, not I."

"Capable she is, very. Seems a strong lass, although a bit too pink to be pretty."

"There you go with pink again." I turned up a cuff of fabric and chainmail to expose my wrist. "We are more white than pink."

He held his long, light blue forearm next to my shorter, thicker one. "Looks pink to me."

My skin did have a redder cast next to his sky-blue.

"We're all pink inside, right?" He leaned forward, hands on the bar. "You ever look up inside a blue girl?"

I hated that I blushed. "I need permission from the Collegium before I'm allowed such…activities."

"Wait for them, and you'll be an old man. Get the girls while they're girls. I might not be as learned as you, but trust me on that."

"We have something more important to talk about."

Merf's eyebrow humped. His patch shifted. He leaned in. "Let's hear it."

I also leaned in. "What do you know about the origin of the Guides?"

His eye narrowed. "Like what?"

"You were simple tradesmen, before the discovery of the Anaxagorum. After that, your offspring showed a tendency to blueness and your people suddenly knew how to throw wards and sniff trails. How did they learn their crafts? Your women's healing skills rival Testa's and the castle surgeons, but they're based on incantations. I even question your brewing. Your ale is superior in flavor to any in the south, yet it's made of basically the same ingredients." When Merf showed no reaction, I continued. "All castlers are taught not to ask, but I'm tired of ignoring the truth of it, the truth you know."

"What truth would that be?"

"I beg, Merf, stop pretending there's not a secret that the twenty thousand people around us are ignoring."

"Jonne...." He let the pause hang. "Things that happened three hundred years ago are a wee before my time."

"Remi saved my sister from a slipperfish and not with a sword and derring-do. Lada saw her pitch a fetish into the water while incanting words she didn't understand."

Merf had been a Guide when younger. He lost his eye to Lake Rado after diving overboard to rescue a mate, and that one open eye suffered burns from extended exposure to toxic water. The man never complained about its loss. "What's the most valuable manuscript in the castle vaults?"

I straightened in shock. "I can't tell you that."

Merf stayed fixed on me, until his meaning sunk in, and then asked, "The usual for breakfast, then?"

***

By the end of the third day wearing my chainmail, I thought I'd never walk again. I went to bed early and woke up as stiff as a dead man's leg. When I ignored the paige's wakening knock, Brillix used the floor key to barge in and pull me to my feet. He walked me to the great hall on the castle's main floor and winked at me to exacerbate my misery. I had not been called to the training yard for the last two days, but that changed when Brillix put a dull training sword in my hand. He worked me until I collapsed, groaning like an old floorboard.

"You need to get your mind off eating and onto your training, Plumpkin, or the world out there will crush you."

I'm not sure my body strengthened, but my resolve did. I decided to tell Lada I would not intrigue with her regarding the Anaxagorum. My fate was my burden to carry, as was hers. That's how we were raised. Whether a sixth sense or coincidence, she asked me to meet her on Ryckerd's balcony with the rogues at three marks past midday.

***

"I am disappointed, Jonne. In my new state of self-awareness, I have begun to think you and I could care for each other, like brothers and sisters in storybooks."

I sipped bloodberry tea—rather flavorless without a sugar stick—from a slender ceramic mug and watched Lada's face try to hide her anger. I said, "My decision has nothing to do with sibling relationships. It's about respecting what I believe, what I thought you believed."

When Lada compressed her lips into a scowl, her whole face sharpened, an axe blade aimed at me. "Will you try to interfere with my agents?"

"The Anaxagorum is not magic, but it is trouble we don't understand."

"I asked you a question."

The sky to the north was darkening again, the sky over us already gray with drizzling clouds. The parapet above provided protection from the light rain. "Ah, yes. Your agents. How many of these surreptitious folk will be accompanying the party?"

"Enough to get the job done, even without you. They each have their own reason for wanting the Anaxagorum to stay close to home."

"Such as?"

"That would be their business."

"And is part of that business to kill me when we're out of sight of the castle?

"Kill you?"

"If so, please do it now and save me from taking another step in this armor."

"Ah, your dark humor often eludes me."

"You've changed, Sister, and desperate people do desperate things."

The distant sky wasn't just gray. It had turned inky. My attention affixed to it. Who knew what kind of storm could burst from such weighty clouds?

Lada continued talking, but I caught only snatches. "Understand, my brother…," "…because it is close-minded not to…," "…a threat to what I want…," "…wash my hands of blame." "Do you hear me?"

The clouds became a flat, black layer above the farms, as if a river of pitch had been poured over the horizon. I waved Lada off.

She didn't stop talking, but the timbre of her voice dulled. "I have never seen so unnatural a sky."

The peal of the bell in the castle's high tower made us flinch. Cast over three centuries ago to warn Northem of an approaching enemy, the huge iron thing had only been rung to mark dusk and dawn for the resetting of water clocks. This was the first time it raised its voice in alarm. BONG! A sound both sharp and deep. BONG!

The cats, in an explosion of legs and tails, swarmed up the faux tree limbs into the safety of their enclosed aeries. Tiny, arm-waving figures in the distance drove oxen and horse teams into byres. Then the farms in the mid-distance caught the fright. Then the ringing of the market bell told us the village saw it, too.

BONG!

As if giant claws had rent the sky, the black layer shredded into thousands of ribbons, each snaking toward the ground at great speed. They slammed into the soil and burrowed along the surface, gathering heads of sod and shattered rock, and then wriggled back into the air, now resembling earthen comets with sinuous black tails. The accumulated material gave the inky substance mass, as proven when the comets began striking farmhouses, wagons, livestock, and their owners. One strike after another threw up a gout of dirt, splinters, and tiny rag dolls. After each strike, the black vapor returned to the sky to be absorbed by the inky cloud.

BONG!

The shouting of men and the clatter of wooden bows against the south stairwell walls knocked us from our stupor. Archers were scrambling to their firing parapets. I struggled to my feet.

Lada, with no feet to struggle to, threw her arms toward me, like a babe to its mother. "Jonne!"

Remi was the only person I'd held in my arms as an adult. The notion of gathering my sister to me would not have come without her prompt, a gesture so primal, so universal, I didn't hesitate. Our arms encircled each other, and I lifted with my legs. Sadness swept over me and almost overflowed into tears. My older sister weighed no more than a child.

With much bumbling, I worked the latch on the door to Ryckerd's chamber and stumbled inside under the weight of chainmail and legless sister. I steered us toward his bed of lichen and allowed us to tumble onto it. I landed with a muted CHINK! Lada landed with a squeal of pain. We both lay still and listened.

Listened.

Lada hugged my left arm. "Oh, Ryckerd, where are you?"

I wondered the same but trembled so violently I could not speak. Ryckerd, no doubt, would've trumpeted brave words and told us what to do. Lada and I lay in each other's arms without moving.

The chamber door banged open and three men rushed into the room and though the door to the balcony without noticing us. Two carried composite bows of horn and glued wood. The third carried a wood and iron crossbow for shooting incendiary bolts.

The castle had never been attacked, and the archers had never fired their weapons at actual enemies.

The sounds of impacts grew louder, closer. One of the men moaned loudly, "How can we harm a thing like that?"

Lada pushed me away. "Help them."

"I don't have a bow."

"You have arms and legs. Hand them arrows. Give moral support. Do not be caught cowering."

I sprung to my feet with more agility than I expected the chainmail to allow. Having a purpose felt like a gift. The three archers were aiming with trembling arms at an incoming comet, as I exited Ryckerd's chamber. My feet froze to the soil covered floor of the rogues' lair, my eyes to the comet. Only one man had the presence of mind to loose his missile, as the comet arced down and slammed into the wall below us. The floor shook.

The castle had been built to confer prestige upon the rising librast and knightly classes in Northem, not out of a pressing need for defense. Engineers and masons from the south were hired to build a fighting castle as great or greater than anything in Tule or the Severed Kingdoms. By the end of the attack, we'd know how they did.

The tremor shook my internal structure much more violently than the wall, and I fell hard to my knees. The archers gawked at me.

"Lance Brother, are you hurt?"

The chainmail. They thought I was a knight.

"Tell us what to do."

Another comet rushed toward us, high and to the left. My finger shot toward it. "Shoot the flogging thing!"

They aimed with purpose. An arrow disappeared into the comet's dirty head, as did the fire bolt, both without effect. The second arrow flew late and swooshed through the vaporous black tail just as the thing exploded in a gout of dirt and pebbles into the tower above. The inky substance that had propelled it evaporated.

No others hit near us. I learned later only one hit closely enough to defenders to have an effect, concussing a soldier in the west round tower. The attack lasted only a few moments, a handful of drops in the water clock. The black ribbons had dissipated, the inky layer gone. My mouth had grown clammy, mayhap because the drizzle had stopped, and the sun had reasserted itself to burn away the moisture. That was a less shameful excuse than admitting fear had done it.

The archers gazed down on me, faces souring. "Blossom?"

I pushed myself to my feet and smiled weakly.

They turned. "We could've used some help, you sniveling prong."

From where we stood on that balcony, we could hear the rattling of the portcullis rising and the thump of the drawbridge lowering into place at the front of the castle. Trumpets brayed. Hooves clattered. The archers peered over the battlements crowding me out of the best viewing spots. I walked up one of the angled beams that passed for a tree limb to the rogues and caught a view over the archers. A squadron of knights from the Order of Man were deploying into battle line and heading toward the wrecked farms. They looked grand and gallant, red and white pennants flying and lance points gleaming, and my diminutive father in the lead, spurring Jules into a charge against an enemy no longer in the field.

I couldn't help feel pride in his audacity, because he'd never faced an enemy of any kind with a blade. He'd accompanied one expedition into Faellar as a young Librast In Situ, but saw no combat. The trip had been aborted due to an outbreak of toadskin among the party. A month after the party's return, the current Librast Superior died young of heart failure, and Father was raised to the position.

Although twice Father's size and half his age, I was critically short on bravado. If my performance on the balcony were an indicator, I was doomed to be a pool of uselessness in the ancient darkness of Dunkelgrau where slavering things tracked the scent of living flesh.

I did feel pleased with myself for not soiling my breeches. I also took comfort in seeing that the inky mass displayed no intelligence, as its strikes seemed random. By the next morning, the damage was assessed: one soldier suffered minor abrasions, two farmers dead, no others grievously injured. The toll came in dead and crippled livestock, and large swaths of ruin through the fields.

I slunk back inside Ryckerd's chamber, hoping Lada hadn't seen me shrivel. She had, through great will, dragged herself to her litter and not seen me.

"I am sure the archers appreciated your assistance."

I snagged her lap blanket from the floor and laid it over her stumps. "You should pay closer attention, next time."

***

A week passed with no further sightings of anything macabre. The elation of surviving the malignant cloud quickly gave way to the profound horror of its existence. If the Anaxagorum were drawing arcane life to it, why didn't the chroniclers of early Northem mention similar incidents during its two-hundred-year residence under the castle? I, for the nonce, refused to attribute the arrival of the inky mass to coincidence. Inhuman creatures had long dwelled under Faellar, but few had been seen in daylight, none near the castle. And where was I heading within a fortnight? Underground where who-knew-what was awakening.

Part II
The Lovely Darkness

Chronicler's Illumination: Dunkelgrau

The ruins got their name from a word inlaid into a mosaic two hundred spans underground. The letters, when transposed upon our alphabet, resembled DUNKELGRAU. They were the first Faellic letters found by the torchlight of Arno I and his small group from the Leper Hill settlement after they roped down from the surface half a millennia ago.

The vault of the Anaxagorum lay at the same depth as the inscription but much farther east. The keening that originally lured the Northmen from their castle to the open pit continued leading them through a league of caves, tunnels, and partially intact urban areas. They found the blood book entombed inside an unmarred draysalt sarcophagus, its lid conspicuously ajar.

Arno's party reasoned that centuries of underground tremors had shaken the lid from its seat. Others back at Leper Hill argued that the tome might have opened the lid through eldritch means, itself. Were the book alive, and if it possessed such a power, then it had had ten thousand years to apply it.

Lexica IX

Father and his bodyguard met us at the departure point where the cobbled quarry road became the wider Baldurgate. Picketed on either side with shady oaks, Baldurgate cut north through farmland to the Cheeky Nobs. A crude path led from there into Faellar. The four supply wagons and their four-oxen teams waited in the gloom under the canopy.

In front stood the vanguard, consisting of Brillix, four other mounted lance brethren, eight foot warriors, eight foot archers, Remi the Warder afoot, the lean flatulent with the ruined pate, and I, the Librast In Situ, astride Thunderhoof. Bringing up the rear were five mounted lance brethren along with various fighters and support personnel, including Pulumbonk, afoot.

The eternally nervous Herbalist Superior had joined at the last moment, as her lieutenant herbalist had taken ill after eating deathshead cabbage mistaken to be hogshead cabbage. (How does an herbalist make such a mistake?) She rode, while her two apprentices walked. Despite the hardships of an expedition, she probably relished the time away from Father.

The fox-faced wild man with the ruined scalp walked next to Remi. He wore the same multi-color vest of stitched-together pelts over a cuirass of boiled leather, only now he also carried a double-headed axe. It wasn't an artfully smithed weapon like Ryckerd's. Its handle was gnarled and wrapped in rawhide strips, and its blades were dead black, except at their cutting edges where they gleamed like silver. I felt at once protective of Remi and jealous of him.

The cook, a hulking, amiable blueskin I was nearly as fond of as Merf, passed my horse on his way to back of the line.

"Naught to worry about, Jonne. We'll be back afore ya know it."

I didn't have a good smile, but I gave him what I could. "I hope so."

The sun arrived with Father's entourage, raising its face enough above the eastern horizon to spill light over the Northern Plains. He sat atop Jules in his full parade armor, a resplendent beetle among men. Visor raised and round, rubicund face clenched in a dramatic scowl, he raised his baton for attention.

"The Anaxagorum will, from this day forward, be removed from the eyes of the world and resealed in its tomb in Dunkelgrau. I, Arno the Seventh, decree it. You band of stalwart heroes have been chosen by history to fulfill this task. You shall not fail me."

I've always been amazed at how well others suffered Father's pomposity. Everyone in the party raised their weapons and cheered. I tried not to visibly cringe, while hoping against certainty he wouldn't call attention to me.

His gauntleted hand swept my way. "My son, Jonne, today fills his sister's shoes."

This time, I'm sure my cringe was visible. Did it not occur to him what an awful choice of words that was?

He continued. "I expect you to abide by his wisdom, when Brillix is otherwise occupied."

I gazed down on the reins in my fist and wished we could get on with our journey. Alas, the Librast In Situ was always consulted on decisions made on behalf of the party, but the inclusion was honorary, as the librast had only meaningful say in the disposition of artifacts and tomes and, later, in the telling of the tale. Good thing. What wisdom did a pampered book curator like me have to lend? Lada received months of training before her first outing as Librast In Situ. I'd received a few days of lectures on basic exploration and edible fungi. The nuances of close combat for which I had lost my instincts had come back, to a point. Were an enemy to stand squarely in front of me without moving much, I stood a good chance of striking him. My knife throwing was my one source of pride among this group. I could hit even medium-sized, moving targets at five spans with considerable frequency.

Father rode up to me and said loudly enough for those nearby to hear, "I cannot be there to lead you, boy."

"I shall do my best."

"Let us hope your best is good enough. Your sister's was not."

Many times in the coming days, I chided myself for not taking up for Lada's honor. The slipperfish attack was not a failure on her part. My guilt never lasted, as I had only to think on the mischief she and her mystery agents planned with the Anaxagorum. I had no idea what the plan was or whether I could stop it, or if I would want to.

I did say, "You forgot to mention the Valens powder."

He turned Jules and rode back to the front of the line. "I am distressed that not one of you has asked about the medicinal power for my daughter. Forget it and and you will be banished. All of you."

As he bloviated about the prosperity of Northem under his guidance, I surreptitiously scanned the other party members to identify possible accomplices to Lada. She had told them not to harm me, but she couldn't guarantee my safety if I interfered. "If someone discovers you have informed Brillix or one of the knights," she had warned, "you will very probably invite a knife in the dark."

Did she watch from Ryckerd's balcony? Mayhap Theodoric hunkered nearby, green eyes peering through the firing embrasure. I raised my hand, should either care to see me.

Father wasn't one for sentimentality, so without a slap on the shoulder for me or praise for the adventurers risking death for him, he thrust his baton into the air. "To Dunkelgrau!"

I didn't expect more from him, but I wanted more, although more of what I'm not sure. The man had trouble acknowledging quality in others, so I'd always done my best to find it myself. I knew who I was with manuscripts. I knew I had a knack for communicating in writing, for perceiving meanings beyond the words, and applying knowledge to practical uses. I have also been aware that I have an above average ability to recollect and quantify items, written or physical. But leadership, combat instincts, situational awareness, courage? If I have none of those, my term as Librast In Situ will be short and shameful.

Father's herald raised his bannered clarion and blew the three, long notes known as the Mother's Call. Winged things flurried from the canopy of oaks. Instead of forward, as the call to battle, the Mother's call meant "come back to me, my children."

I thought of my own mother. She had, but an hour ago, hugged me and kissed, not me, but a green ribbon with which she gifted me for good luck. I wore it secured by a pin around my neck between my gambeson and my chainmail coat.

Brillix, Lance Master of the expedition, gestured to his lieutenant who blew the Traveler's call, one short blast followed by one long blast repeated three times. It simply signaled "onward." Hoof and foot raised. Oxen heaved against their yokes. Wheels groaned into their first rotations, and the timberman on foot beside me began his steady tap on the marching drum. Dop Dop...Dop Dop...Dop Dop. As individual segments propel the caterpillar, each muscled body within the party set the whole in motion toward the east along the bumpy cobbles into the rising sun.

Remi walked between the timberman and the scabby wild man, draped with pouches, a satchel, and cape, and wearing her headdress of three red-and-white great ruyk feathers splayed downward to the bottom of her silver-gray bob. I rarely paid much attention to adornments on women, but I loved the feathers on her. She strenuously avoided my gaze.

Much of my gear rode in a wagon, so Thunderhoof, even with my being encased in armor, was far from overburdened. I thought to offer taking some of Remi's pouches but didn't. Chainmail couldn't protect me from her barbs. I fantasized for an instant that she smiled up at me, and I drew her onto Thunderhoof behind me, her arms around my waist, body pressed to mine. I don't know why I indulged such whimsey, as it only made reality uglier.

***

The shaded road ran straight through the farmlands for two leagues, and then another league through grassy hills ranched by a gentry growing rich on oxen, pigs, horses, fur-bearing shooms, and meat-heavy albons. Shooms were rodent herbivores made round and puffy by a thick coat of plush fur. Albons were floppy eared ungulates resembling the cattle breeds of the south, only they had tails like horses and bristles running along their spines, red for males, orange for females.

Where the cobbles and the oaks of Baldurgate ended, the hypnotic track through the round, rock hills of the Cheeky Nobs began. The change of colors stunned the eye. From somber greens and browns, the landscape turned to bare rock hillocks worn smooth and swirled with vibrant oranges and yellows. I felt I was entering liquid butter petrified in mid-churn.

Cutting a proper road through the Cheeky Nobs would require time and manpower Northem did not have, therefore adventurers made do with rattling through the swales between nobs. The rock was smoother than the cobbled road but rarely flat, so wagons frequently yawed at worrisome angles.

During a time waiting on the wagons behind us to traverse such a stretch, Remi sat on a curving rock incline crosslegged with her gear around her. When I snuck a glance, she caught my eye. I glanced away but, as if she were physically pulling my eyes, my gaze went back to her.

Her bright cobalt irises contrasted with the black lids surrounding them, beautiful and devastating. Her expression held neither warmth nor chill, when she remarked, "If I had a sister, I would be her ready-friend always."

I had also dismounted and yearned to lie down to ease the weight of the chainmail, now hotter and heavier with the thick gambeson Moonsie's seamstresses had made for me. Instead, I sat up straight, not wishing to lie out flat like pounded goose meat in front of her. Focusing on flexing my fingers was easier than looking at her. "I'll presume you're in league with her."

"In league with whom?"

"You mentioned my sister."

"I surely did not. I mentioned 'a' sister."

"Do you know Lada well?"

"The Ice Witch of Northem? Who doesn't?"

"If you have something to tell me, I ask that you say it...and plainly."

She shrugged. "If I had a sister, I would be her ready-friend always."

I stood to walk, now to ease my bum and inner thighs, and to be out of Remi's aura. "I plan to return to my sister with the Valens powder for her pain."

"The herbalists will do that. She needs your support else wise, Jonne."

Remi had been one of the many unwanted babies given to the service of Gela soon after birth, as others were given to service at the castle or on farms and ranches. What other sister could she be referring to? My romantic fantasy about Remi was loathe to depart, even though I knew I must consider her an enemy. In fact, anyone in the party could conceivably be an ally to Lada's plot.

I was no good at cultivating allies. The only people I knew I could trust were Mother, Father, Merf, and, though it slightly surprised me to realize, Ryckerd. He could be distant. He could be a bully. But there was never a time in my life I didn't know absolutely that Ryckerd would draw his sword in my defense. Lada's, too. I wonder how he would've handled this uncomfortable division of loyalties. He most likely would tell Brillix and dare the conspirators to come at him. My confidence was propped by less sturdy struts than his.

The wagon train bumped and rattled through the Cheeky Nobs until twilight. Red light from Homm, the first and largest of the two moons, turned the churned butter colors to those of butchered flesh. Humu, the smaller, white moon, wouldn't be out for another half-hour, its light too weak to have consequence.

We had no need to scavenge for supplies, as we carried what we needed and the surroundings offered none. Of the three women in the party, only Remi and the Herbalist Superior accepted the hospitality of wagon beds. The other, a brute named Birna from the southern islands of Pushni, her hair whitened and stiffened into short spikes with lime, slept on the ground with the men, her cape for a blanket, her snores as robust as any war horn. Men took turns to stand, six at a time, as pickets around their sleeping comrades.

I took my supper of bread, apple slices, and salt pork next to Pulumbonk, aching to accuse him of conspiring with Lada. That would accomplish little, so I asked instead, "Have any of your fellows in the tavern spoken of the wild man with the grotesque forehead?"

He chuckled. "The man could use a new suit of clothes, yea?" His teeth tore at a scrap of salt pork. "Tell me we'll have a fire and fresh meat tomorrow night."

I craved the same things. "I fear only more salt pork and misery will be offered, until we get back."

"Then so be it."

Pulumbonk first impressed me as a dandy in his rich leather boots and ornate doublet, so he surprised me by showing little displeasure at outside life. He must've stored his fine garments, for he was dressed for the expedition in sturdy boots and a jerkin of leather reinforced with metal buckles.

I remarked wistfully. "I have a fine feather bed at the castle."

"Stone makes a hard bed, but we won't need to worry about our safety. Look at the companions we have around us."

"I'd feel better with thrice their number."

He grinned. "You are every bit as gloomy as Lada said."

"She's called me worse."

"You should assist her with her…needs."

"As you are doing?"

"Do you accuse me of something?"

"I believe you'd do anything for Lada, so yes, I am."

"I have no response to that."

"Then tell me of the wild man. Who is he, and why is he allowed to walk next to Remi?" I was sorry for letting that slip.

"The blueskin warder?" He grinned. "You've the urge for her, yea? You, a man of the castle?"

"The question afoot regards the wild man, not me."

"Want me to talk to her, mayhap put in a good word for you?"

I recoiled. "No!"

"Very well then. His name is Subu, or so I hear others call him. Have you traveled over the western waters to Tulos? Quite hard to believe the ancestors of a farting animal like that are now the well-trimmed landholders of imperial Tulas."

I had not been to the large island of Tulos, but I had read accounts of it written by explorers and merchants. My image of it was of vast, grassy plains hemmed by gnarled forests and overrun with horses. Civilization had never taken root there, so ancient tribes with names like Gurash, Swaytuk, and Jaballdot warred incessantly with one another for women, horses, and ownership of the few viable harbors allowed by the island's sheer shorelines and toothy reefs.

"He's a scalp-taker," said Pulumbonk, face sour. "An unsavory trade for even an animal from Tulos."

I winced when remembering the ruined red pate where the man's hair had been. The man didn't stand much taller than I, but his aura of violent energy made him seem monstrous.

Pulumbonk encouraged my discomfort by adding, "Those aren't pelts making up that vest of his."

When the time came to venture underground, I wasn't sure what or whom I should most fear: the creatures of the dark or a vindictive warder and a scalp-taker of my own party.

Pulumbonk placed his trencher next to him. He seemed finished with the meal, yet a mess of apple bits, large bread crumbs, and groat bits lay uneaten.

I gestured to it. "Looks as if a blind dog had at that."

He chuckled. "I know when I've had enough."

"What a waste." Brillix wouldn't approve, but I dragged the trencher closer. "May I have it?

The Cheeky Nobs provided no distraction for my mind, and I was allowed no reading material on the trip because of our limited storage. Nor were there any twigs or grass from which to fashion curiosities. I considered withdrawing my journal from its leather sheath embossed with the flaming eye of Northem and sketching, but I couldn't waste paper on frivolous pursuits. The light had begun to fade, in any case. I made tiny round forts out of pebbles. Pulumbonk withdrew two pinches of powder from a pouch and flicked tiny fireballs at my forts. When he wouldn't tell me the trick, I flicked pebbles at him and battle was joined. I was actually enjoying myself, until Brillix walked by and knuckled my head.

"No malarky in my camp."

***

Morning came brutally. I had slept less than well: my backpack for a pillow, hard rock for a mattress, and a kick to the foot instead of a gentle rap at the door for a wake-up. Sleeping in my gambeson and boots under my cloak, only to be greeted by a cool, moist morning was barbaric. Having no fire seemed cruel. My chainmail, which I had folded neatly and placed beside me, had disappeared in the night. Before I could inquire, I noticed several others, mostly castlers I'd known my whole life, snickering over their shoulders. Even after twenty years, it hadn't become less painful.

The big cook caught my eye and smiled sympathetically. "Talk to Brillix."

I had no chance to talk to Brillix, as he started lecturing the moment he saw me. "You should never sleep without your armor and weapons where you can find them instantly in the dark." He passed the chainmail to me. When I took it with both hands, he tossed my sheathed sword and bandolier of throwing knives. Trying to catch them all at once resulted in my dropping the lot and then bending to root for them like a pig. I couldn't detect Brillix's sway-back in his armor, but I knew it was there and took a sour pleasure.

I wanted to hate Brillix, but I berated myself, instead. Many an account of expeditions into the wild preached the importance of correct procedures. I failed, though, to make the mental leap that those procedures applied to me. When someone chuckled about Blossom, and not even in a whisper, I felt I deserved the name.

Pulumbonk helped me into my armor. "Having a bum ear doesn't make you stupid. Can you hear out of it?"

"Every word."

While I buckled my belt and slung my pouches, Remi walked past.

"Unless you want to die like a feast-day albon, don't do that again."

The remark was a decided upgrade from "die dog."

All the parts of our caterpillar lined up, and the whole trundled forward at sunrise. As I rode, I debated whether or not to include the fumbling of my chainmail in the journal I kept of the expedition. It seemed a revelatory expression of my character at that point in the tale, so in it went.

The sun rose, and the morning warmed pleasantly. We rocked and creaked and heaved our way farther across the Cheeky Nobs. The clop of horseshoes on rock and shouts from the path ahead brought us to a halt. One of our scouts, the elder Fletcherson triplet, Certe, appeared. Brillix waved for me to come to the front and hear what the man had to report.

Certe's brow was heavy with concern, but his voice was low and even. "We come across corpses not far up. Animals, great ruyks by the look of 'em, kilt by blades but not a dead rider among 'em."

Brillix absorbed the news, heroically erect in his saddle, one hand at the saddle horn, one resting on his armored thigh. "Ruyk this far south?"

It made no sense. The Ruyk were tundra dwellers of the far north in a harsh land they called Krak-ala-mok, which meant The Place of Punishment. The great ruyks they rode might have been named after the Ruyk tribe or the tribe after them. Even they don't know. The animals have round bodies, two powerful legs, and glossy red, oval heads like the groats ranchers raise in Northem for meat and eggs, only much larger and fiercer. While we try to breed away the tiny forearms of the groat, Ruyks breed their beasts to be larger, stronger. The three clawed fingers of a great ruyk can shred a man. Enormous herds of the beasts roam the north grazing on tundra weed, a plant that grows during four months of the year and lies dormant for the other six. The nomads, also known as Ruyks, use every part of them, from feathered crests and tough, glossy black hides, to flesh, bones, and hooves.

Ruyk shamans have passed cautionary tales from generation to generation about the Writhing Soil living unnaturally to the south in Faellar, and traveling there is forbidden. Where an empire once flourished stretches a realm only reptiles and raptors, insects and underground abominations that never emerge into the daylight call home. Faellic ruins have been found as far west as the disease-belching Fumus Mountains and as far east as the Axehead Mountains, a place devoid of life where gigantic blades of rock jut from the ground at belligerent angles. Between Krak-ala-mok and the Cheeky Nobs lie eight hundred leagues of ruins covered by lush grassland and scrubby plains, which forms a veritable wall between them and the rest of the world.

Only one tribe of Ruyk is friendly. They scoff at the shamans' warnings and venture into Faellar twice a year to meet a caravan from Northem, trading steel weapons and iron implements for gleaming black hides and the striking red-and-black crest feathers. Our scouts and traders say the Ruyk tribespeople smell alternately of freshly sliced tomatoes or manure and that their single women braid living insects into their hair.

I was curious as to their culture but in no hurry to meet them in person.

We caught up to the other two scouts, Berte and Aethelbert, an hour later, after passing more great ruyk carcasses. The three brothers were unlike most blueskins, as their coloring was deep indigo, and they were fiercely loyal to Father. The men were of the same bloodline as the Guides, only they knew the land, not the lake. The younger two were squatting with palms to the rock next to their mounts, when we arrived.

They all had scars on their cheeks that rose from the flesh in the shape of a circle with an X growing from it—many Guides scarred themselves with arcane symbols, claiming the symbols weren't magical but spirit shapes that came to them in dreams. The shorter one, Aethelbert, spoke to Brillix. Although I rode next to Brillix, the scout never looked at me.

Aethelbert held the bridle of Brillix's horse. "A mound of Ruyk riders two hundred paces 'atta way, recently kilt. More great ruyk carcasses, too. The Ruyk don't leave their naksies (companions) unburied, so they gonna be back."

"You think the Ruyk are collecting their dead in that pile?" asked Brillix.

"Bring yer weapons to hand. We gonna sniff about."

The man didn't wait for approval. He and his larger brother, Berte, gave their horses' reins to the older Certe, and then scrambled away, not along the path but over a smooth rock hillock that seemed too steep to climb. They managed it, not with ease, but with proficiency.

Brillix circled his hand in the air. "Lock down the wagons."

The teamsters blocked their wagon wheels and hooded their oxen, the beasts' horns slipping through pre-cut holes.

Over my armor, I wore the twilight-blue cloak and hood of the Librast In Situ. From a strap on Thunderhoof's saddle hung my helmet, a handsome cap of domed steel, a fixed face mask with tear-drop eye holes and generous brass piping for decoration and reinforcement. The first things Brillix and the other fighters did were shed their cloaks and don their helmets. The first thing I did was forget my helmet, pull the hood of my cloak over my head, and squat next to a wagon with the intention of hiding under it should things get bloody.

A man-at-arms cried, "We've no spears!"

Without a spear or lance, a man afoot fought at a disadvantage against a mounted opponent.

"Calm down," Brillix said loudly enough for those around him to hear. "Riders in this terrain are at more of a disadvantage than us, so use the weapons you have."

Like him or not, I did respect Brillix's sanguine competence. He swatted the party into positions around the two middle wagons, one holding food, the other holding the Herbalist Superior's gear and the sheathed Anaxagorum. I hated the possibility of losing the other two wagons and their poor, clueless beasts, but we couldn't guard all of them at once. One forsaken wagon held a cask of Red Hand Ale, the one thing to look forward to in the evenings. The other held tents and cooking equipment. Brillix placed me at the rear left of the second wagon next to Remi.

She sorted through her shoulder satchel, eyes flicking from it to me and back. "You don't know what you're doing, so when the 'doing' starts, stay out of my way."

"Out of your way where?"

She almost softened. "Under the wagon. You'll have some protection there."

I would not cower in front of Remi, or so I told myself. To my knowledge, she had been on only one previous expedition. She acted as if she'd been on many.

Someone toward the front squeaked, "The sky!"

Remi and I craned to see. Inky blackness suffused the thin cloud cover turning it into a flat, dark layer over the horizon ahead, not as expansive as the one that appeared over Northem. The inky ribbons that descended from it were also fewer than the number that attacked the castle. I looked at the wagon behind me. Did this one carry the blood book or was it the other? I half expected a sound, a shudder, a something from the wagon, but I had no sense of it as Lada had.

Remi's eyes never left the cloud. "Fascinating, and with so little moisture in the air."

Howls came from the middle-distance around us. Possibly human. They grew louder. The ground began to vibrate. Then came a maddening clicking, as that made by the toenails of heavy animals on rock.

A realization chilled me. The things coming for us might well be in league with Lada and her agents. I wheeled, nearly sure Remi would be raising a blade to strike me. Instead, I saw a young woman of my age and same level of near-hysteria coiled like a spring.

"What is it?" I asked.

If she had been a cat, she would've leapt straight up in the air. "Sweet Gela's toenails!"

I bounced back a step. "Sorry."

"I guess so! You scared me bloodless. What's wrong with you?"

My eyes couldn't hold hers for long, so they turned skyward. "We should never have taken the blood book from the imperial capital."

The heel of her hand struck my shoulder. "Our ancestors should never have let it leave Northem."

Wisdom told me, they should never have plucked it from the depths of Dunkelgrau, in the first place.

My job was not to fight but to witness. Still, my hand felt happier on the cool, metal handle of the throwing knife I eased from its sleeve in the bandolier of six. I had sharpened the tips of the light blades until each could sink deeply into unarmored flesh. While I threw them with deadly accuracy in practice, I wasn't sure I'd remain steady when something bore down on me with teeth or blade.

The inky layer advanced on us at a terrifying speed. With it, the sounds. Paws pounding. Harness rattling. The human howling took a shape as it neared, not just war whoops but also insane screams, men filled with both bloodlust and anguish. They seemed to come from every direction at once.

Remi's voice tugged me from my overheated imagination. "If you must stay standing, guard me while I prepare a ward."

I mulled the definition of "guard." How did one do that? I looked to the man to my right, an archer, but he was too busy readying his quiver to do any guarding.

Remi pulled from her satchel a star made from twigs lashed with grass and threw me a disgusted glance. "Draw your sword, Jonne." She breathed on the little star and raised it to the sky. On the words, "Dolki horendun!" it floated from her hand to a spot just above the wagon we guarded. Another glance at me, this one self-satisfied and a bit mocking. "Find something in your library to explain that!"

She fished in her satchel for what I assumed to be another ward, when the howling stopped. The clicking of toenails, now closer, now more of a scraping, a ripping at rock, grew on the other side of the round hill I faced. The oxen, though hooded, strained at their harness.

A beast's head, egg-shaped and shiny red with hooded eyes as green as sunlit grass and a frill of red and black feathers encircling it, broke the crest. A great ruyk. Its head rose on a long, muscled black neck that grew from a stout, round body sleek with short, licorice hair trimmed here and there with red and black feathers. The thing skidded downhill toward me on two massive hind legs. Arms reached from its chest, three-fingered talons ready to clutch. A rider waggled side to side on its back, spear raised, torso girded in leather buckled with raw iron. An inky vapor trailed the beast, like the earthen comets that had attacked Northem.

My peripheral vision showed blurs in similar colors and with vaporous tails bearing down on our caravan, causing the oxen to stamp. I only felt concern for the enemy charging me. I forgot the knife in my hand and fell back on my usual recourse: to stare stupidly.

Remi thrust another star trinket at the oncoming Ruyk and shouted, "Dolki horendun Remi non!"

Beast and rider blew backward two paces, as if struck by a handheld hurricane.

"Jonne!" Remi shouted. "The rider!"

What I couldn't do for myself, I did without thinking for Remi. My knife flew toward the man's upper chest, with the intent to slow him enough that I might finish him with my sword, as the drill masters had taught me. The fellow rose to his knees but slipped, so the tip of my knife dug into the unprotected flesh of his throat. With a violent jerk and a splutter of pink foam at his lips, the man was done.

Remi bent over the beast, trinket held within a hand-span of its face, her mouth delivering a stream of what sounded like nonsense. The great ruyk quivered but did not try to rise. She called without turning to me. "Here!" Her free hand pointed to the soft spot under the beast's chin. "Drive toward the brain!"

I had slaughtered albons and beheaded groats, so the grisly aspects of this procedure didn't daunt me. How to aim the blow did. Remi sidled to the left. I took her cue and squatted shoulder-against-shoulder with her, placed the sword point and drove it in with both hands. The strike was more merciful than the one it intended for us.

To my right, arrows flew into a great ruyk without slowing it. The beast closed, until its hand-talons grabbed the archer next to me and its mouth bit into his neck. Its rider jabbed down at a second archer with a spear only to be dragged from his mount by a man-at-arms and skewered.

To my left, one of the knights in the rear guard knelt to avoid a great ruyk's talons and thrust his sword upward into its belly. Two lightly armored blueskins—the clinker and the cook, I believe—tore the rider from his saddle.

On the other side of the wagon behind me, a powerful flash strew spots over my vision. I later learned it was Pulumbonk. With a luminast trick, he had blinded four onrushing enemies, so his companions could deal safely with them.

A foresight? An uncanny presence of mind? Something turned my head from Pulumbonk's flash and urged me to move quickly to the left. A spear thudded into the wagon where I had just stood.

"Dolki horendun Remi non!"

Another miniature hurricane flew at three assailants charging us on foot. I aimed a knife at the nearest one, knowing before I released that the blade would strike true. An opponent's head usually presented a hard target to hit, but my knife pierced this one's forehead, killing him instantly. I had no time to throw at the others. Remi pounced on one with her poniard, and I on the other with my short sword. The act felt as if I had performed it dozens of times.

Shouts of pain and victory rose from every point in our defensive circle. Though I didn't realize it immediately, the fight was over. Remi and I stood at the ready, waiting for anything else to appear. My tongue had swollen, and my mouth felt full of glue. I sucked water from my flagon, noticing Remi did the same.

She licked her lips. "Dry days are bad days for warding."

Brillix's voice from the head of the caravan called, "Tend the wounded. Stay alert."

Relief shivered through me. "I'm alive."

Remi, glancing around the wagons, panted, "We are at that."

My gaze fell upon the corpses of the men I had just killed two paces away, and I sagged to my knees gagging. They did smell of sliced tomatoes, and the image made my reaction all the stronger. I'd grown up seeing dead bodies in the grove of Gela, where we placed them for nature to reclaim. I'd never seen any I had myself felled.

A soft thump behind startled me from my sickness. Remi's wondrous smile spread, her top row of teeth brilliant against lavender lips. She hauled herself up to the wagon seat and, on tip-toe, swatted at something on the tented top. A dun-colored star bounced into the air and fell near where I knelt. It was the fetish that had hovered over the wagon.

I stared at it. Such items weren't supposed to float in mid-air, at least not by the intent of nature.

Remi hopped down next to me. "It's but twigs and grass, not much of a danger to a fighting man, such as yourself."

I toed it across the yellow rock closer to her. "Twigs and grass, mayhap, but what is it's function?"

She turned playful. "Reckon through that yourself, librast."

Before I could answer, a presence manifested behind my shoulder. "I see you dispatched some of the enemy." Brillix stepped into view. "Or was it she?"

Remi put the star into her satchel. "He helped."

I prickled. "I dropped two with my knives. Killed them." My body trembled as the words came out. "The great ruyk, too."

Brillix addressed Remi. "What did you cast?"

"An agility glamour. It will have benefited everyone within ten spans of it." She looked directly at me, her front teeth peeking curiously from under her lip. "Or did you think you were suddenly a natural at this?"

Brillix smirked. "Almost smells of magic, eh?"

He continued around the wagon's rear to check on the others. I stared at Remi, wanting to ask, but not daring to utter a word.

Her chin rose, as if in victory over me. "Brillix appreciates my little tricks. Your father would put me back in the pillories because of them." She yanked the drawstring of her fetish bag. "It's time for people's view of blueskins to change, Jonne. Wouldn't you agree?"

"I've never thought any less of blueskins."

"And that's why I think more of you." She nodded to the dead men in front of us. "Don't forget to retrieve your knives. They don't grow on bushes."

If there were any other feats of inadequacy I could perform in front of the woman I wanted to impress, I couldn't think of one.

Lexica X

A request passed mouth to mouth from the head of the caravan to me: Come see Brillix. I enjoyed feeling important in front of Remi who was kissing one of her grass-and-twig fetishes before replacing it in her satchel. On my way up the line, I passed men embracing to celebrate their survival, one dutifully cleaning his blade, and two crouching next to a third whose face drained to white as his blood spread over the rock under him. No one called for an herbalist, as the dying man was beyond their ministrations.

I felt elated not to be him then horrified that I could easily be him in some battle to come. Pulumbonk believed in a divine entity that took an interest in his life. Such silliness became suddenly desirable, although I had no faculty for connecting with it. Children of Northem, in the castle, village, and the blueskin community, were taught to accept death without dwelling on the mystery of it. "Worry not about what comes after life," taught the Sisters of Gela, "for the answers will only reveal themselves after your body falls from you." I didn't know the man dying at my feet, but I wondered if he had a god or was alone with the pain.

All of the wagons and their oxen remained mostly undamaged. At the front of the caravan, I found Brillix, three knights, and little Certe, the elder scout, standing over two figures on the ground. One was a man on his knees wearing a coat of rough hide fitted with iron studs. Shaggy hair as orange as Lada's hung toward the ground from his bent head. Subu, the vulpine scalp-taker, squatted behind the wretch, his fingers deep in the orange hair and his knife at the man's throat.

Brillix addressed me while gesturing to the captive. "Hold witness, Librast." He nodded to Certe. "Continue."

Certe uttered a string of gutteral noises that were the language of the Ruyk. I barely heard the captive's reply, but Certe translated for our group. "As I told ya, this fella's from a tribe I do na' know. His people losted their hunting range to another tribe up in the Krak and comed south with their families."

"Into the Cheeky Nobs? Nothing to eat here."

"Harken to me, Brillix. They did na' plan to come this far. They had na' choice. The animals comed under some magic and—"

"Not magic," corrected Lance Brother Poonal, the long-chinned knight tasked with guarding the Anaxagorum.

"Say what ya will, but something's controllin' the beasts' minds, and it is na' the riders."

Brother Poonal said, "Ask why they attacked us."

Brillix addressed the scout. "Ask for his whole story. What led them here?"

When Certe asked, the captive remained still. When he asked again, Subu yanked the man's head up by his hair. The Ruyk's eyes went wide, mouth fell open. "No kill!"

"The black cloud is connected to this," I said.

Brillix dismissed me with a wave. "We can see the obvious ourselves, Jonne."

The captive was nervous to the point of shaking apart. Words whispered out of him in gusts, as if his recent memory had shattered, and he needed to search for the pieces. One phrase...then another...and another. The scout translated at intervals.

The man's tribe was known as the Arakks. They had only emigrated into Faellar a few months ago and not more than thirty leagues into it, when they found a source of clean fresh water and an abundance of vine fruits and burrowing mammals he called "keedy geats." His people didn't like the change from hunting to trapping, fishing, and gathering, but they ate well, and they're children were safe. Their idyll ended two weeks ago, when their great ruyks began behaving strangely. They became distracted and frequently unresponsive. Some wandered south in the evenings. Then more. One hundred warriors rode out to bring them back, but the farther south they went, the more headstrong their mounts became. When they caught up with the strays, the jittery, snorting things attacked their masters and had to be killed. Yesterday, the riders themselves became disoriented and hyper excited. They attacked the Northem caravan in a state of delirium.

I almost remarked that it had been two weeks ago that the Anaxagorum had come ashore with Lada, but I supposed Brillix would find that "obvious."

Certe the scout finished with, "Their beasts comed fer us, like they knowed exactly where we be."

Brillix waved him to silence. "Enough. It pains me to hear you desecrate the language so."

Certe scrubbed at his nose with the heel of his hand. "The day ye learn to sniff a trail, I'ma learn yer castle talk."

Subu tied the captive's hands with a rope and tethered him to the second wagon. I heard him warn the man, "Raise a stink, and I'll scrape yer pate clean of that orange mop, gally boy." He noticed my watching and nodded with what seemed respect. "Yer the man of words?"

"I am that, yes."

He stepped to me and placed a hand on my shoulder. His breath smelled of old meat, and the scarred pate up close was fearful. The agony of having one's scalp removed by blade and through the long months of healing must've seemed unending. Two mottled green eyes and a long nose turned to me. "I am The Subu. S-U-B-U. Write me good in yer stories."

"I…I record what I witness,"

He turned without remark and retook his place in line next to Remi. I found Thunderhoof tethered to the front wagon. A pair of bloody streaks suggested he had been raked by talons, and an inspection of his rear hooves revealed blood and the torn hide of another animal, meaning he had given as good as he had gotten. I scooped a dollop of albon fat from the bucket on the food wagon and rubbed it into the wound. Thunderhoof showed his approval with a toss of his head and a nuzzle against my hands.

Our caravan started forward, at least another day in the Cheeky Nobs before us. We settled into the monotony of the trek and passed the day without further event. While taking our meal that evening, Pulumbonk and I verbally danced around each other trying to ascertain what Lada had said of us to the other. He asked what she was like when alone, whether she mentioned him in her talks with me, did she have a sweetheart? My questions were never so obvious. I asked for his thoughts on honor and loyalty to family, the contents of the Anaxagorum, and if he were the only one to find it so alluring. He evaded mine, and I evaded his, so we learned very little. He said, "If you love her, you'd help her become whole again."

Blood connected Lada to me but I couldn't say love did. Mayhap I should've cared more that she wanted her legs back, but I didn't. The only person I knew I loved was Mother. Lada had always been too focused on her studies to spend time with me. We teased and fought a fair amount when very small, then Father trained that out of us. Ryckerd had taught me a few things about battle craft and outdoor survival, but he was five years older and never a companion. All of us would defend our family, but none of us knew how to love it. Lada had been playful with

Brillix and palpably angry when he withdrew his affections, so she still had some emotions in play.

Pulumbonk, eyes set dreamily on the stars, mused, "I should like to be the one who finds Valens powder for Lada."

"Do you even know for what you are looking?"

"A purple powder found on draysalt when underground."

"Not a powder in its natural form. It's mold that forms on some surfaces in the Faellic underground."

He patted one of his satchels of fire-making ingredients. "Molds are full of marvelous secrets."

***

On our third day, we made it past midday before we noted the inky mass collecting in the sky to the west. It came quickly over us and shredded itself. Without loose rock and soil to give them mass, the vaporous ribbons whirled around us and through the sides of the wagons, doing naught but causing the horses to kick and our bowels to clench. The soundless attack lasted no longer than it took a man to make water.

Farther on, a wagon's wheel shattered, forcing us to spend a third night in the round, rocky hills. Rain sprinkled briefly in the evening, and the black vapor appeared again, only to dissipate as the rain abated. Whispers among the party said we were all thinking the same thing: Was the mysterious inkiness inside the raindrops beading on our cloaks? Could it do to us what it did to the Ruyks? My mental state seemed sturdy enough, for the nonce.

We ate at dawn and caterpillared forward at first light. The hills grew gentler in grade and opened to scrubland. Our wagons rolled easier along the path worn in the soil by previous expeditions. The plain before us undulated but without serious gradients. Vegetation stood mostly at knee height and rarely over a man's head. The plants came in various hues of drab greens and yellows, their names cataloged and shelved in the top-most underhall of the castle.

Less than a league in, we saw the first webs. They were silver-white, many the size of cloaks. They hung in some of the taller vegetation. Not spider webs, these didn't show the geometry spiders weave. The fibers criss-crossed without design. Farther along, larger swaths of vegetation were hidden under drifts of the ghostly stuff. One could imagine the wind throwing up watery spray from Lake Rado, turning it to silk, and then blowing it over the land. Texts in the Northem archives mentioned such a phenomenon three hundred years ago, when Festur was rumored to have penetrated the blood book.

I could just see around a knight in front of me to one of the scouts riding up to Brillix and pointing. Their voices didn't carry, but their bodies told the story: shrugging shoulders, hands over mouths in consternation, longing looks toward home. No order to stay alert needed to be given. The entirety of us became one nerve.

I had come to Dunkelgrau at ten, as a Librast Initiate, and again at eighteen, as a newly sworn Librast Custodian, to serve a mandatory military role. I, with others my age—all of us coming to our majority—were sprinkled among veteran adventurers to guard a work force installing a better system of nets, ropes, and pulleys for conveying men and supplies into the rend in the earth to the dark ruins below. The assignment was uneventful, but I have a physical memory of the gnawing in my chest each time I peered into that black slash in the soil.

That was over two years and several hundred sugar cakes ago. I had a strong sword arm then and a younger man's conceit. Since the horrors of Emperor Draman's crusade in the south began last year, I've learned how quickly can fall a kingdom and a culture, a sister and a brother. With the advent of the inky cloud and the webs, I can practically taste poison on the air, one ready to wither the enlightened civilization begun by Julius the Wise in Tulas, cultivated in Kamsala, Atmaa, and Qnok, and advanced in Northem. Was it all for naught, all doomed to lie as another layer of ruin atop Faellar? For all we knew, Faellar rested atop the ruins of an even older civilization.

I studied again the party members around me. Who among them could be ignorant enough to think the Anaxagorum could be plumbed without consequence? Many were foreigners I had no clue about. Ten were knights and sworn to preserve Northem's archives and advance its mission of enlightenment. I didn't suspect them. The few men-at-arms and archers from the castle and village militia might be enticed by the power of the book, but it was the blueskins, Remi, the clinker, the cook and a few others, I worried about. If the legend were true, they were tied to the book by their blood.

Should Draman and the followers of Askerat prevail in the south, they will come for us. Loyalty to Northem's mission needed to be assiduous by all. Should one of our Guides decide to sell the secrets of crossing Lake Rado, Northem will fall. Ignorance will hold dominion over the world and brutes will be kings. The thought made the salt pork I nibbled while I rode seem drier.

Mayhap in another ten thousand years, the blood book will call again, and other righteous men will prepare to descend into the hole that was us to re-inter it.

Father, why didn't we leave the cursed thing in the south?

***

At late morning of day four, I saw the first row of draysalt spires in the distance, webs fluttering from them like tattered, white banners. By noon, I could see all one hundred and three of them jutting from the ground. Though this was my third expedition out there, the sight flattened me. As the old chronicler had written, the lengthening shadows cast by the waning sun did look like a demonic phalanx of spear points advancing across the plain. Another three hours brought us to the lip of the pit.

The site was as I remembered it. Even though two hundred spans long and forty wide, the slash in the ground didn't become visible until one crested the slight rise hiding it. A wooden platform, with its booms, windlasses, and pulleys, stuck out like a tongue from the near edge of the chasm, as if to lick the darkness below. The nightmarish Raka Infante that dwelled below made a habit of stealing the ropes and netting, so we transported that gear to and from Dunkelgrau in the wagons.

A corral of stones and tarred pine poles built by past expeditions remained intact a goodly-walk from the hole. The teamsters parked the wagons near the enclosure and all of us dismounted to set up camp. Most of us went right to work clearing the corral of webs. Not sticky as I had thought, the webs were dry and only slightly more solid than smoke. They parted when tapped and gathered easily into large puffs.

I led Thunderhoof to the farthest point in the corral from the hole and checked his hooves for imbedded stones. The Ruyk captive had warned of seeing "beings cavorting among the spires" during the Arakk warband's ride south, so Brillix took five knights out to investigate. Everyone else had chores to do.

Ten of us gathered armloads of un-webbed hawk sage that grew in abundance over the plain and heaped it into the large crib inside the corral for feed. Within an hour, others had hung kettles over fires, erected four pavilions and eight tents, and hammered together the field forge. A crew worked until twilight to lay out the ropes, thread the pulleys, and spread the net in which party members, supplies, and the Anaxagorum would be lowered to the floor two hundred spans down.

We dined for a third night on roasted great ruyk meat, as the battle in the Cheeky Nobs had been serendipitous in leaving us more carcasses than we could butcher.

Darkness was full upon us, as we finished supper. The chirps and buzzing of insects out in the scrub rose to a drone. Families of jabber rats would be slipping from their burrows to feed on them, and by midnight, they'd be clicking and cooing about their hunts for all of their neighbors to hear.

I knelt within the firelight shared by my pavilion and that of the knights, scouring my wooden trencher with gravel. A quantity of thoughts paced my mind, all regarding what I might say to Remi to win manly respect, something Ryckerd might say. "You fought well today," would seem pretentious coming from a man who required a woman to spur him to action. I thought to tell her I admired her headdress of great ruyk feathers, but she might think me weak, if I complimented her too often, or that I had impure motives. I wished I could promise to protect her, but that day might never come.

I had been hunkering in a crosslegged ball at the back of the herbalist's pavilion. When I raised my face from the cradle of my hands, I noted the two herbalist apprentices snickering.

"Ready to go home, Blossom?" one asked.

That propelled me away from them and into the ring of tents to search for a stick to carve, but the only ones to present themselves were thin and brittle. I collected instead some grass and twigs, and sat in the deep shadow of the cook's wagon, with its winged doors open and work counters lowered. I felt the pull to go home although not necessarily to Northem. I fashioned a tiny house with a front door. Were I to win Remi, I would be happy to live with her in such a humble dwelling. I wondered as I had many times if she had noticed my ear and then crushed the little house with my fist.

The veil of sleep didn't fall, so I ambled about camp with no clear purpose. The food wagon and the other three wagons set in a square formed the nexus of the layout. Two pavilions for Brillix and his knights, a third serving as an armory, and a fourth for the Herbalist Superior, her two apprentices, and me formed the first ring around the wagons. Around that was a second ring of eight smaller tents, and beyond it, a third ring of lumen poles, the fruits spiked atop them casting their gently pulsing orange light out to ten paces. Lumen fruit only retained its phosphorescence for five days, so we'd be using lanterns and torches soon.

I tip-toed toward the slash, wondering how I'd feel seeing it again. The small tents held three men and their gear. I stepped between two of them, the one on the right buzzing with two men's snores, one higher pitched than the other, as if a big bee and a less big bee were sharing the tent.

Just past the tents, a guard stood in a dark spot between the light from two lumen poles. Oddly, he was looking toward the camp, not away, as if he were guarding the outside from us. Common sense said retreat, but when he wiped his eyes, I hustled through the lighted area and over the rise that blocked the view of the slash and the plains beyond.

There, barely catching the pulsing light, stood Remi. Her cloak was elsewhere, leaving her moss-green tunic and tight breeches in full view. Her arms were raised, hands fussing with something in her hair, causing the hem of her tunic to rise. Enough orange light reached her to reveal the gentle curves of her backside before losing them to the shadows. I could see them. I couldn't. They were there. They were gone. I was mesmerized. She seemed to be settling a tiara of unknown material onto her head.

Pulumbonk stood close, one hand holding rust-colored strands of snoutbush—so named because of its resemblance to the long, droopy snout of an albon—his other hand shaking a single strand free for Remi's use. Why hadn't she come to me for such assistance? Had we not fought side by side? Had we not kissed happily once? And Pulumbonk, was he wooing Remi now that Lada was an amputee? Love had no place for the legless, it seemed.

I turned to slink back to my pavilion when the blue-skinned cook and the clinker, appeared from behind a tent and crept next to Remi. The clinker was a trap-and-gadget man, small-framed and irritable. The cook was his opposite, hulking, slow, and agreeable. They stopped only long enough to receive a star fetish from Remi. Each tucked the thing into their doublets and moved on without a word.

I followed the two around the camp, surprised at how normal the coat of chainmail was beginning to feel. Its weight hadn't lessened, but it's burden on me had. The large cook resembled Merf from behind, only his long hair was braided, not ponytailed. The clinker was one of the few blueskins to crop his black hair above his ears. I imagine long hair has a tendency to catch in gizmos and gadgets. They made whispering stops with seven others: three more blueskins, the spiky-haired female brute from

Pushni, one of the herbalist's apprentices—a perpetually sour young man I had never liked—and two heavily armed adventurers from Qnok I had yet to hear speak. Their rounds made, cook and clinker returned to the food wagon.

Seeing someone as ensconced in castle doctrine as an herbalist apprentice now talking secrets with suspicious people disturbed me. Intuition told me I'd just beheld the conspirators and should alert Brillix. Lada's warning about knives made me hesitate. Maybe Remi and company weren't up to anything sinister—but that seemed the reasoning of a coward.

When I returned to my pavilion, I learned that the sour herbalist apprentice, who was also one of my tent mates, stood first watch with seven others around the camp. The Herbalist Superior and her other apprentice were already snuggled under blankets and cloaks atop beds of hawk sage. Before descending to my own bed, I exited my pavilion and rounded the food wagon to Brillix's pavilion on the other side. To my relief and consternation, he was still on patrol. That solved my dilemma of whether or not to tell him my suspicions, but it also spurred my heart to an anxious trot not having him around.

Clouds had slipped in to absorb much of Humu's red light. Homm, the smaller moon, had just risen to peek from behind her big brother. Both would disappear two hours before dawn. Time passed, but sleep would not come, only thoughts of knives and conspiracy. The insect drone almost lulled me, until the cacophony of jabber rat songs slapped me to full wakefulness.

Had we passed midnight? Neither the apprentice or Brillix's patrol had returned. An itch between my shoulders insisted I rub myself like a bear against the ground, but the gambeson and chainmail thwarted relief. I crept outside again. Moonlight, still trapped between layers of clouds, failed to do more than reveal my hand at arm's length. The pulse of the lumen fruit ringing the camp at least defined silhouettes: the side of a tent, a cooking pot hanging from its tripod.

I could barely make out the sentry standing closest to the pit. Interestingly, he continued to watch the camp. Wouldn't things in the darkness below constitute a greater threat? Crouching in a dark spot between lumen poles, I heard a voice incanting strange words. It was Remi's, soft but no doubt hers. My feet searched for accommodating bits of earth without dry twigs or scraping stones. A cat in chainmail, I approached the crest of the hummock hiding her.

No longer spritely and feminine, her voice was low and dark. "Malka este ulo nathrak. Toors bansento obrillat sak."

The language sounded similar to her warding incantations, the same aggressive consonants and staccato meter. Dread ran up my spine on needly feet, and I thought to back away. Then, three sung notes, watery and lovely, needful and heartbreaking rose from the hidden platform. I ached to see her, but peering over the hummock raised the risk of being seen.

I rose.

Drok!

She was kneeling on the platform with her back to me as naked as a newborn. The lumen light kissed with orange the curve of her shoulder and the trembling muscles of her outstretched arm, the feminine roll of a hip and the toes of a slender blue foot. Then dimmed. Then kissed again.

Pulumbonk knelt next to her, where I should've been. He held a bowl of water, eyes glancing about nervously.

I had seen Remi dance naked at festivals for the last two years, but she had been caked with mud and stained with bloodberry juice, her hips draped with garlands of white hatcha blossoms. The eerie beauty of her completely uncovered aroused parts of me both physical and spiritual, and stole all but a squeak of my breath.

I must get to the four knights still in camp. They'll know what to do.

Although Remi's guards might hear me move, I had to do something. If I could reach the knights, they'd deal bloody justice to all the conspirators, but...

That would include Remi!

What had been but a squeak of breath burst forth like a tiny trumpet. The guard near the hole tensed. I blundered back a step into the pulse of the lumen fruit. The flash of a blade leapt from his silhouette, and the figure came at me. Some day I'd need to think for myself in a martial situation, but that night I thrust my arms out and stood there to receive his malevolence with no other plan. A tent line tripped him, slamming the man to the ground three spans away, his sword landing near me. It was a broadsword, a real torso splitter, and I should've tossed it farther into the darkness. Instead, I drew my short sword and hesitated my advantage away. The man was a member of our party, and my mind had trouble categorizing him as an enemy. As a dark form on the ground, he sprung at me, conical helmet driving into my abdomen. He was one of the archers. Down I crashed. He was atop me in a blink, my sword now in his hand.

As abruptly as the snap of fingers, the air around us turned green, a pale light the color of sickness and decay subsuming all other light. The flesh of my ungloved hand looked dead. To my knowledge, Gela had never produced such a light. The man atop me rose to his knees and stared. I squirmed onto my belly and crawled toward camp. I had the presence of mind to shout, “Alarm! Alarm!” then scooted backwards to watch what came next.

My attacker, still kneeling, had hunkered into a ball, one arm raised, a twig-and-grass star fetish silhouetted in his hand. Whatever he needed protection from would be coming for me.

It announced itself with the tearing of roots and the crumbling of soil to my right, and then behind me, and another farther right. A fourth drew my eyes left. The smooth curve of a sphere pushed through the dark soil into the green light. Three thumbs higher and the empty eye sockets of a human skull gazed at me. Even in such an extreme circumstance, my scholar’s mind wondered.

What race left their bones in the soil above Faellar? Ruyks? Those who built the settlements under Northem?

The mind doesn’t long wander when human remains are pushed through the soil by living plant roots. The spidery little roots hawk sage leaves in the top soil and the sturdier roots of broad-leafed diamond grass rushed into the empty brain cavity of the skull and lifted it higher. Those roots entwined to form a green rope. Other ropes snaked over the ground to wind together into the thickness of a man’s neck. Tendrils scurried from the neck then round and round the skull, until they formed a thick helmet covering all but the dark sockets. The vegetation grew higher and more massive, carrying the skull a span and then two spans above the soil, forming a torso and, from it, arms—one, two, three—that tapered to whips, not hands.

The guard who had attacked me kept his eyes averted and the star fetish held high. I didn’t move for fear of drawing the thing’s attention, yet in my peripheral vision, I detected other man-plants rising. I had no doubt there were more. My focus fixed on the eye sockets of the nearest skull, as they filled with a viscous brown liquid, mayhap sap, mayhap something less natural. The liquid congealed into a ball in the center of each socket. From the ball grew flat, oval projections, as petals opening to reveal an ovule serving as an eyeball. The petals lit with a fulgent green and, to my horror, waggled like the fingers of a hand, as the skull surveyed the world it had just entered.

My scooting retreat came to a halt when I backed into a lumen pole and froze. Heavy footfalls behind me—two, three men—halted near me.

"What horrors be these?"

"Call the luminast!"

"This green is no light I've seen."

A fourth set of footfalls came charging. A war cry rent the air, and a white surcoat blurred by me. The man was a knight, his battleaxe raised, his target the nearest man plant. A two-handed blow severed the limb sent to intercept him, but the two others wrapped like whips around an ankle and his neck. The thing pulled the knight from his feet and dragged him to it, a tendril squeezing his scream to a wheeze and then to silence.

Another man charged to his aid, only to be tripped and dragged to another man-plant. An archer fired, his arrow sinking deep into the neck of a third creature. It didn't slow the thing, and tendrils enwrapped the archer. I could see his eyes bulge as he slid across the ground in front of me.

Other men charged from the tents into the green light. More tendrils whipped with airy swooshes.

Perhaps my being recumbent rendered me less of a threat to the man-plants, for they ignored me and advanced on the tent area. Great muscular roots shot before them, like long toes, their tips spiking the ground, and their lengths contracting to pull the man-sized abominations forward.

My legs didn't consult my brain before raising me erect. I yelled, "Remi! What are you doing?"

Remi continued incanting. Pulumbonk hopped to his feet. "You're supposed to be with Brillix!"

I had not time to process that. An approaching man-plant lassoed my ankles and pulled me to my back. My hand slapped at the soil to my left seeking the guard's dropped broadsword but my fingers touched only rough grass. My pouch of throwing knives lay in the pavilion. The only weapon I had was my belt knife, the kind most people wore for cutting meat at meals. Sliding fast along the ground toward the thing in a panic, I never had a chance of finding it.

Did I reflect on my life in those blurring last seconds? Did I see my mother's face? My brother's or sister's? No. I was thinking that being strangled by an eldritch plant seemed an unfair way for a man of words to die.

I won't call it a miracle, as the Askerati would. I won't call it luck, as many blueskins would. I'll call it a favorable turn of events.

The man-plant had dragged me to its base, another of its tendrils already tightening around my neck. I couldn't breathe, but a broken neck might kill me before asphyxiation did. My eyes worked fine, bulging as they were, and they filled with the silhouetted figure of a woman, her nudity revealed only in flashes, when bare skin and green light met. A wide eye. A glimpse of silver hair. A mouth wide with the words, "Cest ese estraka non!"

Air seeped into my lungs as the tendril released, and the man-plant halted, limbs drooping at its side. The woman settled astride me in a position suggesting pleasure but delivering safety. She then lowered her torso against mine. Damn the armor for depriving me the warmth of her flesh!

Yet her breath was hot on my ear. "Lie still."

I wrapped her in my iron arms and listened to the battle resolve itself in war cries followed by screams of pain and the cracking of bones. Through gambeson and metal rings I could feel the trembling of Remi's body. My cheek counted the rapidity of her hot breaths. My right hand, of its own volition, travelled up her back to cup her head and hold it snugly to mine.

The battle sounds diminished to a hush, and then her words in my ears, "Do not judge me evil, Jonne."

I hadn't time to note my reaction, for a new set of sounds drew both our gazes across the ground, over a collapsed tent to a sight neither of us would forget. It wasn't the figure of the man or the exploding of plant material that awed us. It was the flaming double blade of an axe arcing back and forth through the air to the growls of its wielder.

"Addra, addra! Forenza krak!"

With every strike, a tendril dropped to the ground or a skull spun through the air. Only on the blades from ancient myths could fire join with steel to create devastation neither could achieve on its own.

The guard who had hunkered nearby scuttled on all fours next to us. "The man is a witness. Can your wards protect us from his blade?"

Remi's reply was airy. "I don't know."

"If he lives, we can never return to Northem…to anywhere."

The growls and snickering of the axe ceased. The red of the metal cooled to the same black and green of the hand and arm of the man carrying it. The green light blinked off, and the halted man-plant near me disintegrated into a heap of plant matter. The axeman came closer. Others crowded about us, some brandishing weapons to defend themselves. I assumed they were the other conspirators, as they bore no wounds. Pulumbonk glanced nervously from me to the approaching warrior.

The spiky-haired woman growled, "Run off, you! Eleven be us, each with quick arms and killing steel."

The shadowed man entered the pulse of the orange lumen light. I recognized the ravaged pate and the vest of scalps. His face was mostly dark, but I could tell it turned my way.

"Come to me, word man."

I hesitated.

His free hand extended. "Come now."

I was brave enough to stand but not so brave as to stand at full height. I sidled left to protect kneeling Remi. "We should parley before more blood is shed."

He might not have heard. He certainly didn't care what I had said. His eyes scanned the others dispassionately. "Ye can meet yer ends now or scurry into the dark to be hunted later."

Nobody moved. I felt Remi's hands on my shoulders, heard her voice. "Go to him. You were never meant to be harmed."

My gaze remained on Subu. "This is a time for reason."

He heeded me not. One ropy arm leveled his axe, so it pointed at the center of the group, Pulumbonk. "I've come for treasure, but ye have—for reasons I don't care to know—ruined our chances for that." Red heated in the axehead. "So I'll take vengeance, in trade." Tiny flames danced along the cutting edges. "And I'll have me a new vest by morning."

Lexica XI

I could guess the intentions of the conspirators, as they coiled en masse. They had to be calculating the odds of attacking Subu and his fire axe. I didn't budge. The very existence of such a weapon cast further doubt on the reality I had been taught. If they did attack, would I run, cower, or do something I couldn't foresee? An interesting study in human behavior, were the human someone else.

The thud of hoofbeats neared, and the energy drained from the would-be attackers.

Six mounted knights emerged from the ring of tents. Brillix assessed the situation in moments. With Subu, they bound our hands, lined us along the lip of the pit, and forced us to kneel so close to the edge, a minor shift of equilibrium could precipitate a two-hundred-span plunge into blackness. He placed me at the end of the line, not quite as close to the edge, but near enough vertigo teased me. I pleaded my innocence.

"Jonne, what I saw was this scrappy Subu fellow alone and you with these others arrayed against him."

"I was protecting Remi."

"Is she not the very one who raised the things that tried to kill us?"

"But we don't know her side of the story."

"How stupid are you?"

Very, it seemed.

Brillix addressed the kneeling group, as the horizon paled to announce the coming sun. "I'll presume you are part of a conspiracy to steal the Anaxagorum. I want to know why and who else is involved, and you shall tell me in private, one by one. Should your story not meld with the others, you'll be tossed head first into the pit."

Brother Poonal, the hoarse, long-chinned knight, grinned. "Should that not kill you, the Raka Infante will eat your broken parts before your dying eyes."

The line of kneelers, as one, instinctively leaned forward to shift their weight away from the pit.

"Surely you don't intend that for me," I blurted.

"Your father shall judge you."

Relief swept through me. Father wouldn't kill me. Then again, he might do so to show impartiality. Worse, he could ostracize me, and dying alone in the wastes would be worse than a quick drop into the pit.

None of us eleven were fed breakfast. Subu, the knights, and two other survivors ate theirs in front of us. The Herbalist Superior and her apprentice were among the fallen, which left us with one herbalist, the sour one allied with the conspirators. A scout and a wounded adventurer also escaped the killing. Eight total had fallen to the man-plants, and two had died in the Cheeky Nobs. That left nine loyal to the mission and eleven opposed to it. In the middle was I.

I wanted time to talk through this, to hear everyone's story. Knowing Remi's group had tried to kill the rest of us, no amount of talking would matter to Brillix. He made us sit for hours. My mouth watered, and my under garments grew stinging wet from a bladder that had lost its patience.

Brillix led each conspirator to a pavilion for questioning, starting with the cook. I had never gotten to know the man as I had Merf, but I had enjoyed a goodly number of meals from his pots and spits at the Fingers. I hated that he might be killed.

Next went the clinker, and then the sour herbalist, the spiky-haired woman from Pushni, Pulumbonk, the two laconic adventurers from Qnok, an archer named Zir, and the two other blueskins, until it came Remi's turn. The woman had not said a word or allowed a word from me, after my cowardly display in front of Brillix. Surely I could've proclaimed my innocence in a less sniveling way. The infuriating thing was, I was on the side of right, not she. When Brillix led her away, she wished Pulumbonk well but didn't even look at me.

The sun moved but a few marks before she returned to the kneeling line, fully dressed. The next to go was the man between Remi and me, a blueskin whose name I always got wrong. Gref? Krof? He worked as a shipwright's apprentice. The man had always comported himself in a friendly, if not crude, way.

With the space open between us, I turned to Remi, willing her to meet my eyes. When she didn't, I whispered, "In the castle, they told stories of necromancers to disobedient children."

Her face turned a quarter to me. "So they believe the living can raise the dead at the castle? That's magic, you know."

"They told the stories to make the point that there were no necromancers, no monsters, no magic. We had to grow up wise enough to battle such notions."

"You're calling me a necromancer then," she accused more than asked.

"Perhaps you didn't see them, but human skulls were the first things to break the surface. Then the roots bound to them." I wanted desperately for her to tell me that she hadn't known that, she hadn't intended harm.

She gazed ahead, into the middle distance, mayhap at a tent, a place decidedly not me.

The shipwright's apprentice returned and knelt next to me, shaking. He spat as Brillix gathered two others he'd already questioned and marched them back to the pavilion. "He don't even know why we blueskins want it."

I presumed he spoke of the blood book.

Remi peered around him to me. "Do you?"

Without thinking on it longer, as I should have, I answered, "For its secrets."

Her expression said "disappointment," but her eyes never left me. "You were foolish for casting your lot with us."

"I was trying to protect you."

"I'm accountable for what I did. You could've saved yourself."

I was so happy she didn't think me a coward, I smiled. "I still think I can reason this through with Brillix. Nobody needs to die."

The shipwright apprentice cast a hot glance. "Only a castler could think that."

Our conversation ended. It seemed a long while before Brillix led his two charges back to the edge of the pit. Some, like the man next to me, avoided looking at him. Some, like Remi, challenged him with glares. I must've looked like a scared rabbit, as the next turn was mine. He stopped in front of the shipwright's apprentice, but set his eyes on me. The angle at which he stood belied his sway back. I looked away, as I felt guilty for finding pleasure from his imperfection. His body didn't move, although I didn't know if his eyes left me or not.

I glanced up just as he pivoted, placed a booted foot in the apprentice's chest and shoved. The man's howl of terror only lasted a few seconds. I didn't hear his impact, but I imagined all the horrible things it must have done to his body and the sight of the Raka Infante appearing from the darkness to sniff his corpse.

Brillix said to me, "You're next."

I practically wet myself again. "Into the pit?"

"Come along, Plumpkin." He gestured for me to rise.

In the pavilion, Brillix bade me sit in one of the two chairs, luxuries only the commander had. The place smelled of tent:

damp canvas, earth, and body odor, and, poetically, fear. Brillix offered me a cup of ale, which I accepted warily.

My voice took a while finding its legs. "Why did you execute that man before hearing my side of the story?"

"We can't have them thinking you influenced me in the decision. Better to let them think you're one of them, so we might keep you alive."

"You...then you don't believe I've cast my lot with them?"

"You did an honorable thing, protecting the woman you fancy. Not smart, in light of things, but honorable, and I must respect that. I'm also giving you the benefit of the doubt. I harken to Tetram's treatise on the imperative of nobility. Do you know it?"

The question stunned me. "I'm surprised you do."

"Tetram states a basic tenet of our civilization, mayhap of all civilizations, that, 'There must be a noble class set above the rest to rule, or chaos shall ensue.'"

I savored my ale. The cup was my first in five days. "I harken to Fechunard's reply to that in which he writes of 'The Nobility of Flies.'"

Brillix looked puzzled.

"I doubt you knights were taught this, as it runs counter to the role you play in enabling the ruling class."

"Nobility among flies is ridiculous."

"Is it? Fechunard writes: 'The fly born in butter does not think less of the fly born in feces. Both are flies, and both were born to do what all flies must do.'"

"So you preach equality? That's naive."

"It works for flies."

"But we're human and somewhat more independent in our thinking than insects."

"Are you saying rulers can't rise from a low birth?"

"No, I am asking if you would accept a crass blueskin to be the first man in Northem? Do you think any of them care a turd about Tetram or Fechunard?"

"I believe some do." That was a prevarication.

"Have you guessed why this cabal of blueskins and foreigners tried to take over our expedition?"

I felt toyed with. "The secrets of the Anaxagorum tantalize many people."

"You are not simple, Jonne. You know that, despite what those in the library think, there is dark knowledge out there that does not abide by the rules of Gela. Those who control that knowledge would no longer need to follow the guidance of rational men, like you or I. Inevitably, the only thing to follow the collapse of reason is chaos."

My respect for Brillix's intellect rose. I dared look him in the eye. "I have not agreed with this mission from the beginning. Trying to hide the Anaxagorum, the way the rulers of Faellar did? None of us knows if it can be hidden. Or more precisely, if it can remain hidden."

"Enjoy your ale, Jonne, because from this moment until I say otherwise, you shall assume the role of a captive. You will hunker with them, you will listen to their whispers, and you will relay their secrets to me."

"You're making me a spy?"

"I'm keeping you safe. The instant they think you're my ally, they will kill you. I would, because you'd be the easiest and most logical first kill, if they try to escape."

"Four days back to Northem," I thought aloud, "assuming no more broken wheels or Ruyk attacks. I can manage that." Every part inside me exulted at being spared the horrors of Dunkelgrau. The feeling dulled, as I foresaw serving as a minion to Brillix for the rest of my life.

Brillix motioned for me to up-end my cup then led me out of the pavilion, back across camp. Before forcing me to kneel next to Remi, he whispered, "You and I are not flies."

***

We prisoners were fed, allowed to shed our wet undergarments, and answer nature. All but I were bound at ankle and wrist, then laid like cordwood shoulder to shoulder in one of the pavilions, their heads alternately toward the entrance or away. Subu set me with my back to the center tent pole and a chain with a lock around my waist.

Brillix brought my leather-bound journal to me, then tossed the pouch of pens and ink into my hands. "You have one hour to jot notes of recent events, and then you should sleep. The rest of you should sleep, as well. You'll need your strength for the journey to come."

I was ready to head back to Northem that moment. We could rest once we were away from that accursed place.

Outside the tied-open tent flaps, a knight stood guard. I had enough light and an eagerness to write, for putting everything on paper would help me reason through the right and wrong of it.

Before I put nib to paper, someone whispered, "Will ya show us to be criminals, then, booker? Mad dogs to be hanged and bled out?"

Another added, "No fair yer writin' of this without understandin' our purposes."

Remi surprised me by saying, "Leave him be. Jonne's a fair man and will give a fair account."

"He's a castler," hissed another. "And he don't know 'fair' from 'feck ya.'"

Remi said, "Our mission's a success. The Anaxagorum goes back to Northem, and our people will know what we've done here."

"So," I said, beginning to understand, "learning the secrets of the blood book isn't the end in itself, is it?"

"'Tis a means to an end," Remi said. As an acolyte of Gela, her elocution was groomed from childhood. "You've already guessed that we blue folk have had a glimpse at its contents long ago. The teeny bit of knowledge our ancestors gleaned came with a price. It turned us blue, and it turned us different."

"We gonna learn more, this time," the first voice said. "Then, ain't no fifty Northem knights can scare us no more."

"I'll tell the tale according to facts," I said. "That's as fair as anyone can be."

"If you write of what has just been discussed," said Remi, "take care with the words you use, or Lada will bleed with the rest of us.

***

I didn't know I'd fallen asleep, until someone kicked my feet. "Get up and grab your kit."

My first act was to check my notes. No ink had been spilled, and the words were all legible. Satisfied, I joined the confusion of the others.

Long-chinned Brother Poonal and another knight kept kicking feet. "Up with you. Brother Hanfred will untie your bonds. You, too. Up."

Poonal unlocked the chain at my waist, and I groaned to my feet. Every muscle ached. Light lingered in the sky but the shadows said "late afternoon." A sturdy breeze had picked up, and on it rode countless strands of white web waiting for a limb or shrub or human to catch them. They collected on the sides of the wagons and tents, and swathed the knights who began to resemble cocoons.

Only I and five others were unbound, a wise move on the part of the knights to keep us manageable. Remi remained prostrate on her side, hands bound in front.

I squatted next to her. "Are your bonds too tight?"

"All bonds are too tight."

I wormed a finger between the rope and her wrist. It was snug but not cutting. "Remi," I whispered. "While I might not support this conspiracy, I will support you, on my life."

I could see she wanted to be defiant, but her glare softened and her eyes fell from mine, for a change. "Your kindness is your beauty, Jonne." Hands bound palm to palm, she extended her arms and wiggled her fingers next to mine. When I offered my hand, she held it between hers. "I have done something grievous, therefore I shall take the punishment."

"Not if I have a say."

Poonal rapped me on the shoulder and squeaked, "Out you go, Jonne."

I stepped out of the tent to where Pulumbonk stood pulling webs from his face. I felt fairly confident my life was safe, and the promise of Remi's touch lifted me, so beginning the trip back was a merry moment. One step outside the tent and a skein of white wrapped my face and clogged my smile.

Pulumbonk combed web from his jerkin. "If only this wisp were worth coin."

I fingered a strand from my mouth. "You'd be well shod in fancy boots till forever."

Pulumbonk whispered. "You'll keep Lada's part in this secret, yea?"

I spat more web. "Of course."

Brillix, sword in hand, its naked steel resting on his shoulder, waited until the chosen were untied. "Grab your undergarments from the drying line, then get your kits. Check them twice, then check them twice more. We're descending tonight into Dunkelgrau."

"What?" The cook, one thick, blue leg already free of his breeches in anticipation of dry undergarments, tried to pivot and twirled to the ground.

My heart sank. A moan went up from the still-bound prisoners. The ones standing gawked at Brillix.

"We'll send half of you to the platform at a time. This lot will be led by Subu, and Brother Poonal. You will go down first. I'll lead the next group. Hardy Udrakk, the fighter from Atmaa you managed not to kill, will assist me. The rest of my lance brothers and Aethelbert will stay above."

Aethelbert was the only scout of the three brothers to survive. I noticed him by the food wagon preparing his own kit. He glared at the conspirators and me. "Be glad I'm goin' away fer the nonce, else wise I'd bite yer throats out and listen to ya gurgle while ya die."

The hatred in his eye said he could do just that. If he wasn't joining us, he must be preparing for a run back to Northem. A lone scout could make the journey in under two days. Reinforcements could arrive within a week, not that the possibility helped me feel better about the change of plans.

Brillix continued. "Should anything happen to Brother Poonal or I, nobody will winch you back up. You'll die in the dark."

The cook groaned. "I'm na' trained to go down in the dark."

Subu, who I hadn't realized was standing behind me, commented as if we were embarking on a stroll through sunlit fields with the family. "Pull yer pants up and quit yer snivelin'." He sang the rest, a song I was unfamiliar with. "Into the lovely darkness go we wretches three, wandered away from the light of day to where the treasures be."

Lexica XII

Twilight was in full mantle when Brillix and Subu the Scalp-taker, pushed their six prisoners to the platform constructed over the chasm. Although I was a spy among the conspirators, Brillix regarded me with the same murderous glare he directed at them. He seemed amused. "Enjoy the view."

I had no intention of going anywhere near the railless lip. The spiky haired Birna from Pushni stood in her chainmail vest and iron-studded girdle with the toes of fur boots right at the edge. The two laconic warriors from Qnok, in their expensive breastplates and helmets, lined up beside her. I had yet to know their names. Apparently the three needed to show everyone their scorn for fear.

Brillix and Subu did not join us on the platform. They looked down on us from the slight rise that blocked our view of the camp. The five other prisoners, including Remi, remained bound in the knights' pavilion.

Perhaps it was an initiation rite for the newcomers to Dunkelgrau or the knights' revenge on those who had killed their companions because the evening went from peaceful to terrifying in a snap, as only they knew it would.

A stream of saffa bats erupted from the pit, like magma from a volcano. Red wings on black bodies blurred the air, their flapping a roar in our ears. On and on they came, as if endless. With them came a dank guano stench we couldn't escape, no matter how low we hunkered. With their large, spade-shaped ears and no eyes, coal-black bodies, and those translucent red wings that resembled freshly carved meat, they were made for nightmares. Their talons could grasp and kill a jabber rat. I only raised my head when the last of them flew free of the pit and onto their hunt.

Up the rise from me, Subu crouched ready for a fight, bright eyes wide. Like most of us, the Dunkelgrau experience was new to him. He had recently returned from Verdana, a Faellic ruin I've heard described as green above, gold below, a contrast with this waste. When he recovered his composure, he spat at Brillix's feet to show his appreciation of the prank. The knights had a hearty laugh, but then it was back to stern faces.

Even at midday, with the sun straight above, one could not see the bottom of the pit, so with its being twilight, the space eight paces to my front, where the platform ended, seemed the end of the world.

Brillix pointed to us on the platform. "My group and then the carts will follow you. Interfere with our mission again, and you'll not see daylight."

We recovered our weapons and backpacks from a pile, and then went to work.

Brillix and another knight swung the boom in from the chasm until it stretched directly above us. We then spread the thick netting flat over the platform and laid upon it the six-by-six sheet of bound planks that served as a pallet. Standing atop it, we gathered the four corners of the net and looped them over the hook dangling from the boom. The series of pulleys and the lead counterweights at the end of the boom eased the burden for the two men on the windlass. They heaved on its spokes. Pulleys clattered. Ropes groaned to tautness. The net turned from shapeless to a four-sided pyramid with us captive inside it. We wove our arms through the netting to maintain balance, as the floor yawed left and right before finding its balance. Outside the net, the knights leaned into the counterweighted boom end and our conveyance swung over empty space.

I closed my eyes, as the windlass gears clicked, the rope netting creaked, and we started down. For the first time in over a week, I thought of the Traillus. Why a book on morals, etiquette, and wisdom written by men over six hundred years ago would make me feel braver facing the darkness, I don't know. Mayhap it helped by simply reminding me such things existed. I would be more inspired if it had been able to save itself, as the Anaxagorum had.

A peek showed we were fully below the surface. I'd read of the entry to Dunkelgrau and, although I couldn't see it, I knew the relatively small slash in the ground opened into an immense, domed chamber. From the floor, passages led in three directions into parts of the city still accessible. All had been thoroughly swept for treasure by earlier expeditions, so I hoped Subu would find something of enough value to satisfy him. Nobody wanted a scalp-taker with a battleaxe rimmed with eldritch fire to feel cheated.

Brother Poonal tapped Pulumbonk's shoulder. "Light stick."

Pulumbonk produced a tightly rolled tube of paper the length of a forearm and dipped his fingers into an oiled bag on his belt.

Holding the tube outside the netting, he snapped his fingers to conjure a small flame in his palm, which stood straight in the still air. Once lit at both ends, the tube tumbled downward, casting sputtering light as it fell.

I thought immediately of the Raka Infante who lived in the ruins. They had the limbs and torso of a small human, but they could sense living things in the dark and scramble up nearly sheer surfaces. They fed on fungi, green lichen, insects, and rodents. Twice a month, they came to the surface to snare jabber rats. When present, human meat was a delicacy they couldn't resist. We'd surely encounter them before long, as they dwelled in the caverns along our path. Even though Brillix found it unlikely, I felt sure we'd touch down in the middle of a slavering horde ready to test the savoriness of our meat.

The Raka wore no armor. They had bumpy, pale skins and strong skulls. For weapons, they used clubs and sharpened poles, or flails made of braided roots with large shards of Faellic red glass attached to the end. Slings of jabber hides served as their only missile weapons. The Raka were fearsome even unarmed for they were heavily muscled and paralyzed the weak-willed with their horrifying countenances. Although broad of build, their faces resembled malformed human infants with chubby cheeks and high foreheads, black pits for eyes and tiny teeth. To our advantage, the Raka Infante were stunned by bright light and unimaginative in their attacks. The thought of seeing such a fiend in this place terrified me, but I pressed my face to the netting for a view below, nonetheless.

Pulumbonk's light stick cast an impressive amount of illumination, and we gasped at what it revealed.

The gigantic face of a man carved from black draysalt watched us with pupil-less eyes from forty paces away, a long nose above a long beard on a long face. Looming from the shadows a distance to either side of him, two other faces: one wide-jawed and mustached, the other round faced with thick lips pouting from a curled beard.

"That must be Thessidore," I whispered.

"Tis Thessidore," Brother Poonal confirmed. "Flaginus and Emda to either side."

Most of us in the net knew the names. They were three of what scholars had named "The Eight Kings of Faellar." Arranged around the circular plaza directly under the opening in the surface, they rose stoically one hundred and fifty spans. To be fair, members of the third expedition into the hole noted one statue had obvious breasts and a tapering female waist, a possible queen, but the reference remained "eight kings."

Subu, stroking the ruin of his forehead, regarded the statue regarding him. "What riches have ye seen, old man?"

Our pallet, which had descended smoothly thus far, abruptly dropped several spans. Then wrenched to a halt. We lurched one way, then the other. Breaths caught and arms hugged the netting more tightly. A dozen heartbeats later, we started down again past the folded hands of the kings.

We descended along the falling drape of their robes to an interruption of the smooth lines where carved teeth appeared. They were curved and needle-like, the kind a carnivorous fish would have, and holding them, jaws rimmed with lean lips. The kings were knee-deep in the mouths of monsters, giant fish mayhap or toothed lizards. The monster heads hosting the jaws revealed themselves in stages as we lowered: broad-skulled, gaping mouthed, featureless bumps where eyes might be, and finally a base of curling projections of carved draysalt that could represent the waves of a sea or the tongues of a fire. I had seen the motif of water and fire in renderings of architectural details from Faellic ruins and from illustrations in books. Faellic paper was of a type our age has never seen, as it had lasted nearly ten millennia, even now resisting crumbling when touched.

As we neared the bottom, everyone angled their heads for a glimpse of the ground. The best I could see were parts of three more statues and a section of the mosaicked plaza. Magnificent in craft and color, the plaza depicted a landscape of trees, hills, and grassland made from matte green and brown stones. Rivers, the twin moons, a fiery volcano, and many walled cities gleamed with stones as lustrous as sapphires and rubies. Faellic letters in the center of the scene, although their shapes didn't match our alphabet exactly, did spell something like DUNKELGRAU.

Scholars presumed the inlaid landscape to be Faellar and the surrounding statues to be important personages, mayhap gods or rulers. Were they contemporaries of one another? Or where they representatives from many ages? Perhaps they were something else entirely. As to the monstrous mouths swallowing them—or spewing them out—they were almost surely metaphorical, mostly likely religious. If the creatures had once existed, I hoped they had died with Faellar.

Our conveyance began halting in short, jarring lengths. The men on the windlass knew it was close to touching ground, because red paint marked the rope at two hundred spans. It came to a stop with a soft thump. The netting around us slackened, and the hook descended within easy reach. Two of us slipped one side of the netting free of the hook, and it collapsed to the ground like a mess of sodden hair.

Brother Poonal, visor lowered, sword and triangular shield raised, stepped out first. Subu followed closely behind, his dread battleaxe at the ready. I didn't notice until a cone of light shot from the netting that Pulumbonk had prepared another of his geode lanterns. The cone swept in an arc to the right, and then back to the left, glinting off the helmets of the two adventurers from Qnok as they stepped out, oval shields up, and then catching the spiked white hair of Birna who bounded forward, falchion sword on high. The cone slid back to the right, continuing three hundred and sixty degrees, until it again lit the way ahead. Pulumbonk crept out, the hulking cook shadowing him. As the last to leave, I reattached the netting to the hook, pulled my sword, and trembled into a crouch.

Birna, finding no resistance, went to all fours, her shield on the ground in front of her, the falchion atop it. "O greet Brumba, share your power with this cub so eet may grow strong to betta' serve you." Brumba had been the mighty bear god of Pushni for as long as people had inhabited the island. Twas a shame this beast of a woman couldn't see Ryckerd. There was a bear god.

The groans and rattles of the lowering contraption would have announced our arrival to anything nearby, but that didn't mean we planned to shout up to the men on the surface. They'd wait a hundred-count before raising the pallet. Until then, we stood back to back, trying to see in all directions. The Raka Infante wouldn't charge into the glare of the light stick, but as the saying goes, "Prepare for anything."

A faint clatter from above and the sudden rise of the pallet told us the windlass had engaged. I followed the thing's ascent, until it became a little square against the sliver of gray sky. We were now painfully alone in another world, with only the sightless eyes of eight dead regents to watch over us.

As shameful as it made me feel, I wished Brillix were were near to tell me what to do. For lack of anything else to do, I adjusted the straps of my backpack.

Along with our armor and weapons, we each carried a needle and thread tucked between two flaps of leather for patching shoes; strips of salted pork and dried albon rolled in groat bladder, four tins of salted goldtail fished from Northem streams and the River Erle; two barley baguettes; a tin of bloodberry jam; six spans of thin, knotted rope; and three spans of wire strung with tiny piddle bells for warning traps. For hygiene, we castlers and the warriors from Qnok carried toothbrushes and a delightful mixture of salt and clove, as well as a fine vegetable oil soap from Tule. The others made do with a frayed brinnel-branch twig and a pinch of salt for their teeth, and a purse of ashes for soap. Our cloaks we rolled and strapped to the top of our packs.

The water clock, pickaxes, buckets, and the boiling cauldron, a barrel of potable water, as well as the herbalist's supplies, and the tightly secured Anaxagorum would come down last in the two-wheeled carts. I wasn't sure why, but they also carried bags of volcanic ash from Qnok and six iron rods three spans in length that stuck from the cart like stiff tails.

Long-chinned Brother Poonal whispered. "Let's have a look about."

We split into two groups, each with a bullseye lantern to pierce the shadows. The light stick in the middle of the floor burned on, flickering orange over the statues and the plaza. My group, with Pulumbonk, Birna from Pushni, and Brother Poonal, crept north along the periphery. The other group with the cook, the warriors from Qnok and Subu went south. We then walked rightwise around the plaza, scanning the rubble-piled bases of the statues and down each of the three passages as we encountered them. It was Birna who stumbled over the body of the shipwright's apprentice.

"Brumba doon!" she called in her tongue across the chamber, making all of us wince. "Here's Brillix's ill-thought work. This fighter could'a been of good use in this dank belly of the world."

The cook added from across the gloom. "He could'a took my place, that's for sure."

"Voices down," Poonal hissed. He glared at Birna, his fractured voice trying to reach across the chamber. "Your head comes off, after another squawk like that."

"Ah, sure, wheezy man," she shouted back. "You gonna take it?"

"Good Gela, people," I whispered. "If we must remark, we should do so quietly."

Birna scoffed. "Anger don't come in 'quiet,' Plumpkin."

That she used Brillix's nickname gave me another layer of shame to wear. I mumbled, "I believe it can come in 'less loud,' though."

The clatter of the windlass drew our eyes up. The square bottom of the pallet swung into the sliver of sky, and the second group started down. That would be Brillix, the clinker, Remi, the sour herbalist apprentice, three archers, and Udrakk, the loyal warrior from Atmaa. The man's sturdy build reminded me of my brother, Ryckerd. He was a refugee from the persecution of Emperor Draman and his Askerati, as well as a veteran of Dunkelgrau, which made him twice as valuable as we newcomers.

The first thing Brillix asked when he stepped off the conveyance was of Pulumbonk, "Do you have your flying light on you?" When Pulumbonk said he did, Brillix gestured impatiently. "Let me see it." Pulumbonk withdrew from his satchel a ball of paper with a wick secured to a wooden handle by twine. Brillix nodded his approval. "If you want to leave this place, don't lose that."

Pulumbonk, forever wilting in Brillix's presence, bowed. "No worries there, by all."

The second thing Brillix said was to me. "Put your helmet on."

The steel and bronze pot had been hanging comfortably from my belt, but tended to rattle as I walked. The face plate limited my vision somewhat, but it also gave me a sense of security and held my warm breath near my face. As the underground was markedly cooler than the surface, I welcomed the face plate and the thick gambeson that otherwise made me sweat during the day.

The third pallet came down with the two carts of supplies, their wheels wrapped in leather to deaden their clatter. Lance Brothers Brillix and Poonal cautioned us to silence for the fifth time, and we entered the eastern passage in this order:

Subu, Brillix, and Udrakk of Atmaa.

An archer. Pulumbonk. A second archer.

Remi. The two nameless warriors from Qnok.

The sinewy clinker pulling a cart.

The cook pulling a cart.

Myself. The herbalist apprentice.

Brother Poonal. Spiky-haired Birna. Zir, the third archer.

Two bullseye lanterns plied their beams left and right ahead. One lantern swept the path behind.

The iron lanterns held candles made only in Northem and exported south before Draman's rise to power. Twisted hairs from a shoom's tail formed the wick. While the fur coat of a shoom was prized for its softness, its tail was long with hairs that flared to resemble spiky bushes when the animal was threatened. The candle was made from the milky excretions of skeenar trees that thrived in the Faellic highlands along the river Erle. Whites from the eggs of domestic groats acted as a hardening agent allowing the milky excretion to be shaped. Northem candles burned twice as long as the tallow and lard varieties in the south, and had no scent. They and Faellic treasure had made Northem rich.

While those in the front and rear rows could see, the sides of the passage were completely dark to me. Earlier expeditions had named this portion of the eastern passage "TheThree-eyed Tunnel," as its entrance lay between two kings, one with both eyes, one with a patched eye. From what I could see, it was an unadorned archway of sedimentary rock six men wide and a lance-pole high. Packed earth formed much of its floor, although precision-laid pavers of an ancient street peeked through in patches.

The sole of my right boot creaked with every step, something I'd not noticed before. It wasn't loud but those before and behind me could hear it, so it provided a marching rhythm in the absence of the timberman's drum.

Creak, dop. Creak, dop.

At one hundred paces, the light caught a white-painted, square spike protruding from the side of the passage. The numeral 1 showed in black on the facing side. We stopped, listened, moved on. By the time we reached spike 5, I felt we had been underground an hour, but it could have been much shorter or longer. There yet was most of a league to go, before we reached the open sarcophagus. I didn't understand Father's logic in replacing the book there. How could we bury it any better than the Fael?

Onward we went, slowly but none too quietly. The leather-wrapped cart wheels made little noise over the pavers, but the contents frequently rattled, and the occasional cough or sniffle echoed. Were someone near me to speak at a normal tone, I would've flown from my skin.

The two bearers held their torches high, so the tips of the flames licked the ceiling. Drippers were slimes that dropped onto passing creatures, whether Raka, saffa bat, cave cricket, or the occasional human. If they found exposed skin, they drew fluids from the host until the dripper had its fill or the host wiped it away. They couldn't kill a healthy human outright, but the diseases they carried could. Drippers retreated from fire.

Every fifty paces the light caught the mouth of a narrow tunnel cut into the left or right wall, where earlier adventurers had probed for evidence of ruins and treasure. Near spike 17, I stubbed my boot on something and sent it clacking and clocking down the passage. The line froze until someone identified the object as a broken, wooden cup. Some of the others cursed me with hisses. Some sighed in relief. Pulumbonk thanked his god, Unathar. I felt happy to come across signs of others of our kind. It reminded me that humans had been this way and come out alive.

We stopped at spike 59, all of us struggling with lack of sleep. Packs slid from shoulders and bodies plopped to the ground.

Brother Poonal explained hoarsely. "The Weeping Temple is another hundred paces on, but we will camp here tonight." He held one of the lanterns and shined it to the side wall, the beam illuminating a hand-cut entrance into a dark room. "Relieve yourselves in there. Pulumbonk will set a twilight lamp inside, but we will not have any illumination in the passage. If Raka are hunting in this section of the ruins, they can only come at us from the front and behind. Hand your piddle bells to the clinker, and he'll see nothing gets close without tripping up a riot of noise."

The strand of piddle bells we each carried looked harmless, two spans of wire holding eight little bells. In the clinker's hands, the strand became part of an alarm system of criss-crossed trip lines. I didn't understand why a fire was a bad thing, if the Raka were blinded by light. I asked Brillix as he passed.

"Raka are like moths to a...no, they're like you to Remi: they find the subject irresistible, no matter how dangerous."

We laid out our cloaks for sleeping in the same order as we had walked. The treacherous herbalist and I were nearest to the latrine room. For now, that was convenient. Later in the night, after it had hosted several visitors, it would be less so. I knelt to place my backpack for a pillow, when Remi entered the dark room.

Shortly thereafter, she exited and then knelt next to me and the herbalist. "The skalds never sing about the ugly parts of adventures, do they?"

The herbalist apprentice was a slender man a few years older than I. A cleft had formed between his eyebrows from his being angry apparently since birth. "I should be lighting aromatic cones of dried rosalette back at the castle, not readying my bed next to a shite hole."

Remi said, "Nobody forced you to come."

I asked, "Did La...who recruited you two into this plot?"

Remi held up her index and forefingers, the universal sign for no, shut up, think again, not now.

The herbalist said, "You think I'll be the one to feck the ginny?" He rolled up in his cloak. "Nice try, Blossom."

Remi's finger tsked me. "You can't ask such things, Jonne."

"I can, because I should like to know."

"The less you know, the less some fidgety someone will want to stab you in your sleep. You're not exactly a man of blades and battle."

I winced. "Mayhap you misjudge me."

She smiled sympathetically. "No, I don't."

"I'll do my part, as I did in the Cheeky Nobs."

"You were brave for me last night, but I wish you hadn't been. We were told you were scouting with Brillix. I would not have allowed the attack on the camp, if I'd known you were in it."

Her confession moved me. "I'm sorry we castlers have given you reason to hate us."

I melted when she laid her hand on mine. "There has been one among you who has been often kind to me."

The aura from the twilight lamp in the latrine made it feel she and I were the only ones in the world at that moment. My thumb caressed her little finger. "Our kiss during the festival, it meant more to me than you know."

She gazed upon our hands. "When Lada told me of the other girls you'd kissed, I felt betrayed, that you were like the rest of them, above accountability."

The urge to kiss her seized me, but cowardice disarmed it. I settled for the bold act of not letting go of her finger. "I will not let them harm you, when we get back."

She lifted my hand to her cheek and nuzzled. "You are too optimistic, but I thank you for it."

"I optimistic? I'm putting forth a fact. If I can't protect you, I shall share whatever fate they bestow upon you."

"Seems you already are."

"I suppose."

Her expression grew concerned, and a finger pointed to my face. "What is that on your lip?"

Before I could raise my finger to check, Remi bestowed a peck on my lips. I must have grinned like a dripspittle. Her smile was enchanting.

"Nothing to say, word man?"

"Well…pibbly bibbly."

Her hands came together in a silent clap. "You remember!"

From the front of the group broke a series of three crisp barks. I couldn't help smiling, as it had to be Subu passing wind, probably posing as he did when I first saw him in The Six Fingers. Giggles rippled through the group.

Though not from Brillix. "Enough! Make them silent, from now hence."

Brother Poonal added, "Do you wish to bring the Raka upon us?"

I sensed the smile in Subu's voice. "Let 'em come."

To Remi I said, "Now is certainly not time to break foul so enthusiastically."

She shook her head in amusement. "You mean 'fart'?"

"I prefer a more colorful metaphor."

Her upper teeth came to the fore. "Such as?"

"Very well. A clever wit could say, 'fogging,' or 'blowing the meat horn,' or my favorite, 'making post prandial remarks.'"

Remi's smile turned coy. "I like learned men."

"Is that why you kissed me?"

She became bashful. "I've told you why."

"My heroic good looks?"

"You make me feel good."

"I shall always try."

She released my hand. "Time will tell. That you kissed two other girls that night tells me you see others as toys."

"They kissed me."

"Do not try to make me feel stupid twice."

She rose and picked her way through the dark, past the two carts and the sleeping cook and clinker, back to her spot a million leagues from me.

I didn't think I would sleep, but I did, at least until, sometime in the dead of night, the piddle bells rattled their alarm.

Lexica XIII

I had no sooner sat up than a rush of small, heavy bodies battered my cheeks and launched my heart into a breathless sprint. The sickly green light that had emanated from the man-plants illuminated the scene. Saffa bats filled the passage, the violence of so many wings in so small a space driving me back to the ground. My companions awoke screaming. I remembered my helmet and had it in place over my chainmail hood and its chin strap pulled snug in a matter of blinks.

The perpetually sour herbalist exploded with a gust of curses foul enough to make a skunk blush. Other shouts of dismay joined in. I lay directly behind the cart with the Anaxagorum and the long iron bars, so I could see the bats tearing at the elum-soaked bag containing the tome. Were it not lashed to the cart, the combined efforts of the bats might have carried it off.

Up the line and past the carts, a kneeling figure struggled to stand against the torrent. A female cry of pain and a glimpse of strap-and-buckle boots confirmed it to be Remi. I crawled toward her, past the cook who covered his head with his hands then lifted them quickly to say, "Have a care, Jonne." When I came alongside the clinker crouched by his cart, he shouted for me to go back to my place in line. I wish I had said something like, "You're one to give orders, you traitor," but being clever while terrified only happens in sagas.

Remi met me crawling the other way. I took her hands to stop her, but her eyes didn't open. I shouted over the cacophony of wings, "Where are you going?"

She pulled her hands free and tried to crawl around me. When I blocked her, she attempted to crawl over me. I rolled her onto her back and pinned her with my body. Her eyes snapped open, but they saw past me. I outweighed Remi, even without thirty pounds of armor, but she summoned a preternatural strength and began to push me off.

The clinker shouted behind me. "Let her get up, booker!"

I needed a moment to understand why she would want to get up, and then it became obvious. She couldn't lift me decisively, and I couldn't pin her, so we wrestled back and forth, until I hugged her arms to her body with all my strength. Her mouth stretched, as if with pain, and out croaked words in the vile language of the blood book.

"Baaral nak othron eescoos!"

They say words can never physically hurt you. I felt that, should these words continue, they might. Unexpectedly, her incantation wilted to a long, hopeless groan.

I tried soothing her. "Tis Jonne. Do you not know me?"

She went limp in my arms.

The tempestuous flight sputtered to an end, as the last of the bats abandoned us for a place farther up the passage. My ears rang with silence. A few figures rose to their feet. Then more. Remi lay panting. I removed a glove and fingered away beads of blood from multiple cuts to her cheeks where her cloak couldn't protect. The warmth of the her skin was, inappropriately, thrilling.

Voices muttered up and down the line. Brillix called back. "The book. How fare's the book?"

The clinker toed the still-cowering cook, until the man stood, head almost touching the ceiling, and examined his cart. "The bag's near ripped asunder."

Brother Poonal inspected it. "The book is unmarred, its bindings secure."

As they talked, Remi contracted into a trembling ball. Her fingers enwrapped my hand. "It wanted me, Jonne. The book, an object of worldly material…it shouldn't be able to summon a person to it. But it did…and I tried to go to it."

Lada must not have told Remi about her sense of connecting to the book in Tule and aboard The Drowned Hag. "It's not just you. The tome seems at times to be aware and willful."

She gripped me harder, trembled more fiercely. "I fear my incantations have connected me to it."

I whispered, "This is why we wish to hide the thing from the world. It isn't meant for us."

"But it is, Jonne. I know it as I know the reality of pain. It is meant solely for us."

Brillix appeared above us. "What's this?"

I looked up, trying not to quaver with the lie I was about to tell. "The bats knocked her off balance, but she's unharmed."

"She's bleeding."

"From but a pair of cuts."

He checked the water clock in cart one. "We've not slept more than four hours, but I imagine further sleep will elude us."

The cook looked up, thick lips smiling hopefully. "I could sleep more."

Brillix addressed the group, "Tis near morning, so take your water ration and a bite or two. When the clock's down three fingers, we'll move into the Weeping Temple." He returned to the head of the party.

The herbalist muttered next to me. "I'll eat and drink when I wish."

I felt protective of Brillix, knowing the man was doing his duty as a leader. I considered saying that, but defending him out loud would seem strange for a hostage.

As if on cue, word passed down from Brillix, through Pulumbonk, Remi, the clinker, to the cook, and finally to me. "Jonne the Booker to the front."

When I arrived, Brillix bade me sit and, in a voice loud enough to carry to the whole party, said, "Tell me of what you have recorded thus far, booker."

He held up two fingers to hush me before I answered. A wink at Subu signaled the scalp-taker who then began a conversation at normal volume with the loyal archer in the second row.

Brillix whispered to me. "Why was your girl standing, Jonne?"

I glowed at the thought of "my girl." "She was...trying to cast a ward."

"She could've done that kneeling."

"Caught by surprise, mayhap she—"

"Mayhap she was trying to get to the tome. If so, I need to know."

"Why would she do that?"

"Have you forgotten? They killed some of us to have the book to themselves."

I nodded. "True." My next words, if not chosen carefully, could belie my being more concerned about Remi than the mission. Brillix had kicked a man to his death in the pit, so would he hesitate to kill Remi, if she presented a threat? "Brillix, she professed a fear for the book, when I went to her aid. I believe she finally comprehends the danger of the thing."

He considered a moment. "I hold you accountable for her actions."

***

The tunnel widened after spike 60, and I could see the foundations of stone buildings to the right and left previous expeditions had excavated. As they were not built of draysalt, little more than crumbling bricks or the spaces where bricks had been held testament to their one-time role in the ancient city.

Anything of value in the site had been removed long ago. Nonetheless, hearing the crunch of Faellic dirt under my boots and breathing the air of the ancients helped me feel connected to the culture I had read about for so long.

I walked lighter in my armor and pack, for Remi glanced back frequently to share a smile. The joy didn't last.

Should we return to Northem, the Collegium would stand Remi at trial with her fellow conspirators. Death or banishment could be the only verdicts, and, despite my brave words, I had no confidence I could alter them.

The transcendent power of feeling affection for another had finally been made known to me. I had been a hard bulb germinating in darkness, now breaking the soil to unfold tender petals to the sun. To be crushed under the boots of happenstance so soon thereafter made me want to believe in a god, so I might drive my sword into his dark heart and bring pain to creation.

I wished I could simply enjoy the glory of the moment. I didn't want to be gloomy Jonne. Happy Jonne would be so much better, but, for the next many paces, despair chased hope around my heart, and I could think of nothing else.

A hint of light and the distant sound of cascading water lured me from my reverie. Another few paces and we disgorged from the passage into a chamber whose vastness stretched into shadow in all directions. Large patches of moss that could live without sunlight gave off a phosphorescence not unlike that of lumen fruit. Where there grew moss, there shown light. It washed the scene in aquatic blue-green, like that which a diver might see when swimming among the underwater Seraphatic ruins off the coast of the Sotte Wald. Whatever lesser structures waited in the gloom to be discovered would have to be patient, for the titanic centerpiece of the chamber demanded time for comprehension.

The Weeping Temple was a draysalt structure unlike any other found in Faellar. A colonnade of towering, flat draysalt sheets rose like black sword blades almost as high as the Eight Kings, but they supported no ceiling or other structure. They might have been decorative, as they served no obvious purpose at ground level other than to line a promenade to the entrance of the main structure. It was a tower of the same girth as the lighthouse in which The Six Fingers made its home. Three of the tower's four sides were concealed by rock and debris that had solidified around it over the millennia. Its face remained visible, rising all the way to the rock ceiling. Were one to stand on the surface above it, he or she would see the spire top of the tower. It was catalogued as Spire 93 in the Northem archives.

Arno I and his band named it the Weeping Temple for the waterfalls that tongued over the lips of aquifers at many levels in the chamber and ran down the face of the tower. A lake of crystal-clear water at the base had threatened but not succeeded to submerge the promenade in the five hundred years since its discovery. Ripples on the water's surface carried the blue-green light on their rims and created ever-expanding concentric rings that might hypnotize one who gazed upon them too long. A causeway of crushed rock and logs hauled in from Northem ran from where we entered the chamber across the lake to a small, dry island and then to another, until it connected several islands before reaching the black opening of another passage in the far side.

Brillix ordered, "Fill your flagons."

Remi threw out her hand. "No! We must keep moving."

Brillix stiffened. "Are you countermanding me?"

"I'm trying to save our lives."

Brillix held up a hand to stop those preparing to leave the line to gather water.

Remi explained. "Magicka requires moisture to carry it. My wards worked only weakly in the Cheeky Nobs because of the dry air. Should an eldritch force re-summon the saffa bats in this place, the magicka will be inexhaustible." When nobody responded, she made a lifting gesture with her hands to encourage understanding. "They will tear us to pieces."

Brillix didn't hesitate with his decision. "Then let us make haste to the Temple Tunnel." He pointed to the dark passage across the cavern. "We have water enough, for now."

The line started forward, every eye watching for movement from the shadowed cave ceiling where the bats nested. Cart wheels crunched dirt. Armor jingled.

Birna of Pushni grumbled behind me. "I gotta have a piss."

Brother Poonal clenched a fist. "Hold it."

"I'll not make it across this lake, you hear me? And I'll not wet me britches again."

"Keep moving," said Brother Poonal.

The archer with them said, "I could use a piss, me-self."

I turned, feeling safe to speak my mind in my helmet and chainmail. "Did you not hear the warder?"

Birna smirked. "You again, Plumpkin?"

She carried a vicious-looking falchion, its long blade resembling a large cleaver set within a primitive handle. Her movement was too fast for me to dodge, and the weapon's iron-shod butt drove against my stomach, causing me to stumble backwards gasping. When Poonal raised his sword, she dared him to strike.

After a moment, he nodded to me and the herbalist. "Go on. I'll stay with them for this little bit."

Birna grinned at her small victory and walked back the way we came before squatting and reaching her hand up her kilt to move aside her undergarment. The archer did his business where he stood. Brother Poonal watched the darkness above.

I moved at the pace of the line, slightly bent and still sucking air.

The herbalist complained. "Idiots. Nothing could keep me here a dash longer than necessary."

I found it intellectually interesting to note how far a motivated line of people can move in the time it took others to empty their bladders. Fifty paces, I reckoned. The trio behind already looked small and dark in the middle of the narrow causeway. Poonal jogged to catch up with me. Kilt down and pants buttoned, the others followed at a recalcitrant amble. With the strength rebuilt in my legs over the last fortnight, I would have run.

I saw it at the same time as Brother Poonal. We were sixty paces on, half way to the Temple Tunnel, when a large ball of darkness in a cloud of pale green detached from the shadows above. My fear drove me forward, but my curiosity repeatedly turned my eyes toward the event.

Brother Poonal, yet twenty paces to the rear, stopped to exhort his fellows onward, as they were separated from him by a goodly distance. They did not see the dense swarm descending on them, nor would they. By the time I turned from checking the way forward, the swarm had engulfed them. Two pairs of feet remained visible. Green light glinted from Birna's falchion as it swung through the swarm and shreds of bat fluttered into the air. The archer's bow swatted ineffectively. I considered shouting "Halt!" to the party, but my body was hustling selfishly away from the swarm.

Poonal, too, seemed torn between helping or fleeing.

I felt small when he chose the heroic path and hurried to them. My pace slackened, prompting the herbalist to shout, "Don't even think it, Blossom!"

"You're a traitor," I said and stopped to shout to Brother Poonal.

He was already hurrying toward me, but to a man in a chainmail hauberk with steel leg and arm guards, "hurrying" could only be an aspiration. The swarm lifted. One motionless body remained on the causeway, Birna's, from what I could see. The archer's body dropped from the swarm and splashed into the lake, his lamellar cuirass easily identifiable in the green light. My moment of nobility expired, and I turned to catch up with the party. It had moved too far for me to reach it at a run, but I sped up, nonetheless.

Poonal shrieked behind him. I didn't want to turn, but I did. He took one hack at the swarm before the bats engulfed him. Taloned feet lifted his visor, and the cries coming from him as they had at his face horrified me. While I am not a brave man, or a skilled fighter, I am often clever. I knew I couldn't outrun the swarm, but I might survive longer than Poonal because my helmet's visor was fixed in place.

One doesn't think through crazy plans when one enacts them. I drew my sword and thrust it with all my might into the particulate soil. It went in one and a half hand-breadths. I seized the pommel and lay upon it with my considerable weight, driving the blade another hands-breath deeper. My body balled up and my arms enwrapped that blade, as though it were my mother's leg. I can't say with surety what I did next, but I believe I might have whimpered something about how unfair the world was.

The things were on me. A mathematician might contemplate the disparity of mass between an armored man and a quantity of little winged creatures and therefore stay somewhat detached from the moment of his destruction. I stayed very much aware. First came the dank guano odor, then came the tearing feet. My armor and helmet protected me, for the nonce, but how long before they dragged the sword free and took me away? If they couldn't kill me through a vulnerable place in my armor, a drop in the lake would drown me without question.

I should've contemplated my life, my family, but I thought of nothing but holding onto that sword.

The sword began to come free, hesitantly at first, but then whisking from the soil. I continued hugging it to me but only because I knew not what else to do. My body hung rigidly in what seemed a single grip. The gravel path fell away, and I wondered what Pulumbonk would say to his god Unathar in such a moment.

A force like the back of an enormous hand shocked the swarm and my body within it. White light burned away green light, and the combined shriek of the swarm deafened me. The swarm shuddered. I dropped to a breath-stealing crunch on the causeway.

My eyes opened on Pulumbonk's sensible boots. I rolled to my other side to see the strap and buckle of Remi's. The cook and the clinker thrust their hands under my armpits, pulled me up, and hustled me away. Once running on my own power, I pulled free.

Pulumbonk held aloft his geode, lancing its beam into the heart of the disintegrating swarm. Remi stood behind him, a star fetish at arm's length. I actually saw the barest outline of the force she projected. It glimmered like flawless glass bent back on itself into a half-bubble. I had seen no evidence of the wards she cast in the much dryer Cheeky Nobs. Brillix stood with them ready to do whatever brave men do at times like that.

Eyes still on the cave above, he shouted, "Now we go!"

Pulumbonk tucked his geode under his arm and long-legged it back to the party. Remi, although the shield she projected vanished, remained frozen as she was, arm up. Brillix seized the thick collar of her doublet and tried dragging her. Her body toppled backwards as stiffly as a statue. Even at twenty paces, I could see Remi's eyes were closed. When she began to emit the sickly green glow, Brillix leapt back and lifted his sword to strike.

I wailed, "Nooo!" and followed my outstretched arms toward them. "She is our only warder!"

He stayed the blow but continued backing away. "What's happening to her?"

We passed each other going opposite directions, I for once, not heading toward safety.

I lied, "She's casting an aura to help her resist."

Within heartbeats, I knelt and patted her cheek with leathered fingers. "Tis Jonne again. Awake! Please!" She didn't respond. When I added, "Must I carry you?" her eyelids fluttered open, and she rolled to all fours where she teetered, the green glow evaporating.

Only when I tilted her chin up did recognition light. "Jonne?"

"You're scaring me bloodless."

"That's my saying!" she said, amused in a drunken sort of way.

"I know. Come now!"

She allowed me to lead her by the arm up the causeway to the passage, now glowing with lantern light. Brillix waited at the end of the line, a safe distance from the lake. I told him of Birna's need and the events that followed.

"We lost three fighters because one couldn't hold her water?"

"And we shall lose our one warder should she not get rest."

"We're not stopping, booker. Carry her, if you wish."

Remi stood by, head low, shoulders slumped, and no evident will to argue her own case. Both carts were filled, so I couldn't place her there. I did remove her pack, pouches, and water flagon, and hung them from the six iron rods. She stumbled along beside me, one arm locked in mine.

I worried for her, but I felt marvelous about myself. I had done something brave. Now I was doing something noble.

Brillix sent two men back to act as the rear guard behind Remi and me. One was Zir, the treacherous archer who wore the old-style conical helmet and a hawk's talon on a necklace. The other was the loyal warrior from Atmaa, Udrakk. He wore top-quality gear: armor similar to the lance brothers, and a red helmet with a chainmail face guard that left only his eyes and nose showing. In a word, he was "sturdy." He needed only to walk behind to intimidate us.

"Dis blue one should be killed," he said, eyes challenging me to disagree.

"But Brillix said that—"

"I know what da man say. Walk on."

Remi gazed into her own world. I nodded a welcome to Zir.

He returned the nod and echoed Udrakk with a gesture that said, move on.

Five paces along, Udrakk remarked, "I suppose da lass is fetching, but, for the love of steady bowels, cannot be healthy to kiss blue lips."

***

We walked for hours with only one stop. The passageway hosted us most of the way, as welcome breaks in the monotony were infrequent. The chamber known as the Marketplace greeted us with the almost indiscernible foundations of twelve structures around a small plaza. The round plinth of a post for who-knew-what rested in the center. Once through the Marketplace Tunnel, we came a half-hour later upon The Well where a large cavern yawned over an unadorned black hole in the ground. Next to it rose the nub of a single structure still defying obliteration after so many millennia. Patches of purple mottled it and the solid rock brim of the hole.

"The mold," announced the herbalist. "Why aren't we stopping?"

Brillix called back, "We can collect it later."

The herbalist threw his hands up and looked at me. "Later? Best we do it now, don't you think? Bringing back mold for Valens powder is my primary mission. It's everybody's mission."

I said, "I thought you were here to steal the blood book."

"Are we trying to be funny, Blossom? Are we?"

When I kept walking without answering, he turned to Udrakk and the archer. "It's worth a fortune."

"I don't need a fortune worth of da awful stuff," said Udrakk. "The Librast Superior pays me heavy in gold."

The herbalist looked to me again. "Tis your sister's pain we're trying to help."

"We shall collect it later."

He raised his voice. "You're all lucky to have me along, you know. You get hurt and...."

Brillix came stalking back through the others.

"I'll be silent," he said, holding his hands up in protection.

Brillix whipped out his poniard. "If I come back here again, I'll snip your tongue."

The herbalist's furnace cooled. The line moved onward.

The Well Tunnel led us on a snaking path for over two hours by the water clock. Footsore and aching, we stopped at the terminus of the passage. The lead lantern's beam fell on a simple round chamber with a low ceiling. A band of Faellic letters had been engraved at eye level without embellishment. The only words of the long phrase known to us after five hundred years were, BLOOD, DISTURB, and ETERNAL WOMB.

In an alcove on the far side lay the sarcophagus. I had read about it, heard it described in midnight stories, and had an image of its being grander than the squat rectangle of featureless black before me. Its lid lay on the ground behind it, probably in the same place Arno I and his group had set it. A precisely cut space in the otherwise solid draysalt had once held the Anaxagorum, and with some effort, would again that day.

After a brief rest, a ration of water, and a tin of salted goldtail for me, the party went to work. Subu, the warrior Udrakk, and I were posted in the passageway at the rear of the carts with Remi who had become a lump of girl sitting propped against the wall. I sat next to her, hoping to sleep.

During supper, I learned the purposes of the iron rods and bag of volcanic ash. The men from Qnok, home to the volcanic Mount Chandra, planned to mix the ash, crushed rock, and water into a slurry they called creta. With lengths of the rods driven into the rock floor and wall abutting the sarcophagus and wooden forms made from the dismantled carts to hold it until it dried, the creta would form a layer of something harder than rock. A sarcophagus for a sarcophagus.

I hoped it held the blood book fast, at least for my lifetime. One trip into Dunkelgrau was enough. Having nothing to do, my imagination obsessed on the cup of ale I'd quaff as soon as the hoist lifted us to the surface. I appreciated the water I had, though. Most of the reserve cask was being used for mixing the creta. An emergency ration at the bottom of the cask and whatever mouthfuls were left in our flagons would have to suffice, until we regained the Weeping Temple lake.

Every muscle in my body craved rest. The men hammering in the round chamber had to be marvels of physicality. Near me, Subu and Udrakk took turns standing at the ready while the other sat crosslegged. I removed my leather gauntlet with the intention to hold Remi's hand, but I decided that would be presumptuous. I closed my eyes and thought of ale, until the more alluring image of Remi outlined by lumen light pushed all else aside. One part of my anatomy came forcefully to life and strained at my undergarments. If somehow Remi were pardoned, I was at the age when the Collegium should grant me coital rights. I remained lost in carnal reverie, until a ghost of Remi's voice jarred me.

"I must have water."

I groaned to my feet and offered my hand. At the water cask on cart two, she held a cup under the bunghole, while I tilted the cask. Cup half filled, she drank greedily and placed the cup back to the bunghole. "More, please."

"We have but little left."

"One more cup."

She looked so weak, how could I say no? I let her fill to nearly the brim. She raised the cup and upended it over her head, letting the precious water drench her hair and bead on the feathers of her headdress.

"Are you mad?" I plugged the cask.

"Needful." Her expression added nothing to the meaning.

"Remi," I whispered. "If you can't fight off the call of that book...."

Just then I noticed the green aura around her. Damn Brillix for being right.

I called, "Subu," but weakly. He would kill her.

Remi—eyes closed, face expressionless—began to invoke. "Dolki extrumus Anaxagorum non!"

Panic kicked me. "SUBU!"

Subu and Udrakk had been watching the rear approach, but both leapt to my side.

"She communes with the book!" I was shocked to see my sword in my hand.

"How?" Subu asked, weapon raised but unsure of what to strike.

Brillix and the work crew had removed the Anaxagorum from the cart as soon as they began mixing the creta. It now nestled into its niche in the sarcophagus.

The pretty woman, once dear to me, now horrifying, thrust the star fetish into the air above her. An invisible force drove me and my companions into the passage wall. Remi glowed pale green, as she walked toward the round chamber completely contained within a translucent bubble.

Udrakk roared, "Alarm!"

The green light filled the passageway around us, but the round chamber at its end still burned with the yellow light of lanterns. Heads turned. Men shouted. Weapons appeared. Nothing withstood her warding aura. The carts scooted sideways as she passed them. An arrow directed at her head bounced vertically into the ceiling. The laconic warriors from Qnok came at her one after the other swords raised. I heard the slightest puff of air from her mouth, an airy pwah! The bubble around her bulged to punch one warrior onto his back and bulged again to bounce his companion against the chamber wall.

She halted in front of the sarcophagus, grim and untouchable. With the words, "Ana rasa," the heavy tome floated from its niche and landed on her awaiting hand. She turned and re-entered the passageway, carrying the thing as though it were a pie.

Brillix shouted, "Block her with the carts."

Before we had the chance to try, she expanded her protective bubble and crushed the carts to splinters and wheels.

My hand extended as she passed. "Remi!" Then the bubble pressed me to the wall, and she was beyond me, pushing past Subu and Udrakk.

The scalp-taker raised his double-headed axe and invoked the eldritch language. "Addra, addra! Forenza—"

The translucent force jabbed like a fist and knocked him to the floor. His axe clattered down the passage.

Remi continued away from us, back down the long, snaking passage toward the Well, a sphere of pale green, the Anaxagorum riding happily on her uplifted palm, and we helpless to stop her.

Lexica XIV

Twelve exhausted men, many laden with weapons and armor, set after Remi. She seemed to glide effortlessly down the passageway inside her bubble filled with green light. We, in contrast, panted, ached, and foundered with every step. At one hundred paces, the hulking cook wobbled into a heap. The laconic warriors from Qnok were flawless physical specimens, but they paid in fatigue for their beautiful, heavy armor. I, heart near to bursting, went to my knees shortly after them. Brillix showed his quality by being only one of two who made it over two hundred paces. Subu, who was built for running, was the other. Although I yearned to stop, I got up and stumbled to catch up. Whatever transpired, I had to witness it.

Subu stripped off his scalp vest and the leather cuirass, exhorting Brillix. "Strip. We can catch her."

Brillix panted his disgust. "I'm a Knight of the Order of Man."

Subu's side whiskers spread with his grin. "Be a warrior, shiny man."

The two locked glares for an instant, before Subu charged off, bare-chested, battleaxe ready. Lean though he was, every bit of him welted with muscle.

His words echoed back. "Addra, addra! Forenza krak!" The edges of his axe blazed.

I caught up to Brillix who had doubled over wheezing. He noted me and spat. "A true fighter needs no magic."

"I rejoice that Subu has regained his."

The passage ran straight here, so we could see the enchanted axe's attack bounce off the ward. Subu growled, "Ah, yer a nasty hump," and prepared to strike again.

The surface of the bubble fisted him onto his back. Whatever was inhabiting Remi paid no heed and glided onward.

I didn't understand even the basic knowledge Remi drew upon to cast her wards, but I did wonder how long a cup of water could sustain a ward of that power. It should fail soon in the dry passageway. Even then, she would likely be fast enough to outrun us, especially as a supernatural energy powered her. I had no doubt that energy came from the blood book. If not, why hadn't this type of thing occurred in the last many trips to Dunkelgrau?

Brillix caught his breath. "Go back and gather the others. We can all rest here."

"You understand this is not Remi doing this."

"Unbind your heart from your duty. Go."

I headed back to sweep up the tired men littering the passage for seventy paces, my youth the only thing keeping me on my feet.

Pulumbonk had apparently gathered his luminast's gear, as he was just joining the others. "Your Remi has ruined most everything!"

"The blood book is responsible."

"Which makes Lada responsible." His long fingers covered his face. "Oh, yea but I'm daft for listening to her. To cinders with her and this book!"

"I thought you fancied Lada."

"I do," he wailed. "Isn't it horrible?"

So that was the price of desire? I yearned for my days of anonymity in the sub-basements of Northem Castle. But being alone after feeling the molten euphoria of connecting with one you desire would never be satisfactory again. I feared all the yearning in me could not save Remi, for the book would probably destroy her, when it had no more use for a human vessel. Then again, I feared for my own safety more than hers. Shameful.

The carts and water cask lay smashed far behind us, their parts scattered among cast-off packs and other gear. The flagons we carried with us had enough water to wet our mouths. I had one tin of salted goldtail tucked in my purse. Others had left theirs behind in their packs. Yet the party, to a man, agreed to head for the Weeping Temple after a short rest. We could fill our flagons in the lake and make it to the Plaza of the Eight Kings in a few hours. Logic said we would find Remi there, as the knights on the windlass would not raise her without us. Then again, the Anaxagorum had linked with a mortal vessel and surely planned to use her to some end. Could it lift her to the surface? Lada was the only other to have physically touched the book outside of its elum-soaked shroud. Mayhap it would seek to absorb her, as well as Remi.

How foolish was I to guess at its intentions?

The group caught its collective breath, caring not that the passageway hung heavy with the odor of unbathed bodies. Revived, if not refreshed, we headed toward our first landmark, The Well.

Brillix had yet to chastise me, which made my dread compound every second he waited. The man had more on his mind than me, so mayhap I'd be spared. He was facing a failure with the Anaxagorum, not only for losing the book, but for letting it take over a vessel to transport itself. He would almost certainly risk us all to recover the purple rocks from which Valens powder could be scraped. Father might strip him of his titles, if he also failed providing Lada her medicine. I hated stopping for anything, but how could I face my sister again, if I didn't? If Brillix were a failure, I was a catastrophe.

The inbound journey from The Well to the Sarcophagus Chamber had taken us over two hours. The trip back out, unencumbered by carts or caution, took one. What I saw when we arrived in the chamber of The Well would crawl through my memory for the entirety of whatever lifetime I had left.

I travelled in the middle of our group, so I didn't see her first. The gamey, guano reek of saffa bats told us the cavern of The Well was near. A hint of green light heralded the Remi-thing's presence within, as it seemed anything or anyone under the power of the blood book glowed with such light.

Brillix called for, "Torches!"

The cook and I carried the only two torches not left on the carts.

"Eyes high!" Subu called back.

Not seeing what they were seeing created anxiety so intense it nearly choked me.

Pulumbonk stepped between the cook and me, a pinch of his secret powder in his fingers. One snap, and a flame bloomed in his palm.

The cook cocked an eye. "How do you do that with none of the dark words?"

"Training. Not magic." He passed the flame under the heads of our torches.

I squinted, as they flared. "Why torches, Pulumbonk? You have your geode gadget."

"It doesn't work against the bats."

"It sure did when you saved me in the Weeping Temple."

"They have no eyes, Jonne."

"But I saw—"

"That was Remi's ward what kept them at bay. Light alone has no effect, yea though I tried."

The cook, nodding his head, trying to be positive, said, "If fire can roast a groat, it can roast a bat, I'd say."

We held our torches high and advanced behind the men in front. Brillix, Subu, and Udrakk made up the first line. The warriors from Qnok stood in the second. Behind them, the remaining two archers nocked arrows wrapped in cloth saturated with Pulumbonk's powder. Behind us, the luminast fumbled in his satchels for something, as he walked. The wiry clinker took up the rear with the odious herbalist.

We disgorged from the passageway into the cavern. Brillix shouted to the archers, "Ignite!" To the fighters nearby, he said, "Down!"

Green light illuminated a large part of the area in front of us, but the fighters blocked my line of sight to all but a blur of darkness in the air above where the Remi-thing must have been. The archers turned, passed the tips of their arrows over our flames, and the specially impregnated cloths spouted fiery plumes that caused me to recoil. Their arrows arced over the front rows, sizzling as they flew. They illuminated thousands of saffa bats hovering in place, so closely packed, they couldn't avoid being hit. Two bats were struck, but the entire mass quivered, as white-hot bits exploded through it.

The bats, I realized, formed two distinct masses, not one. Hanging in their grasp was the Anaxagorum, glistening red, and no doubt controlling the creatures carrying it. They were its wings. The fighters remained crouched, as the archers prepared another flame shot. How could anyone not stop and gape, as I did?

I could see the Remi-thing framed by the men in front of me. A tableau macabre. An obscenity against womanhood.

The multitude of bats gripped the Anaxagorum by its spine. Beneath the book, on its knees, face upturned, the blue-skinned Remi-thing. The covers of the blood book suddenly spread open, like the wings of an unnatural bird. From the spine dangled a thick sheaf of fat, red pages that looked for all the world like flaps of living tissue. The Remi-thing grasped a cover by each hand. Then it began to feed on the pages, like a chick under a mother hawk.

The mouth and the overbite I had found so adorable had become pure animal in their function, mandibles tearing at the fleshy pages as fiercely as a beak into prey. Blood ran from the book covers, matting the Remi-thing's hair and dissolving its clothes as it flowed: along its arms, over its shoulders, down its back, atop its buttocks, and over its heels to cover its feet. As it ate, the pages began to disappear.

Brillix thrust his sword forward. The fighters sprung as one. Hundreds of saffa bats detached from the mass to engulf them, before they took five steps. Steel flashed. Shreds of black fell from the air. Shrieks, mayhap of hate or pain, compounded one on another until the noise became as searing as the torch in my hand.

"Where are the cursed torches?" Brillix yelled.

I had heard no order to advance and looked at the cook. He mirrored my perplexity.

Pulumbonk shoved us forward. "Thrust into the flurry."

We stumbled forward, torches out, lungs sucking breath. I stopped behind Brillix whose sword snickered and snacked through the living cloud.

I called, "I'm behind you! Don't kill me!"

"To my left! Stand to my left, and do what you can."

I tentatively poked the torch into what looked like a blanket of quivering wings and gnashing teeth. Bats hissed. I thrust harder, so the flame contacted several bodies. A hole formed in the mass where bats disengaged whatever linked them and scattered.

"That's it, Jonne!"

I thrust and thrust, something hot and red and delighted growing in me. "Burn, you fiends!"

An arrow shot past the Remi-thing's head.

"The ward is down," Brillix shouted. "Rush her!"

Logic deserted me. "No! I can talk to her."

Brillix paid no heed. Who would to such foolishness?

I learned later it was Pulumbonk who threw the fire bomb, the one he had made too powerful in his haste. Flame exploded in the midst of the bats. Fiery pellets rained over us, nesting in my chainmail, between the fastenings of Brillix's shoulder armor, on the bare flesh of Subu's nose.

The bats flew apart. As did we. Shrieking. The air turned caustic. Our throats burned. My torch spun from my hand, leaving me as useless as a sack with no bottom. I spilled to the floor and wept, as I hadn't since I was six.

The bats dissipated into the darkness above. The blood book was gone, covers and pages. Only what had been the Remi-thing remained. It licked its lips, firelight twinkling on the red sheathing the once-blue body. Sleekly feminine. Magnificent and horrific. Its face whipped in our direction, taking in the swords, the axe, the fire-dappled armor, all through closed lids.

Even out of our armor, we wouldn't have been fast enough to stop the thing, when it bound for the well.

The well was a plain, circular hole of featureless black in the ground. I fancied, for a moment, that the space of the hole had always been nothing, would always be nothing and could never be displaced, so the world had to form around it. A cylinder of nothing encased by a planet. Into that space dove the Remi-thing, the torchlight catching only a blur and the glimmer of crimson toes disappearing.

All that remained in the chamber were a veil of caustic smoke, twelve panting men, and a memory I would live with forever.

Brillix didn't miss his chance. "This is on you, Plumpkin. This is all on you."

Lexica XV

The light of my one torch couldn't reach most of the cavern called The Well, only the wall just beyond the actual well that curved up into the high shadows. The rock floor surrounding the well stretched flat and smooth out to ten paces, as if it were poured creta. It looked unnaturally smooth and level, but I detected no grooves to suggest paving stones. The material might have been a lighter variety of draysalt, because it was unmarred, as no natural expanse of rock could be. The pitiful nub of a cornerstone that belonged to a long-destroyed building rose to knee height six spans from the hole. The floor spreading beyond ten paces looked as one would expect of a subterranean chamber: mounds of flowstone toothy with conical stalagmites turned rust-colored by mineral drips.

The purple patches of moss rimming the lip of the well and flecking the flowstone caught every eye in the party, except mine. My attention was glued to Brillix.

He turned to me, his voice large in the emptiness. "Put your nose in that hole." When my mouth hung wordlessly, he said, "Prove to me you're something more than a love-sick, little, fat boy."

Three weeks of reduced food and almost constant movement had burned some of my blubber away, but what does that matter to a man looking for an insult? I picked up the torch and crawled slower than drying mud to the edge of the hole.

He prompted, "Look over."

I did, heartbeat in my ears. The walls of the well were visible six spans down and as smooth as the area surrounding the opening. Below that lay a dark as black as the end of time. How could anyone survive a dive into it…and, fortune aid me, what horror might leap out of it?

Brillix stepped up for a peek. "We're not sure this oubliette has a bottom, but who knows what might happen with the Anaxagorum in control of a warder?"

I scooted away from the rim, as fast as my palms and knees would take me.

Brillix walked to the boundary of light and scratched at the nearest patch of purple flowstone with his sword tip. "We will need to collect some of this rock, before we return to Northem."

I knew it. There we were with no food or water facing a trek back through hours of dark passageway, and he wanted to chip at rocks. I actively loathed Lada.

"Allow me to clarify, booker. You will collect them."

"You won't help?"

"Nobody will. We shall leave you with torch and sword to watch the well."

I had no reply, unless the terror in my eyes did the job.

Pulumbonk couldn't face Brillix, so he looked at me. "He'll be killed. What of the Raka? The bats?"

"The blood book, and therefore the bats, have no further interest in us. As to Raka, they've migrated to another warren of tunnels."

The cook, big lips in a tight frown, asked, "How do you know?"

"I've seen none of their spoor, but more telling: we would've encountered them by now, if they were hunting these tunnels."

The cook looked around at his mates for support. "That's good news, don't ya think?" But they all kept their eyes on Brillix.

The knight passed his sword in an arc to include them all. "We shall hasten to the Weeping Temple and fill our flagons."

Relief beamed from every face but Subu's.

Brillix continued. "All but Udrakk, Subu, and this loyal fellow here…;" he patted the shoulder of the archer not aligned with the conspirators, "…will return with full flagons to Jonne."

The first word I had heard from the fighters from Qnok was when the bigger one said, "Nay." The word expanded in the gloom.

"You've not let me finish," Brillix said, sword directed at the man. "After you've dropped the water with Jonne, the rest of you cabal of conspirators will return to the Sarcophagus Chamber and fetch the packs of food and remaining torches and—"

Groans and glares all around.

"And you will wait with Jonne, until I return."

"That could be days," whined the cook.

"At least three. You will fill the bags we brought for the purple rocks. You will protect each other. You will watch this shaft for Remi's return."

The herbalist flared. "You plan to leave us here to die? You—"

Brillix's blade wagged up and down. "That tongue is due a snipping."

The clinker, half the size of the cook, tensed. "You do, you plan to leave us to starve."

Brillix sighed, as if enduring children. "How will I take the Valens rocks back to Northem, if I don't come back for you?"

"You could wait weeks to do that," the clinker pressed.

"And do what in those weeks? Sing songs and eat jabber rats?"

I was surprised nobody knew the type of man he was.

Brillix explained slowly. "I'll not go back to Northem failing in this. Plain enough?"

The big fighter from Qnok said, "Why obey, when execution is planned for us on return to castle? I fight you now."

Brillix replied, "Rudis." (So the man had a name!) "We do not execute heroes. Hold here for three days, until reinforcements arrive, and we all go back as brothers in arms."

"Ya mean," began the cook, "ya won't tell of our betrayal?"

"Yes, but only if you work with me to earn it."

The cook exchanged smiles with the clinker.

Subu declared, "I came for riches."

"You were warned these tunnels are picked clean. A fat purse of the Librast Superior's gold should be generous enough."

"The purple rocks are worth a fortune in the south," Subu said and stepped next to me. "So I shall stay with the word man and collect my own share."

"I need fighting men," Brillix said, laying his sword blade against his palm.

"Not if ye speak truth about the Raka being gone, or were ye lying?"

Their eyes remained locked for a long silence. Brillix gestured to Subu and me but addressed the group. "Gather their flagons. We leave for the Weeping Temple."

***

How can I describe the next few hours? I would need a word stronger than terrified, a color darker than black, and a sound for when there was no sound.

The party of ten had not been gone long when Subu's ropy arm leapt out and snatched the torch from me. When I tried to stand, he placed one modest-but-iron-hard hand on my head and held me in place. "Stay," is all he said, before heading down the passageway back to the Sarcophagus Chamber.

"I shall come with you."

Before he and the torchlight disappeared, he left me with two, fat, ugly words to fill the darkness. "Do not."

I knelt in disbelief, for how long I know not. Long enough to run a hundred versions of the question "why?" through my head.

Why are you leaving me?

Why did you act as if you would stay?

Why are you going back to the sarcophagus?

Why did I let you take my torch?

Why couldn't it have been Myrle or Eela who lured me into the supply shed to steal my heart at the Festival of the Twin Moons?

I lowered myself to a seat with great care. The well was near. When darkness is so complete and a literally deeper darkness awaits one misstep away, reason vanishes and the logic of nightmares arises. I didn't think for one heartbeat about watching the hole for signs of Remi. I thought of kings in the toothy mouths of monster fish, of eyeless things that existed in places unknown to light, of blood coating Remi's arms and running, spreading, filling the well, and bubbling up through the slash in the surface. Going mad was not a possibility. It was an inevitability. I would forget who I was and shriek forever in the darkness, mayhap to catch my name in the echo.

I considered talking to myself, but hearing my voice say one word out loud was enough. "Jonne" sounded so deafening and yet so tiny, I clapped my hand over my mouth.

I tried to be rational— "Subu will come back," "The others will come back"—but having no sensory input made such thoughts slippery. I told myself I was too intelligent to panic, but I wasn't sure with what weapon to fight it. The silence was so total, my ears strained to hear anything. The nothingness roared back. I hugged my knees to my chest. Time didn't exactly stop, but it slowed to the pace of my breath. How many breaths were in a mark? It seemed I breathed a week's worth.

Then came a light crunch. An animal? A human foot? A red woman's foot? If there was a fear worse than that of nothing happening, it was the fear of something happening. I scooted away from the hole, along the wall, the sound of earth crunching beneath my bottom. I'd welcome the pale green light, but for all I knew, only the book's black vapor exuded from the well and was, at that moment, surrounding me. I had never touched the Anaxagorum, but that gave me no assurance that it couldn't take me over and bleed over my body and tell me to cast myself into the hole.

I stiffened at the sound of another crunch. Definitely a footfall. Not far from me. A short, crisp rip made me gasp. Two more. Riiip Rip! Flatulence had never sounded so welcome.

"Subu?"

Mayhap twenty paces from me, I heard whispered, "Addra, addra! Forenza krak!"

It would've been a modest light any other time, but in this place, it was a starburst. Subu's axe edges lit and cast a nimbus of red light that barely included me and the well three paces away. Subu looked demonic where he sat crosslegged, orange whiskers bright, axe standing in front of him, and every scar on his head thrown into high relief by shadow.

"Young booker, what did ye contemplate while lost in the darkness?"

"You've been there this whole time?"

"What did ye contemplate?"

I was so relieved to see again, I blurted, "I think, everything!"

"What else can ye think, when yer world's become nothing?"

"I didn't expect philosophy from a scalp-taker from Tulos."

"Anything's possible, ain' it?"

"Within reason, I suppose."

"This ain' about reason, word man. It's about possibility, like what yer mind saw when yer eyes were blind. Anything coulda' been in the space around you, striped women as tall as towers or mountains floating on clouds or axes that come to fiery life with an utterance."

"Are you testing me for some reason?"

"If ye are to write about—" a fist thumped his chest— "...The Subu and living books, reason can na' be an obstacle."

"I'm not here to write solely about you."

"But ye are here to write what ye see, yeah?"

"That is true."

His grin said he was quite amused by himself. "Then wait and see The Subu do what The Subu do."

"I would eagerly write of how you came by such an axe and its words of power."

"Two men know the story, and I ain' gonna make it three."

"Hungry?"

He licked his lips. "I'd eat both yer legs, were ye to offer."

"How about half a tin of goldtail?"

His eyes lit. "Ye've got it on ye?"

"Seemed wise to carry a bit of food. Half for your story."

Subu studied me a moment. "Uh, yeah, then. Half yer food buys half me story."

I withdrew the tin from my belt purse. "Shall I write that The Subu is trustworthy?"

He walked to me, took the tin, and twisted the top off. "Ye shall," he said, as he fingered what seemed a fair share of the gooey white meat out of the tin and into his palm. Sitting next to me, he sucked the blob into his mouth.

"Better tasting things have come out of me stink hole."

To remain edible for months, the fish had to be broken down in a caustic solution and then tinned. Salt made it only a bit less awful, but we both ate all we had and licked our fingers. Even had we water, the aftertaste would've remained caustic.

"Listen, then, word man," began Subu. "I spared a man's life for his axe and the utterance I heard him speak."

"Do you not worry he'll try to get it back?"

Subu took a deep breath and uncrossed his lean legs. They stretched straight out from a fur kilt bolstered by leather pteruges, calves and feet wrapped in puttees, soles studded with iron. "He no longer has a tongue to make the words."

He seemed fearless. "Do you pray to any gods?"

Subu looked up, as if seeing through the rock ceiling to the heavens. "There's somethin' bigger than us, fer sure, but whatever it be, it don' give a squat about us."

"You sound like a Northman."

"That a compliment? Ye Northmen are too arrogant in yer knowledge to see the world as it really is."

"And how is it, really?"

"Floating in nonsense."

***

I thrilled to the glimmer of torchlight in the tunnel, which heralded the arrival of the conspirators before the scuff of their boots did. Into the chamber of The Well emerged Pulumbonk, Rudis and his yet-to-be-named companion from Qnok, the cook and the clinker, the angry herbalist, and Zir, the archer in the conical helmet.

Before anyone spoke a greeting, the herbalist, face in a perpetual scowl, said, "Still here waiting, are you? Joke's on us all, for that carbuncle Brillix is on the surface laughing at us, right now, eating, telling the story to the other knights, and laughing some more."

The clinker said, "Ah, plug it up, ya itchy crotch, or we'll eat you."

The cook added, "An herbalist needs about five marks per pound over a fire."

Subu stood. "Let's start a fire, then."

The herbalist tossed a bulging flagon to Subu. "Eat yourself, sellsword."

Pulumbonk handed my flagon to me and sat down in a knot of long legs and arms. I recalled Lada's comparison to a praying mantis. "He'll come back. Lada will have him lashed, if she finds he tarried while she was in pain."

I said, "I can't say I'm pleased with my sister in this moment."

"So you want her to suffer?"

"Not forever, although a little more suffering for what she's done to us would be justice."

"Ye lot needs to be off to fetch the food," Subu said, eyeing the men sinking to lumps against the cave wall.

"You go get it," grumbled the herbalist.

Rudis, his beautifully etched armor dull and scratched, sat stiff-backed against the wall. "First, rest. Then, we go. All we."

Two hours of snoring was all Subu could endure before kicking the feet of the sleepers. "Now, we go."

Before the herbalist could complain, Pulumbonk said, "Best to have it done. We can rest on our return."

"For three days," grumbled the herbalist. "Or more."

Subu handed me the torch. "It has but little fuel left."

I took it and glanced at the black eye of the well. "I am to stay, then?"

"Ye have a sense for the girl, and she for ye. Who better to know her in the dark?"

I asked Pulumbonk for some of his magic light.

"Magic? You know better, Jonne. I need the stick and powder I have left. Mayhap, you'll find your god in the dark."

They left me again to fill my eyes with naught but mystery and speculation. I sat alone next to the well. Mayhap it was good for the mind to take away the obstacle of sight for a while. Having the torch was some comfort, until I realized my tinderbox lay in my pack in the Sarcophagus Chamber.

If a god presented itself, I was ready to listen.

Subu had sounded almost reasonable when he spoke of darkness being the absence of obstacles to thought. Being once again in total darkness, I could only see the absence of all things being the summation of death, and dead I was not. Being terrified reminded me of that. In any case, after a long stretch saying nothing, hearing nothing, I detected no god.

I flinched when the thinnest of voices said, "Jonne."

Close? Mayhap. In my head? Mayhap. Only in my imagination? Likely.

"Jonne," it echoed.

It came from the well, and it was soft and feminine and life-saving.

"Remi?" I breathed.

"Be brave...." The voice quavered, as if struggling for its existence. "The Raka come."

Curiosity is closely akin to bravery, for I crawled—one hand forward, then the next, and the other—until the ground disappeared under my fingertips the well's rim. My voice was little more than a trembling of air.

"Remi?"

The well replied with that nearly sub-aural murmur deep, empty places make, but no Remi.

I scooted back to my spot and contemplated how to be brave. If Remi wanted me to be brave, I would be, but I couldn't quantify the word in my present context. I did "brave" the best I could, by pulling my sword and trying not to wet myself.

Time only became relevant again when a distant-but-clear voice in the passageway, asked, "Jonne? Prepare for guests." Twas Pulumbonk.

I shot to my feet. "Yes! I am here. Hurry!"

Light, too weak to be more than one torch, tickled the mouth of the passage. Lithe Subu emerged first, carrying not only his backpack but mine. Lanky Pulumbonk followed. The sturdy men from Qnok came next, light dappling their armor. Then appeared the cook, the clinker, and the herbalist.

More than one person visiting me at a time in the past turned me inward. I was practically dancing. "Come in! Come in!"

The archer Zir came last, immediately groaning to a seat upon entering. "My legs are done!" He cuffed the herbalist on the shoulder. "Might I have yours?"

"Do you think me a Tulian whore willing to share my legs with a snot like you?"

Zir set his bow and backpack agains the wall next to him. "I'm not gonna say you fellows don't look—and smell—lovely, but the grouse is right." He stretched his legs before him with a groan. "We must remember to bring more women, next time."

After walking for hours with Zir behind me, I learned he thought about women often. Not in the longing way I did, but from a genuine affection for women as company, and not necessarily salacious. The clinker was that man. When the rest of us yearned for food and rest, he'd tell us he needed a good rut with, "a blue gal about yay big with a pillowy arse and a mouth with a wet smile."

When Pulumbonk came to sit by me, I surprised us both by embracing him with my best hug. "Tis good to see you."

"And you, my friend."

Saying "friend" was so easy for him.

Subu, who had assumed command without trying, declared, "We've food enough fer six days, if we eat but third rations."

Rudis of Qnok added, "Any man steals from another and into the well he is thrown."

Subu continued, "We'll rest now and gain the Weeping Temple when we're up and bouncy again."

The big cook fussed with his braid. "At least we'll have plenty of water."

The silence grew fat, until I dared share my news. "I heard Remi, or a voice I believe to be hers."

Subu said sleepily, "She come to ye in the dark? Smack them blue lips over ye?"

"She warned of Raka coming."

I heard the men sit up.

Rudis asked, "Whence come they?"

"She was thin on details."

"You know the lore, booker," said Subu. "Where do they nest?"

"Nobody knows. Dunkelgrau consists of myriad tunnels and chambers twining together, so their nest could be anywhere but, also, they could hunt anywhere."

Subu pressed, "What did this voice say, word by word?"

"'Be brave. The Raka come.' I recall naught else."

Rudis said, "We are too weak to fight. We rest now." He pointed to the two passage entrances. "Post man there and there. No Raka sneak on us."

Subu nodded his assent. "Jonne, ye and The Subu will watch first. Mark the water clock. After four intervals, we move to the water and light."

"We should conserve our torches," Pulumbonk said and snuffed the one burning.

The herbalist, scrubbing his nose on the back of his hand, asked, "So we just lie here in complete dark? Is that it?"

I took my backpack, felt my way to The Well passage entrance, and sat. "Try it by yourself, sometime."

"Not all of us are like you, Blossom. I actually prefer light and people."

***

Knowing we could tell the passing of time with the water clock gave shape to the darkness. That didn't stop me from falling asleep. For one blink or a hundred, I know not, but I awoke before Subu caught me. The man might take a finger, or mayhap my entire hand, for such an offense.

"Anything, Subu?"

Even the recklessly brave can sound weary. "Nothing."

"You sleep. I can stay alert."

His reply came only moments later in soft snores. How would I see the water clock in the dark? It rested next to Subu, as did his axe.

I crept toward the intermittent dripping, until my fingers touched the basin over which a funnel marked in increments let pass its droplets. Carefully my hand dipped into the top of the funnel, finger meeting water half way down. My poor memory of the clock's measuring marks left me doubting how much time had passed.

I looked toward where Subu's axe should be and whispered, "Addra addra, forenza krak." No result. My hand was on its way to touching the axe's haft but scurried off at the thought of startling Subu. The dark was safer.

Counting to ten thousand would keep my mind occupied and would approximate one hour, so I began quietly, "One, two, three…."

I didn't make it to one hundred before I dozed, waking abruptly when my chin sagged to my chest. That happened twice, and my concept of time grew fuzzier. I stood and leaned against the wall, so it didn't happen a third time.

The cook, always a loud sleeper, outdid himself with the volume of his snores. Hearing anything approaching in the passageways couldn't be assured, but it kept me from nodding. After a time, he must've turned onto his side, as his snoring eased. Others snored lightly. One wheezed as he breathed.

After a time, I heard muffled speech. Not a conversation, this was one voice murmuring just above the threshold of audibility. I didn't know the voice, but I could deduce by the inflections and omissions of certain words, the speaker was Rudis or his companion from Qnok.

The litany ended with, "May the passing cloud reveal my paradise."

I knew the phrase from Durdell's Follies of Faith, an examination of the cults and religions of Arqonias written in Northem a generation ago in the Year of the Harmonious Wind, my year of birth.

One of the men from Qnok was praying to Askerat.

Emperor Draman had declared all beliefs outside of Askerat heretical. Mayhap he sent these men to spy on us secular Northmen. They couldn't have known we had taken the Anaxagorum, because the two had arrived in Northem as adventurers two weeks before Lada's raid. Twas, in fact, they who brought us the news of Draman's usurpation of the throne of Tule. Mayhap that was their only mission, and they stayed in the north for the reason other southerners did: a chance at the wealth of Faellar. I wondered what Father was paying them and the others, for none would find treasure on this outing. I would inform Brillix of my suspicions, should I see him again. Until then, the pair of fighters shared the same peril as the rest of us.

My mind busied itself trying to deduce the men's objective, which was maddening without more information. So I thought again on the existence of gods. If magic were part of the world, then could not gods also be? Academically speaking, the question fascinated me and confounded me.

I went back to counting, something true and unchanging. Two would always follow one, and counting would always take us into the future. At one thousand, I tried to convince myself four hours had passed. Everyone needed their sleep, so I was loathe to wake them early. Another count, this time to two thousand, seemed an eternity.

I nudged Pulumbonk's supine form with my boot tips. He sat up with a yelp, thus starting a chain-reaction of men waking with their own style of horrified comment. A torch flared. Soon each man had groaned to his feet, splashed water on his face, and poked a shred of salted pork or gooey goldtail in his mouth.

Subu asked of the clinker, "Chisel."

The clinker, the same size and just as muscular as Subu, asked peevishly, "Now?"

Subu took the chisel and its attendant hammer, stepped to a purple patch of flowstone, and began pounding.

"We have no time for this," said Rudis, towering over Subu.

"Go without me, then."

The herbalist apprentice didn't pass up the opportunity to fulfill his mission for the Librast Superior, and began scraping at the purple-covered rock floor with a special, broad-tipped knife.

The rest of us sat. I dozed enthusiastically.

***

Subu took the lead, the fighters from Qnok close behind him, and Zir with Pulumbonk on their heels. The herbalist, now smug that his mission was accomplished, and I came next, with the cook and the clinker in the rear.

We reached The Marketplace and its simple plaza surrounded by the foundations of small structures. We ate salted pork, took a few mouthfuls from our flagons, and sat for ten marks of the water clock.

The long walk to the Weeping Temple began. With luck, we'd have full flagons and be in the Plaza of the Eight Kings begging Brillix to lower the pallet in a few hours. No signs or sounds of the Raka Infante. No saffa bats. No appearance by Remi, either by voice or body.

Brillix would be furious we had abandoned our vigil over the well, but he'd simply have to listen to reason. Besides, all of us would most likely be dead before we saw him again.

Lexica XVI

None of us knew whence the Raka would come, if they came. We had not noted any side passages off of our main path other than a few short, exploratory tunnels. The sole veteran of Dunkelgrau with us was the clinker, and he had not encountered them on either of his expeditions.

Pulumbonk had given his flare to Brillix, so the knight and the warrior, Udrakk, could signal the surface for their own extraction. We had to hope they were safely up there now and would hear our calls. If they had been, or we were, ambushed by Raka Infante, then all the shouting in the world wouldn't matter.

Subu, or as he seemed to prefer, "The Subu," led us from The Well past the hundred and ten white-spike markers to The Weeping Temple. I heard the falling water before I saw the chamber. The memory of Brother Poonal's screams begged me not to take another step. But I did. One after another with the companions fortune had chosen for me. Pulumbonk knocked his already-sputtering torch against the passage wall until its pitch-soaked wrapping fell free and could be stomped out. The nine of us paused in the gloom, listened.

When we didn't hear the thrash of wings or movement of bodies, we stepped into the chamber and the aqua-glow of the underground moss. The causeway connecting the islands in the lake seemed longer than before and the exit into the Morning Tunnel that led to the way out impossibly far. We moved as quietly as possible, although our boots crunched the rocks packed between the logs of the causeway. The cook had a new cough he stifled poorly.

I had not time to study the cavern on our first, harried crossing. Nine waterfalls issued from tunnels at varying heights, the longest falling straight from the blackness two hundred spans up where the ceiling must be. The splashing waters drummed at our ears and, in places, pelted us with droplets.

The sloping walls forming the dome I recalled as being smooth, but they now showed themselves to be lumpy with gray outcroppings and pitted with niches about the size of a warrior's shield. I tried to imagine the temple and its towering colonnade of blade-like pillars as it looked millennia ago, shading Faellic citizens walking among them under a blue sky. Mayhap the city had always been this way, built underground in giant chambers, like this one, The Well, and the Plaza of the Eight Kings. People would've walked in perpetual gloom

Half way across the chamber, strewn across one rock island, lay pieces of Brother Poonal's armor: a tatter of red and white surcoat here, a steel pauldron there, a blood-encrusted shoe just a few thumbs from the water's edge. No sign of Birna's remains.

"How do bats strip a man like that?" asked the herbalist.

"And where is the man?" I asked. "Bats aren't meat eaters."

"His weapons be gone," noted Subu.

The clinker, pickaxe at the ready, said, "Probably at the bottom of the lake."

Subu turned to all of us behind him. "Pulumbonk, prepare yer light sticks."

"I've but one, and it should be saved for—"

"Don't ya smell it?" Subu scanned our faces. "There be animal scent in here...and it ain' bat."

The cook, his pickaxe slung and his gleaming cleaver ready in his hand, asked, "Then why ain't we runnin'?"

"Shine a bullseye up there," Subu pointed to the closest wall.

Zir the Archer carried the one lantern we had salvaged and directed its beam to the wall. The light revealed only a gray outcropping, nothing unusual. Until it moved. Two arms, two legs appeared, fingers and toes gripping the rock face to carry the gray humanoid torso out of the beam.

"Hide the light," Subu hissed and gestured for us to follow him.

The cook patted the cleaver absently against the quilting of his doublet, as he walked. "That a Raka? I wonder if they cook up good."

The herbalist groaned. "Brillix knew. He knew they'd get us."

"Plug it," the clinker snapped, his own pickaxe readied.

The single lantern beam directed our progress forward, all ears attuned to the dripping gloom, all weapons at the ready. As before, mist gathered on the eye slits of my helmet and moistened the blade of my sword. Even inside the leather and steel of my gauntlet, my fingers chilled. I detected no animal scent.

We made little noise, so it must've been our scent that stirred bodies to skitter in the shadows around us. Fingernails and toenails clicked against rock. A heavy pant made by many throats rose in a gutteral runh, runh, runh repeated in unison. Human armies had to beat war drums to intimidate their enemies. We couldn't see all of them, but we could hear them gathering above and in front of us. To come near enough to attack, they'd need to splash into the lake and swim to us or drop from a great height directly onto our path. They were flesh and bone, so I couldn't imagine their not taking grievous damage, if falling from high points.

The splashes began around the perimeter of the lake. The glowing moss of the cavern did little more than highlight the spray thrown up by churning limbs heading our way.

The herbalist squeaked. "How many are there?"

I tapped Pulumbonk on the shoulder from behind. "The light stick."

"We can't move while it's lit."

"Why not?" snapped the herbalist.

Pulumbonk asked, "You want to melt your hand carrying it?"

The cook spluttered. "I don't want to die in a cave full of bat droppings!"

Subu shouted, "Light it, afore we're overcome!"

Pulumbonk's head shook in disagreement but held up the light stick and conjured fire into his palm. "The ground is wet."

"I have chain and leather gauntlets." I sheathed my sword. "I'll hold it."

Pulumbonk's expression said I was crazy, but he handed it to me and lit both ends. Light seared my eyes as it leapt out to fifty spans around us. The water frothed with over a hundred swimming Raka Infante on either side of us. They shrieked at the light and ducked under the water. We hurried toward the far tunnel.

The light stick, after but a few moments, grew unbearable. I tossed it from one gloved hand to the other. "It's too hot!"

"I told you!"

"What do I do?"

"Don't get it wet."

That was no help. I knelt and set it on the driest spot I saw. The men in front quickly outran the light's protective aura. They had the directed beam of the lantern the archer held.

"We ain' stoppin'," Subu shouted.

Pulumbonk stared at me, as if shocked I wasn't doing anything to correct the problem. I glanced from him to the herbalist and to the wide eyes of the cook.

From behind me, the clinker hissed. "Yer the smart one."

The most urgent problem was keeping the stick from soaking up too much moisture. That I solved by drawing my sword and laying the handle under one end of the light stick. At least the stick's whole length was not in contact with the moist ground.

Now, how to carry it without my fingers? The solution came quicker than expected. I drew two throwing knives from my bandolier and used them as tongs. I couldn't move fast without fumbling the stick, but I could move. My cluster of five frightened men tried to close the gap with the other four at a motivated shuffle.

Raka had drawn themselves onto the dark causeway ahead, blocking Subu's group's way into the Morning Tunnel. They stood not quite so tall as a human but had deeply etched muscles and rudimentary but nasty looking weapons. I didn't hear the invocation, but there was no mistaking the red glow of Subu's axe blazing to life.

Some Raka had swum outside the intensely bright circle of the light stick to the sides of the causeway. The sides were sheer but only six hands above the water at their highest point, so the Raka could heave themselves onto it without much difficulty. The two warriors from Qnok, while not talkative, were articulate with their blades. Claw-tipped gray hands thrusting from the water were hacked off. Bodies climbing onto the causeway were kicked back.

Ahead of them by several steps, Subu danced with his axe, its fiery head etching red loops in the gloom. I couldn't yet see their faces, but the wounded Raka shrieked at a pitch not unlike a human infant's. Had I an extra set of hands to cover my ears!

It seemed forever, but we closed the gap and brought the circle of intense light around the entire party again. The Raka shrank back. We closed ranks and pressed forward.

The all-metal throwing knives had heated through and began burning my fingers through my gauntlets. "I can't carry this any longer!"

Pulumbonk plucked two more knives from my bandolier of six and took the sparking light stick. I transferred my hot knives to my armpits for a few moments to let my fingers cool.

Raka armed with clubs, sharpened poles, and flails with wicked red shards of Faellic glass at their tips clogged the tunnel mouth. Another group had mounted the causeway thirty paces behind us. I caught my first sight of a Raka face and wilted. Their heads were hairless and smaller in proportion to their muscular bodies than I had imagined. Their noses were no more than bumps, their eyes no more than punched holes. Their mouths were blood-red gaps, lipless and lined with tiny, sharp teeth.

Be brave, Jonne.

I whirled around to throw a knife, as the cook and clinker hurried past me to be closer to the fighters. The purse hanging from the clinker's belt caught on the sheathed poniard on mine. Although I was the heavier man, he stumbled free, while I spun to the ground. My momentum set me into what seemed a slow-motion roll over crushed rock, over the edge of the log bulwark, and into water up to my shoulders.

People with gods might attribute my luck to a miracle, as the mounded rock foundation under the water was sloped, not sheer, so I didn't sink. I felt like a frog too fat on flies to get over the slick log, now at eye level. I threw one elbow upon it but found the rest of me laboring too slowly to pull myself up and regain my feet ahead of the Raka approaching from behind.

"A hand, I beg!"

Pulumbonk slowed.

The clinker kept hustling. "Leave him. He's a poncey castler."

I would forgive Pulumbonk anything, should we have a future, for he tossed the light stick at the closing Raka, which shrank them into a shrieking huddle. Long fingers wrapped my wrist. Others slipped beneath my armpit. He was no Ryckerd, but his strength, combined with my spastic effort, was enough. I crawled up. Rose to my knees. Was pulled to my feet. We caught up to the others who were blocked from moving into the safety of the passageway by Subu, the archer, and the battling Qnok warriors.

Subu left them and pushed past the rest of us until he was out of the tunnel mouth and on the causeway with nobody within reach. "Here I've room to fight!"

I felt simultaneously thrilled at having his protection and sorry for any Raka who closed with him, but my empathy was academic. All Raka needed to die.

I drew my sword. Pulumbonk drew his, one from the same Northern smith as mine, Moonsie, the perpetually amused armorer with the big-busted lady tattooed on his bicep. Legs widened, we stood half-ready for a fight, not knowing whether to help Subu, watch the ceiling, or prepare to kick away swimmers.

The danger came from above, where the sloping wall was only thirty spans over the causeway. A gray blur landed on the back of the cook, its stubby hands under the man's chin. The cook's cleaver banged to the ground. One muscular jerk by the Raka broke the big man's neck, and the two bodies fell backwards into the lake. The Raka sidestroked the much larger corpse into the darkness.

I wanted to shout, "Hurry!" but the herbalist beat me to it. The Qnok warriors and Zir were doing what they could to gain entrance to the passage, as evinced by the screeches of their foes. Zir held the bullseye lantern in one hand, while fighting with his short sword in the other. Its beam highlighted targets for the warriors and blinded the Raka looking into it.

Another Raka crashed onto the clinker, collapsing them both to the causeway surface. Being the closest, I had an instant in which to forgive his leaving me or let him die. I had no Remi or Lada to spur me on, so I calculated my thrust, taking valuable moments no veteran would waste, and drove the sword into the Raka's muscular neck. Its thick fingers slapped at the wound, giving the clinker time to roll free and hack his pickaxe into the thing's heart.

Instants later, the few surviving Raka in the passageway melted away, and our group lurched into the mouth of the Morning Tunnel. Subu took his time, continuing to fight on the causeway behind us. He swayed and ducked and swung, and Raka and parts of Raka splashed into the lake to the left and right. He glanced back at us, whiskers wet with blood, eyes wide with ecstasy.

Subu fought until his arms tired, and then retreated to the relative safety of the passageway. The Raka Infante shrank back into the aqua gloom.

He halted in front of me panting and grinning. "Ya see that, word man? Yer chronicle would be dull without The Subu."

***

Under the guard of the fighting men, the clinker, herbalist, Pulumbonk, and I knelt on the causeway to fill the party's flagons. We finished as the intense blaze of the light stick on the causeway sputtered and failed. We had hours to go before we reached the Plaza of the Eight Kings, but none of us called for a rest.

The Raka Infante had the smell of fresh human blood in their tiny nostrils, so they would surely follow us. We had one spare candle for the lantern, one half-spent torch, and no more of Pulumbonk's wondrous light sources to last us until we gained daylight. If Brillix didn't send the pallet down to retrieve us, we would die by thirst, hunger, or tiny teeth.

The weight of the full flagon of water slung over my shoulder and the food in my backpack gave me some solace. Recalling the expertise the fighters had shown in dispatching the Raka also brightened my faltering hope to at least a spark.

We came across two dead Raka lying across the passageway floor where they had bled out. Farther along, a third Raka, sitting against the passage wall panting, met our lantern beam with a pitiful wail. Rudis put the thing out of its misery with a well-aimed blow.

I found it hard to imagine such a hideous thing having gentle traits. Did it love its offspring? Its mate? The incongruity of face and body seemed a product of evil, not of Gela. Some scholars posited that they were the degenerate progeny of the Fael. Possibly but unlikely. Mayhap they were created by the Anaxagorum during its long slumber in Dunkelgrau. It seemed certain the Remi-thing had called them to the Weeping Temple to ambush us.

As painful as it was, my mind clung to thoughts of the woman I had kissed. Would I some day forget the magic of that moment? How would our children have looked? Blue? Pink? Black hair or silver? Were Ryckerd, Father's first born, to have a son, he would, by custom, name him Arno, as dynastic names were bestowed every other generation. Were I to have a son, even with Ryckerd dead or missing, I could name him as I pleased. Pulumbonk's heroic act on the causeway made me put his name on the top of my list. Were I to have a daughter, I'm not sure what I'd name her. Not Lada.

***

The last two hundred paces to the Plaza of the Eight Kings presented a formidable obstacle to men so exhausted. The clinker, who had not thanked me for my assistance, suffered unrelenting back pain from receiving the full weight of the leaping Raka. The warriors from Qnok, though neither complained, tended contusions they'd received through their armor. Subu, "The" Subu, asked for unguent and dressing from the herbalist for a gouge across his neck. Zir had taken a spear thrust to his lamellar cuirass that broke a rib. Pulumbonk looked bewildered. As to me, the chainmail felt as heavy as the first day I wore it. The cook, for once, was the only one at peace. That he'd been eaten presented a cruel irony. I had liked him.

After all the exertion and with our only light source at the front, the passageway became a suffocating umbilical. I removed my helmet. The chainmail coif I let fall back onto my shoulders, the heavy gloves went into my belt. The cool felt miraculous.

Breaths were more refreshing. My fingers ruffled my sweaty hair, and I felt almost good.

Both of my hands went to my face to wipe it free of sweat, when something slapped onto them. Twas as if someone had spat a glob of mucous on me the size of a griddle-cake just off the fire, because it scalded the backs of my hands. I pulled my hands from my face, the glob still adhered to them.

"Dripper!" I exclaimed and turned to the herbalist for help.

He couldn't see me, but he could see it glistening. "Get that thing away from me!"

Drippers were reported to be as gray as the stone to which they clung, but this one pulsed with pink luminance. It sucked at me, a sensation that burned like the sun. Jerking my hands apart resulted in the blob giving up my right hand to engulf my left hand. The pain became excruciating.

"Someone do something!"

The lantern swung its beam to me. Pulumbonk pulled his sword and tried to tempt the thing onto its blade, but there were no juices to suck from steel. I flailed my hand. The others backed away.

My mind stayed clear enough to remember. "I need fire! Light a fire!"

Pulumbonk shoved his hand into his pouch. Before he could produce a flame, I heard "Addra addra, forenza krak!" and The Subu appeared with his axe edge flaming. One touch produced a sizzle and the thing jumped from my hand into the air, mayhap to regain the ceiling. Pulumbonk swiped at it. The clinker's hands flailed to keep it off. Rudis grabbed the thing out of the air, threw it to the ground and pinned it with a boot.

"Finish dat ting!"

Rudis lifted his boot, and The Subu pressed his blade against the part still showing. The thing sizzled and collapsed on itself, until only a greasy black ball no bigger than a pecan remained.

Rudis stepped close to me. "Wear you helmet, gruggard."

I didn't know the word, but I got its intention. Pulumbonk examined my hand, but it was the disinterested herbalist I wanted. A tug at his sleeve pulled him about.

"Salve, I beg."

The herbalist glanced at my hand. "Salves are for real wounds on real men, Blossom."

Pulumbonk and I gawked. How could someone say that to one of the few companions they had in a tenuous situation? Mayhap I would understand personality types better, one day.

Of all people, the clinker took my side, saying to the herbalist, "He's hurt. What's wrong with ya?"

The herbalist's mouth puckered in distaste. "Look at you telling me what to do. I—"

The Subu rapped him on the head with his now-extinguished blade. "Give him the salve."

The herbalist did.

***

We stopped at a latrine to rest. Used on the way in, this one had acquired what veterans called "camp bouquet." It was hardly worse than the smell of our bodies. The plaza remained our destination, but inactivity for thirty intervals by the water clock would be paradise. The Subu and Zir watched the rear. The Qnok warriors watched the way ahead. Pulumbonk lit the stub of our one twilight candle and placed it in the latrine entrance, its glow able to serve both those within and those resting in the passage. I stepped to the other side of the clinker to get away from the herbalist and sat, back to the wall.

I was pleased Pulumbonk sat next to me. "I owe you a kingdom, or at least, a lifetime of orange cakes for saving me."

He appeared happy to have something on which to focus. "You're Lada's brother."

The lake water from my flagon tasted as purely delicious as any water ever. I chose not to think of the dead bodies now in it.

Pulumbonk stretched long legs before him, the boots he'd bought for the expedition nicked, scuffed, and dulled by filth. "To think, those would've been my lovely Ruprecht's, if I hadn't stowed them at The Six Fingers."

"You showed foresight."

"Twas Lada's idea."

"She has a good one, now and again."

Pulumbonk rested his chin on his knees. "I risked my life hurrying through a brewing war to catch passage on The Drowned Hag, so I could see Dunkelgrau. Foolish, yea?"

I asked the group at large, all conspirators except The Subu. "Was it worth this?" When nobody answered, I addressed the herbalist. "And why you, a man of the castle?"

He chewed at a fingernail, shrugged.

The clinker's eyebrows spiked, as he turned to the herbalist. "Yer a spoiled dripspittle, and greedy for what pelf the book might've brought you. We blueskins wanted the book for equality."

"You're rich in your tradecraft," explained the herbalist. "I, too, should be rich."

"This ain't about wealth."

Rudis, the bigger warrior from Qnok stepped over Pulumbonk's legs on his way to the latrine.

I whispered into Pulumbonk's ear. "I overheard him praying to Askerat a few hours back…or days. He thought we were asleep."

"Him? Them?" Pulumbonk's mouth hung in incredulity. "Askerat is a common man's god. Those two are well-trimmed."

"Mayhap they're spies for Draman."

Pulumbonk considered the possibility. "Let's be glad they're here and, for the nonce, on our side."

When Rudis exited the latrine, I closed my eyes and enjoyed the silence.

Pulumbonk tapped me with a knuckle. "I feel your loss, Jonne." When I turned to him puzzled, he said, "Remi. I noticed how you were with her, like me with my Lada."

I snorted, "Your Lada."

He heated, "Yea, my Lada. She had my heart at first meeting."

"I believe she seduced you to join a conspiracy you didn't believe in."

"I believe in it. She made an eloquent argument for bringing the Anaxagorum's knowledge to humankind."

"She wants her legs back."

"She has feelings for me."

"We have never been a 'feeling' family, Pulumbonk."

"Do you not love Remi?"

I studied my salve-coated hand. "Not much of her left, is there?"

"You'd dive down that well, were there a possibility of saving her."

"Pulumbonk, I…." My words trembled out. "She spoke to me from that well, told me the Raka were coming…but how? Mayhap her mind is still her own, only her body…she's as blood red as the book was and, I fear, forever gone to me." I didn't mean to sound so desolate.

"I have prayed that we shall see better of this, and that love will not be denied."

"As if prayer has ever helped anyone," I said. "Let events pass as they may."

***

My chin rested on my chest, and my mind floated happily away, when The Subu barked, "Eyes to the rear!"

Zir said in a hush, "The eldritch light."

My eyes snapped open. What had been utter darkness in the passage behind us now lit with a distant glow of pale green, the silhouettes of Raka within. I nudged Pulumbonk. "The green light!"

He moaned, "I have no more tricks to fight it."

"There, too!" The herbalist pointed to a second group of red mouths and spearpoints enshrouded by a glow in the passage ahead.

"Raka!" growled Rudis.

The shorter of the two warriors knelt next to Pulumbonk, lantern in hand. "Light it!" His voice was boyish and at odds with the hard face hosting it.

Pulumbonk raised a flame in his palm. Another few heartbeats and the beam from the bullseye lantern stabbed the eyes of the approaching group ahead. Gnarled hands flew to shield black eyes, and the group stopped.

At the same moment, facing the passage behind, Subu uttered his words, and the red from his axe blushed the walls. Zir nocked an arrow on the string of his composite bow. Leading the rear group of Raka glided the blood-red Remi-thing, its feet barely toeing the floor to propel itself.

The clinker hefted his pickaxe. "Let me kill three, and I die happy."

Pulumbonk lit our last torch and drew his sword. The herbalist crouched and waited, poniard in hand.

Another fight so soon seemed cruelly unfair. "Nooo. Can't they leave us be?"

Rudis swatted my shoulder. "Your weapon!"

The sword came slowly from its sheath. The two groups of enemy closed to within fifteen paces of us, so we were blocked front and back.

The Remi-thing, glistening red from matted hair to bare toe, put a hand to its mouth and exhaled a black stream into it. The hand slashed across the air, leaving a band of inky smoke. The smoke solidified into words in Faellic letters. As I watched, they turned into letters of the common tongue.

VALIANT WARRIORS

A second swipe of its hand spelled,

STAY YOUR HANDS

Only I spoke. "Remi? Does any part of you remain?"

The thing's bloody eyelids opened. Gray irises around black pupils found me. Red lips parted long enough to exude an urgent nothing that hadn't the strength to become words. Eyes closed. Mouth shut. I wanted to run to it.

The hand slashed a new band of vapor.

THE GIRL IS MY VESSEL
FORGET HER

The Subu asked, "What the piss are ya?"

It spread more bands of vapor.

I AM WHAT THE WORLD HAS LOST

Seeing Faellic letters so nimbly translated made me forget everything else. Northem had thousands of manuscripts awaiting meaning.

I SEE NOT CONSPIRATORS
I SEE NEW FRIENDS
AID ME
BE AS LORDS AMONG MEN

I glanced at Pulumbonk who was also speechless.

The Subu finally asked, "Become friends? With them mewling shorties at yer back?"

THEY ARE CHILDREN OF THE DUST
AS ARE YOU
THEY COME TO PROTECT ME
NOT TO HARM YOU
DO THE SAME
OR DIE WHERE YOU STAND

"Well," the herbalist began, eyes trying to connect with one of us, but all stayed focused on the Remi-thing. "Lords among men? That means rich. You do understand that, yes?"

The shorter warrior from Qnok, Rudis' companion, swatted his shield with the flat of his sword. "Nay! You are abomination to my god. You will die here!"

The Remi-thing's mouth fell open and out gushed a stream of black vapor. It, with no more mass than wood smoke, blew through our ranks to the group of Raka facing the warrior. The vapor entered the first rows of Raka through their nostrils and mouths, and they howled their nightmare howl.

I thought of the vapor hurling comets of earth at Northem's walls, of its guiding the great ruyks and their riders into battle, and its animating the man-plants. The vapor had no effect on humans, but the Raka could be propelled like missiles. Four of them flew across space to crash into the Qnok warriors, knocking Rudis onto his back and clutching the other to drag him back to the awaiting mouths of their kin, as if by living grappling hook. They tore off the man's helmet and drove a spiked pole through his head. He was theirs to consume later.

Rudis grabbed for his sword.

The clinker seized him by the belt. "They'll kill all of us."

Rudis whirled an arm at the clinker who released the belt and leapt back. Sword out, Rudis coiled into a crouch ready to charge.

The Subu addressed him matter-of-factly, "Ye'll fight alone and die for naught."

Rudis hesitated and then slammed the weapon back into is sheath. He hammered the passage wall and rumbled to the sky beyond the ceiling, "Award me vengeance anon!"

Was there an Askerat to hear him? I might maintain my conviction that gods played no part in the lives of humans, but I was looking at a very real, very red something that defied natural laws. If it were a god, why did it need a human vessel? How had humans defeated it in the past?

The Subu addressed the entity. "I'm a mercenary, ye bloody thing." Then he bowed low with a sweep of his arm. "Make me rich, and I'm yer man."

The tension eased. The others, one by one, assented to serving the Remi-thing. I feared, with good reason, the blood book would bring woe to the people of Northem, especially the castlers, due to their rejection of phenomenon like it.

It drew another vaporous band in front of me.

YOU CAME TO BURY ME
I OFFER FORGIVENESS

The silence awaited my answer.

"Will you spare the girl?" I asked.

NO HARM CAN BEFALL HER
AS LONG AS WE ARE ONE

I tried to recreate Remi's face from the red thing with its eyes closed and overbite hidden behind tight lips. I thought of Mother and Father, Lada and Ryckerd, Merf and the noble rogues, of the beacons of reason that were Northem and the mysterious lighthouse we called The Six Fingers. No matter how I answered, I would betray people and traditions I held with affection. Either way, I'd betray myself.

"Keep her safe and I, too, am your man."

Part III
The Six Fingers

Lexica XVII

I had been terrified from the moment I entered Dunkelgrau, but curiosity nudged fear out of the way. This was history-in-the-making. The Remi-thing, walking in the middle of over fifty Raka Infante washed in pale green light, led the way to the Plaza of the Eight Kings. The Subu and the rest of us followed. I couldn't get close to the blood-red body, but the passageway carried my voice clearly.

"What do we call you? I know the girl as Remi, but I think you are something else. The Anaxagorum? Do I call you that?"

How it might respond while walking was a mystery, but I kept inquiring.

"If you are, I'm more than a bit excited to know more about you. I...actually many of us...believe you to be a compendium of the arcane, possibly magic, which is extraordinary, but perhaps this is merely conjecture. You are, well, you are alive with your own will and...do you know I'm a librast with the library at Northem? My sister Lada brought you back from Tule just over a fortnight ago."

The clinker addressed me over his shoulder. "You're prattling, Blossom, like a girl."

"I'm trying to learn something...as a man with a working mind should."

"You think that's funny? I'll show ya funny."

"I'm only trying to explain."

His grin wasn't friendly. "If you didn't have that scalp-taker watching over ya...."

I suppose The Subu was watching over me, which was certainly a comforting realization. I ignored the clinker and raised my voice for the Remi-thing. "Do you plan harm to humankind or good?"

The thing and her Raka marched on.

"Most of us don't believe in gods, but if you're one, I know that I, at least, would welcome a chance to understand what role you expect us to play in supporting you."

The red body, standing taller than the Raka, swiped a band of inky vapor in the air between its head and the passageway ceiling. The band hung in place. As I got closer, it spelled out the role it wished from me:

A SILENT ONE

The Subu startled everyone with a yelping guffaw.

The clinker swatted his thigh. "Now that's funny!"

"Laugh if you will. This…entity…could be an ally."

He turned his face forward. "Only a pea-wit would trust this thing."

"You were certainly eager to get your hands on it, as I recall."

He snorted, "When I thought it just a book of spells."

From behind, the herbalist whispered, "If you think any of us expected this, shake the cobs, Blossom."

"I have cobs in my mind? Get the hubris out of your eyes."

"Chickpeas?" He laughed. "In my eyes?"

"You're thinking of hummus."

His face reddened. "I know that." Then he shouldered me into the passage wall.

I turned to the clinker. "Would you like to exchange places?"

"And walk next to that spoiled little ponce?"

To the herbalist, I said, "You're stuck with me."

"Better than that blue-skinned prong."

The clinker pulled me back a step and took my place next to the herbalist. "What'll we chat about, ponce?"

I fell in next to Pulumbonk much relieved.

From ahead, Rudis barked, "Silence, gruggards."

He marched ahead of The Subu, right on the heels of the Raka, sword in hand. I hoped he didn't do something to get us killed. I understood his desire for revenge and asked of Pulumbonk, "Do you not feel anger at Lada for what's she's done to us?"

He weighed the question. "Nay, not anger. I'm mystified, confused, I'd say, by what she thought we could accomplish."

I wanted to discuss Lada's motives but could talk no longer to love-stupid Pulumbonk without my sister present to defend herself.

Presently, Pulumbonk said, "I am somewhat angry, I suppose."

At least he had some grasp of reality. I felt somewhat angry at myself for babbling so at the Remi-thing. Curiosity had turned me into a babbler. While not my place, I ached to ask The Subu of his plan of action. What would we do when we got to the surface? What if the thing wished to present itself at Northem Castle? Did he think his battleaxe could harm it?

Mostly I ached to be back in my soft bed looking forward to easy sleep and another morning of sugar cakes and anonymity.

***

Daylight shone through the slash in the surface above the Plaza of the Eight Kings. We humans ran over the inlaid stones to be in sunlight again.

The herbalist screamed to the sky, "Anybody up there?"

Zir joined him. "If there be a good soul among you, lower the pallet!"

The Remi-thing and her Raka bodyguard stayed on the gloomy periphery. When I expressed our desire to get to the surface quickly, it replied:

REST UNTIL DARK

The Subu paced around the floor, finally stopping far across the plaza from me. He held up a helmet belonging to one of the knights who had stayed above. "We're wabberjacked, lads. Fellas up top have been butchered, prolly by our mole-eyed friends." He called across the plaza. "Red Lady. Yer monsters do this?"

"How do you know they're all dead?" asked the herbalist.

The Subu glanced up to the platform holding the windlass. "Not too spry at answering ya, are they?"

The herbalist glanced from face to face. "We're stuck down here. Why doesn't that scare the spit out of everybody?"

It did me and, by the expressions around me, the others, as well, except Rudis. He had stepped within twenty paces of the Remi-thing, which stood as still as a small statue at the base of one of the towering kings.

He asked it, "You dare assume the powers of God?"

The Subu called to him. "If ye stir 'em up, ye and Askerat best be able to swat 'em back down, cuz I ain' helpin'."

Rudis remained focused. "Fight me, and I show you the power of a real god!"

Zir hollered, "We need ya, Rudis, for we are but a handful."

Rudis didn't move. Mayhap he wished to show his lack of fear, as he did by standing at the lip of the platform before descending into Dunkelgrau.

"Why ain't the Raka attacking?" asked the clinker, his skin light blue in the sunlight. "We've no chance vanquishing fifty here where they can surround us."

I explained what seemed obvious. "They won't attack unless we provoke Rem…the Anaxagorum."

Pulumbonk said, "I prefer Subu's name, The Red Lady."

Heads nodded, except for the clinker's who continued glaring at me. "How you know what they'll do?"

"I pay attention."

"And I don't, ya ponce?"

"Explain to me the significance of the green light surrounding the Raka."

"To scare the shite out of us." He grinned, looked around for supporting chuckles.

I explained, "Things under her thrall emanate the green light."

Pulumbonk shook his head in puzzlement. "I thought the black vapor did that."

"I believe the vapor is an expression of the book's will. When exerted upon a subject, the Raka, the man-plants, even the Ruyk, they glow green."

The herbalist asked, "Then why hasn't she enchanted us?"

The clinker glanced from him to Zir to me. "Who says we ain't already?"

"Do you see the green light around us?"

The four men looked.

Pulumbonk asked, "But what about the Ruyk? They are men, as we are, but they—"

"I believe the Ruyk and their beasts have a preternatural bond. Mayhap that makes them vulnerable to influence through their animals."

The clinker snorted. "They were sure 'nuff stupid to attack us in the Cheeky Nobs."

"Not stupid," I corrected. "Their simple lifestyle doesn't require as much abstract thinking as ours, therefore they may not have the breadth of acuity to fend off a psychic intruder. The book guided them to attack us."

The clinker said, "You don't know any of that."

"Let's say he does," the herbalist posed, before asking of me, "Tell us then, why won't she attack us now?"

"So far, she…it…has only attacked when threatened."

The clinker studied the Red Lady who remained immobile forty paces away. "If you're sayin' she's got some special brain power, why don't she think herself a pair of real wings and go on her flogging way?"

"Allow me to posit that the thing is genderless, not a she but an it."

The clinker smirked. "You know, booker, why don't you deposit yourself up your own arse?"

I started to define "posit" for him, but Pulumbonk shook his head.

The clinker wasn't listening. He was gazing at blue sky. "I tried to build a pair of wings outta wood and linen. Woulda' worked, if I hadn't dislocated my shoulder flapping."

As the daylight shined strongly, I sat on the plaza and scribbled notes about what had happened since my last entry. A day ago? Two? What I had witnessed in that time seemed more fantastic than real. Three veteran fighters killed by normally indifferent saffa bats. Raka nesting in the Weeping Temple where they'd never been seen. Bright, capable Remi doing the bidding of an inanimate tome and then consuming its fleshy pages to become the tome! It all defied reason. Who could and could not be controlled by the Anaxagorum? The implications to the existence of civilization were formidable. And fascinating.

I considered not recording in my notes that I had joined the others in siding with the Red Lady against my kin and home, but that would be breaking the oath I had made to the Collegium to document factually. The Askerati could lie and follow superstition.

What had been bright, midday sun faded to gray sky above me. A glance at the Red Lady revealed it seated cross-legged and immobile, flanked by its pit-eyed bodyguard hunkered on all fours. A thin column of black vapor rose from the thing's mouth past the statues, through the slash, to a point higher than I could see. I nudged Pulumbonk.

He gazed on the thing he'd help unleash and shook his head. "I make bad decisions."

***

The sky had turned inky, although evening had yet hours to arrive. The black vapor stopped issuing from the Red Lady, and when it stood, the Raka stood. The Subu remained across the plaza from us. The others came to full alert from their dozing.

Six Raka, shrouded in green light, broke from their mates, leapt upon the bases of the two closest statues, and scuttled over the king's bodies all the way to the tops of their heads. From there, the distant forms sprang onto the sloping wall and made their way to the top of the dome where the slash of gray sky waited. My neck stiffened, as I watched for a long interval before hearing the welcome clacking of the windlass. The square silhouette of the pallet swung into view.

The clinker grinned. "The bloody minx might be friendly, after all."

"We go up first," said the herbalist directly to me. "Don't let that thing stop us."

"Why would it listen to me?"

The Subu trotted over to us. "We go up first."

The herbalist pumped his fist. "The axe speaks!"

Pulumbonk couldn't look The Subu in the eye, so he gazed at his hands. "We know your axe is mighty—"

The Subu snapped, "Yer a head taller than me, yet ya can't look me in the eye?"

Pulumbonk focused on Subu's chin. "Can we defeat all these Raka? And might she not summon more?"

The Subu called to the thing. "Halloo there, Red Lady. We're goin' up the rope before ya. Problem?"

The thing didn't respond. All human eyes watched the pallet click the last few spans to the floor. It thumped to a stop, the net collapsed and the cable went slack, soon coiling on the ground as the windlass kept clicking.

The Subu shouted, "Yer bright boys need to stop their winching."

I addressed the Red Lady by making a cranking motion and saying, "Stop winding."

The winching stopped. We rushed aboard, Rudis breaking his staring match to join us.

The thing spread a message before it.

COME SPEAK WITH ME JONNE BOOKER

I looked to my companions.

Pulumbonk whispered, "Speak to her from here."

"I can read your words from here."

Another swipe of the thing's hand spelled:

TIS REMI WHO NEEDS YOU

I was in mid-step when hands seized me by my bandolier.

One belonged to Subu. "Nah ya don't."

The other belonged, surprisingly, to Rudis who did not speak.

"Talk to me," I called.

As the thing had done to Rudis's companion, it launched four Raka through the air straight and level, like missiles, knocking the three of us to our backs on the pallet. The Raka clutched me. By a thin rope of vapor, the Red Lady tugged us free of my companions. Raka were amazingly strong, lifting me as they would a log and running me across the mosaic to where the thing sat. The rope from the windlass pulled taut, the netting formed its pyramid with the others inside, and the pallet started up.

Struggle as I could, I only came free when the Raka released their grips. They rejoined their companions around the motionless Red Lady. I asked, "What do you intend?"

The pallet grew smaller, until it was naught but a patch of black against the sky. Mayhap the answer was obvious: it would hold me hostage, so my companions wouldn't bounce off as soon as they reached the surface. I tried, as I had countless times in the past days, to imagine what Ryckerd would do. My conclusion was as always: I couldn't do what Ryckerd would do, whether it were to attack the Raka, threaten the thing, or dash for the rising pallet.

I passed my hand before the Red Lady's face. "Remi? Are you yet alive?"

The eyelids blinked open, shocking me that they looked frightened. The lips moved to make three words in Remi's voice. "Stay by me."

My heart rejoiced and ached simultaneously. "Of course!"

The eyelids shut. The lips returned to repose. A hand spread vapor between us.

STAY OUT OF MY WAY

I argued, "You said that Remi needed me."

The Red Lady hesitated before swiping more vapor.

PERHAPS SHE DOES

I DO NOT

If normal women were hard to understand, ones inside living books were impossible.

Presently, the clicking of the windlass resumed, and the pallet became larger, more detailed, and, soon, resting on the mosaicked floor again.

The Red Lady didn't stop me, when I boarded the pallet alongside it and a dozen Raka. The ones left behind sprung like squirrels to the statues and skittered up to the top of the dome faster than the pallet could take us. I didn't know what awaited us at the surface, but I felt exhilarated exiting Dunkelgrau. When the pallet stopped, I jogged across the platform and up the rise to good, healthy ground far from the pit.

The Subu shouted at me from where the four wagons still rested. The tents and pavilions were in various stages of collapse. Brillix, the knights, the horses and oxen were nowhere in sight. Shreds of white web drifted on the breeze. The sun, barely visible through the dark cloud mass directly over us, rested at four o'clock. In the distance at every direction, the sky was blue.

"They left us?" I asked.

The face of a dead Raka, mouth open and dull red, gazed up from a patch of scrub, its body shrouded under white web clinging to the grass. I brushed the web away with my sword and stepped back. While the head was intact, all that remained of the body was a spine and ribcage lacking most of its ribs. The few that remained had no flesh on them and plenty of tooth marks to explain why.

I turned to the clutch of Raka with the Red Lady. "You...eat your own."

Pulumbonk called from the ruined camp. "Jonne!"

I jogged in my armor through the ankle-high scrub, noting scattered bones not of human origin. When I arrived next to Pulumbonk, I gazed upon what held the attention of the others: a strew of mostly eaten Raka corpses, the shredded, bloody armor belonging to one of the knights from the Order of Man, and the blood-filled boots of the loyal archer. No sign of Brillix, Udrakk, or the other knights.

"We can na' blame 'em for leaving, can we?" The Subu said, amused.

"Do ya think they took all the livestock with them?" asked the clinker. "If those Raka shit-drips ate my horse, I'll have me some baby skulls for the mantle back at the Fingers."

Poor Thunderhoof. "Mayhap they've but run off."

The clinker had begun sifting through the detritus of the camp. "You go right out there and look for them, booker."

I scanned the vast, rolling plains, the black spires the only landmarks. Not many places for a horse to hide. Mayhap Thunderhoof could find his way home, but that was fanciful thinking. I had other things to worry about, such as the Red Lady, now surrounded by her full contingent of fifty Raka, waiting twenty paces away, facing the south and Northem.

The Subu called from near a wagon. "Dried ruyk meat here. Water barrel's half full but top off fast and let's get on."

The herbalist's eyes shifted under his heavy eyebrows. "We ought to head out on our own. That thing's not even looking at us."

"Go ahead, castler," the clinker said, trading his fingerless gloves for a pair of handsome gauntlets from the dead knight.

I had joined The Subu to load a spare duffel with meat and chipped fried potatoes nobody had told me about. He and I shared a handful in secret, his face brightening at first taste. Three of them passed my tongue before we closed the bag.

Delightfully salty and crunchily delicious, they were everything the tinned goldtail wasn't.

Pulumbonk gathered extra flagons of what I thought was water. He passed one with a whisper. "Ale."

I thrilled from top to toe. "You've saved my life twice now." I quaffed deeply and slung the flagon over my shoulder, happy to carry the extra weight.

Rudis checked his gear, grabbed a spare flagon, and stood impatiently. Zir gathered arrows to refill his quiver and then helped the clinker by carrying one end of the food duffel. The Subu hoisted his personal bag of purple rocks in addition to his backpack, water bottle, and heavy axe. No taller or heavier than I, he was remarkably sturdy. I changed the stockings I'd been wearing with spares from my tent. Boots back on, pack filled to the brim with writing satchel, food, dirty stockings, water, and my share of the purple rocks destined for the castle, a flagon of water on one hip, one of ale on the other, I stepped next to The Subu. The herbalist joined, and when we started for Northem, so did the Red Lady and its bodyguard.

I whispered over The Subu's shoulder, "The Red Lady said neither she nor Remi could be harmed while they are one, yet your axe seems quite powerful."

"It'll split solid rock, but it could na' bite through the ward of yer lady friend."

"Remi learned her tricks from ancestors who read the Anaxagorum, so I suppose we shouldn't underestimate her power."

"Two things you must learn about The Subu, word man: I never overestimate my abilities or underestimate them of me foe. And I never say no to strange, bloody women who might make me rich."

"So we just follow it?"

"The Red Lady is a proposition, and we'll follow her till a better comes along." He looked at Rudis. "I reckon ye want to kill it. Show me the profit, and I'll help ya. Get in the way of profit, and I'll kill ya."

***

The Subu's confidence impressed me, if it was confidence and not foolishness. He marched at the head of our line, behind the thing and its Raka, but a mere two steps ahead of Rudis. The heated exchange between the two after Subu's condescending remark about profit practically led to violence. Rudis took umbrage at being considered cheap enough to work for profit or weak enough to be vanquished by The Subu. Knowing Rudis could strike the scalp-taker from behind at any time kept me aquiver.

We trudged over the web-strewn plains under the inky cloud mass that remained directly overhead, no matter how far we walked. The Red Lady might have her black vapor, but she couldn't do much against a castle brimming with defenders. When the Northem militia of villagers, farmers, and tradesmen took up arms alongside the castle's garrison and remaining Knights of the Order of Man, nearly two thousand fighters could take to the ramparts or to the field. Fifty Raka could be destroyed in one charge of mounted knights or one volley of arrows. That the thing marched straight toward Northem without a trace of worry distressed me.

Pulumbonk walked beside me. "Lada kissed me before we left. Tis painful to think another might never warm me."

The image of my sister's kissing someone only sickened me for a moment, as it led to the memory of Remi's kiss. "Kissing is a grand and terrible business."

Pulumbonk gazed beyond the horizon. "The fire adept who trained me in Haramdum said women controlled fire more surely, because they were made of it."

I chuckled, "An uneducated observation but not untrue."

"Jonne, what do you think will happen to the world in the coming years?"

"I can't imagine a blood-soaked, eldritch being can bring much good."

"I figure our chances of even seeing the future are thin, yet...I must wonder: could I give up wise Unathar to serve bloodthirsty Askerat?"

"Stay in the north and believe what you wish."

"What if the Red Lady helps the emperor to cross Lake Rado?"

"What if the Red Lady destroys Draman and all of his followers?"

"But what if she doesn't?" The man was more negative than I.

"For all the help Unathar has given you, I'd question his existence."

"Unathar is a benevolent god and would accept you, if you let him."

His remark offended my notion of self-accountability. "Gods aren't in play here. The potential of the blood book is. Will it work alone or enlist those who can channel magicka? I think of the modicum of power Remi could summon when casting her wards multiplied many times."

Pulumbonk weighed the notion. "Learning to harness such power has its appeal…and its terrors."

"Yet, what frightens us most is the loss of women who may or may not care for us."

Pulumbonk's head shook slowly. "I've always had a taste for fine things. I left my lovely boots in my locker at The Six Fingers, you know. My filigreed doublet, as well. I would be happy to wear forever a pauper's rags, if I could be with Lada."

How far would I go to be with Remi? I cursed myself for thinking again, what would Ryckerd do?

Night had settled fully as we talked, although Gela gifted us with a gibbous moon that lightened the landscape ahead and behind us, just not under the inky layer. The breeze continued but carried no white webs, so the ground stretched as a sea of serrated grass blades in silhouette. Glancing back, I could see only one of the black spires of Dunkelgrau poking above the horizon. I had expected the sight to reassure me that I had survived the horrors of the underground.

The herbalist kept his ugly mutterings to a minimum, while we marched, and the fearful whining of the cook had been forever snuffed. The Subu and Rudis said nothing. Zir rhapsodized about a paradise of shallow river waterfalls flowing into a pool ringed with giant trees near his home in Ralkswald. The clinker groaned intermittently from the pain in his back. Only Pulumbonk and I carried on a conversation. The others must have thought us weak baby boys needing the care of women. Or, mayhap, they were yearning for the same.

I found myself gazing upon the lovely shape of the Red Lady, her skin no longer blood red but the same blue gray we all shared in twilight. In the dark of The Well, The Subu had suggested the absence of light could open the mind to possibilities. That black evening, I could, for an instant, believe the female shape to actually be Remi and that, one day, I might come to know her in the glow of lumen light on the soft bed in my chamber.

The Red Lady abruptly stopped, sat, and disappeared among the gray bodies of its cohort. We humans watched from twenty paces to its right. Presently, all of the Raka lay down, invisible in the grass, leaving the thing exposed, hands folded in its lap.

The herbalist grumbled, “Flog me, what’s it doing now?”

The Subu, Rudis, and Zir scanned the horizons. Pulumbonk, the clinker, and I focused on the thing.

Presently, Zir said, “Setting an ambush you think?”

Rudis replied, “The hiding, yes. It stinks of ambush.”

The herbalist gaped incredulously and swept his arm over the empty plains. “An ambush for whom?”

The Subu watched forward. “For whatever’s out there.”

Pulumbonk’s patience ran brittle. “What do we do? Just sit here? I have…I have no more powder, only my sword.”

“Perhaps the Ruyk come again?” asked the clinker.

“Could it be jabber rats the thing is detecting?” The herbalist asked.

Pulumbonk offered, “Who knows what benighted things live in a place like this?”

“Reason would suggest a force from Northem has caught its attention,” I said.

“What reason?” asked the herbalist. “Tis way soon for the relief column, if one comes.”

“Then where does reason lead you?”

“Brillix’s group?”

I nodded. “Could be. But do four or five men constitute a threat to the…to it?”

The Subu said, “Brillix’s brain might be a bit stiff in its cradle, but it’s a practical brain. If he’s got horses, he’s long gone. No horses, and he’s gonna keep moving.”

“What if he’s got wounded?” asked the herbalist.

The Subu kept his eyes on the horizon. “Badly wounded men do na’ make it far.”

Not all of us heard it, but I couldn’t mistake the three short blasts of a horn in the distance.

The Subu threw up his hand. “Eyes high! To the south.”

Three long blasts answered the other.

“Tis the Friend’s Greeting,” I said, excited at the implication.

All of us stood, but only those of Northem knew the horn signal.

Zir the Archer asked, “What’s it mean?”

The Subu and Rudis turned to me.

“Brillix and his survivors must not be far ahead, and they’ve met friends coming from the south.”

The herbalist’s eyes opened as if he’d seen a mountain of gold. “If they’re friends, they can only be Northmen!”

"Stands to reason," said the clinker, ready to flee, "but I'll believe it when I see it."

The Subu held up a hand. "Don't rabbit off just yet. I plan to stay with the Red Lady, till I see what we're up against."

Rudis, in a move I didn't think possible for a heavily armored man, lunged three paces and bashed The Subu in the face with his shield. The scalp-taker fought to remain standing, eyes blinking away blood and blurs. Rudis, sword not yet drawn, ripped the battleaxe from his opponent's hand and whirled it into the scrub. Then his heavy, straight sword sung from its metal-ringed scabbard. The Subu stumbled backwards, finding his orientation.

"You will protect this thing not!" Rudis raised his sword and advanced.

"No, Rudis!" I wasn't sure if I were protecting The Subu or trying to keep our small band from becoming smaller.

The shout caused Rudis to hesitate long enough for The Subu to pull two blades sheathed at the small of his back, a short, curved sword for slashing in his right hand, a sturdy dirk for stabbing in his left. Rudis advanced aggressively, his shield before him and parallel to the ground to deny The Subu an easy rush. He held his sword high and ready to hack. The Subu surprised us by dropping his slashing sword and diving under the shield for the slower man's ankles, easily missing the sword swing meant for his body. He hugged Rudis's legs together. When the armored warrior toppled to his back, The Subu drove the dirk into his unprotected groin. Half of everyone alive could've heard Rudis's scream. The Subu wasted no time straddling the man and finishing him with a merciful stroke. Rudis's arms flopped to his side without a quiver.

By the time The Subu wiped his blade on a tuft of grass, we had turned our attention from him to the figure sprinting toward the horn calls.

Zir pointed. "The herbalist!"

The clinker prepared to run. "We should go with him."

Pulumbonk glanced from The Subu to me and back.

I was torn.

The Subu swept his dirk before him. "Go, if ya will."

My body answered before my brain did. I lurched forward with Pulumbonk. My foot didn't land its first step when The Subu said, "Not ye," and I went into an awkward half run. My gear threw my balance, and down I went with a crunch into the scrub grass.

"Yer gonna stay, word man. Who else gonna witness The Subu's deeds this day?"

I realized how close Pulumbonk and I had become, when his face melted in anguish, and I felt it in myself.

"Sorry, Jonne. But Lada...." He turned and ran.

I gawked at The Subu. "Those are my people. We'll be safe with them."

"Will we?" he said and began searching the grass. "Help find me blade."

"But you beat the Raka on the causeway. With the Northmen, you can—"

"We had the advantage, and the Red Lady did na' control them. Ah!" He pulled his long-hafted battleaxe from the grass. His right hand caressed the leather-wrapped wood. "Magic is real, young'n. Once ye've tasted the power, ye get a hunger for it." He turned to the Red Lady still cross-legged and motionless. "I'll wager that thing sets a bountiful table."

I sank to a squat with him. "What do we do?"

"Wait for fortune to tell us." He grinned. "Did you see The Subu defeat Rudis?"

"Of...of course."

"Write it just as ye saw it."

I hadn't identified that as a priority. We went to our knees and watched the horizon, or at least I did.

The Subu's gaze angled skyward. "The Red Lady's callin' fer help, I wager."

The thick inky cloud above us was dissipating into ten smoky fingers that probed to the east, west, and north.

"Why are we not running south? Seriously."

I can't say I'd seen worry cross The Subu's face, until that moment. He called to the Red Lady. "Yo! Share yer powers with me, and we'll stand with ya." After a moment, he added. "Do ya hear me?"

When it didn't respond, I said, "Why would it share anything with us?"

The Subu shrugged. "Did na' hurt to ask." He took a deep breath. "Right then, we go south."

I sprung up.

"Save yer energy, or ye'll drop after thirty paces."

He set our pace at a fast walk. The Red Lady didn't hurl Raka at us or try to entwine us in vines or vapor, but our flight didn't go unhampered. We tried to find bare spots to walk on, but the scrub was widespread, knee-high, and tangled. The vining roots of hawk sage and the toothy blades of diamond grass clung to our ankles and sawed at our boots. Light raindrops pinged the top of my helmet.

"There's leper's luck fer ya," The Subu cursed. "Wet things won' burn so easy, when I hit 'em."

"Your Red Lady's magicka will be stronger."

A drizzle pattered around us, a natural one, I supposed, as the inky cloud had completely dispersed into the ten wispy fingers, now independent and moving away. The filmy clouds above it seemed benign.

"Me lady? Yer lady."

"You're the one who wanted to follow her."

"Yer the one who wants to put the sausage to her."

"Not to the Red Lady...and that's not all I want to do to Remi. Wait, I don't want to 'do' anything to her."

"Nekkid, word man, you wanna be with her nekkid, or yer made wrong."

"I don't want to talk about this."

"Philosophy, then? Finkleshit's Treatise on Stupid Stuff, perhaps? Or ye can hold forth on how noble flies be."

"What? How do you know about that?"

"The Subu has ears."

My breathing came less easily. "You were eavesdropping on my conversation with Brillix...in the pavilion...however many days ago that was."

"The Subu has ears."

"I'm done with...this conversation."

"Ye really think we folk who ain' from the castle are as low-born as flies?"

"I didn't say that."

"Ye did."

"I didn't."

"Ye called me a fly."

Was he trying to pick a fight?

He continued. "Is all right by me. Flies are fast and clever and do what's needed to survive."

I had no breath to reply.

His hand sliced toward the southwest. "We flies gonna buzz that way, so we don' get caught between two swatters."

"No," I wheezed. "Straight. They're friends ahead."

"Ye tell me that when they shoot arrows at we two fellas runnin' right toward them from the shadows."

I shook my head at his reasoning, but he knew I'd do whatever he did. With a mighty gout of spiritual pain, I divested myself of the flagon of ale, and toward the southwest we stumbled. He slowed to shrug out of his backpack and let it drop to the ground. The duffel of purple rocks remained over his shoulder. I started to shrug off my own backpack.

"Nay ye don'. Yer carrying food fer the both of us now."

I didn't ask why he didn't drop the rocks, but I did take a moment to unroll my cloak and cast it over shoulders and backpack. The evening grew darker, and the view south blurred with rain. I thought my senses were teasing me, until I stopped and felt it again. The ground trembled.

The Subu crouched. "Yer kin are near."

To underscore his words, a horn call of two short blasts followed by one short and one long. PAH PAH, PAH PAAAH!

The Subu asked, "What's it mean?"

"Battle line."

"Brillix must'a warned 'em what's waiting."

"See?" I asked. "The Northmen didn't shoot them with arrows."

We both leapt when lightning branched across the mid-distance. Not far to the southeast, it reflected off the spearpoints and helmets of men in three ranks, horses in front, footmen behind. They became a blob of moving dark, once the lightning faded.

I pointed, as if The Subu couldn't see them himself. "Good Gela, there they are!"

The Subu shrunk. "They've a flogging army! How'd they get here so soon?"

Even if Aethelbert the scout had made it back to Northem in one day, a force this size would need at least a day to organize and two or more to get through the Cheeky Nobs. Had we been in the timeless dark of Dunkelgrau for four days? I would've guessed three.

Another streak of lightening brought more details and a surprise. Fifty knights and men at arms rode abreast in the front, lances high. Following them was a rank of about fifty men wielding halberds, glaives, and bill hooks. In the rank behind them marched archers with crossbows and composite bows, the bowstrings of the latter would be less effective wet. Eight lieutenant banners of varying colors bobbed among the footmen. Two lieutenant banners waggled at either end of the cavalry rank, both in the red and white of the Order of Man. A gonfalon standing taller from the center displayed the commander's blazon of a black, cat's paw inside a ring of red fire.

I shivered, as if struck by the lightning above. "Ryckerd!"

Lexica XVIII

Excitement yanked me from my knees to a high squat, the desultory rain still pinging my helmet. I only hesitated because The Subu didn't rise with me. "Why tarry?"

"I ain' in no hurry to get shot." His gaze flashed from me to the dark ranks of fighting men two hundred paces away.

"You'll be safe with me."

His hand seized my booted ankle.

I twisted free. "You're not one of the conspirators, but...Subu, I'm going to my people."

I headed for the Northmen, fighting through the hawk sage and diamond grass. I didn't look back at The Subu for fear my kinsmen would vanish if I glanced away. Lightning reconfirmed their existence by finding steel helmets and lance points. Evidently, one of the ships had rescued Ryckerd from the Tulian fanatics. I felt small for not holding more hope for him. History was filled with heroes and villains guided by the wind of good fortune, but I didn't expect it to blow beyond the pages of the past. Yet, in this world of Raka and blood books, real misery and real death, it had carried my brother to me.

The Subu had taken us farther to the right of the advancing Northmen than I had guessed, so I approached them on their flank, instead of face-on. They headed straight for where I last saw the Red Lady and might leave me behind if I didn't hurry. Off of my shoulders slid my backpack, which brought a welcome spring to my legs.

The next lightning illuminated the coats-of-arms for the wealthy personages who sponsored militia groups. Sponsors supplied training and weapons for the men in their formation, whether they be tradesmen, craftsmen, hunters or the like. The lead farmer, for example, had a bright green sickle and a sheaf of golden wheat for heraldry, and each man he sponsored wore that symbol and color.

My arms flailed above me. "Yo, friends. Tis Jonne the Booker."

"And The Subu!" called a voice behind me.

The sinewy man with his bag of purple rocks and big axe stopped alongside me. Wide-eyes and black blades pivoted toward us. Coincidentally to my shout, a horn blast brought a halt to the three ranks. Aerwart, a wealthy shoom rancher, now a lieutenant surrounded by men wearing yellow-and-brown livery with curled shoom-tailed blazons, threw out a gauntleted hand.

"Hold there!" Aerwart had a fist of a chin draped with a heavy mustache.

Crossbows from the third rank aimed my way. The Subu didn't wait for the lightning to cast light on us and summoned the fire of his axe. We stood with hands raised within its red glow, a visored soldier and a frightening wild man with a flaming axe wearing no livery to identify them.

"Who comes?" Aerwart called.

I tilted my helmet back on my head. "Tis—"

"Jonne the Booker?"

"Yes," said one of Aerwart's halberd men. "I know that cake-eating face."

Another piped up. "Tis Blossom!"

Aerwart waved us toward him. "Come on, at the quick."

We hustled the twenty paces to him. All eyes followed the glowing axe head. Aerwart motioned us to follow, as he pricked his horse toward the front of the line. The gathering smelled of warm horse flesh and fear sweat.

As we passed the crossbowmen, The Subu grinned his scary grin. "Call me friend here 'Blossom' again, and ye'll have to march on one leg."

"No, Subu, really, I...." I didn't finish because the damage was done. I appeared too weak to stand up for myself, and mayhap, I still was.

"Lance Master," Aerwart called. "See who comes!"

Within moments, I stood red-faced and huffing below my bear of a brother, one white plume flanked by two red ones denoting his rank as Lance Master. "Ryckerd!"

Of all people, it was Pulumbonk who held Ryckerd's attention. The luminast stood on the other side of my brother's destrier, watching the other direction. Both faces turned to me, Pulumbonk's in delight, Ryckerd's in amusement.

"So there you are." His helm resting on his saddle pommel, his almost-smile nestled in his beard, and his deep brown eyes on me, he was impossibly but inarguably my brother, alive and close enough to touch. Before my excitement came to full flush, he addressed me as if I were just any other spy in from the field. "Tell me of this Red Lady."

The Subu and I gawked, I because my brother showed no joy in our reunion, and The Subu because nobody saw his glowing axe for the first time without commenting.

Ryckerd's squire, recognizable by the blade-like metal wings on his helmet, brought his horse close to Pulumbonk and handed down a satchel.

Ryckerd addressed the luminast. "So none of your wares are any good because of the rain?"

"The light sticks won't last but a few seconds in sodden grass. My geode lantern can highlight but a small bit of ground ahead of you."

"And you can't ride a horse. You're seeming less useful to me." Ryckerd scanned the dark before him. "Prepare a light stick and stay close." He turned back to me. "He says you speak with the thing. What dangers does it present?"

A "good to see you, Jonne" would've been nice. "Extreme."

"Details, Jonne, not opinion."

Pulumbonk leapt in. "She summons things."

"It." I corrected. "It was a book, and I believe it still is, a book with an agenda. It—"

"How will it fight? How do I fight it?"

Three horsemen trotted to a stop in front of us, a fresh blueskin scout, a man-at-arms, and Brillix, the white and red plume of Lance Captain bobbing above him. He surprised me with a smile. To Ryckerd he said, "When we have the thing in sight, we'll sound one long horn call for you to hold. Three short, you attack."

"Good," Ryckerd said. "May fortune ride with you, brother."

Ryckerd's true brothers were those he trained with. The trio wheeled their mounts and cantered off, Brillix throwing another smile to me over his shoulder. It seemed a genuine smile among comrades, not the chiding kind he usually gave me.

I said to my brother, "You're attacking? We should withdraw to Northem—"

He held up an armored hand and addressed Pulumbonk. "Lash that light stick to the end of a spear and put Jonne's helmet above it to shed rain. You'll precede us by twenty paces."

My hand rose protectively to my helmet.

Pulumbonk gawked at Ryckerd, but my brother's expression was unyielding. "I know of the conspiracy, luminast. You're getting off easily."

"Ryckerd," the name came out more of a shout than I intended. "Listen to me, for once. This rain, its moisture will be a boon to the thing."

"Tis certainly no boon to us," he said. "But we have the numbers." His eyes fell on The Subu's axe and the grinning fox holding it. "What trickery is that?"

"No trickery," I said. "Magic."

Ryckerd's brow rose. "This from you?" When his squire chortled, Ryckerd silenced him with a wave. "Magic is your true assessment, Jonne?"

"It is. The book wields glamours, as well, ones we can't underestimate."

"All the more reason to kill it now."

"Good luck with that," The Subu said, "or are yer weapons eldritch, too?"

"You," Ryckerd jerked his head toward the rear, "join the second rank, on the wing where you can wield that weapon." To me, "You join the wagons. They'll be along soon."

"I can fight."

"Your job is to survive and witness." When I didn't move, he added, "Very well, stay in the center of the archers' line and away from contact."

I almost asked if he knew about Lada's part in the conspiracy but .... "Good to see you well, Ryckerd."

He swept his arm toward the rear. "No heroics. Stay alive."

Part of me was glad to be safely tucked away. Another part felt it wanted to prove Ryckerd's little brother could do more than slice cakes. I handed my helmet to Pulumbonk who looked like a man condemned. "Good luck out there."

"Please pass my love to Lada, if—"

"I will." I turned to leave the front line of horsemen.

"Wait," The Subu said. "Has nobody told the big man about the green glow?"

Pulumbonk looked to me. I looked to Brillix. Brillix looked to Ryckerd.

Brillix, for the first time in my experience, sounded halting. "Yes, sir, there...there is a green glow around some creatures we encountered, but we don't understand its meaning."

I raised my hand. "But we do. I do." I had Ryckerd's full attention. "Things enchanted by the thing emit the green glow. You'll have no trouble seeing them in the dark."

Ryckerd considered for a moment. "If we can see them, we can strike them."

"But," asked The Subu, "can ye kill 'em? The Red Lady used to be yer Remi girl, and she threw a ward na' even me axe could break."

Ryckerd said, "Keep that talk to yourself. That thing is not getting past us tonight."

The Subu took me by the arm. "Back we go, Jonne Booker, like good little boys."

I walked backwards, eyes on Ryckerd. "I would've told you of the green glow."

His attention had shifted to Pulumbonk who picked his way into the dark scrub ahead, holding the spear with the light stick lashed to its top, as though it were a commander's banner. My helmet wobbled on the spear point doing little to shield the light stick from the rain and zero good protecting my head from whatever else might fall that night.

Ryckerd called to him. "Keep walking."

I began to call again, but The Subu tugged me along. "Yer brother's got a mind full of war now."

We cut through the rank of horsemen, who regarded us as if we were stray dogs, and then we angled right, crunched through the scrub to the end of the rank of foot soldiers and halted. The Subu planted the butt of his axe and waited for what came next.

The halberd man at the end of the rank looked the scalp-taker up and down. "I'm the wing man for this line. Find another place."

The Subu sidled one step to the left. "How's that?"

The soldier, the cobbler's eldest son, steamed. "Who in the gray lands of—"

I raised my hand. "No cause for offense. Tis by Ryckerd's order."

The man glared. The Subu grinned. The man turned to the front grumbling, "I don't like strangers on my flank."

I said, "You'll be happy to have his axe nearby, I promise you," and then started for the third rank to lose myself amidst the archers.

"Don' ya go too far, word man," said The Subu. "Stand there toward the end of them archers where ye can see The Subu."

I took a spot between two crossbowmen, men my age who were horse grooms full time, and soldiers only on nights like tonight. One chuckled in surprise. "Blossom? Take your gloomy mug elsewhere. We're fighting men here."

"I'm Librast In Situ now, if you don't recall."

Both men wrinkled, as if regarding a spoiled cabbage.

One said, "It speaks!"

The chuckler said, "Shame about your sister. She could stand near me anytime."

Three short horn blasts called from the darkness near where we'd left the Red Lady. Brillix must've been in view of the thing. Ryckerd's cornifer answered with the call to advance. Moments later, Pulumbonk's light stick flared into a tiny sun atop the spear, my helmet a black speck above it. Light spread over a swath of ground, and the little army started forward, the mounted men moving as one, steady rank. The under-trained rear ranks moved unevenly, a bulge of quick soldiers here, a sag of slower soldiers there, like two lengths of string being pushed forward sideways. The lieutenants did their best to align the ranks, but all that accomplished was keeping the strings from bunching into knots.

The horsemen presented a reassuringly solid wall. As all beasts journeying to Dunkelgrau, each horse had its fetlocks bound with elum-soaked cloth to keep the hawk sage and diamond grass from harming them. I worried they yet might trip while running through some of the thicker clumps, but I assumed Ryckerd had weighed the risks. I focused on keeping myself from doing the same.

The Subu didn't march as the others. He assumed an amble the tunnels of Dunkelgrau didn't allow. His wide shoulders wagged right and left, like the head of a flower on a tight stem. From behind, his fur-wrapped helmet, leggings, and cuirass made him seem something of the soil. The eldritch axe had yet to flame up, but I was hot to see what the man could do in a pitched battle with such a weapon. I planned to do little more than watch and stay out of the way of sharp things. Without Ryckerd's watching, my desire to play warrior had receded.

With the next blast of the horn, interesting things began to cascade.

A blob of pale green rose from the scrub in the distance, where The Subu and I had been just a half-hour ago. The rain ceased. Another green cloud appeared in the eastern sky, growing larger. A third appeared in the western sky. Yet another bloomed at ground level on the southwest horizon. Whatever the Red Lady had summoned was answering.

Ahead of me, materializing from the shadows, three riders reined in their mounts and joined the front rank of horsemen. The red and white plumes on the central figure denoted Brillix.

"Ryckerd!" I shouted to warn him, but his cornifer sounded the "advance quick" call.

The earth under my boots shuddered as the weight of fifty horses shifted from trot to canter. The giant shapes of man and mount pulled away, grew smaller.

Lieutenant Aerwart, fist-chin and droopy mustache hidden behind his visor, rode in front of The Subu's rank of footmen. He signaled his line of men forward by raising his lance over his head. Its ruff of red cords under the blade, now blackish in the twilight, signified a foot commander's rank. The lieutenant of archers, also mounted and with a red-ruffed halberd, took the cue and ordered us to, "Maintain pace!" which was a purposeful walk, at the moment.

Ryckerd's cornifer blew one long note and, even as the radiance of Pulumbonk's light stick waned to a sputtering point of light ahead of us, the dark rank of horsemen farther on broke into their charge. The soles of my boots vibrated. The two moons did what they could to aid the riders, but the clouds, though thinner, sucked much of their light.

My ears told me what my eyes could not. A sudden shriek of Raka Infante and a moist sound like drumbeats on flesh marked the moment of impact. No more than three heartbeats passed before silence resettled. The horses had passed through the little creatures and would be wheeling to reengage.

The cornifer for the footman, his horn deeper in tone, sounded the double-quick, and our two uneven lines lurched into a trot. Our armor chunk-chunked with every step, a metal drumbeat that echoed the cadence of our hearts.

My eyes flitted over the firmament, from one cloud of pale green to another. Details became clearer as they neared. I expected saffa bats, but the approaching silhouettes suggested larger creatures with wide wing spans and tiny bodies. The ground-level cloud hadn't come close enough for me to see anything but a nimbus of green. If we didn't vanquish the Red Lady before the others converged, we were in trouble.

"Remi, I'm sorry," I groaned to myself.

I drew a knife from my bandolier. If the Red Lady attacked me, I didn't think I could make myself harm it, but combat behavior, as I was learning, wasn't something one planned.

May fortune stop my hand from dealing the killing blow.

A break in the clouds allowed moonlight to flood the plain. Ryckerd and his mounted men had turned for another attack, but instead of riding back into the Raka, they seemed stuck in place, the movements of their horses spastic. I couldn't dwell long on the mystery, for my feet snagged in particularly recalcitrant hawk sage, and I slammed forward into the ground, knife lost in the dark scrub.

Cries of alarm sang from both lines of footmen, as most tripped along with me, even The Subu. I tried kicking free, but the plants grew tighter. With my poniard, I sawed and hacked, until I could regain my feet. As soon as I did, more plants, or mayhap their roots, twined around my ankles and held fast. The ground all around had come to life.

For the Red Lady to be able to control the Raka, the plants, and the approaching things, a huge amount of power and concentration would be required. At least, that's how my human brain assessed the situation. I had to remember, the Red Lady was no lady but a book, and I had no good idea of how a book could control anything. If it required magicka to perform its tricks and moisture provided a conduit for magicka, this night was, as I feared, its ally and not ours.

Lieutenant Aerwart barked something from The Subu's line. Our own lieutenant, the commander of archers, relayed the order. "Stand fast! Prepare your weapons!"

All of us were preoccupied with freeing our feet, so he swatted the nearest archer with his baton and repeated the order to prepare. The men responded. Arrows were nocked, bolts seated. I continued sawing at roots and ripping up what I could, until I formed a clear patch around my feet.

The crossbowman who had disparaged me and proclaimed his lust for Lada, tapped me on the shoulder. "Do mine!"

I wish I had said something akin to, "I should let you die where you stand," but I went to work clearing the area around him and his friend on the other side of me. The more of us free to move, the better.

The commander of archers saw me. "Keep at it, bashful Blossom, and earn the right to stand with us."

Again, I found myself happy to have something to do other than wait in dread. I had to clear most of the area one pace around the man to prevent the twining things to find their way back to his ankles, and, even in the cool of evening, I began to sweat. My sword-swinging muscles were better attuned than in many a month, but my weed-hacking ones were coming up wanting.

Before going to the next man, I looked to the north. Horses struggled in place and sent up a great complaint, clearly audible from such a distance. The silhouettes of armed riders milled about, occasionally a sword arm rose and fell. Ryckerd's troops must be amidst the Raka who had survived the charge.

The green clouds from east and west had come closer, alarmingly so. They were, in fact, saffa bats, tens of thousands of them. They were providing wings for a legion of new Raka, each one hanging from a mass of bats acting as its wings. There were hundreds of Raka armed and beginning to shriek their war cry, a hideous sound a human baby might make if on fire. The nimbus to the north had yet to reveal its contents, but it was wide enough to suggest a hundred or more something-elses heading for the Red Lady's position.

The commander of archers pointed high to the west. "Section one, action there!" He gave the same order to section two, but to the east.

The men near me held crossbows at the ready but gaped so broadly, I wasn't sure they'd remember to use them.

Lada's fancier croaked, "What are those flogging things?"

My revenge on him was to withhold an explanation. Let him wonder. Let him quake. I had. Back on my hands and knees, I hacked and ripped at more writhing plant matter, sensing that any moment, something could land on me.

The commander of archers bellowed at me. "Leave them be! They can't flee with their feet bound."

What a horrifying splash of reality that their leaders didn't believe in these men. I stayed on all fours, listening to the men mutter about doom or call for their mothers. Legs trembled visibly. The man nearest me said nothing, but the wet darkness spreading along the thighs of his red trousers spoke volumes.

The commander shouted, "Fire! Fire, you poltroons!"

I sprung to my feet and saw the face of the man in the wet trousers. Eyes as big as great ruyk eggs, mouth slack, composite bow hanging at his side, he looked the way I must have at the Battle of the Cheeky Nobs. The first of the airborne Raka were nearly above us.

I cuffed the man on the shoulder. His fingers dropped their arrow but his eyes leapt to me. "Don't think, just listen," I explained, drawing an arrow tailed with a beautiful cerulean blue feather from the quiver at his side. "Take this." He did. "Nock your bow." He nodded vigorously while bringing the arrow's notch to the bowstring and laying the arrow's shaft over his thumb.

The wave of bats swept down to within fifteen spans of the ground, the Raka dead-eyed and red mouthed and eager to drop into the fray. One chubby one swinging what looked like Faellic red glass on the end of a vine caught my eye.

"There!" I pointed. "Aim for that fat belly."

He raised his bow and drew the string to his ear.

A Raka's eyes had no pupils, so knowing where they were looking posed doubts. This one swept in our direction. Out swished my sword. The archer's arm trembled under the tension of his bow. Missiles leapt into the air around me, some into targets, most into nothing.

"Shoot now!" I yelled.

The man's bowstring twanged, and the arrow streaked to just above the Raka to one of the bats carrying it. The mass of bats never shuddered, and released its passenger eight paces away. Momentum carried the Raka through the air onto the archer. The baby-like thing shrieked in something like ecstasy, as it whirled the sharp glass across the archer's throat. At least I can write that he died fighting.

The Raka hit the ground and rolled into my shins. I dispatched it with a downward thrust and then ducked, for the air was awhirl with black wings and red mouths. Most of the attackers were too high to strike with my sword. Being little good with a bow, I watched for Raka on the ground and not too distant. I cut down one trying to get to the rear of Lada's admirer. Another perched on the back of a nearby bowman and ripped at the man's face. I hammered his head with the pommel of my sword and finished him as fell to the ground stunned.

As soon as I recovered, I saw another Raka holding a sharpened sliver of metal like a sword. Its bats released it a few paces away, and it hurtled right for my face, weapon raised. My sword and free hand rose instinctively to block. A crossbow bolt suddenly sprouted from its side and the muscled gray thing spun off trajectory into my shoulder, spinning me to my knees.

Lada's admirer hooked his crossbow's string onto a device on his belt, put his toe into the stirrup at the nose of the bow, and then stood up straight while stepping down, using his whole body to draw the string back to its firing position. "Defend me while I reload!"

I stood back to back with him, scanning this direction and then that. Down the line, where most of the archers were still immobile because of the plants, a gray ball of five or six Raka covered three men whom they'd knocked to the ground. One was very much alive and stuck fast. When the gray ball and its compliment of dripping mouths crawled over him, his endless scream slashed part of me open, and all the bookish notions of heroic battle spilled, never to be recovered.

The crossbowman, as impolite as he might have been, proved a skilled shot. He missed sometimes, but when he hit his mark, the results were spectacular. Raka that had been struck dropped their weapons and clutched at their wounds or plummeted as inert bombs into the ground or went into such spasms as to throw their bat couriers off course.

I finished the wounded ones, slashed at bats that came too close, and did my best to free the feet of other archers at every break in the action. The fight to survive kept me from wondering if Ryckerd and his men were having any success.

While the Raka seemed without number, our two ranks dwindled after every wave of attackers. Those of us in the archer rank who could, tried to join the line of footmen. More heavily armored and armed for close combat, they fared better against the Raka and fell less frequently, but inevitability would catch them. I say "them" because, in the chaos, it never occurred to me that I might fall. "They" were the victims. When my time came, I wouldn't need to worry about the grammar.

Mayhap the Red Lady's power had stretched thin, for the writhing scrub at our ankles became less tenacious. The Subu used his freedom of movement to seek out targets, instead of providing one of himself. The men murmured when he first invoked the fire from his blade. They cheered when he began etching fiery arcs in the air, causing bats and Raka to explode into flames, and wheel away screaming. I thought him oblivious of his surroundings. When a nearby glaive man went to his knees under the weight of three landing Raka, The Subu swept them away and jerked the man to his feet.

Four men near me fell to heavy wounds in the next few moments. Lieutenant Aerwart, now afoot and fighting almost as energetically as The Subu, tried to swat the survivors of both ranks into a circle, but many were still rooted, some too wounded to move, others simply couldn't hear or see him through the storm of wings and blades.

I thought of the beacon of reason that was Northem snuffed by an onslaught of magic, should the Red Lady, guts filled with the arcana of the Anaxagorum, prevail over us and find disciples across the land. If we librasts survived, we would have to rewrite the books to reflect a new reality, one in which strong minds and good intentions would not be enough to maintain a righteous age for humankind. Of course, such thoughts were at the back of my mind, for in the forefront were my sword, my companions, and the knowledge that mortal muscle could not sustain.

That wave, the third wave of saffa bats and Raka, thinned around us. One breath of relief was all we were granted, before the ground shuddered. I turned tiredly to see a herd of great ruyks, emitting a green glow, charging at us from the south. They had no riders, but I'd seen what their beaks and fore talons could do to a man at the Battle of the Cheeky Nobs. Aerwart must have seen them, for he arrayed eleven men with pole arms into a line between us and the oncoming herd. Other men bunched up behind them or stayed, stunned and stupid, in groups of twos and threes. Charging flesh fared badly when meeting a line of resolute spears and halberds, but when the chargers numbered over a hundred and the defenders barely more than fifty, resolve could be crushed.

I hardly registered the impact of the beasts, although there was a great crash of feathered heads against metal bodies, of talon and tooth on steel. My eyes had glued to The Subu who stood alone twenty paces from the end of our line. He was wiping blood from his eyes when he saw the beasts coming at him. The Subu might someday know death, but he never knew panic. Feet planted wide, he held the eldritch axe upright before him with both hands.

Arcane words rattled from his throat. "Addra, forenza, krak, e-methoom!"

The butt of his battleaxe hammered the ground, and a wave of red turbulence twenty paces wide rushed before him. The great ruyk in his way were swept away in a bluster of flailing legs and whipping tails, like so many puppies before an ocean wave. The force of the magical discharge catapulted The Subu back several paces where he bounced onto the soil.

I flew to his side. He allowed me to help him to his feet, then left to search the scrub for his axe.

"No time!" I seized his fur cape. He saw how vulnerable we were by ourselves, so we tumbled back to the knot of struggling men centered around Lieutenant Aerwart. The great ruyk not stopped by their spears or by The Subu's energy blast had surged past to engulf the islands of isolated soldiers. They would soon turn and surround us.

I needed to learn those men's names.

The great ruyks relentlessly battered Aerwart's line of eleven men. The Subu, sword and curved knife drawn, and a handful of other footmen deployed to the wings to form a semi-circle to stop the beasts from slipping around our flanks. The four archers protected by them frantically sought targets, fired, and reloaded.

Like them, I held one of my remaining throwing knives but feared loosing it into one of my own, as friendly bodies jerked to and fro to the rhythm of the fight. Lieutenant Aerwart's exhortations provided a constant point of reference for men locked into worlds existing of only them and their assailants.

The beak of a great ruyk found a defender's neck, lifted him, and thrashed his body back and forth, disrupting the whole line. Another man fell to his knees and was crushed backwards by the weight of his attacker. I didn't need to be a veteran to know we were crumbling and soon to be on our backs being ripped to pieces.

Lada's admirer, one eye swollen shut, the other crazy wide, shouted at me. "You brought this on us!"

A great ruyk collapsing from a massive halberd blow to its neck, fell into the crossbowman who then fell into me. My legs were braced in the right direction to keep us from falling. Instead of showing gratitude, he jerked away from me, as though I were another enemy. The crossbowman threw down his weapon and bolted for the south. After five steps, he tumbled to the ground screaming. A wounded Raka in the grass had thrust a spear into his thigh, and began dragging itself closer to finish him. I had my knife ready and a clear shot, so the blade twirled and sunk deeply into the thing's back. Its arms cocked back trying to reach the blade, but the exertion exhausted it, and into the grass it sunk.

Lada's admirer drew himself into a ball and wept. Seeing the great ruyks behind us with dripping beaks and eyes searching for new prey, and a dark swath across the western sky from where a fourth wave of bats and Raka approached, I felt like giving up, as well. Order had disintegrated. The last of the footmen and archers were on their knees trying to hold back talons and teeth. Aerwart lay on his side, clasping his neck. The Subu had disappeared. I trotted to the downed Raka and retrieved my knife, as I had been trained to do.

Great ruyks were fewer in number, but those still moving were energetically tearing at the bodies of the fallen. The fourth wave of bats and Raka drew between us and the moons. I lay face first in the scrub, hands over my head. Running would make me a target.

I recalled the utter blackness in the chamber of The Well, and wondered if that's what awaited me in the next moments. Pulumbonk was out there somewhere, but I doubted Unathar was anywhere near to help. The Subu might have been dragged off, which horrified me. If he could become great ruyk food, how could I not?

I heard Raka shrieking as they did when they were about to drop on a victim. More frightening was the rumble gaining urgency under me. The ground quaked with more and more intensity, until my teeth rattled. More great ruyks to pick our bones? Then I heard human war cries.

I rolled over. The sky over me had grown dark with descending bats and Raka, but the sight that astonished me were the horses. They seemed to be everywhere. On the horses were men in armor, wheeling and hacking and leaning from their mounts to help the footmen. Bouncing atop one of their helmets were one white plume flanked by two red.

Ryckerd's voice bellowed, "Cast now!"

As if the ground I lay on suddenly coughed, a wave of energy exploded into a dome around us, sending out a spray of drops from the sodden scrub. All flying things caught by it were either bounced out of view or splattered in mid-air. Raka landing on the dome clawed at it for traction but slid to the ground. Knights of the Order of Man, surcoats spattered with blood and dirt, along with their mounted men-at-arms, trampled or speared everyone of them within reach.

I can't say how long it went on, but I know I grinned through the entirety of it. Then, at the end of that measureless moment, the Raka were gone, the sky was clear of bats, and men half lit by the moons cheered.

I stumbled toward Ryckerd who sat his horse with the majesty of a victorious commander from legend. His eyes glanced from the sky to me.

"Still in one piece, Jonne?"

I hadn't thought to check until then, so I quickly scanned my limbs and patted my torso. "I believe I am."

"I'm glad that is so."

"By Gela, what was that blast?"

Ryckerd's eyes remained on the sky. "You didn't think I'd come without warders, did you?"

The blast had been a ward, of course, an exceptionally powerful one due to the amount of moisture. He had brought one or two of the four warders remaining at Northem, as I should've known he would. "A victory, yes?"

"No." Ryckerd's sword pointed toward a receding shape in the sky.

Black against light gray clouds hung a human figure carried by twin masses of saffa bats heading south toward Northem. I had no doubt it was red in color.

Lexica XIX

Pulumbonk considered Ryckerd's timely arrival a miracle. He attributed his own survival to a divine act, as well. I survived to write this because of a good turn of fortune and see now that wanting a god of my own when under duress was cowardice. If the Anaxagorum had its way, every manner of superstition and half-truth could be pandered to those who didn't know better. Even magic must have a logic to it. I see none in religion, and perhaps that's why it appeals to so many.

Ryckerd's unmiraculous appearance can be traced to a concatenation of events that followed one another logically. Father had sent the Drowned Hag and the Bloated Shrew back across Lake Rado after only the loss of an hour at Northem. Logically they would return to the jetty where Ryckerd made his last stand. If they didn't find him there, which they didn't, logic dictated they split up and search along the shores, for where else could he go? If he had been killed or taken prisoner, they wouldn't find him, and he wouldn't have been so stupid as to flee into the city of Tule. A tactically astute man, he would've stayed near the shore to watch for rescue ships, most likely by following the shore to the base of the eastern cliffs, where the narrow path gave a small group a chance against a larger one. The group would have nothing to eat, but my brother, knowing the nature of our father, would expect rescue soon. The Tulians feared the lake and had no watercraft of their own, so merely attempting a rescue promised a high probability of success.

No god had intervened. No magic had been invoked. A bit of luck and an assembly of reasoning minds had saved the day.

The same applied to the battle. The Red Lady simply outplayed us and escaped unscathed. We had failed in our objective but learned a little more about our foe. Its powers were limited to the manipulation of simple minds and vegetation. How it conjured the black vapor or what the vapor might be capable of in a different setting remained a mystery.

After the battle, a courier was dispatched to warn Northem, but he would have trouble beating flying things that wouldn't be slowed by the wagon-tipping Cheeky Nobs. Even if the rider did arrive before the Red Lady, how would the defenders of Northem prepare for a willful book that looked like a blood-soaked woman with bats for wings?

***

I learned from Ryckerd that Thunderhoof and most of the expedition's livestock had escaped the Raka attack on the camp over Dunkelgrau and headed home. He had dispatched two drovers to guide them back to Northem. The news came as a happy surprise, almost as surprising as when Pulumbonk hugged and kissed me on both cheeks once reunited after the fight, which I have recorded as "The Battle of Midnight Wings." Such intimacy was customary in his homeland of semiarid Atmaa. May it never become so in Northem. While I did embrace him with much the same enthusiasm in the chamber of The Well, that was a one-time slip on my part. Composure should never be willingly lost.

The Subu has startled me by wriggling from under a heap of bodies near where I had fought. He stood, shook blood from his whiskers, walked concentric circles around the battlefield until he found his battleaxe, and only then asked how I fared.

The actual number of soldiers engaged that night was one hundred and seventy-one. Of them, most of the mounted men came through with minor wounds, only five dead. The spearmen and archers had been devastated, thirty-nine killed, thirty-three incapacitated by wounds, and the rest of us bloody and walking but shocked.

"I had no time to muster a larger force," Ryckerd confided as we rode toward home, I on a recently ownerless horse. The timberman's drum set our pace. Dop Dop...Dop Dop...Dop Dop. "Father sent far too few of you to Dunkelgrau. Had he seen the bloody thing in the firelight of the Imperial Library, he would've guessed its potential."

I half-heard him. The morning sun had done little to dispel my memory of dropping Raka and clutching plants, or that Remi had literally flown out of my life, but I welcomed its light, as if it were another lost brother.

"Jonne," he said. "Keep your mind on the day, not last night."

"Forgive me."

"No apologies for being frightened, but don't let it consume you. We'll dissect the battle later to learn its lessons."

Having my brother to myself warmed me. "I'm pleased you believed me about the blood book's magical nature."

"I know you, brother Jonne. Neither you nor Lada would leap to such a conclusion without good reason."

"You must tell me of your battle with the Tulians on the jetty, so I might record it."

"Not a battle, more a blind exchange of arrows. I was very proud of the Tulian loyalists. They knew when the ship's boat left us, it would not be coming back. Not but one man among them had any fighting experience, yet they followed without question to engage our attackers."

"Who were also Tulians, yes?"

"Some of the city guard, religious fanatics who deserted their king and backed the usurping bastard Draman. They flew shrieking like crows when we burst through the mist upon them."

"Were the loyalists rescued along with you?"

"You can interview them at the castle, if you wish. There's no going-home for them."

I was elated at going home and had to fight the urge to show it. "I'm glad you are with us again and safe."

His barely-there smile peeked from his beard. "Thank you for spending time with my rogues."

"I find them preferable company to most people."

"That they are."

I shared his smile, an atypically warm moment between us. "Ryckerd, I fear we'll be unable to help Northem."

"Let events follow as they may."

That wasn't very encouraging, but it was reassuringly Ryckerd. I turned to assess our procession in the sunlight. Knights with dirty faces and sagging plumes, men-at-arms looking hollow-eyed after their first engagement were all I could see. They blocked my view of those on foot or stacked in the wagons. I hoped Pulumbonk fared well. I also wished to slap him for being so feckless as to join Lada's conspiracy. He had yet to apologize for it.

Lada also needed to be slapped, but I would not be the one to divulge her role in the conspiracy. Ryckerd didn't seem to know of it. The clinker and apprentice herbalist didn't appear to be stalwart secret-keepers, so their tempers, if nothing else, could bring them to point fingers. Brillix almost surely would say something.

The Red Lady, far from her source of Raka Infante and saffa bats, would have few allies to call on, if she intended to penetrate Northem castle. With luck, it would fly south, across Lake Rado, to manipulate the Askerati. They might be too arrogant in their superstitions to adopt magic. Mayhap the fire worshippers of Haramdum would welcome the thing. That would be a formidable marriage.

For The Subu, I had no worries. The world could crumble in space, and he would find a plot of it on which to remain standing.

Remi, though, thinking of her had become too painful, so I shut her out. That lasted less than a mark.

Thoughts of her intruded as I fought to focus on recording all the things more important for this history than my mewling over a girl. I had plenty of time, as getting through the Cheeky Nobs with wagons of wounded took longer than it did with wagons of just supplies. Pulumbonk sat with me when we stopped to rest or to unload the wagons and manhandle them through steeply angled passages. He radiated joy at believing Unathar had deemed him worthy of staying alive and at the thought of seeing Lada again.

He would say, "Tis a good day to be alive!"

I would answer, "What if it's our last day?"

He hated when I said that and tried to argue his right to joy. I never engaged, as I expected the coming days to reveal horrors. I did look forward to one of Merf's hearty albon stews and an orange cake or two. I did not look forward to suffering Father's outrage at our failure, or suffering Lada's, for that matter.

Evenings were a welcome change from the last week. The Subu joined Pulumbonk and me for meals around a shared fire, the two of them revealing themselves to be quite accomplished at telling ribald stories that made me laugh out loud more than once. The Subu told of a frog with a large penis and the lady swan that followed him everywhere. Pulumbonk spun a tale of a man tasked with finding the mouths of rivers and engaging them in conversation.

The days hinted at the coming of autumn with crisp nights and cool days under sunny skies. The orange and yellow veins in the round, rock hills of the Cheeky Nobs practically glowed. I longed to get out of my armor, but it kept me comfortably warm instead of oppressively so, as if I should complain. One or two of the wounded drew their last breaths on each of the six days back. The moaning of those remaining provided an appropriate serenade for a journey of the defeated.

Brillix spent most of his time keeping the minds of his men from dwelling on what had happened and focused on what needed to happen once home. I heard him speak of taking discarded rigging from the ships and tenting it over the exposed parapets of Northem castle, in case of another aerial attack. His nights he spent among the wounded, comforting where he could and unknowingly making me feel small for disliking his exemplary qualities. Not until the last day on the road, as we entered the calming normalcy of the rolling ranch land along the Baldurgate road and heard the first clops of hooves on cobblestones, did he speak to me.

"You're almost home and still alive. Are you as surprised as I at that?"

I felt the words were spoken as a comrade and not a critic. "Many things have surprised me these past days."

He nodded soberly, "I too, but we've met them spryly and find ourselves yet alive."

I asked, "Will you report the conspiracy?" While Pulumbonk seemed to have forgotten his complicity, I'm sure Brillix had not. "Father will have those few surviving killed."

"Can we not report it?" His expression allowed only one answer.

The blueskin clinker's desire for equality gave him a legitimate reason to want the power of the book for his people. I hated to see him hang for it. Then I remembered Remi's midnight incantation and the murderous attack of the man-plants on my unsuspecting companions. Books I'd read made the dispensing of justice seem a clear-cut act of logic. In reality, it proved messy.

As we passed the first habitation, we were hailed by a shoom rancher on horseback at the gate to his estate. A pair of much younger men inside a pen on a hillock behind him sorted shooms and placed the selects into a cage on a wagon, presumably for shearing.

"What news?" the man shouted.

Brillix stopped to arrange for some of our wounded to be taken into his home. The man agreed eagerly and, though I couldn't hear his words, carried on in an agitated fashion. Brillix reported to Ryckerd.

"The rancher says a trio of boys from the village are camped at the ford and telling wagons bound for the market to turn back."

"Why?" Ryckerd asked.

"Something's afoul at the castle, but he knows not what."

A heavy rap on my shoulder prompted me to rotate. The knight behind me had tapped me with his lance and leaned forward. "What's that he says?'

I shook my head. Why pass the news and frighten the entire column?

A knight and two mounted men-at-arms broke away and galloped over the cobblestones to scout. We waited as the wagon with our most needful wounded rumbled by and through the gate leading to the shoom rancher's lavish home. The apprentice herbalist rode on its tailgate and grinned at me as he passed, something I'd never seen him do. Mayhap he knew he'd be above persecution in the next weeks while serving the wounded, more of which were possibly to come.

On the cornifer's signal, the column trundled forward. We'd travel more than a league before entering the arbored section of road leading through farmland. A view of the castle wouldn't appear until at the end of the arbor two leagues farther. My stomach filled with nervous wings. We hadn't heard the castle bell, so I took that as a good sign.

I lost myself in the timberman's beat, hoping thoughts of Remi wouldn't follow.

Dop Dop...Dop Dop...Dop Dop.

But they did.

***

I wondered if Pulumbonk's good mood would survive his first sight of what I had just seen. It was blocked from him until the rear of our procession caught up to the rise I'd just crested. Mayhap he had deduced what lay ahead by what we saw when passing the farm fields. Not a bush nor a blade of grass remained in sight, only dirt and trees pulled up to their highest branches into the soil. Gela's domain was being plundered.

The trees forming the arbor normally obscured a view of the castle up to the quarry road. Well before that, we noted the trees that should have stood tall beside us were tilted and noticeably shorter. The effect became more dramatic as we rode. Noble oaks looked as if a giant had knocked them aside. Farther on, they looked as if the giant had burrowed underground and pulled them down by their roots, until some were no taller than bushes. Without their obstruction, those of us in the lead saw Northem Castle a league out, when we topped the crest of Buckleberry Glen.

The knight riding next to me gaped. "What manner of skragging is this?"

I offered, "The same kind of magic you saw last night, only on a larger scale."

The knight's face soured. "I don't need you to tell me that."

"But you asked—"

"What makes you think I asked it of you, Blossom?"

"Librast In Situ, Brother—"

He looked as if he might backhand me. "Ah, but you're a dense plog!"

Knights recognized no equals but other knights.

We were, however, equals in our confoundment. All of us, whether mounted or afoot, stared at the phenomenon on Leper Hill. Alone in an otherwise blue sky shimmered an enormous dome of blue-gray mist, as if a giant's glass bowl had been upended and set over the castle. The castle was only a suggestion of itself. Something mud-colored inside the mist draped it like a blanket, the great keep and its surrounding towers still standing but completely obscured.

I, like many of us, couldn't conjure a remark appropriate to the moment.

Ryckerd found voice. To his steward, "Tell the wagons to get the wounded back to the nearest farms, then send a rider to the Fingers and bring the blueskin skragging women. We'll need their healing powers." To me, "Jonne, to my side quickly."

I urged my mount past the two knights behind Ryckerd, thrilled to be needed. "Yes?"

"The day is dry, yet look at this. Does the thing not need great amounts of moisture to engineer such as this?"

The day was dry. I was about to confess my befuddlement, when it occurred to me. "The lake. It's using Lake Rado."

Ryckerd was not one to emote when surprised. He took his time to respond. "An alarming possibility."

"Mayhap worse. It might be in the lake. I watched it dive into a bottomless well and come out—"

"We shall go closer to discover the nature of what covers the castle."

I hated the idea. I loved the idea. Curiosity was a duplicitous companion.

The horsemen moved forward. The able footmen were ordered to follow at a distance. The wagons made their slow turns and headed back to the nearest farm, Windhelm Vegetables and Curios, known for their enormous cabbages and the brightly colored purses, packs, and bed covers crafted by the lady of the manor and her daughters.

Ryckerd allowed me to stay at his side and, after a little way on, he leaned toward me. "Should this be the end of Northem, I want you at the docks. Take what survivors you can and sail to the south. You must keep the memory alive, even if only accompanied by blueskins."

"They are Northmen, blue or not."

"But they carry none of the intellectual property that is us."

Interestingly, they were the caretakers of what had been gleaned from the Anaxagorum centuries ago. Mayhap it was their turn to rise to prominence. None of that was a priority to me. My safety and that of my family was top of mind.

Another ten marks forward and the blanket covering Northem Castle revealed itself.

"Roots!" gasped a knight.

I saw it to be so, as every visible point of the structure had been cocooned by intertwined roots and vines, leaves and bark. While we halted to take it in, one high point that must've been the west tower collapsed to half its height, the crunch and crumble audible at a quarter-league out.

Ryckerd and I reacted in unison. "Lada!"

He turned and projected to all. "Brothers of the Order of Man, this is the hour we fulfill our pledge. The rest of you, Northem has suckled you, as well, but I leave it to each man—of the castle or village, the tavern or the farms—each of you must decide whether you assist or run."

"To the fray, I say," said a knight, "whatever it might be."

Ryckerd raised his sword. "To the fray!"

I echoed, "Whatever it might be."

I hesitated to say farewell to The Subu and Pulumbonk, but Ryckerd wouldn't have it.

"Keep up, Jonne."

I glanced back while spurring forward. All of the mounted men followed. The footmen hesitated, although Lieutenant Aerwart exhorted them from his horse, his red-ruffed lance held high. I would've been none too quick to advance, were I on foot. Being on horse gave me the illusion that I, with luck, could escape. I didn't realize how much luck that would require. Pulumbonk I saw not. The Subu, whether he could see me looking or not, raised his axe in my direction. For reasons I've yet to understand, I felt I was betraying him.

The ethereal dome of mist and the writhing mass of vegetation gripping the castle appeared very real as we drew closer, but my mind had trouble accepting it. This was the stuff of fables and nonsense. How did men with steel weapons fight those?

At an eighth-league out, we broke into a canter. My heart lodged in my throat, as I detected a sound more disturbing than what my eyes saw. The enwrapping foliage creaked with exertion, not the noise of movement but of tightening. Toward the barbican, stone crumbled. At many points I couldn't identify, timbers snapped. The Red Lady was squeezing the castle to death.

Lexica XX

We saw no Raka Infante, no saffa bats, no man-plants by the time we halted on the narrow rode leading up to the barbican gate, or where the gate should be. Nothing waited to do us harm, although the loamy reek of the vegetation inside the enormous bubble of mist slathered us as completely as the moisture in the air. We saw no way into the castle, for the main gate and the east and west sally ports were clogged with knotted vegetation. I could almost feel the tension of the mass quivering inside me. Its groans were ceaseless.

Father and Mother, Lada and all other inhabitants of the castle had to be trapped inside. If not, we would've seen Father outside casting orders and proclamations.

The village and the blueskin compound at The Six Fingers had not been touched, so someone suggested we try finding a rope and grapple.

"And do what with them?" one knight asked. "The castle is wrapped sides and top."

The hoofbeats of a new rider turned our heads. The Subu reined in next to me. Pulumbonk, arms around the scalp-taker's waist, grinned at me, eyes wide with what could be exhilaration or horror.

The Subu addressed Ryckerd. "Get a rope and grapple, and I'll get ya inside."

The knight who had proposed such straightened in vindication. "I told you."

I brightened at men I suddenly saw as friends. "A pleasant surprise this."

Ryckerd darkened. "That's Aerwart's horse."

The Subu explained. "I done the man no harm, but I taught him a lesson about making up his mind too slow."

Seeing our puzzlement, he elaborated. "The man weren't sure he was gonna join ya, so I pulled him from this horse and come in his stead." He ticked his head toward Pulumbonk. "This long-legged loper ran half way with me."

Ryckerd considered The Subu, a face-off between hulking bear and circling fox.

"His axe," I said. "It could help."

Ryckerd asked of The Subu, "Can it?"

"If it don't, nothing ye got will." He didn't await approval before dismounting in the fluid motion of a seasoned rider. His homeland, Tulos, was the land where horses grew, after all.

The dismissive knight looked down the road to the village. "I see no help coming from our friends below."

Were I a blueskin at the Fingers or a tanner in the village, I would be in no hurry to confront such a thing on behalf of the castlers. Yet, for whatever reason, there walked The Subu in his wide-shouldered sway, across the carpet of emergent vegetation to face the mass blocking us. I could tell by the creak of saddle and stirrup that those around me were leaning forward in interest.

The Subu set his satchel of purple rocks at his feet and looked at me. "Keep yer eye on these lovelies."

He uttered his words of making and flames rippled along the axe's cutting edge. He widened his stance, raised the weapon high over his head, and with an explosive "Kee-haw!" brought it down on a thick cable of intertwined greenery. It sliced deeply, fluids within hissed into steam, and the cable fell away.

Ryckerd shouted to a brace of men-at-arms. "Get that rope and grapple."

The Subu scanned the network of large and small cables making up the vegetable cocoon, then held up a hand. "Hold that!" He slung his axe by its loop over his shoulder, bolted forward, and leapt onto the wall of muscular plants, hands and feet finding easy purchase. "The Red Lady's given us a ladder."

"What's your intention?" Ryckerd asked.

The Subu looked down on Pulumbonk. "You climb as well as you run?"

"I spent eight years in a forest."

The Subu, hanging with one arm free, gestured to the column of horsemen. "Ye metal clankers don' got a chance on this. We'll cut through the top and raise the barbican. Ye lot try hackin' through the front."

Ryckerd pressed, "Why are you so keen to be here?"

The Subu spoke as he climbed. "Cuz ain' nobody in the world seen such a thing as this."

We watched as Pulumbonk found handholds among the ropy structures and followed The Subu to the top of the right barbican tower. Their leather and fur armors weren't light, but they weren't the heavy carapaces of the knights' hauberks.

The Subu called down to me. "Don' go nowhere, word man."

Ryckerd ordered us to dismount. He unhooked the hand-axe from his saddle and stalked to the barrier. His knights followed then awaited his next actions. I held the reins of five horses. Ryckerd hefted his axe, eyed a particularly thick cable of intertwined grasses and vines, and sunk the blade into it. Twice more he hacked but the cable remained but half-cleaved.

He eyed us grimly. "This will ruin our blades, but if we are to find our loved ones…."

A knight wielding his own hand-axe stepped to the barrier. "Let's get to it."

Before another blade struck, a great groan shivered through the vegetation. Stone crumbled inside the cocoon. Above us, the left of the barbican's enwrapped twin towers dropped a few spans, until it drooped like a broken shoulder. After a tense moment of uplifted eyes, Pulumbonk's face appeared from the still-covered, right tower top.

"That just tore a hole through the greenery we can drop through. See you in a blink." He disappeared.

The soldiers attacked the barrier with fury. The ground under the road to the barbican sloped down to either side, so only ten men could chop at a time. Ryckerd ordered a trio of men-at-arms to gather saws and wood axes from the village.

I watched the sky, expecting to see the Red Lady and her bats circling. Why did she want to destroy the castle? If she wished to eradicate the documents within, she'd need to enter the sub-levels and do it by hand. Mayhap burying them and their keepers would be enough.

One knight at the barrier stopped chopping. "I'll not risk breaking my blade on this."

"Agreed." Ryckerd gazed down the road toward the village. "Jonne, ride down and hurry them along."

I handed the reins of four horses to a man-at-arms and mounted, happy to have a purpose.

Ryckerd continued as I wheeled. "Once you find them, hie yourself to the safety of the Fingers."

"But I should witness what happens inside."

"Dead you can witness nothing. Be off, and tell your friends among the Guides to ready the ships."

Lada had successfully argued with Ryckerd, but I had never done more than anger him. I caught him in mid-turn. "There's a girl, Ryckerd, a blueskin, the acolyte dancer, Remi. The book inhabits her and—"

"Get on with you!"

How would I explain to him that Remi might survive, once she'd transported the book to its destination? He wouldn't believe me. I shouldn't believe me.

I spurred my horse. "Tell her I'll await her at the Fingers."

Exiting the dome of mist brought immediate warmth from a fully risen sun. I wiped water from my eyes and nose, but my armor remained bedewed after my short ride to the village.

The men-at-arms were where I knew they would be, Meeper's Cut Shop. Meeper and his family had disappeared. Not being blueskins, they had probably sought safety among the farms. Most of the village was deserted, except for a group of twenty rough men, blueskins and white, armed with spears, axes, and swords. They seemed to be watching for looters, as they had surrounded the three men loading saws and axes onto a cart.

The burliest of them, Hak the Blacksmith, threw up his hand, as I approached. "Ya come to join these thieves?"

The men-at-arms were better armored and armed, but being outnumbered seven-to-one they had raised their hands. One looked hopefully to me. "Tell them, Jonne. We're trying to save the castle."

"Morning to you, Hak," Hak was a blueskin friend of Merf's, and he had spent many a breakfast at the same table with me at the Fingers. He returned my wave.

"We can't let anyone, even castlers, run off with honest folk's goods, Jonne."

"Anyone have any coin?" I asked of the beleaguered men.

"We're equipped to fight, not shop."

My stomach clenched at the thought of failing Ryckerd. "Hak, this is about more than saving the castle. This is about saving the lives of every man, woman, and child, whether blue, white, pink or leaf green."

"Me and every pink skin down here are sore-tired of not having a say in the goings-on around here."

"You want to have a say, then take up a saw or axe and join those cutting their way into the castle."

"Sorry, lad, but that's your castle, not ours."

Ermle the Dyer, arms stained muddy purple to the elbows and smelling of the stale urine used in his trade, said, "Yer father's no friend to us, the bloated little tick. Let him boss his way out of this."

Hak waved him silent. "He don't mean that, but your papa went and stole that blood book from Tule without asking none of us."

A little blueskin with a lisp said, "That ain't what'th at the heart of the matter." He glared at me. "Your papa's a right nasty prong to the blue'thkin, like hi'th papa before him and on and on.

All the men awaited my response.

I felt like an ant entrusted with too big a crumb. "What if I pay you in goods many times more valuable than the rope?"

The group looked to Hak. "I would think Meeper will find that acceptable."

I turned my horse. "I'll be back in moments."

What I intended to do would get me cuffed if not murdered by The Subu. Ryckerd was pacing before the vegetable barrier, when I rode up. The others waited beside their horses or stroked dulled blades with whetstones. When Ryckerd turned, I said, "Your tools are coming."

"More quickly would be best," he said.

I slid from my horse, slung The Subu's bag of purple rocks over my shoulder, and pulled myself back into the saddle. The purple mold that went into making Valens powder would've fetched three gold pieces per ounce at the castle, meaning I was taking a full purse of gold from the man who asked me to guard it.

No villager or blueskin had ever possessed any, so when Hak opened the bag, he gawked at me and then showed the others.

"Does that make the purple powder?" one asked.

Hak looked up at me. "This is too much to pay for tools."

I said to him, "Keep it all," and then to the men-at-arms, "Hurry back with what you have."

The vigilantes crowded around the bag. The men-at-arms mounted and pulled the cart behind them. They regarded me as if they knew not who I was. Self-preservation should've driven me, as ordered, to the Fingers and relative safety, but I watched them ride up the castle road wishing I were with them. As The Subu had said, Ain' nobody in the world seen such a thing as this.

I hesitated for such a while, one of the vigilantes said, "Ya best get up there. Only a coward won't help his own."

I felt slapped. "My brother ordered me to the Fingers."

The man eyed me up and down, shrugged, and joined his fellows who were splitting up to continue their patrols.

"I'm obeying an order," I called after him. If I was a coward it was for not wanting to face The Subu. With a tug of the reins, my horse turned toward the towering, black lighthouse and the tavern built around its base.

Pern the Fisherman, along with his teenage son and young daughter, scuttled along the side of the road, their belongings in heavy sacks. They fished for goldtail in the Erle River that ran from the Axehead Mountains all the way to Lake Rado. The castle wasn't visible from the river, which made me wonder how they knew to flee to the Fingers. Who knew what other secrets the blueskins had learned from the Anaxagorum a half-millennia ago?

The grounds outside the tavern teemed with blueskins who had come in from the village or, like Pern's family, from fishing or trapping, or from the remains of the Dunkelgrau expedition. I noted the clinker and the foreign archer, Zir, upending tankards near the main entrance of the Fingers. The scout and warders who had served with Ryckerd's force at the Battle of Midnight Wings embraced family who were ecstatic to see them.

Merf I didn't spot until he hustled into the sunlight from the tavern followed by three others, all carrying food in crocks and trenchers to the people outside. The tavern could easily have seated them all, but the assembly seemed to be organizing to depart, people being sorted into groups, baggage being set in different piles. Here and there were bursts of anger, but for the most part, the blueskins cooperated with members of their Guides who had taken charge.

Blueskins owned oxen but none owned a horse, so I stood out. Merf handed trenchers to a pair of woodsmen and waved as he trotted to where I waited outside the crowd.

He stroked my horse's muzzle. "Thunderhoof didn't make it back?"

"I've not seen him." I glanced over my shoulder to the globe of mist and the specks crowded inside it at the top of the road. "I'm to tell you to have your Guides ready the ships."

"We are, but for our own people." He noted my shock. "My friend, you're welcome to join us, but—"

"You're going to leave us?"

"We built the ships. We pilot the ships. We go first. Sorry, Jonne."

"We'll be needing your skragging women, too, as there will soon be wounded." Assuming any living thing made it out of the castle.

"We plan to wait and watch. If the castle crumbles, we board and take our chances with the Askerati plogs in the south."

"The castlers have protected you all these years." My words sounded thin.

"Your knights were used to intimidate us, and you know it."

I supposed I did.

"The magic book that you vilified us for touching has come back to have its say."

I stared up the hill.

He slapped my thigh. "Most of us will welcome you, as you've chosen to be among us so often. When did you eat last?"

The strip of dried albon I'd gobbled after the battle had burned through me. "Forever ago."

"Get your mount to the livery, and I'll bring you something hot." He winked. "Maybe toss in a sugar cake, eh?"

My mouth gushed at the thought, but seeing the blueskins working together for their common survival shamed me.

Ryckerd would severely reprimand me. The Subu might kill me. The words leaving my mouth surprised me. "I hope to see you again."

I turned my horse and spurred to a gallop. Pounding up the cobbles toward the village felt good. The village and its marketplace went by as a blur in my periphery, as my eyes stayed affixed to the figures at the castle barbican. The horse, whose name I knew not, seemed to relish the chance to be the mighty beast Gela had made her and bit long patches of earth with single strides.

Moisture slapped my face, as we shot through the dome of mist. I wiped my eyes to see the nearly fifty riderless horses staked by their reins to either side of the road. The gateway had been cleared, most likely with the help of The Subu's axe from the other side. Two men-at-arms watching the horses leveled their lances at me.

"Tis Jonne the Booker. Have they gone inside?"

"Mayhap ten marks ago."

I tried to make a fast, smooth dismount, but the right stirrup held my foot, and I hung upside down from the left flank, my helmet dropping from the back of my head and clattering to the cobbles.

One man-at-arms looked at the other. "Thank Gela, reinforcements have arrived."

The other man rolled his eyes and stepped in to help work my boot from the stirrup. My leg came free, my boots clapped the road, and I danced out of the arms of my saviors, trying to regain my footing and a modicum of dignity.

One man said, "Your brother doesn't want you in there."

"I don't believe I have a choice."

Ruined plants carpeted the road through the barbican gate into the outer bailey. Sunlight beamed through the hole torn in the canopy by the collapsed tower, but it did little more than accentuate the Dunkelgrau dark of the interior waiting for me farther on. Hesitating to consider what I was doing would've been unwise, so I strode in, sword out.

"No shame in staying out here with us, Jonne."

But there was. A few steps deeper into the cocoon and every noise sounded thunderous. The dread I felt only two nights ago in the passageways of Dunkelgrau returned. Ten paces farther, and I had to stop to find what light there was. Somewhere ahead waited the gate into the great keep, but a dull red glow to my right marked the way down to Moonsie's armory. From there I could reach the castle's wine and milk cellar and, beyond that, the central stairs of the great keep that could take me up to Lada's and my rooms or all the way down to the fourth sub-basement where the Anaxagorum had been temporarily kept. Lumen fruit sconces would light those areas.

Even with the light from the forge's fire pit, I kept my left hand to the curving wall as I descended. "Moonsie?"

The embers were dying but numerous enough to heat and light the room, the tongs and hammers on their hooks. "Moonsie?"

Something scraped the dirt floor in the armor storage room ahead of me. Rats didn't frequent the forge, as there was no food. When the sound didn't repeat, I dared whisper, "Tis Jonne the Booker."

A yelp lodged in my throat, when Moonsie's face appeared in the black doorway. He wore an open-faced helmet, a line of dried blood bisecting his face. "Jonne, what misfortune this?"

I inspected his face at a double arm's length. "You were attacked?"

"Nah, falling rubble is the danger in here, but there's no way out."

"The barbican is clear."

Relief flushed his face, as he motioned to others. His son, an eight-year-old wearing a man's helmet as wide as his shoulders waggled into the red light. Behind him, Moonsie's sturdy daughter, draped in chainmail and wearing the same kind of helmet, followed, scooting the boy along. Wife and infant came next, mother in a simple pot helmet, bent low and cradling her babe. Moonsie, usually chatty, stopped to place his hand on my shoulder and bow his head in gratitude. He hurried his family through the door and up the stairs to the courtyard.

I plucked an unlit torch from its sconce and held it to the embers. The way through the door into the wine cellar came clear. I saw nothing disturbed, only row after shadowy row of hump-backed casks receding under the low, arched ceiling. Fluid dripped somewhere, its sound mostly lost amid the groans of tightening plants and the crumble of bricks. The pavers in the floor vibrated continuously.

Once into the hallway of the basement, I hurried to the central spiral staircase and listened. I heard no voices, no movement. At least, the stairs felt like home. Ryckerd had made me a wooden sword when I was six, and I had many a duel with monsters and mad men trying to force their way up the stairs to my family.

Faced with the decision to venture farther down to the galleries of scrolls and tomes or up to the more familiar floors where the leading families lived, I didn't hesitate. I started up, torch and sword in hand. The enclosed spiral staircase of stone was intended to be traversed with tapers, not torches, as the smoke filled the space quickly and made me cough.

Exiting to the airy ground floor was a relief. The aroma of freshly baked bread met me. While mostly open, the floor was lanced with load-bearing posts. Bound to them by vegetable cables, to the walls, and to the stone floor were men and women, eyes and tongues bulging. I knew them all. Most were male, but I noted two women, both wives of knights, a dropped poniard at the feet of one, a bejeweled mace near the other. My family was not among them. Crumbled stone littered the floor.

I hurried to the grand stairs up, passing the open entrance to the kitchens and scullery. I saw no bodies but noticed dropped utensils and a tipped cauldron. The grand stairs followed the gentle curve of the outer wall, the fluid sweep of the carefully cut white stones mirrored by the integral carved balustrade, a testament to the stonemasons' skills of yore.

The second-floor hosted bed chambers for four families. I announced myself with the barest of whispers. No reply. A central spiral staircase ascended to the next three floors, but I cared only to reach the top floor where the Librast Superior's family lived. I didn't expect to find Lada, Father, or Mother, but I had to see for myself. One step. One breath. Another step. Another breath. My heart beat at thrice the rate.

At the fifth floor, I made my most courageous act of the day by pushing open my parents' door. The chamber looked empty but normal, except where a ceiling stone had fallen through the green canopy of the bed. Next, my chamber, where a fallen ceiling beam and a heap of rubble dominated. The door to Lada's chamber lay open. As suspected, she was not there. My second most courageous act was entering Ryckerd's chamber and, after a deep breath, peeking onto the balcony. The blanket of vegetation blocked the sun, but my torch found reflective eyes watching me from every branch and aerie.

I whispered, "Take heart, my friends."

I had just reached the staircase to head back down when I heard a loud ripping of foliage from the opposite side of the floor. I rounded the central shaft quietly, although my torchlight announced me. A smaller, more claustrophobic spiral staircase led to the grand parapet above, the highest point of the castle. Sunlight blew from the tiny door. Someone or something had made a hole in the cocoon up there.

Footfalls, barely louder than falling leaves, tapped slowly down the stairs. If Raka or man-plants showed themselves, I would fling the torch at them and risk the dark of the stairway down to the ground floor. No gnarled Raka foot or plant tendril appeared, instead, a humanoid foot: bare, blood-red, female.

The message of the corpses on the ground floor suddenly came clear. They had all been armed and threats. I placed my sword on the floor. A second red foot heralded a supple calf and the nude body with Remi's face. The Red Lady's eyes were closed, but it turned instantly to me. Its hand swiped.

DESTINY CALLS JONNE BOOKER

I shuddered, mouth open but speechless.

HOW WILL YOU ANSWER

I dropped to all fours, the chainmail over my forehead clinking against the stone floor, armored hands over my head. Flesh soles trod the pavers next to me and passed my trembling lump. They made little noise, but I heard them as if they were those of a giant. Six, seven, eight steps, enough to carry it to the stairs down.

Remi's voice, small and desperate, called to me. "Come. Jonne. Please."

Lexica XXI

Remi sounded weak but alive. I could not be weak.

The Red Lady entered the central spiral staircase, I four paces behind. Apparently, I was correct about the sickly green light affecting only those under the thing's thrall, for it, by itself, emitted no light. I held onto my torch. Without my sword, it was my only weapon, other than the two throwing knives remaining in my bandolier. Flame might be the best counter to the vegetation, in any case.

"Remi?" I whispered, hurrying behind. "Are you unhurt? Can you exert your will? How can I help?"

If Remi were trying to respond, the Red Lady stifled her. Down we walked, smoke stinging my eyes, round and round past the fourth floor, the third, the second. As we exited the central shaft and headed toward the grand staircase, I noticed what I hadn't before. More of my people hung purple and swollen in the grasp of vines. Over five hundred lived inside the walls, so I held hope others had survived in the lower levels. Ryckerd, Brillix, and their group almost certainly had ventured downward.

The groan of tightening vegetation had ceased. The floor no longer vibrated. Mayhap the cocoon had accomplished its mission, or the Red Lady couldn't risk entombing itself. A network of twining vegetation remained adhered to the ceiling but showed no inclination to move.

Once on the ground floor, I paid closer attention to the faces of the dead. I knew them all, of course, guards, a few knights of the Order who'd been left behind, armed cooks and attendants, a paige, three wives of leading scholars, and an elderly scholar who had evidently tried his luck upstairs and died of fright, for no vine grasped him. I discerned none of Ryckerd's company but did see the terrified eyes of a woman and two children peeking from a half-opened doorway. They seemed unharmed and probably would've appreciated a wave of acknowledgement from me, but I failed them.

The Red Lady entered the wider, zig-zag stairwell to the underhalls. It never changed pace, descending purposefully but unhurriedly. I peered onto the first sub-level. Most lumen fruits had been knocked from their sconces and squeezed to dim husks, leaving the space in heavy shadow. I saw soldiers dangling from the ceiling and clasped to the walls. No movement. No sounds. If the level held survivors, my torch found them not. The next level told the same story. But on the third, I heard voices.

A male whispered urgently then stopped when my boot sole creaked. I poked my head through the opening onto the level.

"Tis Jonne the Booker."

Pulumbonk's voice was unmistakable. "Praise be to Unathar!"

As was The Subu's. "Git yer tail over here."

The Red Lady disappeared on the turn of stairs below me. The woman within her must've sensed my stopping, for her voice hobbled out. "Stay. With me."

The Subu croaked, "I'm in a bad way, word man, and ye owe me."

My heart pulled me downward. My conscience pushed me outward. My feet hesitated. If I could've torn myself in half, I would have. Remi was but a voice and mayhap a ruse by the Red Lady, but that voice was the only connection I had to her. The Subu and Pulumbonk were flesh and blood. Lover or friends? I hungered for both from a lifetime's lack of either.

My tongue said, "Remi, I shall follow," but my feet took me into the dark circular hallway toward my friends' voices.

The torchlight found them. Pulumbonk sat against the wall hugging his long legs to his chest. The Subu's axe lay on the wooden floor in front of him. The Subu hung upside down from brown cables that had burst through the far wall, run along the ceiling, and then lassoed his ankles. His frown smiled at me.

He ticked his head toward Pulumbonk. "This one's too afraid to cut me down."

Pulumbonk held out his hands to ward off my judgement. "The vines come for anyone holding a weapon."

I glanced back at the stairwell. Then to The Subu's axe. Idle roots covered the ceiling, waiting for a reason to come to life.

The Subu's face had gone purple. "One cut with my livid blade will free me."

I addressed Pulumbonk. "You've stayed by him, although Lada likely waits below?"

"A hurtful choice, but could I leave him?"

Of course he couldn't have. My limbs knew the right action. I placed the torch into a lumen sconce and put my hands to the battleaxe, lifted it a span from the floor and incanted the words of making. "Addra addra, forenza krak!"

No flames appeared, but a thick, brown root whipped at me from the ceiling. I dropped the axe and leapt back, and the thing retracted among its brethren.

"The axe don' know yer touch, booker. Ye'll need to bring it to my hand."

I toed the weapon until it rested right beneath him. "Then I shall raise it to your hands and drop back."

"Nah, ye won't. I'll need ye to help me guide the blade."

I gulped and tried passing the torch to Pulumbonk. "Mayhap this will ward the roots away while I do this."

He shrunk back. "But they…those things…could think that a weapon."

The Subu said, "Are ya stupid? Do ya see them attacking Jonne?"

Pulumbonk took the torch.

The Subu's bright eyes angled toward me. "I'll drop me right hand. Ye raise the handle to it, and then we make our cut."

A single cable of several intertwined roots hung a half-span from the ceiling as a noose around his ankles. One well-aimed blow with that axe might sever it, but—

The Subu said, "Cut one of me feet off, and I'll hobble on me stump, catch ya, and slice ya into bacon, which I ought'a do for snatching me loot bag."

I waited for a sign that he was joking.

He snapped his fingers. "Now take that handle like this. I'll grab it and, when she lights, yer gonna use the blade like a knife. Slice, don' whack. Ready?"

I aligned my hands before grabbing the handle. More to myself than anyone else, I said, "I go," and lifted the axe.

He wrapped his fingers around it and made the words of making. Flames raced along the blade's edge. I raised the weapon and before I could place it on target, roots reached from the ceiling. One wrapped my ankles and pulled me upside down. Another found my left wrist. A third tightened about my neck so hard, my airway closed, my eyes felt as if they might pop from my skull, and I thought of nothing but getting free and…

…of taking one breath. Just one. By all that was good and fair, one breath before the pressure in my skull broke my head open.

A man screamed. He might have been far away or right next to me. Didn't matter. It was only a curiosity happening elsewhere while I died. My body convulsed. Once, twice, violently, thrice. Orange burst before my eyes. A dark hole opened under me, and I began to fall. I knew it to be The Hole of Forever where names became irrelevant and existence fell into the past tense.

The pain in my head was excruciating but, of a sudden, my eyes were gazing upon Pulumbonk above me.

"You were right," he said with a manic grin. "They don't like the flame."

I lay on my back sucking air, while he held the torch to the cable around The Subu's ankles. The thing retracted. Then jerked. The Subu rose a hand's breadth and then dropped. The cable sizzled, and the roots forming it began to separate. When the plant matter erupted in blisters, the noose uncoiled and the entire length chased itself along the ceiling and out through the wall, back into the soil beyond. The fire worked better than I expected.

The Subu's hands must've been numb for they did little to break his fall to the floor. His eyes blinked, as if they couldn't stop.

"Ah, me noggin!" He draped his arms over his abdomen. "Me whole self's gone floppy."

Pulumbonk knelt but stopped before touching the man. "Your blood's sloshed out of balance, but—"

The Subu's head shook impatiently. "I know that. Give a man some space."

I rose to an elbow, as Pulumbonk retreated closer to me. "Pulumbonk, many thanks. I thought the world had done with me."

He knelt and looked about panting. "You always think that. What...what do we do next?"

I eyed the stairwell. "We go down."

The Subu rubbed feeling into his arms. When I rose, he said, "Not so fast, word man. We're luckier together."

Pulumbonk and I looked at each other. Pulumbonk asked, "We are?"

"Who has walked out of the mouth of the dragon these many times together?"

He had a point, but my feet were already turned toward the stairs. The Subu made no move to follow me, all of his attention on the axe at his feet.

"Don't grasp it for swinging," I said, "Try carrying it by its strap." I trotted to the stairwell.

Two pairs of feet tapped behind me. I descended at an unwise speed, boots slapping risers in the gloom. I had forgotten the torch and put my hand to the wall for balance. A glow caught up with me, meaning Pulumbonk had the sense not to forget it.

The last time I had come to the bottom of these stairs, I had overheard Brother Poonal forbidding Lada and Brillix to approach the vault temporarily holding the Anaxagorum. Could I have done anything differently at that juncture to change the course of events to a situation less apocalyptic?

If there were a prologue to the end of times, it waited in the hallway before me. Ten figures caught by torchlight swayed from nooses, arms at their sides, boots a span from the floor, weapons barely visible on the stones beneath them. The creaks of the twisted vegetation holding them were arhythmic and hideous. Not even longing to reach a lover or family could keep me moving forward, as the only way to pass was to push through the thicket of limbs and protruding eyes.

Pulumbonk panted behind me.

The Subu stepped to my side. "For those who speak of dignity in death, this."

Orange lumen light peeked through the hanging bodies, marking the arched door into the vault at the end of the hall. From it leapt a woman's scream followed by an exclamation that could only have come from Lada.

"Mama!"

Father's voice, in all its miniature imperiousness, shouted. "And who are you, shameless woman?"

The Subu brushed past me. "That thing is in there." He reached for his axe, then hesitated.

I stepped in front. They were my family, after all.

Right arm leading the way, I pushed the first corpse out of the way, as if it were a side of beef in the market. Then another. The lynching roots groaned. Gases squeaked from relaxing bowels. Saliva dripped from mouths no longer vigilant. I angled my eyes down, as I knew these men, if not with familiarity or affection, with respect.

By the seventh corpse, they seemed less men and more like weighty fruit from a cursed tree. I parted numbers eight and nine to reveal the last body, the biggest of them. I didn't want to see the face, but seeing the cat's paw signet etched into the man's scabbard collar, I had no choice. It was impossible for Ryckerd to be dead, but there he hung. My eyes fixed on his face. Who was there to save me now?

Mother saw me through the door. "Jonne? On my life! Do not approach. Run!"

The vault room entrance lay five paces away and gave me a partial view of the chamber. Healthy lumen glowed brightly from undisturbed sconces set at intervals along its curving wall. In a rectangular cavity in the marble floor resembling a perpetually open sarcophagus, knelt Mother eyeing me head-on, her enduring frown in place, but her hands steepled to beseech me. The cavity was fashioned to receive and protect the most valuable items in the library. Other shadows pulsed in the light.

I hurried forward, not halting until completely through the arched entrance.

Tears I wasn't sure she could produce ran down Mother's cheeks. "My insolent boy! Hie from here!"

To my left overlooking the cavity, rose luminous marble shelves containing scrolls and wrapped books, drying powders, shoom-fur gloves for turning delicate pages, a red shoom blanket, and extra tapers, the usual. Out of place was Father, in his red house coat, pinned against the shelves by an unknown force, his eyes wide, lips pressed shut, feet a half-span above the floor. Only strong magic could achieve that.

To the right of the cavity opened a space to accommodate a blocky throne of marble cushioned with red velvet pillows, a fallen reading podium, and three figures: Brillix, alive but pressed against the right wall in the same attitude as Father; Lada, seated in the throne with a blanket over her truncated lap; the Red Lady, statue-still facing her.

The Red Lady, without an utterance or gesture, propelled me with an invisible force and held me against the ceiling over the entrance, where I could do no more than watch. The pressure it exerted made breathing slightly more difficult but was otherwise harmless.

The Subu had set but a toe in the chamber, when the thing coughed a ball of energy that knocked him back into the hallway and hung shimmering in the entrance. I could only hope Pulumbonk was also safely sealed out of the room.

Remi's voice, pitifully small, "Tis I who hold you, Jonne, for your protection."

The world seemed asymmetrical when Remi spoke to me but the Red Lady paid me no heed. Asymmetry might be a word to describe what came next, but it wasn't the best word. Horror? Wonder? Execration? I'll settle for "history."

Mother didn't seem to be constrained by anything other than fear, for she watched with fingers still steepled, tears still rolling. Father's eyes bulged with such urgency to participate, they might shoot across the room. Brillix did as Brillix does, watching soberly for an opportunity.

Lada was the heartbreak. She had lost enough weight to fit into the bed shirt Mother had sewn for her twelfth birthday. Neither woman fancied cats much, so the shirt featured embroidered radiant suns intermixed with green boughs of fir, an appropriate pattern for a girl on the verge of womanhood. At that moment, on her throne of velvet and marble, Lada could have been my little sister with whom I shared stories read aloud, who reported my every infraction to Father, and beamed at always being right.

Her hair had not been trimmed or washed, from what I could tell. Her usually bright, blue eyes appeared drained inside lids of misery red.

They fastened to me. "I did not want this, any of this."

I acknowledged with a blink. It was the last time I communicated with the sister I knew. The Red Lady stepped within touching distance. Lada sucked a bottomless breath and tried to retreat, flesh and spirit, into the marble backrest.

I shall no longer use "Red Lady," as the word "lady" was never coined to describe this corruption of the human form. I cannot call her Remi, as I had once kissed that girl. An entity of blood and arcana was this, and it climbed onto the marble throne, vile thighs straddling the lap within.

Lada stared at the expressionless face three thumbs away and heaved with sobs. Her words were moist. "I do not want you."

The entity pinned Lada's arms to her side. As it leaned in, I wished with all my will that Lada would close her eyes, but she didn't, or couldn't. The bloody lips parted and attached to Lada's in a perversion of a kiss. Bloody hands held Lada's shoulders. Red drained from the entity, slowly, continuously, from the crown of its head.

As if being painted from top down, Lada began turning red. Her orange hair grew dark, moist. When the color spread past her eyes, her lids shut. Her cheeks filled, and the color ran on, covering her chin, coating her neck, and disappearing under the happy fabric of her bed shirt. Ten heartbeats and I could see her pale white hands, just visible where they were pinned next to her thighs, gleam with crimson to the fingertips.

As my sister disappeared, Remi appeared. First, her beautiful silver hair, dry now but limp. Then the soft blue of her cheeks, her black lids and lashes, an eager top lip, a shyer bottom lip, a hint of white teeth. I dared think of her as "my" girl, as more of her was revealed. Or released? Reborn? I blushed at her nakedness under the light in front of others. The ward she held me with became an embrace, and I savored it.

Remi's lips remained attached to Lada's, but her shoulders drooped. Lada stopped trembling. Her hands pulled free and grasped Remi's shoulders. Instead of passively receiving, she actively sucked in the contents Remi carried. The process went faster, until Remi's body sunk in Lada's hands, and the last red left her toes.

The thing in Lada's bed shirt leaned forward and placed Remi gently on the floor between it and the cavity where knelt Mother.

Mother's hands formed a mask over her nose and mouth, disbelieving eyes free to stare. "Lada? My daughter?"

The bloody entity's eyes opened. Her lips formed a smile, not one of victory or satisfaction, but one of relief after a lengthy discomfort.

It spoke to Mother. "Hello, Mama." Then to Father. "Papa." To me. "Brother." Its head turned around toward Brillix, still pressed to the wall. "Perfidious lover." Her hands gestured to the room at large. "I can be Lada to you, as she yet lives within me."

It took a long, deep breath, and pink cheeks replaced red ones, blue eyes flashed, and orange hair regained its luster. A pale hand finger-combed through it. "We are well aware of our past with each of you, and we shall maintain an accord. But, be warned, our life is dedicated now to teaching, so we shall leave you soon."

The thing threw off the blanket over its lap. It stood on lean, athletic white legs running from bed shirt at mid-thigh to white marble floor.

"Honor that accord or see how unforgiving we can be."

Lexica XXII

I remained pressed to the ceiling above the entrance to the vault, Father to the marble bookcase to my left, and Brillix to the wall to my right, behind the marble arm chair. Mother remained kneeling in the sarcophagul rectangle ahead and below me. Near her, Remi lay naked, unconscious, and unattended, and my inability to assist infuriated me. She lay no more than a half-span from the feet of...what name do I use?

"What do I call you? The Anaxagorum?"

"Lada's prettier."

She looked like Lada, right down to the freckles on her cheeks and the earnest glint in her blue eyes.

Mother's out-stretched hands protested. "A mother knows her own, and you are not—"

"The flesh you see is of you, Mama. The mind within has expanded beyond your recognition."

"But...." Mother's hands went to her heart. "I feel so little of you."

"I would release Papa, if I thought he would be any comfort to you."

"You cannot keep him pasted up like that."

With no discernible sound or gesture, Lada lowered Father. As soon as his toes touched the floor, his mouth began running. "And what do you mean by treating us this way? Whatever you are, I am still your father and—"

Lada rolled her eyes and pinned Father back to the bookcase, lips pressed to silence. "I have always wanted to do that."

Mother kept one hand on her heart. The other reached toward Lada in supplication. "How can you hurt him so?"

"He is not being hurt." Lada grinned in self-amusement, something she rarely, if ever, did. "He is not hurt. He is inert."

I didn't expect humor. "I agree with Mother. You are not wholly my sister, therefore the name 'Lada' is only a half-fit."

"What would you have it be?"

I knew as soon as she asked. "Ana Lada." I liked the musical quality as I spoke it.

She took no time to ponder. "Then, Ana Lada I am."

Brillix, from his place on the wall, said, "She deserves no name."

Ana Lada seemed amused. "Let there be no misunderstanding about who is in charge here."

The energy ball blocking the doorway vanished.

"You, in the hallway, you understand, do you not?"

I couldn't see their reactions, but Pulumbonk was no doubt scared beyond answering.

The Subu did not suffer from such interdictions, so his voice rose from below and assuredly. "Ye've nothing to fear from me, ye eldritch minx. I wish only to learn from ya."

"Eldritch minx." Ana Lada rolled the name with a simultaneously charming and disconcerting chuckle. "I liked you the first time I sensed you, Subu: 'true to yourself but as gamey as a field pig,' Come inside, and bring the long-legged shiverer."

"Ha!" The Subu guffawed. "Long-legged shiverer. I think I'm gonna like ye, too."

My position above the entrance gave me an overhead view of the two as they entered. Lanky Pulumbonk stumbled in, pushed by the lean animal Subu.

Brillix came free and floated to the floor. I next, the pressure holding me becoming a helping hand that lowered me.

I went immediately to the bookcase, where it was not blocked by my muted, glaring father, and grabbed the red shoom blanket meant for readers in the cold room. "How have none of you thought to do this?" I crossed in front of Mother in the sarcophagul cavity, knelt next to Remi whose blue skin had pimpled, and spread the blanket over her. I peeled back my chainmail hood and put my good ear to her back. Twas a glorious moment when I heard a heartbeat, slow but steady.

Ana Lada directed that self-amused grin toward me. "Find something you value more than sugar cakes, Jonne?"

I felt her levity misplaced.

"Remi is not yet with us. Her spirit needs time to re-inhabit her host, but...will you want her when she does?"

"Yes!"

Would I?

Ana Lada rotated to take us all in. "The time is here for the world to know high magic again. While gods vie for your souls and nature nourishes your bodies, and scholars, such as you, Papa, train others to believe only what they can see and touch, I exist to confound you with things that should not be. Can there be a rainbow stairway to the twin moons? Why should not water think for itself? Or flies turn into faeries or dragons ride volcanic fire from the center of the world to the surface? What if gold could be plucked from the surface of sun-dappled lakes? What if?"

She let the question hang.

"'What if' is the gift I shall give to existence."

The Subu rapped the butt of his axe against the floor. "Yer japing, eh? Gold plucked from water?"

"'What if'", she continued, "Is what spurs the preeminent species of the world to creativity, and creativity brings about evolution to the next level—of civilization, of awareness, of ability."

Pulumbonk, of a sudden, raised his eyes to her. "Lada? Do you not know me?"

"Yes, Pulumbonk, but you do not know me. I am only partially the woman you desire. Think on that."

"I risked everything for you."

"And you will have your chance to do so again, all of you will."

Brillix balled his fists. "Take risks for you? I'd slay you here and now, if I could."

"You have no choice but to serve, as I have no choice. I do not know who made me, but I know my purpose is to flood the world with magicka and to teach its properties."

I asked, "Why have we no choice in this?"

"You all played a part in awakening me, and because of that, we are bound to one another. I am powerful, but I am fragile. There are places you can travel where I cannot. In those places are fonts of magic too long dry. As each is opened, more magicka will be available to those few who can wield it, and those few will hold the future in their hands. Magic users will soon rule the world. Some will use their power for good, others for evil, never in equal shares. With the magicka will come things from other realms that do not want to be here. Humanity will face extinction."

"This thing plans to destroy us," stated Brillix. "She admits as much."

"I only stage the threat of destruction. Humans will have to unite, to be more creative and more resourceful to regain the balance."

The Subu made a great show of scratching his head. "So, and I mean no disrespect, Annie"—typically, he had to coin his own name—"but yer saying we gonna unleash magic only so it can be beat down again?"

"This is nonsense!" Brillix said.

"If only your muscles were brains, knight. Listen to me."

"I believe not a word."

Her flesh blushed to almost crimson. "Have I ever lied to any of you? I could have lied, seduced you to my aid in the bowels of Dunkelgrau, but I did not. That is not my purpose."

She whirled on Brillix who had another comment nocked and ready to fire. "Stay silent, until I have had my say."

The Subu chuckled. "The man do like to—"

She snapped. "You as well!"

"A'right, keep yer little shirt on."

"I speak to all of you. Without magic, humanity loses its desire to create and feeds its desire to destroy. Look at the Askerati in the south. They will burn and kill, until every person believes as they believe, and then, they'll turn on themselves. You in the north have tried to separate yourselves from the others of your kind, not to unite and build something better, but to preserve an imperfect past.

"Remain as you are, and you will focus on how to tear each other apart, building your castles, forging your steel, and claiming to be the mightiest. That is the industry of death, not life. The Fael fought me and buried me, and within a millennia, buried themselves."

Pulumbonk gazed at his boots. "I'd much rather go home to Atmaa." Dull with mud and scratches, like the rest of his garb, they were a far cry from the resplendent regalia he had worn on arriving in Northem.

"Mayhap your journeys will take you there, for all you, together, are charged with roaming every land, known and unknown, to find other sources of magic: eight fonts that tap into other realms and eight more artifacts of living arcana, like me. The balance will tip and kingdoms will fall. Necromancers will arise and monsters will pour into our world. Then…."

She left her next words unsaid for so long, Pulumbonk asked. "Then what?"

"Then I shall lead the Renewal."

"And we are to follow?"

"If you wish, but it is now that I need you. I am the hand that reaches but you must be the fingers that seize. We will reach into lost places and retrieve what has been forgotten therein. If you prevail, your species will take a step toward being wiser, more powerful and…." She glanced at The Subu. "Richer in pleasures you have yet to discover."

"If we fail?" I asked.

"Your kind will stagnate, decay, and die out to make way for who comes next. You will become a memory, like the Fael."

"We'll prevail," stated The Subu, as he turned a triumphant smile to Brillix. "Ya see, ya lolly? We're gonna be kings!"

"The world needs to be done with kings, Subu. You will be, instead, my fingers, my six fingers."

The Subu turned to me while inspecting himself. "Do I look like a finger to ye?"

If she included Remi, I counted only five.

"Upon each of you I will bestow a gift that will make you as individuals stronger and you as a group unstoppable."

"Gifts?" echoed The Subu. "I like the sound of that."

Ana Lada faced me. "You first, brother Jonne, Blossom, Jonne the Booker."

"Bestow your gift upon Remi, not me."

She eyed me from toe to head. "I became acquainted with your essence, when I was carried into this vault a month ago, already fated to be Lada." She studied her bare arms. "Lada's was the first flesh to touch me in five hundred years, you know. That is when we bonded, that night in the burning library. Quite the dramatic setting." She lowered her arms. "On my first whiff of you, I identified you as: 'puffy eater who defeats himself,' but I am not beyond being surprised. You have shown resolve and a hungry mind."

I glanced from Father to Mother to The Subu. What did one say to that?

"More importantly, you exhibit unflagging loyalty to the vessel that carried me here. Hold still." Black vapor snaked from her mouth. I closed mine, but the vapor entered my nose. A slight tickle. No scent. "You will never be at a loss of memory, as you observe events to come. Truth will always be clear to you, but there will be many who will deny it, and you, as well."

"What…what does that mean?"

With a fingertip upon the crown of my head, she urged me a step back.

She beckoned to The Subu. As he stepped forward, his axe unthreaded itself from his shoulder and sailed across the room, past me, and into my surprised mother's hands. The Subu leapt back, fists up.

Ana Lada glanced at Mother. "I know it is heavy, but it will not burden you long." To The Subu, who remained on guard, she said, "I've always sensed you were fearless, but mayhap you are just shy." Her hand beckoned. "Do not fear the vapor."

"I don' fear it." He advanced hesitantly, hand held protectively over the ruin of his scalp. "But I'm wary as a cat of it."

She exuded the vapor. "Subu, also known as Rawhead, also known as Pleebus of High Ranch."

He jerked back. "Ah, really? Pleebus? I hate that name."

"Subu," she continued. "Your axe will never be out of your reach again, in fact, few things will be. Even at thirty spans, any object you could normally carry can be summoned."

He smiled. "Women?"

"Non-living things."

He pushed his forehead close to her face. "I'd rather ye make me look like a whole man again."

"I am allowed only to give what I give."

The Subu held her gaze, fingertips to the scars. "Ye got yer legs back."

"Know your gift, Subu. Now fetch your axe."

He started to walk past her.

Her bare arm blocked him. "Do you really need to walk to it?"

He considered for a moment and then extended his hand. The weapon flew from Mother's hands to his. "Ah!" he cried and studied the axe, as if seeing it for the first time. "That's a thing, ain' it?"

When she turned to Pulumbonk, he dropped his eyes and made no effort to resist the vapor. "Conjuring fire and light need be tricks to you no more. They will flow from you."

He glanced up in puzzlement.

"Hold your palm out and burn me."

"I...I can't do that."

Ana Lada seized his right hand and raised it palm out. "Do you want to burn me?"

"Not...not really."

"Say 'yes.'"

"Uh...yes?"

A gout of fire hid her face for a moment then vanished. She smiled, unharmed. "Others will not be so happy when you do that."

His face radiated pain. "With what trick might I have you?"

"There is no such." She offered her Ana Lada smile. Mayhap it was the smile of surety by one who knew what he did not. "Rely on your friends. Be kind to trees. Try not to incinerate either of them."

Brillix received her, as a wall receives a wind.

"I am not your enemy, knight. I am, in many ways, your best ally."

He offered nothing.

"What a hero you are about to become, Lance Captain, the kind you read of as a child and have always tried to be. No living thing will ever surprise you, even in the deepest dark. No foe can hide its weakness from you, but there will be many, many foes. Be the armored glove for my fingers."

His expression belied something noble stirring, but it did not come to words.

"You speak of heroes." Mother was standing. "Yet you killed my eldest son."

"He threatened my purpose."

"He tried to protect his family."

"A laudable trait, but fortune has blown thusly."

Brillix said, "Then I shall cut him down. Such a man should not hang like a butchered albon."

Ana Lada didn't stop him, when he strode from the room.

The Subu hurried after him, "Brilly boy, mind the creepers."

Ana Lada said, "Cut them as you will. They no longer serve me."

When The Subu disappeared into the hall, I said. "But we do."

Ana Lada studied me for a long moment. "You will be serving something larger than me, and do not ask me what, for I know it only as the Stream."

I sighed. "I'll go help them with my brother."

A red arm blocked my way. "We will need a sixth to join us, and the pool of candidates is small. The warrior Udrakk and the archer Zir are bonded to me as you are. Both are capable in combat. Choose one."

Udrakk was capable but not very likable. Zir was likable didn't inspire confidence. "I'll think on it."

I started again toward the door when The Subu chuckled in the hallway, something one doesn't expect from a man surrounded by corpses. "Would ya look at this lot!"

I didn't make a step before Theodoric, Ryckerd's stout, orange alpha cat, planted himself on the threshold. A stream of twenty-two furry bodies, tails high, flowed around him and took up positions around the room, including one on the back of the stone seat, two on the shelves near Father, and the rest on the floor. Every wide-pupiled eye bore into the Red Lady. She acknowledged each one in their turn.

I stiffened when a thirteen-weight of feline muscle attached itself to my back and climbed onto my shoulder—thank fortune for my chainmail! Theodoric's whiskers tickled my cheek, as he bent to acknowledge me with a sniff. I could only watch him from the corner of my eyes when he sat erect and leveled his stare at Ana Lada.

It was Lada's smile that greeted him. "This one considers you a trusted ally, Jonne."

Then I smiled. "He does?"

"He has chosen you as his second, while he entreats with me."

"If Lada is part of you, this cat should be no stranger."

"I know Theodoric, all right, the Emperor of the Balcony." She crossed her hands before her and met his gaze with hers. "Cats are as aware of their place in the cosmos as I am, and that makes them cocksure."

Brillix and The Subu had re-entered the chamber to watch the strange conclave with Mother, Pulumbonk, and my yet-stifled father.

Not that Theodoric needed steadying, my hand rose to the soft fur of his side and held his warmth to my cheek. "What does this mean?"

"He demands the impossible."

"I would think demands by a cat impossible, themselves." I didn't think it possible for the entity to hesitate over anything, yet the expression on what-looked-like Lada hinted strongly at doubt.

Ana Lada shifted eye contact from Theodoric to me. "The demand comes not from the animal but through it, from somewhere beyond this realm of rock and water."

She blinked several times, as if recalibrating what was possible, and then looked over my shoulder toward the bookshelf. The slap of small feet drew my attention to Father who now stood solidly on the floor. I didn't think one could exhibit disgruntlement and bewilderment at the same time, but he did.

"Papa," Ana Lada said, "hold your tongue, and I shall allow you to witness with us that which I didn't think possible." She sighed, "but apparently is," then walked out of the door into the hallway.

Mother groaned out of the cavity on aged knees and put her hand over Father's mouth. He began to slap it away but acquiesced. We all gathered in the entrance and watched the red-headed woman gaze down on Ryckerd. Theodoric remained happily hunkered on my shoulder.

Brillix and The Subu had laid my brother's body on his back, feet together, hands crossed over his chest. A gold coin hid each still-open eye.

Ana Lada kept her focus on Ryckerd but addressed all those present. "I will not say gods do or do not exist. I can only tell you I am a manifestation of the ethereal Stream, as are we all." She knelt and placed a hand on my brother's abdomen just below his cuirass and belt. "It seems I can perform this ability but seven times, before I must give myself back to the Stream and sleep, until you, or whoever inhabits this world in the future, awakens me again."

Black vapor enshrouded Ryckerd. I barely breathed, as I watched. Ana Lada's body bucked. As did Ryckerd's. Her palm pressed against his abdomen. Ryckerd's lips parted to take a lung-filling breath. She rolled off him and into a heap of white legs and bed shirt.

Brillix, knightly instincts intact, went to help the fallen damsel. Mother joined him.

Ana Lada peered from heavy lids. "My dear boy!" With no discernible effort, she rose until vertical and composed. "Brillix coming to my aid. I hope to see more of that."

Mother, usually so in command of her emotions, looked up from Ryckerd with unabashed happiness. "He breathes!"

"Such joy, Mama!" Ana Lada knelt and embraced Mother. I saw no vapor, but she kissed Mother long on the mouth. "May such joy abound in you for the years you have left. You have denied it too long."

When Mother's eyes wouldn't leave Ryckerd, Ana Lada explained. "As with Remi, so with Ryckerd. Spirit and flesh need time to reacquaint themselves, after a separation."

I was the only one to ask, "Sister...er, Ana Lada, are you well?"

"Whole and hale and happily surprised at this turn of fortune."

Father strode into the hallway. "I have held my silence long enough." He stood over Ryckerd a minor colossus. "If he truly lives, he deserves gifts."

Ana Lada gazed down on him. "Death has agreed to be patient with Ryckerd. No wound inflicted by man or beast or demon can slay him again, but this glamour is not endless.

Neither he nor I will know how long the Stream will mend him before it takes him back into its current for good."

"Demon?" I asked.

"Oh, yes, demons," Ana Lada said rolling her eyes. "Terrible storytellers, love to make deals, save the toes of their victims for their kids."

Nobody had anything to say to that.

I asked, "What gifts will you give to Remi?"

"None." Before I could express my outrage, she thrust out her palm. "She has lived within me, Jonne. What do you bet she has learned a thing or two?"

My consternation must have shown.

"Let her be mightier than you without envy, brother. Your relationship will be difficult. It is up to both of you to find the value of it."

I glanced to Remi curled under her red blanket and flushed with jubilation, choosing not to hear the warning of difficulty.

Ana Lada scanned the ceiling and the roots stitched over it. "I withdraw my hold on your castle. It is time to rebuild for what is coming."

In a fury, the mass of roots and vines retreated through the walls and floor, leaving no trace they had ever been there, other than the holes in the walls through which they broke. The bodies they had held dropped to the dark hallway floor.

Father being Father, asked, "And what's my gift?"

"I have brought your son back to life and given your wife a future of happiness. Is that not enough?"

"Make me a tall man."

Ana Lada regarded him in her way. "Instead, I present you the gift of humility, as you recognize those around you, including a blueskin, will influence the world more than you ever dreamed of doing."

Lexica Ultima

Father never gave any antagonist the satisfaction of a reaction, not that Ana Lada expected or wanted one. What he did showed him at his best. I expected him to be in shock or denial about the existence of the magical being in the room with him.

"If you're finished ruining my castle, I have people to save." To Mother, he said, "Stay with our son, until he can walk." He made his way through the hallway of dead men, still an important man with important things to do.

Brillix addressed Mother. "I should stay with you."

"Assist Papa. He'll make a mess of rescuing everyone without you."

"Go," I said to Brillix. "I'll stay with her."

"Very well." Brillix stepped over Ryckerd's still prostrate body. "Thank fortune for bringing this good man back to us." He picked his way among the lifeless bodies of brother knights without looking down.

"I shall stay with you, Jonne," volunteered Pulumbonk.

"I would," began The Subu, "but I'll wager there's food to be found in this castle."

Ana Lada focused on me and ticked her eyes toward the chamber. "Let us gather Remi. I have business with her kin before I travel south. Your friends will be company enough for Mama."

"I think so," Pulumbonk said. "If no more roots take after us."

The Subu swatted a thigh. "I be hungry enough to chew the fat off yer backside, woman."

"Then go, and be a disappointment to us all."

"A'right, I shall."

Ana Lada glanced to me. "Be sure you record his failure in your chronicle, booker."

The Subu let out an exasperated sigh and plopped next to Pulumbonk. "So be it, then. I'll eat the long legs off this one, instead."

Ana Lada exhaled into Remi's face and whispered. "Walk with us."

Remi's eyes fluttered but never wholly opened. She stood, and the blanket fell away, leaving her as naked as an egg, the dark curls of her womanhood in plain view. I averted my eyes, which added much inadvertent touching as I draped the blanket over her again. Getting her to hold it in place was futile, as her hands kept dropping to her sides.

Ana Lada chuckled. "Human modesty."

I used one of my throwing knives as a bulky brooch to hold the blanket together. Getting the front to stay completely closed eluded me, so she remained partially on display through half-open curtains. I took her left arm and kept my eyes forward.

Ana Lada took the other. As we passed the quartet in the hallway, she said to Mother, "I shall take good care of your daughter."

Mother, despite being overwhelmed by that horrible morning, managed a weak smile. "I do not understand who you are."

The Subu snapped his fingers. "Don' pay the minx no mind, lady. There's no understanding her."

Pulumbonk said, "Where should we look for you, Jonne?"

"Meet me at The Six Fingers."

"That's us now, isn't it, The Six Fingers?" Pulumbonk said.

I thought of the six-fingered red hand pressed into the lintel over the lighthouse entrance. How many others had acted as the Red Lady's fingers in the past?

Brillix scoffed, "I remain a Knight of the Order of Man," and offered Mother his hand.

Ana Lada and I left with Remi. Escorting the sleep-walking woman up the stairs went slowly but smoothly. Sunlight through the high windows of the keep met us upon gaining the ground floor. Survivors who had ventured from their chambers to identify the dead watched our progress over the floor and through the massive door to the courtyard, all eyes on Ana Lada's legs. I did my best to shield Remi from view. Crossing the courtyard brought more onlookers. Remi didn't seem to mind, so I felt embarrassed on her behalf.

Once through the barbican I saw with great relief a dozen or so men-at-arms and a brace of knights tending the horses and sharing stories. Not all had perished. Again, every eye glued to Ana Lada. The springing walk and resolute expression belonged undoubtably to my sister, even if other aspects did not.

She raised a palm. "I require two horses and assistance with my friend."

Only one managed a bewildered, "Lady?"

"Just 'librast' will do."

Three men controlled their embarrassment enough to lift Remi and position her behind me on the horse I had ridden earlier. I held one of her arms around my waist. Ana Lada swung gracefully onto another ownerless horse, presenting a peculiar image in her bed shirt.

Every castle tower I could see had collapsed to some degree, one almost totally. A few battlements had broken off, but the structure seemed sound. Thinking of all the dead inside belied its might.

The warmth of the midday sun, however, felt lovely. Seeing it ignite my sister's orange hair exhilarated me. The village hadn't been harmed, so, when putting the castle behind us, the ride felt like many others with Lada in younger days.

A group of villagers, including several of the patrolmen I'd encountered that morning, headed up the road toward us, all moon-eyed and focused on the castle. They parted and allowed us to ride through them, many whispering among themselves as Ana Lada passed.

We followed the road to the left toward the palisade and dwellings surrounding The Six Fingers. Ana Lada's skin flooded with crimson as we neared. Her hair matted to the side of her head, and she became the Red Lady. To my relief, she retained the bed shirt, as no brother wants to see his sister naked. It seemed she could switch between both personas.

Blueskins streamed through the gate of their palisade to meet us. They apparently sensed the arrival of the blood book, the same that had gifted their forebears. Instead of fear in their faces, anticipation. Some touched the Red Lady's legs. Some held their arms wide in welcome. One man began clapping, and others joined, until the air vibrated.

Lada would've hated all the attention and adulation. The Red Lady, eyes closed, enigmatic smile in view, seemed to expect it. Four of Remi's sisters among the acolytes of Gela— one whiteskin, three blueskins—appeared alongside my horse, all wearing simple gowns of variegated green and buff tied under the breasts with a cord of woven grass.

One winced in empathy. "Sister, what have they done to you?"

One, more combative, glared at me. "If you've harmed her, Blossom, we shall find you in the night."

I recoiled. "I would never!"

"Get her off your horse, so we may tend her."

The Red Lady swiped a band of vapor for all of them to see.

LEAVE THEM TOGETHER

The women shrunk away bowing their apologies.

I extended my palm to them. “Please stay with me, as I shall need you.”

The Red Lady dismounted and disappeared into the middle of the crowd. I led our mounts to the livery. The sisters surrounded Remi and were soon joined by others I presumed to be friends.

I explained, “She needs clothing, food…she…I wish to be with her when she awakens fully.”

“You pay for a room in there.” The combative one pointed to The Six Fingers’ second floor which housed a hostel and individual rooms for travelers, and like the tavern and dining halls below, ringed the ancient draysalt tower. “We will clean and clothe her. You stay away, until then.”

I led them into The Six Fingers’s north entrance. The comforting aromas of fireplace smoke and onions welcomed us. I found the Mistress of the Lodge and made arrangements for a room. The acolytes guided Remi away, leaving me alone among the crowded tables. Merf saved me, by taking my arm and leading me to a seat near the enormous fireplace, the odds and ends of adventurers past adorning its mantle. All those lives lost in the dark tunnels had meant nothing to me before Dunkelgrau. That afternoon, they were brothers and sisters.

“You’re not getting away without a meal, this time, Jonne.”

I tore into the trencher bread of gravy-soaked albon and potatoes. After days of goldtail and salted pork, I was in ecstasy. The Red Hand Ale flowed over my taste buds as the sunlight had over my face. This was the life I knew, yet it seemed, of a sudden, someone else’s. I savored the last mouthful from my cup. I wished to luxuriate in the moment, but, unlike what I’d think a champion of magic would do, I fell asleep at the table, cheek on wood.

I dreamt of Remi’s leading a group of blue women chanting and dancing over the surface of a pond. The water bubbled in spots where things I didn’t want to see tried to emerge. My body couldn’t turn. My legs couldn’t run. I began to—

My eyes snapped open on The Subu’s face, battered forehead thrown into a chiaroscuro of bumpy flesh by the firelight. The dining hall lay empty, except for Pulumbonk next to me on the bench. I had slept a fair bit.

The Subu waggled a spoon at me. “Yer a lucky booker, ye are.”

“Why?”

"The Red Lady says I'll bathe in riches. Else wise, I might be more scalded about ye trading off my bag of Valens rocks."

Pulumbonk said, "We just received our food, but, if you're full, Merf said you should go to the south hall. She's there."

I was up and jogging past the intricately carved pillars before thinking to ask if "she" meant Remi. Through the curving hall I went, then through the drawn, heavy curtains opening on the empty east hall. A cluster of people, mostly blueskins, clogged the opening into the south hall. I heard actual chanting, the voice unfamiliar, possibly male, possibly female.

"Dolki horendun, endruss alkay sif."

I didn't understand the words, but I knew them to be from the same eldritch tongue used by warders like Remi, the skragging women healers of the blueskins, and The Subu when activating his blade. Merf, like most blueskins, knew some of the words but had no proficiency at channeling them. Perhaps thirty among the community could make the words work: the warders, the Guides, the healers, and the arborists who claimed to commune with trees. There must be truth in the claim, for arborists were fought over by farmers and ranchers for their luck with the soil.

I stood at the back of the crowd, with only a view of the dark ceiling beyond. Someone had removed most of the lumen fruit. "What am I hearing?"

They were all familiar people who had little to say to me, except for Eela, the serving girl who hated me for kissing Remi and Myrle at the Festival of the Twin Moons. While the others shushed me, she answered.

"You aren't welcome here."

"Greetings, Eela."

She tried to remain sour but succumbed to excitement. "It's the living book, right in there, finally come back to us."

"We know her as the Red Lady."

"We've known her by the 'living book,' as she told none of our ancestors a name."

"Is she teaching? She refers to herself as a teacher."

"To the ones who can learn. To the rest of us, she speaks of kinship, a gift given by her to the first learners. She makes us proud of the blue skins we inherited."

"Is Remi among you?"

Her sourness came back thricefold. "You can find her yourself." She returned her attention to the voice.

I folded my hands at my waist, fascinated to know the Red Lady had a voice of her own. Not a word she spoke was known to me, and the way she enunciated each one sounded part human, part...what? "Mist" might describe it, as certain syllables had a moist fragility to them. By standing on my toes, I could see the thirty adepts, faces alternately orange and shadowed in the pulse of the few lumen fruits. They sat crosslegged in two concentric rings on the wooden floor, a large one surrounding a smaller one surrounding the Red Lady. Heads bobbed to a rhythm only they could hear. A thick hoop of black vapor encircled all of them.

I watched until my toes got tired. Each time I rested, I'd turn hoping to see the acolytes escorting Remi to me, but all I would see was the east dining hall dim and empty. Then I'd rise and watch The Red Lady a while longer. Her speaking to this congregation constituted history, and I should've been attentive to every detail, but...was Remi healthy? Was she awake? Was she herself again? Would she want to see me? Did she hate me? My attempts to save her had been so puny, how could she not find me disappointing?

The thought of wandering the globe far from warming hearths and good food, while she became a powerful sorceress and forgot all about me felt like a mortal wound, or at least one that would never heal. I tortured myself with thoughts of her meeting one of the new breed of magic adepts that would soon rise, one more handsome and exciting in his intellect than I. Returning to the The Subu and Pulumbonk, and drinking myself unconscious suddenly appealed.

I practically heard my patience snap. My legs took me back to the north dining hall where the stairs to the second-floor guest rooms lay. Up I went, anxious I might meet Remi and her entourage on their way down, looking like an over-eager little boy. The rooms were small and marked by sturdy wooden doors, and blurred by as I pounded along the floorboards. Someone had visited the room I rented, but they had moved on, so little-boy Jonne scurried to the next room and the next. I encountered locked rooms, a handful of castlers whose quarters at the castle had been destroyed, and the hollow-eyed adventurers who had passed on the Dunkelgrau expedition and were now stranded here due to the Askerati rampaging through the south.

Downstairs I found the assembly had broken up and followed the Red Lady to the pier to bid her farewell. I felt snubbed again. Both as Ana Lada and the Red Lady, she had seemed to favor me, so her leaving without a word stung.

The east entrance of The Six Fingers led to the cobbled path down to the lake shore. A hazy sky turned the evening darker than usual, prompting those gathered to carry a torch or taper. Everyone of the blueskin community must've been there, as I saw at least two hundred flames, even in the rigging of the Bloated Shrew where crewmen of the Guides hung.

Merf met me on the path. "There you are, Jonne!"

"Seems I'm forgettable."

"Nonsense. She's waiting for you."

My insides flip-flopped, and I rushed down the path. Interestingly, the Red Lady stood not on the pier but at the lake's edge where water met pebbled shore. She faced the congregation, glistening red in the candlelight of the four Gelan acolytes arrayed before her. A fifth knelt at her feet, a freshly trimmed bob of silver hair just touching her shoulders making her known to me. I stopped, afraid to go farther. That was Remi, awake and real.

The Red Lady's eyes were closed, yet she detected me at the back of the crowd. One hand beckoned. One swiped.

COME TO US JONNE

My first action was to observe that she either could not or chose not to speak in the common tongue. My second action was to forget the first and bump through the mass of onlookers. I could only go as fast as they parted, most of them patting me or applauding me, their attention disconcerting after a lifetime of being invisible. The flickering flames caught more smiles than I'd ever seen from blueskins.

"Good on you, Jonne!"

"Write well of us in your histories."

"What a hero you are!"

That's not the way I saw it, but I managed a smile and a nod to all.

A skragging woman, showing the deep blue skin and yellow irises of the aged, gripped me with a surprisingly strong hand. "Don't fail her."

"Who?"

"Fail her, and you fail us all."

She held me a moment longer to punctuate her warning, then released me.

A dozen more smiles, a dozen more torches fell away, and I was suddenly, shiveringly alone in front of the four acolytes and Remi, the Red Lady behind them, the dark waters of the lake behind her. I had always found Remi to be adorable in a cute, kissable way, but seeing her turn to me wearing the variegated gown and a tiara of woven twigs sprouting orange, yellow, and red grasses, I felt sure I was seeing the most beautiful woman in the world. When her upper teeth peeked from under spreading lips, my massive vocabulary vanished.

Her companions must've known her affect on a mortal male, for they took my arms and led me to her.

I extended my hands, and when Remi took them, buzzing bees went to my brain. I had dreamed I would say something manly and romantic when this moment came, but all I managed was, "I've lost weight."

She pulled me close enough to smell her breath, a hint of lime. "I remember everything you did for me."

"You do?" I thought of ogling her body without blinking when she was the Red Lady. "I'm sorry."

"At the Festival of the Twin Moons, I thought, 'if I do not kiss this boy, there will be no kiss.'"

"I thought I kissed you."

"You could not look me in the eye."

"Then I shall try to be a braver man for you."

"No man could be braver." Her smile collapsed to an expression of concern, and she ventured a finger toward my face. "You have something on your lip."

"I do?"

Just as the night of our first kiss, my mouth was one second speaking, the next sealed by Remi's lips, as if mandatory movements in the physical world had been bypassed, so neither of her feet need step, nor her face lean in, nor her hands rise to my shoulders. Thank fortune my heavy gloves were in my belt and my fingers could feel warmth beneath her gown. I had never hated my chainmail as much as I did then. My body had turned to a flame that needed to join with her. There was no lake, no crowd of onlookers, no Red Lady.

A horn from the direction of the pier eventually intruded. The magic seal broke, and Remi stepped back. The most wonderful moment of my life had passed.

"Where are you going?" I pulled her by the hands back to me. "We should rejoin Pulumbonk and The Subu." I chuckled at the understatement, "We have one or two thousand things to discuss."

Remi squeezed my hands. "Later."

"Later? Do you enjoy torturing me?"

Her hand shooed me. “Oh, hush that! I have no choice but to go.”

“Go?” That feeling again of the ground opening beneath me. “You can’t leave now.”

“Ana Lada needs me.”

“I need you!”

“Jonne, our days as normal people are over.”

“There’s a bleak thought.”

“She requires me for but a blink, and then I can return.”

“I’ll go with you.”

“We go to the forests of Haramdum to commune with the fire makers. The Renewal begins there.”

One of the Guides called from the pier, “Your vessel awaits, lady.”

The Red Lady’s hands touched Remi’s shoulders and drew her back.

“Be brave with me.” Remi’s smile was warm but lacking the needfulness I wished to see.

How was it so easy for her to part with me? I expected something more, and then, to my intense pleasure, she supplied it.

She pressed two fingers to my lips. “Mind yourself at festivals, curious boy. These lips belong to me, now.”

The Red Lady called to the Guide captain, “Mir likke es sur geht.”

I smiled broadly and stupidly. “Fare thee well, beautiful girls.”

The Red Lady drew Remi to her side and swiped vapor before me.

YOU WILL HEAR FROM ME SOON

The two females turned and stepped to the water’s edge and then—not into the water—onto the water. The black lake remained solid beneath their feet and lifted them, as a huge liquid hump, until they stood thirty spans above me. A slipperfish? Some other magic yet to be revealed? Whatever it was rode like a wave that never broke, away from the shore, toward the unsuspecting South.

Made in the USA
Coppell, TX
08 July 2026

83732935R00146